Praise for Lexi Blake and Masters and Mercenaries...

"I can always trust Lexi Blake's Dominants to leave me breathless...and in love. If you want sensual, exciting BDSM wrapped in an awesome love story, then look for a Lexi Blake book."

~Cherise Sinclair USA Today Bestselling author

"Lexi Blake's MASTERS AND MERCENARIES series is beautifully written and deliciously hot. She's got a real way with both action and sex. I also love the way Blake writes her gorgeous Dom heroes--they make me want to do bad, bad things. Her heroines are intelligent and gutsy ladies whose taste for submission definitely does not make them dish rags. Can't wait for the next book!"

~Angela Knight, New York Times Bestselling author

"A Dom is Forever is action packed, both in the bedroom and out. Expect agents, spies, guns, killing and lots of kink as Liam goes after the mysterious Mr. Black and finds his past and his future... The action and espionage keep this story moving along quickly while the sex and kink provides a totally different type of interest. Everything is very well balanced and flows together wonderfully."

~A Night Owl "Top Pick", Terri, Night Owl Erotica

"A Dom Is Forever is everything that is good in erotic romance. The story was fast-paced and suspenseful, the characters were flawed but made me root for them every step of the way, and the hotness factor was off the charts mostly due to a bad boy Dom with a penchant for dirty talk."

~Rho, The Romance Reviews

"A good read that kept me on my toes, guessing until the big reveal, and thinking survival skills should be a must for all men."

~Chris, Night Owl Reviews

The Dom Who Came in from the Cold

Other Books by Lexi Blake

ROMANTIC SUSPENSE

Masters and Mercenaries
The Dom Who Loved Me
The Men With The Golden Cuffs
A Dom is Forever
On Her Master's Secret Service
Sanctum: A Masters and Mercenaries Novella
Love and Let Die
Unconditional: A Masters and Mercenaries Novella
Dungeon Royale
Dungeon Games: A Masters and Mercenaries Novella
A View to a Thrill
Cherished: A Masters and Mercenaries Novella
You Only Love Twice
Luscious: Masters and Mercenaries~Topped
Adored: A Masters and Mercenaries Novella
Master No
Just One Taste: Masters and Mercenaries~Topped 2
From Sanctum with Love
Devoted: A Masters and Mercenaries Novella
Dominance Never Dies
Submission is Not Enough
Master Bits and Mercenary Bites~The Secret Recipes of Topped
Perfectly Paired: Masters and Mercenaries~Topped 3
For His Eyes Only
Arranged: A Masters and Mercenaries Novella
Love Another Day
At Your Service: Masters and Mercenaries~Topped 4
Master Bits and Mercenary Bites~Girls Night
Nobody Does It Better
Close Cover
Protected: A Masters and Mercenaries Novella
Enchanted: A Masters and Mercenaries Novella

Charmed: A Masters and Mercenaries Novella
Taggart Family Values
Treasured: A Masters and Mercenaries Novella
Delighted: A Masters and Mercenaries Novella
Tempted: A Masters and Mercenaries Novella

Masters and Mercenaries: The Forgotten
Lost Hearts (Memento Mori)
Lost and Found
Lost in You
Long Lost
No Love Lost

Masters and Mercenaries: Reloaded
Submission Impossible
The Dom Identity
The Man from Sanctum
No Time to Lie
The Dom Who Came in from the Cold

Masters and Mercenaries: New Recruits
Love the Way You Spy, Coming September 18, 2023

Butterfly Bayou
Butterfly Bayou
Bayou Baby
Bayou Dreaming
Bayou Beauty
Bayou Sweetheart
Bayou Beloved, Coming March 28, 2023

Lawless
Ruthless
Satisfaction
Revenge

Courting Justice
Order of Protection
Evidence of Desire

Masters Of Ménage (by Shayla Black and Lexi Blake)
Their Virgin Captive
Their Virgin's Secret
Their Virgin Concubine
Their Virgin Princess
Their Virgin Hostage
Their Virgin Secretary
Their Virgin Mistress

The Perfect Gentlemen (by Shayla Black and Lexi Blake)
Scandal Never Sleeps
Seduction in Session
Big Easy Temptation
Smoke and Sin
At the Pleasure of the President

URBAN FANTASY

Thieves
Steal the Light
Steal the Day
Steal the Moon
Steal the Sun
Steal the Night
Ripper
Addict
Sleeper
Outcast
Stealing Summer
The Rebel Queen
The Rebel Guardian

LEXI BLAKE WRITING AS SOPHIE OAK

Texas Sirens
Small Town Siren
Siren in the City
Siren Enslaved

Siren Beloved
Siren in Waiting
Siren in Bloom
Siren Unleashed
Siren Reborn

Nights in Bliss, Colorado
Three to Ride
Two to Love
One to Keep
Lost in Bliss
Found in Bliss
Pure Bliss
Chasing Bliss
Once Upon a Time in Bliss
Back in Bliss
Sirens in Bliss
Happily Ever After in Bliss
Far from Bliss
Unexpected Bliss, Coming May 9, 2023

A Faery Story
Bound
Beast
Beauty

Standalone
Away From Me
Snowed In

The Dom Who Came in from the Cold

Masters and Mercenaries: Reloaded, Book 5

Lexi Blake

The Dom Who Came in from the Cold
Masters and Mercenaries: Reloaded, Book 5
Lexi Blake

Published by DLZ Entertainment LLC
Copyright 2023 DLZ Entertainment LLC
Edited by Chloe Vale
ISBN: 978-1-942297-77-2

Sign up for Lexi Blake's newsletter
and be entered to win a $25 gift certificate
to the bookseller of your choice.

Join us for news, fun, and exclusive content
including free Thieves short stories.

There's a new contest every month!

Go to www.LexiBlake.net to subscribe.

Acknowledgments

I thought a lot about second chances as I wrote this book. In romance the trope refers to two people getting a second chance at love, but the idea is bigger. In life, that second chance doesn't have to involve the same person—though this one does. Sometimes our second chance is about acknowledging that what we are doing does not work. Sometimes our second chance involves getting out of a toxic situation. It could be facing a truth we tried to hide from. Some of us have to deal with our own mortality. But when we are strong enough to make the decision to change, what it all adds up to is more than a second chance. When we take that deep breath and follow the brave path, we get a second act. So this book is for everyone brave enough to step out on that stage again, to believe they deserve better, to finally acknowledge they are worthy.

And most all, this book is for Phyllis and her "Mo Betta"

Prologue

Dallas, TX
Present day

Kyle Hawthorne stood in the darkness, peeking through the filmy drapes to glance down at the parking lot below. A tiny clown car moved into a reserved space, and he knew his prey had finally come home.

He shouldn't think about the woman he adored as prey, but he'd decided he needed his inner predator if he was going to get out of the trap he found himself in. For a brief while the woman who was getting out of the small torture device she called a car had lulled him into thinking he could be the man he once was. The man who'd gone to college and had a normal future in front of him. The man who'd never thought about joining the Navy and would have laughed hysterically at the thought of being in the CIA. The man who would never have even thought about leaving her behind in the cruelest way.

Julia Ennis had reminded him of everything he'd become.

It had been a different person entirely who'd prompted him to think he could be both. A now dead man had poked and prodded him and made him see that this life was fucking short and if he couldn't have Mae Beatrice Vaughn by his side, it might not be worth living.

Of course, he had to keep her alive, and that could prove to be a hard thing to do.

A man slipped out of the passenger seat. Actually what he did was unfold his big body and climb his way out of the car. MaeBe had always assured him her car would save the world someday, but that sucker had been hell on his spinal column.

He might have to rip this guy's spine right out of his body like the movie *Predator*.

West Rycroft. Straight off the range and into the bodyguard unit at McKay-Taggart. He was going to have to have a long discussion with his uncle about what constituted a proper guard for a woman in MaeBe's situation. It certainly wasn't a baby Dom who was barely out of training both at Sanctum and the office. MaeBe required someone with experience and knowledge, and the will to ensure she followed orders when it came to her safety.

West Rycroft was barely good enough to carry her bag.

Had they used the time they'd spent in lockdown at Sanctum to play? Had West been trying his new skills on the most luscious sub in the world?

He felt a growl come from deep in his throat.

He needed to get a handle on his nasty side or he would scare the hell out of her, and he didn't want that. She would be mad enough as it was since he was supposed to be dead.

Not that anyone believed him. His faked death was the worst-kept secret in the world, and he blamed his uncle for that, too.

MaeBe would have believed him if it hadn't been for his uncle and her friends. She was probably mad at him, but that woman couldn't hold a grudge to save her life. That was part of the problem. Julia had beaten the shit out of her and MaeBe probably thought they should all sit down and talk things through. She was that kind of girl.

Once he'd thought they weren't compatible, but now he knew that her softness was a complement to his hard outer shell. They needed each other, and everything would fall into place when she walked in and he wrapped her in his arms. They would work things out this evening, and she would let him protect and take care of her.

MaeBe and her bodyguard disappeared as they walked into the

building, and Kyle's adrenaline started to flow.

His cell buzzed in his pocket, and he pulled it out. Normally he would ignore whoever was on the other end of the line, but only one person had this particular number, and he wouldn't call if it wasn't important. He had a couple of minutes until she made her way inside, and he would hear the alarm go off.

He'd gotten around that. She hadn't changed the code. They were going to talk about that, too.

"Drake," he said quietly into the receiver. "Have you landed yet?"

"Just touched down about an hour ago, and we're on our way to your location," Drake said. "We should be there in a few minutes."

"Have you found her?"

He'd worked with Drake Radcliffe for years. Drake had been something between a boss and a brother. He'd definitely become a friend. They'd survived Julia together and were the only two people on earth who knew exactly what it had been like to be surrounded by her unique evil.

Julia had been his fiancée, but she'd been Drake's sister.

"No, but I'm fairly certain she's here in the States." Drake's voice was deep over the line. "I've tracked one of her known aliases to Toronto. From there she would likely cross the border by private plane and avoid passport control. I have to think she's going to go for the information my father kept."

Only a few days before, Drake's father had been killed after he'd been outed as a double agent. The elder Radcliffe hadn't actually been a working Agency operative at the time, but he had been active with a group known as The Consortium. It was an illuminati-like team of some of the world's wealthiest corporations who conducted secret wars and influenced governments and were basically corrupt and violent. Like his ex.

Julia had gotten away, and now they believed she was going after what Drake's father called his burn files. The former CIA operative had kept notes on everyone he'd worked for in case he ever needed to blackmail his way out of a bad situation.

Kyle meant to find those files because if Julia got her hands on them, she would be more powerful than she'd ever been before.

"I'm sending you everything I know. I can't work on this

without clueing my bosses in on it, and then we'll have to work against them, too," Drake admitted. "Everyone will want these files. I suspect my dad kept records on his friends as well."

Don Radcliffe had been friendly with some of the world's most powerful men. Yes, a lot of people would want those records, so it was important to keep the fact that they existed quiet. "I'm meeting with my uncle tomorrow, and I've asked Adam and Chelsea to join us. After I get MaeBe on her way to Loa Mali, I'll work nonstop on finding the intel."

"You're going to try to send MaeBe to Loa Mali? Without you? I thought you were going after your girl."

"I am, but I need to make sure she's safe first. She's not like Taylor. I need to make sure Julia can't find her." Drake's girlfriend Taylor was a well-trained operative who could probably take Drake in a fight. MaeBe was a genius when it came to a computer, but she wasn't a field agent.

He was going to be patient with her since he was the reason she'd gotten her ass kicked by Julia. He hadn't read the signs right, had let himself believe the bad guy was dead and gone when he should have known it wouldn't be that easy.

"I don't think this is the right way to turn MaeBe around, man. You should drop to your knees and beg. Whine until she feels sorry for you and then get her in bed and don't let her out until she's willing to work with you," Drake advised. "You have to bring her in. She's got skills. She can help you. She might forget how pissed she is if you give her a job to do."

"I don't want her to do anything but relax," he said quietly, listening for the beep that would sound when MaeBe walked in. "My uncle has had her training in self-defense and moving from house to house. I'm sending her to Loa Mali where she's going to work on the king's cyber security and be treated like a princess. I'm going to explain the situation to her, and she will understand. She's a reasonable woman. Once I tell her how I feel, we'll be okay."

Drake snorted over the line. "Good luck with that, man. And you should protect your balls. I'll see you soon."

The line went dead as he heard the beep as the door opened.

She was here, and he was about to start his life again.

He'd been wrong to try to trick her. He should have been

upfront and honest with her about Julia and how dangerous the situation was. She would have understood.

She was talking to West, but he couldn't quite make out what she was saying. Would she see the present he'd left her on the bar and know he was here?

Spicy girl. One day I'll show you how hot you can be.

He'd said those words to her the day before he "died." The day before Julia had blown up the world again. He'd been ready to start their lives together after a year of circling warily around each other. They'd become friends, and he'd never meant to be more, but somehow this one woman had become the whole fucking world to him.

He loved Mae Beatrice Vaughn, and he wasn't going to let Julia ruin that for either of them. Mae needed him and he needed her, and once he'd taken care of the situation he was going to marry her and they were going to have whatever weird amazing life they could.

"You're getting so damn good at this, girl," that dumbass cowboy player was saying. "Pretty soon you'll be the one protecting me."

Sure she would. She would never see that asshole again after tonight. West was getting kicked out of here in a few moments.

"Somehow I doubt that." She was walking toward him, her voice rising as she crossed the space between them. "I'll be right back."

He stood in the darkest corner of her room as the door opened and he got his first look at her. She'd changed her hair color. It was brown now, and he hated that it wasn't some crazy, not-to-be-found-in-nature hue. She'd dimmed her light, and she'd had to do it for him.

He would bring it all back, work hard to give her the life she deserved.

He would be worthy of all the love and trust she'd shown him in the past. His stupid heart actually clenched at the sight of her. She'd lost weight, likely because she was so worried.

She stopped, and her whole body stiffened.

He stepped out of the shadows. "Hello, MaeBe."

She stared at him for a moment. "Kyle. Death seems to have been good to you. Why are you here?"

She was mad. He understood that. "You know why I'm here. I shouldn't have left you the way I did. I'm sorry."

"You're sorry? Sorry about what? Sorry you promised me the world and then didn't bother to tell me you weren't dead? I understand that. You worked hard to get away from me. I've never had a man fake his own death before. It was a lot. All you had to say was 'Hey MaeBe, I think we're more like friends than boyfriend/girlfriend.' You're forgiven. You can leave now, and don't break into my apartment again."

Now he was confused. "I didn't fake my death to break up with you." He moved into her space. He needed to get his arms around her, to show her they were both okay. He put his hands on her shoulders. "I did it to protect you."

Her head tilted toward him and then she moved, bringing her knee up.

He should have listened to Drake and protected his balls.

Pain exploded in his body, and he dropped to his knees.

"You can leave, Kyle." She stood over him, hands on her hips, and he could see the newly honed muscles in her arms. She'd been working out hard. "As you can see I can protect myself now."

That was the moment he realized she'd pulled a gun on him.

He closed his eyes and wondered how the hell they'd gotten here.

Part One

How they got here...

Chapter One

Dallas, TX
Eighteen months before

Kyle Hawthorne stood outside the doors to McKay-Taggart Security Services and thought seriously about running.

He wouldn't run, exactly. He would walk away with the restraint and control he'd learned over the last several years, but the truth was no matter how slow he went he would be running.

But then hadn't he been running for a long time now?

Those doors were so familiar. The floor-to-ceiling glass with its elegantly etched words hadn't changed since his Aunt Charlotte had redone the office when he'd been in college. He'd worked here the summer she'd overseen the renovation. The summer of chaos, as he and his brother had called it. They'd both been in college, and working for their uncle and aunt had been an excellent way to make some money and avoid working for their stepdad. Not that they didn't love Sean Taggart, but the kitchen had been rough work in the beginning. It had been way more fun to watch Uncle Ian go slowly insane as his utilitarian office was transformed into something designer and chic.

Damn, but the world had been different then.

No. The world hadn't been different. It had been him.

He heard the ding of the elevator and prayed it wasn't anyone he knew. He still had time. He could turn and get on that elevator and walk out into the world and never be seen again.

He could call Drake and tell him to fuck himself and the whole Agency. He could reject this whole forced sabbatical and go mercenary. There were lots of groups who would love to put his ass on the payroll and let him take out all his anger in the most violent of ways.

His stomach rolled at the thought.

He could still see the blood on his hands. Julia's blood. Still see the surprised look in her eyes as she'd realized he'd been the one to pull the trigger, and then an oddly excited light had come into her eyes.

Oh, you want to play, lover? I think I'll like this game. You're mine, Kyle Hawthorne. No little bullet is going to stop me.

It hadn't been a bullet that truly stopped her. It had taken an explosion and a whole house coming down on her to end that wicked witch's life.

Of course once he'd thought she was his future. He'd been a fucking moron, and many, many people had suffered.

"Do you think he's going to kill you? I know the man seems scary but he's not. The key with Big Tag is to give as good as you get. Like fight his sarcasm with sarcasm. When he asks how my broom ride in was, I smile and ask him if he rode in on the back of a brontosaurus from his age. I know that sounds harsh, but it made him laugh, and now we're cool. I spent the first couple of weeks terrified by him, thinking he was this big bully, but he's actually the sweetest guy."

The words had been said with a slightly husky feminine tone, and when he turned, sure enough there was a woman. A young woman who looked like she'd walked off the pages of a goth comic book. She was petite, a good foot shorter than him, with two purple pig tails, and she liked black. She had on a black miniskirt with sparkly suspenders over a black button-up. Dark green leggings and combat boots completed the look.

She was absolutely nothing like the two types of women he'd been surrounded by the last decade of his life. Military women who kept things neat and clean and practical, or the sophisticated crowd he'd run in when he'd been a spy. Women who were polished and thought out every single word they said and action made.

The first he would have nodded and made some simple conversation with. The second he would spend some time figuring out to ensure they weren't here to spy on him.

He had absolutely no idea what to do with the woman in front of him. "Uh, I don't think he's going to kill me."

She was weirdly fascinating. And just plain weird. She had a messenger bag over her shoulder, and the wide strap was decorated with a bunch of buttons, one which proclaimed her the *Mistress of Code*. She seemed to like code and the color green since she had a big button with the words *I Always Play Green* and some weird figure on it. "Confident. I like it. Are you a client or a new hire?" She gasped as she seemed to think of something. "Or a new vendor? Because if you are trying to sell the big guy anything that's not a lemon tart, he might kill you. We should rethink this."

It was her smile that did it. A small uptick of lips that let him know she was fucking with him and probably fucked with every guy in her life. Not in a "I'm looking to screw you over, take your secrets, and then probably murder you on the way out the door" way he'd gotten used to.

In the "I don't take life too seriously" way. Like the women he'd been friends with in college. The ones he'd been comfortable with in another lifetime. In the life he'd had before he'd so brutally destroyed everything around him.

He should walk away from this woman. He was toxic, and his world for so long had been blood and secrets and death. She wouldn't even know how to walk in his world. She also wasn't his type. The last thing he needed was even a casual flirtation.

"I'm the new guy." He held out a hand. "Name's Kyle Hawthorne. I'm starting in the bodyguard unit today."

She was completely harmless. It wouldn't hurt to talk to the cute goth chick while he was here. He wouldn't be here forever. He was giving this two months tops. That should be enough time to satisfy his family and the higher-ups at the CIA that he wasn't going to do something dangerous. And then he would go do something dangerous.

She reached out, that smile turning into something truly

glorious. Her black-tinged lips spread and showed even white teeth, but it was the way that smile lit up her eyes that made him pause. "MaeBe."

Oh, she was playing with fire because for the first time in months he felt his groin tighten as he took her hand in his and felt an actual fucking spark that probably wasn't static electricity. He couldn't help the way his own lips curled up, and the words that flowed out of his mouth could have come from his twenty-year-old self. "Maybe? I would say that's a little presumptuous of you, but I think I'll go with it."

Who the fuck was he? He didn't flirt with cuties. Not when information wasn't on the line.

He didn't want information from her. Not anything beyond why she only played green and what she was doing standing in front of an office filled with hardened ex-soldiers.

Her eyes rolled but it was softened with a laugh as she released his hand and stepped back. "It's my name, Kyle. Not a prediction of the future. I'm Mae Beatrice Vaughn, hence the MaeBe nickname. My mom came up with it, and it stuck with me. I'm in cybersecurity."

"Really? You work here?"

She pulled a key card out of her bag and held it up. "I do. I know it's hard to think about. I should probably be getting ready to DJ a bar mitzvah or something. Or perhaps working in the dark corners of the web catfishing people for cash, but no. I'm here with the good guys. And don't go with it, buddy. I only date weirdoes, and you, sir, are the boss's nephew." She looked at him critically. "You don't look like the big guy."

"Because he's not my biological uncle, hence the we-don't-share-a-last-name thing." He'd been standing in this hallway for at least ten minutes trying to decide if he was actually going in, but now he found himself scrambling behind her so the door didn't close and he was left on the wrong side.

She strode through, her combat boots clomping against the marble floors. "Huh. He told everyone you were his nephew. So you're Grace's kid?"

"I am not a kid at all but yes, Grace Taggart is my mom. But I do call Ian my uncle. It's different when it comes to Sean. I had a dad. I didn't have an uncle. I call Sean by his name since I was pretty much an adult when they met. Mostly."

That seemed like a million years ago. A full lifetime he could never get back no matter how familiar this place was. The fact that a super-adorable woman with what looked like a banging bod worked here now was proof that the place was likely as changed as Kyle himself.

She turned, those dumb, shouldn't-be-so-sexy pigtails swinging. "I didn't think about that. You knew Sean before he was the Soldier Chef."

He nodded. "Yeah. I knew him when he was the asshole who was trying to sleep with my mom. I actually called him that over the phone once. I hadn't met him at the time. I kind of pictured him being this pudgy dude wearing khakis that came up to his nipples and had a pornstache. So I threatened him."

That smile went nuclear again. "Bet you wet your pants when you finally did meet him."

He hadn't thought about that day in forever. He shook his head. "Not at all. I'd talked to him enough by then that I knew he was a solid dude. When I met him, we were at a hospital because my mom was in a coma. I hugged him, and he got us all through that and then we were family."

Why had he said that? He was guarded. He didn't blurt things out.

Her expression softened. "That's great. It doesn't surprise me Sean Taggart's a good stepdad. Big Tag's pretty much every sad-sack employee who needs one's dad. Not that I would tell him that. Not the dad part."

"You?"

"Absolutely. My dad sucks. I think when Ian picked up on that he moved into what he thinks is the big brother role, but he's a dad. It's probably because he's got so many kids. They're like everywhere. But you know that. You probably got to watch them grow up and stuff."

He hadn't. He barely knew his half siblings. He'd been around when they were little. Even when he'd first gone in the Navy, he'd come home on leave and he and David would take their younger sister and brother out to the movies and to baseball games, and then secrets had become his whole world and spies had replaced his family.

"I've been away for a couple of years. In the Navy." He couldn't tell anyone what he'd actually been doing the last three years of his life. Not even his parents, and definitely not his uncle or anyone here at McKay-Taggart.

He rather thought that was part of this whole sabbatical thing. His bosses wanted to see how wrecked he was and if he could still keep a secret.

What they didn't understand was how far he would go to keep his family from knowing how badly he'd screwed up. His family didn't know he'd worked with their CIA contact, Drake Radcliffe, for years. They didn't know he had anything to do with the Agency at all.

They definitely didn't know about Julia Ennis, and they never would.

"You don't look military to me," MaeBe said. "But then there are a couple of former CIA agents who I would never have guessed."

It was on the tip of his tongue to argue with her since he knew exactly who she was talking about. Michael Malone and Greg Hutchins had been on a CIA Special Forces team. So had his Uncle Theo and several other guys who worked for McKay-Taggart. None of them had been operatives. Not a one of them had ever slipped into a bedroom and slit the throat of an enemy.

Now his Aunt Charlotte was another story altogether.

"Well, I guess being able to blend in is good for a spy," he replied. "As for me, all I had to do was know how to swim and duck. How about you? You do not look like an Army girl to me, but I happen to know my uncle only hires ex-military."

She frowned, though he still found the expression incredibly endearing. "There are a couple of us nonmilitary types. Me. Yasmin, the receptionist. Genny Rycroft has been here for years." She waved as the door came open. "That guy. Hey, Beck."

The man named Beck walked through the door. He was a tall, fit man who was probably pushing forty. He wore slacks and a button-down sans tie, and absolutely, one hundred percent was at least ex-military. It was there in the way he moved, in how his eyes had gone immediately for the dude in the room he didn't know. This man had already taken in Kyle's appearance and was asking himself if he was a threat. "Hey, MaeBe. Who's your friend? Are you okay?"

And the man had assessed him properly. This told Kyle two things. One—Beck was trained and likely had been working for a long time. Two—MaeBe wasn't trained in any way beyond whatever she did with code and whatever basics his uncle taught all new recruits. Beck was worried about her being with a new person, which also meant MaeBe probably didn't have great instincts when it came to danger.

"He's the new guy," MaeBe announced. "Kyle. Grace's son."

Beck's eyes narrowed slightly, and then he was all smooth smiles and relaxed shoulders. He held a hand out. "Of course. You're Kyle Hawthorne. It's good to meet you. Your mom and stepfather run my absolute favorite restaurant."

He shook the man's hand but wasn't in any way fooled by the quick change. He would actually bet that Beck had been out of the game for years and that was the reason for the slight slip of the mask. He would also put money on the fact that this man had done his fair share of fieldwork for whatever intelligence agency he'd worked for. He wasn't a simple soldier, but he'd been working here for a while. "Top is an amazing place. I'm happy to be back home. You don't get that kind of grub on a ship, you know."

Beck stepped back. "I heard you were Navy. Special Forces, right?"

"Spent a decade in, and now I'm planning on enjoying civilian life." He hadn't been out of the game for long. He'd lived in a heightened awareness for years.

Not that it had stopped him from missing the most important clue of all. It hadn't stopped him from sleeping with the enemy.

"Welcome, Kyle. You're going to enjoy it here. You're going into the bodyguard unit, right?" Beck asked as he headed toward the inner door. He turned as he opened it. "That's one floor down. I'm sure Wade will be happy to show you around. MaeBe, I'll let Hutch know you're here. I've got some data for you to look at when you have a chance."

"Of course," she replied.

But Kyle got the actual message. Beck saw him. Perhaps not all the information, but the other man had seen enough to know he was a predator and MaeBe was some sweet, soft prey who needed protection from him. She was too innocent to know who she was talking to, and he should stay away.

What Beck couldn't possibly know is how little he wanted to hurt the woman in front of him, how much he wanted to protect someone for once in his life. Even if the person he was protecting her from was himself.

"Well, it was good to meet you." He didn't want to walk away from her which was precisely why he should and quickly. "I should go downstairs and find my new CO."

"Wade's awesome," MaeBe said. "But I don't think he's in this early today. I think he's taking his daughter to something."

The door came open again and a pretty woman with dark hair breezed in. "Are you talking about Wade? He and Genny are going to be late today. Bella has a checkup this morning, and they both wanted to be there. She hates shots. Hey, you must be the new guy. I have your key card and a welcome packet ready for you. Don't worry. I took the condoms out."

MaeBe snorted. "But, Yas, that's the best part."

"Ah, that would be my uncle. I should have known he would have his own version of a welcome pack, but you should understand that I've worked here before," Kyle said as the receptionist walked behind her desk and set her purse down. "I spent several summers trying to learn the weirdest filing system in the world."

Yasmin opened a drawer and pulled out a folder. "Oh, you will find that Genny completely redid that system so it makes some sense now. I also took out the very invasive questionnaires. No one needs to know how you feel about vinyl records or whether you've ever owned a pork pie hat. The boss has strange ways, but I suspect you know that."

He snorted as he took the folder that would contain all of his first day paperwork and security clearance. "I know it so well. I've had many a Thanksgiving with him. The key to any holiday with Uncle Ian is to set him up in front of whatever football game is on and make sure he keeps a beer in one hand and meat in the other. We have a saying in our family. *Beware wandering Ians*. He'll show up in the kitchen and try to give my stepdad cooking tips, and that always goes poorly."

MaeBe laughed at the thought. "Oh, that sounds like fun. This year's my first Thanksgiving here, and I'm looking forward to it."

"You don't have it with your family?" he asked.

Her vibrance dimmed. "I don't have much of a family. I think Big Tag's orphan dinner will be way more fun than getting kicked out of my stepmom's Martha Stewart holiday party for not wearing the right pearls. Anyway, welcome to the group."

"Yes, welcome, Kyle," a deep voice said. "You're late."

His uncle was standing in the hall that led to the main office. Ian Taggart. The man had been in his life for over a decade, and Kyle wasn't sure how he'd survived without him.

God, he hoped his uncle never found out how badly he'd screwed up. "I'm twenty minutes early."

His uncle's lips curved up slightly. "Like I said. Late. Come on. I'll walk you downstairs. You've got a shit ton of paperwork to do."

He nodded toward the women. "It was nice to meet you both."

MaeBe gave him a wave. "You, too. Let me know if you need anything computer-wise."

His uncle started walking. He didn't look behind him, merely expected Kyle to follow. Kyle did look behind him, unable to not take one last look at a woman who shouldn't catch his eye for anything beyond how odd she was.

Oddly lovely. He was lying to himself when he'd thought she wasn't his type. She wasn't this version of Kyle's type. She wasn't the spy's type. She was absolutely the dumbass college kid he'd been's type. That Kyle would have fumbled all over her and tried to figure out how to work his way into her world. He would have flirted and plotted to get into her bed.

That Kyle had never killed a person.

That Kyle hadn't killed the last woman who'd trusted him.

He jogged to catch up.

Ian stopped in the middle of the hall, whirling around and pinning Kyle with a death stare. "You're not into my cybersecurity expert, are you?"

That was fast. "We were walking in at the same time. I just met her. And obviously she's not my type."

Cool blue eyes rolled. "Sure she's not. Stay away. She's a nice kid and you look like a rolling ball of anxiety and murder."

Kyle felt his jaw drop. "I do not."

"Get your shit together before you go after her," Ian announced loudly and then started moving again.

"I'm not going after anyone." No one in the world could turn him around the way his uncle could. It was oddly comforting. No one would fuck with him in his professional life. Drake might joke with him from time to time, but not in the way his uncle or stepdad would.

"Uh huh. I'll believe it when I see it," his uncle countered as he walked past a big office. The door was open, and he stopped briefly. "Charlie, baby, Kyle got a look at MaeBe and his eyes were as wide as mine when I look at a lemon tart."

Charlotte Taggart was suddenly in her doorway looking chic and perfect in a white sheath dress and high heels, her strawberry blonde hair in a neat bun. "Seriously? I did not see that coming. I've been trying to set her up with my yoga instructor."

"I'm not trying to eat the lady for dessert. I didn't have a key card. The receptionist wasn't here yet because I was early. MaeBe let me in. That's all." He should have taken another job. Any other job. Something far away from his family.

Except his chest seemed slightly less tight. He'd slept at his brother's place the night before and listened to David talking about his students and telling dumb stories about the university he worked at, and it had felt normal and sane and comforting.

His aunt gave him a once-over. "Good, because you look very murdery."

"I do not look murdery. What does that even mean?" He looked regular. He looked like an everyday, ordinary dude starting a new job that did not include gathering state secrets and risking his life on a daily basis. No. Here he would only risk his dignity.

Charlotte waved a hand up and down, gesturing to him. "Look in the mirror, nephew. You should spend some time with Kai before you go after her. Oooo, or I know a nice FBI agent. Should I set you up?"

"Do you want me to quit here and now and go back to the Navy?" He needed to put a stop to this.

Charlotte sighed. "I suppose not. Well, I'll let you settle in then."

His uncle kissed his aunt. And kind of started making out with her.

Yep. He was so far from where he'd come.

But closer to home. So much closer.

He wasn't ready to even consider dating someone. Not close. But he rather thought he would be thinking about MaeBe Vaughn quite a lot. If the heat between them was any clue, she would likely be doing the same.

* * * *

"Did you meet the new guy?" Hutch's head popped up over the side of her cubicle and he rested an arm there, a Red Vine dangling from his mouth.

That long piece of candy was part of his daily uniform.

Hutch was one of the coolest guys she'd ever met.

Hutch had kind of saved her. He'd definitely saved her from jail, but beyond that he'd saved her from drifting away from herself, from making the kind of choice that might have killed her soul. Hutch had given her a place where she was valued.

"New guy?" She slid her headphones off her ears and onto her shoulders.

"Yeah, Big Tag's nephew is supposed to start today." Hutch had blue eyes and a ready smile that she so wished made her heart stop.

It was sad because Hutch was pretty much exactly her type. He liked board games and computers, and they could talk tech all night while they ate pizza and decided which craft beer paired well with cheese.

He was the brother she wished she'd had, a piece of the family she'd lost and now longed for. "Oh, yes. I met him. He seemed nice."

"Nice? He's practically a Taggart. Come on. You have to have some intel."

He'd seemed a bit lost to her. She probably wouldn't see him again. She didn't have much to do with the bodyguards. They were pretty self-contained most of the time. Every now and then a laptop went wonky or one of them couldn't get a game to play and it was MaeBe to the rescue, but she didn't think Kirk looked like a guy who played a lot of games.

He looked like a sports guy.

"He was a typical ex-military guy," she replied. "I think he said he recently got out of the Navy. I figured out that he's Sean's stepson, and he's pretty cool with the whole stepfamily thing. He called Ian his uncle but Sean was Sean. Kirk seemed like an okay guy."

"Kirk? I thought his name was Kyle." Hutch frowned. "Or maybe Kurt. I don't know. He wasn't working here when I hired on, and he's been gone for years. I think he's come home a couple of times, but I've never met him. I met his brother at a party once. David's a nice guy. You should meet him."

She shook her head because she knew what he meant. "I will meet him when you meet my friend from the coffee shop."

Hutch stepped back and bowed formally. "Well played, my lady. No meetings. I'm done with the whole dating thing. I am happily single."

He was not. Oh, she had zero doubt that he was happy his ex was out of his apartment and they had cleaned up all the dishes she'd chucked his way. Hutch had promised her he'd managed to duck. It was probably all his military/CIA training. "Are you sure? She's a nice lady and she makes a killer mocha."

"And David is a history professor. He's as geek as you can get," Hutch countered. "Or I can send you downstairs and you can give Kirk/Kyle/Kurt his system orientation. I was going to send someone from help desk down."

He was an evil man. "Please send them. I don't think I have anything in common with that guy. Though like I said, he seemed perfectly nice if you like the type."

She seriously doubted that man had ever played D&D or spent an entire weekend watching *Lord of the Rings*. He likely loved Marvel movies but didn't read comic books.

She'd learned those kind of men never took her seriously. They might think she was good for a night in bed, but they lacked the fundamental thing she required in a relationship—the compatibility to truly be friends with her.

"So you're not going to be inviting him to game night? You know we could use a fourth for whatever we're playing on Thursday. Boomer's out of town for another week."

And she would miss the big guy, but her prep work for food for game night had gotten so much easier. The Boom man could eat. "Do you think we should cancel? If there are only three of us, it doesn't seem like much of a party. Ever since the school year started we lost Theo and Michelle."

She'd formed a game group over the course of her time here. It had started when Hutch had found out she had a European-style board game collection. It wasn't much since she didn't exactly have a ton of cash. But she was starting to grow it, and she loved hosting some friends at her place once a week. Hutch had brought along Theo Taggart, Deke Murphy, and Boomer Ward. She'd brought her friends Michelle Johnson and Harry Tanaka. Sometimes there were seven of them. Sometimes it was her and Hutch. Theo's daughter had soccer practice on Thursdays this season and Michelle's son had tutoring sessions. Harry had started his residency in pediatrics at Parkland Hospital, and Deke and Boomer's work often took them out of town.

She'd planned on playing *Root* this week, but it was so much better with a full four players. With three players, whoever was near the empty sector was at a distinct advantage. They wouldn't have to fight the way the other two would. "We could see if Jamal wants to come."

Hutch shook his head. "He's on vacation. He's heading to Houston to see his dad. Come on. Don't you want to check out the new guy?"

Something told her the new guy wasn't going to want to play. "I'll find a three-player game. I've got a couple of days. I think Harry said he's off next Thursday. We can play *Root* then."

Hutch's eyes narrowed, and he studied her for a moment. "You are the nicest person I know. You invite everyone. Once I caught you trying to invite an assassin to board game night."

"I didn't know he was an assassin." Since starting here at MT, she'd met many colorful people including a guy who'd accompanied Charlotte's cousin, Dusan, on a visit. Apparently Dusan was the head of a Russian syndicate, and he liked to travel with a crew. The man named Leon had seemed super normal. It was only later she'd found out he was an assassin. "I thought he was from out of town and probably needed some friends."

Hutch chuckled. "Oh, I'm sure he was interested in being friends with you. So why is the sweetest woman I know not holding open the door for the new guy? You brought the last one a welcome basket."

She'd felt bad for the dude. Tag could be hard on accountants. Something about Phoebe Murdoch and how she'd run the place. "And Gary is still here. I think it was definitely the earplugs I slipped in along with chamomile tea and tequila. And the card of a good therapist."

"Evasion. The mystery deepens," Hutch mused.

There was zero mystery here, and the last thing she needed was the whisper of a rumor to get back to Charlotte. If Charlotte got it in her head that she and the new guy might be a good match, she would be in for weeks of "running in to" a man she knew damn well wasn't going to work. He was conventionally handsome and likely upright and all-American, and she was sure most women would be panting after him, but she wasn't most women.

She needed some nerd in her guy, and that Hawthorne dude screamed sports guy.

"I'm not evading," she said. "I'm just not at all interested in him, and I don't think he would be a good fit for our table."

"Okay." Hutch backed off. "We can play *Tapestry*. I'll bring beer if you'll make tacos."

She liked to cook and rarely had anyone but herself to enjoy the fruits of her labor. "Will do."

"You want to hang out with me and Deke this weekend? We're going to see a movie before we head to Sanctum for the night."

Sanctum was the coolest place in the world. One of the perks of employment at McKay-Taggart was membership at Sanctum. She'd never imagined she would find such joy and acceptance in the kink community, but Sanctum had quickly become her safe haven. She played most Saturday nights, always with someone outside of her work family. There were plenty of tops there she didn't work with who liked to scene without expectations of a sexual encounter.

She hadn't had sex with any of the men or women who topped her. Yet.

Would the new guy be there? Would he be at Sanctum this Saturday? Normally she would say no because she happened to know he wasn't in the current training class, but he was a Taggart and that meant he could have taken that class long ago.

What would she say if he asked her to scene with him?

"That sounds like fun, but I'm supposed to go to my dad's birthday party." She'd been shocked to receive the invite. Her stepmom usually made sure she only found out about family functions long after they were over. She'd learned early on not to even try to show up for Christmas or Easter.

Hutch's brows rose. "Your dad's birthday?"

"I know. I was surprised, too." She sat back. "I thought about not going, but it's been a long time since I saw him so I'm going to put on a regular, normal-person dress, tone down the makeup, and pretend to fit in for a night."

Her stepmom was very concerned with appearances.

"Good for you. I hope it goes okay, and let me know when you're on the road." Hutch patted the top of the cubicle.

Hutch walked back into his office, and MaeBe turned to her screen. Well, one of them. She had three, each set to a different bit of work. One showed a file she was completing to end a job. Another was a set of documents she was going through, and the third showed a perfectly quiet office building in Seattle where Boomer was on a job. He'd sent her the security tapes to go through. He was hunting a corporate spy and thought they were pulling some hacking on the security cams to hide their activity.

She was pretty sure he was right. She just had to prove it.

Her cell phone trilled, and she glanced down at it. Speak of the devil. Well, not the devil, but he was married to her. She swiped a finger across the screen and put the phone to her ear. "Hey, Dad. How are you?"

"Oh, hey, sweetie. I'm good. Real good." Her father had a soft tone. She'd never seen the man get angry even once. Her mother had been the disciplinarian of the family. "Hey, I needed to talk to you about something."

She could guess. "I promise I've got a perfectly respectable dress to wear on Saturday, and I will leave the combat boots at home."

"About that, honey," her dad began.

MaeBe's heart sank because she knew exactly where this was going to lead.

* * * *

Julia Ennis stared out over the Los Angeles skyline and wondered where Kyle was. It wasn't like she could ask the man on the other end of the line.

"Are you listening to me, Julia?"

She sighed and forced herself to reply. "Yes, Dad. I understand. I'm getting better every day. The group doesn't have to murder me thinking I'm going to make some kind of deathbed confession."

"Do you want to explain what really happened? Because your brother seems to know something."

"He doesn't know a thing about you." She'd fucked up in an unimaginable way, but at least she'd hidden her stepfather's involvement from her brother and Kyle.

Just the thought of Kyle Hawthorne put her gut in a knot. Her hand strayed to the place where the bullet had gone in, barely missing her heart. If it hadn't been for John, she would have been dead.

"I told you that getting involved with that boy would be nothing but trouble," her stepfather said. "He's too much like your brother. You know there's a reason I never recruited Drake, and it's the same reason I would have stayed far away from Hawthorne. He's practically a fucking Taggart. How did you think that was going to work?"

"I thought it would work like all things do. I was putting him in a position where he couldn't exactly refuse. I just didn't have enough time with him." She had to admit that she'd been losing her hold on Kyle for the last few months of their relationship. He'd been talking to his brother a lot.

She'd intended to end that relationship on a permanent basis, but she hadn't gotten around to it. She hadn't been able to decide on how to off David Hawthorne. Then there was the fact that Kyle's stepfather was a public figure and related to one of the most highly thought-of security experts in the business. The Taggart family might investigate any accident she could plan for David.

"You would never have changed his mind," her father said firmly. "I'm disappointed. I thought you of all people have been taught to think with your head and not your other parts."

She was ruthless. She was savage when it came to business. She'd viewed Kyle as a challenge at first, and then she'd seen how the darkness in his soul matched her own.

She wasn't willing to give up on him. Why should one argument screw up the rest of their lives together? She was the only woman in the world who could understand him. If his parents knew what he was capable of, they would almost certainly turn away from him. She could love the whole of Kyle.

Well, she wasn't particularly fond of the part of him that had shot her, but no one was perfect.

However, as a couple they could move mountains. She simply had to get him to see it, to buy into the vision.

"Did you put the money in his account?" Her stepfather sounded like he usually did. Gruff. A bit angry.

He was only truly happy with her when she was working, and now she was sidelined until she could find a new identity and new face.

She liked her face. Her brother was going to cost her everything.

She refused to blame Kyle. He didn't understand, and she hadn't explained it properly. If she had, they would be together right this minute and she wouldn't be staring at her face for the last time. She would have to become someone else. Someone boring. Jane Adams. Even that woman's name was boring.

"Of course I did. It's there, and we'll have the proof that we need to keep him in line," she said. Her father had insisted that they maintain some kind of leverage over Kyle Hawthorne. "I sent you everything you need, but you're not going to use it until we have to."

She might have sent Kyle on a few non-Agency approved operations. Not that he'd understood it at the time, but now he did. It was precisely what had gotten her in trouble in the first place. He'd figured out the person he'd assassinated wasn't a dangerous terrorist, and he hadn't taken it well.

But she could turn it around because she knew everything about the man she loved. Including his bank account numbers. Setting him up was nothing more than an act of love.

He had a streak of bourgeoisie morality that was proving hard to rid him of. At first he'd gone with it, living life on the reckless edge.

Then he'd started visiting home and coming back with all sorts of stupid ideas. He'd questioned some of their ops and even talked Drake into agreeing with him.

So she'd lost both her brother and the love of her life.

She wasn't sure she could fix the relationship with Drake. She could accept that. Losing Kyle wasn't a possibility she was willing to consider.

"All right. When is your first surgery?" her father asked. "I want to know when you can get back to work. There are a couple of situations that could use your unique skills."

So he wanted her to steal something or seduce someone. "I'll be ready to go in a few weeks. Maybe two months. I don't know. John's taking care of the scheduling."

In The Consortium there were a few customs and rules. Women were always used as the principal operatives during any long-term operations. Women, they'd discovered, were far better go betweens than other men. She'd negotiated the end to many a corporate war. If both companies were in the group, that negotiation could happen over a couple of glasses of wine. If one side wasn't, then she destroyed them. Women in the group took on a code name. She was known as Lizzie.

All the male assistants were John. Johns were good for any number of tasks. They handled most of the physical work, though she didn't mind shooting someone every now and then. They were also around for security and stress relief. In her case, hers would be playing nursemaid as well since she would be having a whole lot of surgeries in the upcoming months. John would be the one who would ensure that it was easy for her to slip into Jane Adams's life when the time came.

John had been with her for over a year, and keeping him a secret had been hard as hell. He'd let her know he was there for all of her needs. All of them.

She hadn't needed a John for stress relief when she'd had Kyle.

"John is the only person you need in your life right now," her father growled. "Beyond doctors, I don't want you associating with anyone but him. I'm putting the data you sent about the missions with Kyle in with my other files. You be careful and stay away from Kyle Hawthorne or I'll take care of the problem for you."

"Of course. That's over. I know it was useful to have a CIA operative, but I can move more freely now, and I don't have to worry about Drake finding out." Because he already had. Because the worst had happened and now she had to find her way back. She wasn't going to tell her father that she had no plans to walk away from her future husband. "And I can work on finding another operative inside the Agency."

"I'll work on that from my side. I do want someone else on the inside, but it needs to be the right person," her father replied.

Maybe if she found the right person to recruit, her father would get off her back. And Kyle's. Her father would do it. He would deploy the leverage she'd built against Kyle, and that wasn't how she wanted to use it. She would greatly prefer to use it to force him back to her side when the time was right.

She would have to be patient. He would likely go home to Dallas to lick his wounds.

"Stay out of sight until you can move to the next phase," her father instructed. "I'll contact you. You should know that your mother is hiring a company to look for you."

Her mom. Senator Samantha Radcliffe hadn't been around much. Her career was far more important. In some ways, her mother had taught her a lot. "They won't find anything. Besides isn't my brother busy covering it all up? Can't hurt the family name."

Not that she had the family name. Her biological father had left her behind long ago, left her in the tender care of Don Radcliffe. She often thanked the universe for that one gift. She had no idea who she would have been if she'd been left with her dull father who'd moved on to teach math or something and had another couple of mewling sheep children. Instead, she'd gotten a true spy. She'd been trained to steal secrets from a young age, and she'd learned that nothing was more important than power. Power and money were the only things

41

in life that mattered.

And desire. Love. Sometimes she wished she'd never met Kyle Hawthorne. Life had been simpler back then.

"Your mother is doing what she does. Eventually she'll accept that you're gone and you're not coming back. We might need to arrange someone finding your body so we can give her some closure. I trust Drake won't ever say a thing. He's too worried about his part in it."

"He should be." After all, he'd taken Kyle's side and he'd left her there when the fire had started. It turned out to be a lucky thing, but at the time it bugged her.

"Don't let anyone take your picture or see your face. Am I clear?"

She sighed. "As crystal."

The line disconnected and she went back to looking out over the skyline. The next time anyone important saw her face, it wouldn't be her own.

That might be the key to winning Kyle back. It would prove that she was dedicated to a fresh start, to being open with him this time around. But first, she would make him a bit uncomfortable. Nothing big. Just some minor inconveniences that would make his life less than perfect.

Then when he needed her, they could start over.

Chapter Two

Kyle looked up at the clock and realized he'd been staring at the computer screen for way too long. It was past seven, and his first day of exile was over. Wade Rycroft had been the last of the bodyguards to tell him goodnight, and that was over an hour ago.

His stomach rumbled, and he had to make a decision. Was he going to get on the train or wait until David could pick him up? He probably could have gotten his uncle to give him a ride, but that would mean admitting he hadn't bought a car. He didn't have the money to buy a car yet, and that seemed like opening a door he didn't want to open.

If he got on the train, he could grab a burrito from the convenience store a block from his brother's townhouse and microwave it. If he waited, he could eat a granola bar from the snack basket in the break room. There were some protein shakes in the fridge that were apparently for everyone. Wade had rolled his eyes as he'd offered them up because apparently his uncle had them stocked to keep the group from getting pudgy.

His uncle was an asshole but he'd also provided a nice gym, and that was something Kyle could get into. He could probably get in five or six miles before David was done with whatever faculty bullshit he was doing this evening. If he tired himself out, he might sleep for a couple of hours.

He stood up from the desk he'd been assigned and looked around, taking in the whole of the place, looking for threats. This was what he did now. He took a perfectly normal location and turned it into a house of horrors, constantly assessing risk.

Because he'd improperly assessed risk once and his whole world had blown up because of it.

Don't look at me like that, Kyle. You know who I am. You knew it when you asked me to marry you. You're with me because you know deep down you're just like me.

A chill went up his spine, and he realized he wasn't alone.

It took everything he had not to reach for the Glock he wore in a holster under his arm. His uncle might get suspicious if he started taking shots at the janitorial staff.

But there was no way to ignore the adrenaline that started flowing as he heard someone shuffling along the hallway that ran beside the office. Security was tight in this building, but no system was foolproof.

Had Julia's group decided to hunt him down? Did they think she'd given him her secrets and they wanted them back? Or would it be about revenge?

There was another option—one Drake wouldn't let him pursue.

They could be coming to recruit him.

It was exactly what he'd wanted, what he'd tried to convince Drake to let him do. Let them come. Let them believe he'd taken Julia out so he could take her place and bring down the entire empire. If he got taken out, well, Drake could find a way to finish the job. It wouldn't matter. The Agency would come up with some cover story and then his family didn't ever have to know how low he'd gotten.

The door came open and real trouble walked in.

MaeBe Vaughn strode inside, a beer in one hand and tears rolling down her cheeks.

He felt caught, like a deer standing in the brightest headlights possible right before the truck took his whole-ass body out.

She sniffled and moved past him, not looking back. One hand went across her face, rubbing against her eyes. "Come on, Wade. Don't fail me now."

If he was very still, she might not see him. Or he could hide. He could jump under the desk he'd been given and curl into a ball, and she wouldn't even know he was here. She would do her crying thing and he could sneak away and eat that sad-ass burrito and deal with his brother's cat. Yeah. He'd trained for this. He'd spent years in the Navy and the Agency learning how to elude a dangerous foe, and right now that overly emotional goth girl seemed like the most dangerous opponent of all.

Because he wanted to figure out why she was crying and deal with the situation. It was his first, stupidest instinct to walk right up to her and hug her against him and ask what had happened. Like they'd always been friends. Like it was normal and natural to offer her comfort.

Fuck. He did need to see a therapist because he looked at her and saw everything he could have had if he hadn't been in that car that night. If he'd made different choices, he would have gotten his MBA in management and probably come to work right here but in the business offices. Or for his stepdad, and one night she would have walked into Top and they would have met and talked all night and made all kinds of normal relationship mistakes. He would have forgotten important dates and she would… Well, she wouldn't have turned out to be a traitor to her country and tried to pull him into hell with her.

He wouldn't have been forced to murder that little goth princess.

"Damn it." She stopped in front of Wade's office and let her head fall forward against the door. "What am I doing? Go home, MaeBe. Except your home is currently being occupied by assholes."

It was the sniffle that did it. He could easily have evaded her, but his feet wouldn't move, and after she sniffled he gave in. "Do you need something from his office? I can probably get through the lock."

She screamed, and the beer bottle dropped to the floor with a thud as she jumped and turned.

Kyle held up his hands, showing her he didn't have anything in them. Not that he couldn't do a ton of damage with his hands. "Sorry. I didn't mean to scare you."

She put a hand over her chest as though she could stop the way her heart was racing. "Well, you did a good job. I think I'm having a heart attack."

She wasn't, but she had definitely been scared. "Again, sorry. I wasn't trying to hide or anything. You didn't notice me as you came in."

No one had trained this woman. Earlier he'd seen his Aunt Erin walk in, and though she'd done it as casually as possible, she'd noted where everyone was. She'd likely done it out of long habit of being situationally aware of her surroundings, but it was what he'd come to expect from women in his world. Julia would have known where every living creature was along with the entrances and exits and whether or not the people in said room worked for an evil empire or not.

"I thought everyone was gone." She bent down to pick up the bottle she'd dropped. It hadn't broken on the carpet that covered the floors down here on the bodyguard level. She stood back up, and her mascara had run slightly, giving her a raccoon-like appearance. "I was looking for the recycling bin. This was out in the hall."

Sure it had been. And she'd found it and poured it down her throat. Damn she shouldn't look so pretty with ruined makeup. "Does Wade keep booze in his office?"

She frowned and sighed. "A bottle of whiskey. The bodyguards usually trade bottles of booze for Christmas every year, and Wade keeps his in his office. Or so I've heard. I...this is stupid. I'm going to go."

He should let her. He wasn't going to. "I assure you whatever Wade has in that office is complete shit compared to what my uncle keeps upstairs. Come on. It's the best view of the city. We can get the snack basket and you can tell me why you're crying."

"I don't think that's a good idea. Besides, why are you up here so late? It's your first day."

"Okay. You're a cautious woman. I can see that. You need an exchange of information. I'm here because I don't have a car and my brother is at some faculty event. He's an actual functional adult with job responsibilities that go beyond throwing his body in front of a bullet for whoever's paying him to. I'm lazy and the train station is a couple of blocks away. I also saw some shit during my time with the military so I don't sleep well, and I was thinking seriously about running a couple of miles on the treadmill so I might be able to sleep tonight. Oh, and I'm avoiding Hamilton."

"The musical? I really want to see it."

"No. The cat. My fully functional adult big brother has a cat because he does that now. The cat stares at me like he's judging every second of my life and all the choices I've made. So talking to the chick who has obviously had a day while drinking my uncle's good Scotch and eating the whole snack basket seems like the best of all worlds right now."

"Big Tag's door is very secure. He uses a key card and a biometric signature. Only he and Charlotte and Genny and Hutch can get in. I don't handle that part of security."

She looked like a woman who could handle a challenge. Who kind of needed one. "I bet you're better than that lock."

Her jaw straightened. "Damn straight. I can get in. Is it really good Scotch because if I'm going to lose my job and everything I've built here, I'd like for it to be good."

"Oh, I promise you that Scotch can vote. It's probably older than you."

"I'm twenty-five."

So fucking young. In all reality she wasn't much younger than he was, but his world had aged him in a way she would never be able to understand. "Well then you've got something in common with the Scotch. Unless the old guy's gotten more snobby about his liquor, and then we're in for a real treat. And he won't fire you. He'll yell at me. I'm used to it. Here's the key with Ian—if he's yelling, everything is fine. You'll know he's seriously angry when he gets quiet. When he's silent, that's when he's planning a murder. What do you say, MaeBe? Wanna prove to the old folks we're completely irresponsible and out of control?"

She bit her bottom lip. "Kind of. Except I don't want to upset the only father figure I have."

He could fix that. His uncle was a reasonable man. He slid his phone out of his pocket and hit the number that connected him to Ian Taggart.

The sound of something crashing came over the line. "Travis, do not throw that freaking frisbee in the house. Who raised you? Was it wolves? Kyle, what's happening?"

"I made a bet with MaeBe that she can't break into your office, and if she can we're going to find your stash and drink it," he said.

Ian sighed and his voice went low. "I thought she wasn't your type."

"She's worked her way through someone's beer, and she was going for Wade's whiskey," he pointed out.

"Hey," MaeBe said, her whole face flushing.

"Wade's whiskey is barely drinkable," Ian was saying, and then he paused. "Damn it. If she's drinking, it's probably about her family. Look, I'll call Hutch…"

He didn't want Hutch. "I can handle it. And David's picking us up, so she won't drive home. I'll make sure she's okay."

"Put me on speaker," Ian ordered. He continued when Kyle hit the button that shared the call with MaeBe. "Mae, you can't get through that door. Hutch promises me that no one can. So you're high if you think you can bust in."

"I so can get in." MaeBe was back to standing tall.

"Even if you can get in, there's zero shot of Kyle finding my stash. I've had that office redecorated since his intern days, and you'll never convince me he was the one to find it in the first place. David is the treasure hunter of the family. Kyle's pure muscle."

Oh, so the big guy wanted to push all the buttons tonight. "Guess what, old man. I've been here a day and I already figured out you put in a secret fridge in the break room. Yeah. I caught that paneling that hides it. That's where you keep the lemon tarts, and I bet they go well with that Scotch."

"Hey, now," Ian began.

But Kyle hung up. He'd done what he needed to do. "See, he's not even going to think about you. He's going to be pissed at me. So let's raid the secret fridge and prove to my uncle my brother isn't the only one who can find a treasure."

MaeBe blinked, her tears clearing. "Okay. Let's do this."

He watched as she walked toward the stairs. He kind of couldn't take his eyes off her. Something about the woman drew him in, and he knew that was dangerous.

She stopped at the stairs and looked back at him. "Thanks. I needed this."

His freaking breath threatened to stop because she was lovely. Really beautiful. He'd thought she was cute before, but something about her smile as she thanked him kicked in every protective instinct he had. "No problem. I want that Scotch."

She laughed as she started up the stairs.

He followed her because for the first time in forever he felt something that wasn't toxic, something that wasn't anger. Something good.

* * * *

MaeBe sat back against the leather sofa and looked out over the city. Big Tag knew how to live.

Lucky for her she knew how to hack a system, and her new friend was excellent at figuring out where hidden things were.

He also could order a pizza.

"What the hell is Srirancha?" He had polished off three slices in no time at all. They'd had to negotiate about toppings though. He was apparently a hardcore carnivore.

That would make a cute shirt. She drizzled her beloved condiment over the slice of pepperoni with mushrooms. She'd had to fight hard for that delicious fungi. "It's a combo of Sriracha and ranch. It's delicious. You know when you order from this place you can ask to play Reaper Roulette."

A brow arched over his eyes. "Dare I ask."

"Before they put the cheese on they put a couple of drops of ghost pepper sauce on one slice, and no one knows where it is. But they figure it out fast."

"Hot, huh?"

"The Sriracha I put on pretty much everything registers at 1000 to 2500 on the Scoville scale, depending on the peppers they use in it. The ranch on this particular version cuts some of the heat."

"There's a scale for peppers?"

"How did you live with Sean Taggart and not know this? Yes, there is a heat index for peppers, and Carolina reapers register somewhere between 1.4 and 2.2 million."

He hissed at the thought. "Damn. Have you ever done this roulette thing?"

"It was so hot I could feel steam coming out of my ears," she said with a laugh. "I'm pretty sure I drank a gallon of milk, and somewhere in all of that pain, I saw like dead relatives and stuff. The crazy thing was we'd played it the week before and no one said anything. So I thought it wasn't a big deal. I thought it was all bullshit, but what happened was Boomer got the slice and he didn't think it was all that hot so he didn't say anything. Something's wrong with Boomer. We need to study him medically. He went on to eat two pizzas after he ate the reaper. I was in a fetal position begging God to take me."

Kyle…his name was Kyle, and she wasn't going to forget it because he was actually pretty cool…took a sip of the ridiculously expensive Scotch he'd found by running his hands over the panels of the walls of the office until he found the hidden safe.

How he'd cracked that sucker she was afraid to ask.

Captain America had a bad-boy side, and it was totally doing something for her.

Mostly taking her mind off that damn phone call.

"There it is. I thought we'd chased it away with pizza and Scotch and crimes we won't go to jail for, but there it is." He pointed with his pinky as he held the crystal rocks glass.

She sighed and sat back. He'd been open with her about the not sleeping thing and that he feared his brother's cat's judgment.

Perhaps it would be easier to talk about this with someone who didn't really know her. It might also help if he was an asshole about it. She was starting to get some warm feelings toward this guy that she shouldn't feel. Dangerous feelings. He still wasn't her type, and she was sure she wasn't his. If he blew off her pain, she would be able to view the guy the way she had from first impressions.

"My dad called." She took a thoughtful sip of the Scotch. Even as emotional as this discussion was going to make her, she wasn't about to disrespect the Scotch. She let the caramel flavor tease her tongue and then waited for the burn to warm her chest. "So the short story…"

"I want the long story."

"It's not that long, and it's pretty ordinary. Do you have a good relationship with your bio dad?" She'd never met Grace Taggart's first husband, and no one talked about him around the office which seemed pretty normal since Grace and Sean had been married for over a decade.

"He died when I was a kid. I remember it being good. He was a good dad. My brother had more time with him. I mostly remember how hard it was to lose him, how hard my mom worked to keep us on steady ground," he said quietly. "It's why I'm all for her marriage and happy to be part of the family. I don't see it as... I wouldn't say David thinks it was disrespectful for Mom to remarry. Not at all. He thinks Sean is great for our mom, and he loves our siblings. I think he worries it's disrespectful for him to love Sean as a stepdad. Like it erases our dad, but it doesn't. It gives us more family."

If only that had been her problem. "Well, my father didn't handle things the way your stepdad did. My dad has always been gentle and kind and utterly in need of someone to lead him through life. I didn't know what to call it for the longest time, but now I know my dad requires a strong top, and not in a keep-it-to-the-club way."

"Yeah, I don't like to think about parents like that. In any way. It's why I do not go to Sanctum. Never will. If I can run into my parents or aunts and uncles while they're wearing fet wear, I say no."

She hadn't even thought about what a problem that would be for him. "Huh. I guess you don't get that part of the employment package. Not everyone's in the lifestyle."

"Sanctum's not the only club in town, and you're getting distracted. You got a call from your father. Your dad needs a strong hand. What happened to your mom?"

"Cancer. He was great with her. He never left her side, did everything she needed, was there for me. I had graduated from college and found a place to live in the city. When I went home for the holidays, he'd already met someone, and he was married by New Year's Day."

"So she wasn't as welcoming as Sean?"

"Not in any way. She has two daughters. They were twelve and seven at the time, and she pretty much took one look at me and decided I was a bad influence. I was told if I wanted to be a part of her family, I would need to change the way I dress and my hair color, and she didn't think it was a good idea for a girl like me to work in such a male-dominated field. I was advised to get a new job if I ever wanted to find a husband."

"Seriously? And your dad married her?" Kyle asked.

"Oh, yes, and asked me to get along. He begged me to get along with her. He tried compromising. I would be allowed at family functions if I would dress normally and play down my hair. I tried that twice, and it was uncomfortable to say the least. My stepmother actively hates me. She seems to think if I'm around she doesn't have full control over my dad, and that's important to her. She rules her family with an iron fist, and my dad doesn't have the willpower to fight with her. I don't even know if he loves her. I think she was strong enough to lead him and he followed."

"But he called you today. Do you talk to him often?"

"Less and less as time goes by. He's always working or doing something with the girls. I see my stepmom's socials, and he's close to her daughters." There was an ache inside her heart that she was pretty sure would never go away no matter how nice the people she worked with were. She was starting to find a family here, but it could never wholly fill the space her father had occupied. "My dad's sixtieth birthday is this Saturday, and they're throwing a big party for him. I got an invitation."

He stared at her for a moment. "Did he call to ask you not to come?"

He was good at extrapolating. "Apparently one of my stepsisters thought it would be funny if I showed up. I guess she didn't think about the fact that I would send back the RSVP card. Needless to say Evelyn wasn't amused and rescinded the invite. My father offered to meet me somewhere for breakfast, but I turned him down. Mostly because he canceled on me the last three times we made plans. I shouldn't let it get to me, but I did today. I would have gone home and drank my own beer and shot things online, but my roommate is having a party, and they can get out of hand. I couldn't stand the thought of fending off coked-up morons all night. I was planning on sleeping on the cot they keep for overnights. Sometimes we have to monitor an op overnight, and we take turns sleeping."

"You need a new roommate. Or a new place to live. I thought it was awful when I had to move in with my brother, but beyond the whole place smelling like books and that mangy cat of his, he's pretty much the most boring roommate in the history of time, and that's how I like it." He sat up, pouring himself another bit of Scotch. "As to your dad, I'm sorry about that. Having solid ground to walk on is so important. You were mourning your mom and lost your dad, too. Do you go to family functions that aren't planned by your stepmom?"

She hadn't expected his empathy. "I tried for a while. I've got a couple of aunts and uncles, but they live close to Austin so it's hard to get down there. I'm lucky I have friends. I had a medical procedure, simple thing but I needed someone to take care of me for a couple of days. I asked my dad and he said no."

"You were hurt and he didn't take care of you?"

"They had a family cruise planned and he said he needed time to get ready. I stayed with a friend." Those old wounds suddenly felt so fresh. Open and bleeding, but in a slow, painful way.

"He's weak. If my stepfather had ever suggested my mother not pay attention to me and my brother, she would have left him. I'm sorry he wasn't strong enough to take care of you the way he should have. He sucks."

She sniffled and laughed because that was a simple truth. "He does suck."

"My stepdad is so afraid of my mom that he sent someone else in to convince her that me going into the military was the best thing for me. I was in college at the time. Grad school, believe it or not."

"You went to grad school?"

"Well, I didn't finish," he admitted. "I was damn glad I'd gotten through my undergrad so I could go in as an officer. Your stepmom would have liked me. I was studying business."

"There's nothing wrong with a business degree. It just wasn't for me. Why did you need the military?"

He was quiet for a moment, and she wondered if their sharing was over. Then he set the glass down, and his eyes went to the windows and the lights outside. "I was in a car accident with a friend of mine. He was driving but it was my car. I drank too much, and he had to get us home. We got hit and he died. I found myself in a self-destructive spiral and needed to find some discipline. My mom wanted me to go into therapy, but I wasn't anywhere close to being ready for that. I talked to one of my stepdad's sous chefs at the time, and he convinced me the Navy was the way to go. As I'm still alive and not incarcerated, I think he was right. But now I'm back and I have no idea what I'm doing here."

"I thought you were being a bodyguard."

"Not the career I thought I would have. I don't know how long I'm going to be here. I'm in a state of flux."

She was starting to find this man fascinating. "Why did you leave the Navy?"

"I had an op go wrong, and now I don't trust my own instincts. It was time to leave. It was time to try something new, but new feels like old—as in I have no car and no house and I'm living like I did when I was in college. I think I'm having an early midlife crisis."

She could understand that. "I live with a woman who still parties like she's nineteen and doesn't know what silverware is. She steals plasticware from restaurants because that way we don't have to clean anything. I don't have any forks. I thought I would have forks by now."

He chuckled, and the darkness seemed to have fled. "David has lots of forks. They match and everything. We should all learn from my brother. Except for the tweed jackets. How does he think that's cool? They have leather patches on the sleeves."

He started talking about his brother and MaeBe sat back.

And realized she was in real trouble with this man.

Chapter Three

Kyle Hawthorne was the most frustrating man she'd ever met.

She looked over to where he sat at one of the tables arranged around Top's private banquet room, a beer in his hand. He wasn't sitting with the rest of his team. He'd selected a place toward the back of the big space where he could almost disappear in the shadows. She was worried he might disappear altogether.

"Hey, how's it going with the lawyer? I heard things went weird."

She turned to her side and Kori Ferguson was standing there, a drink in her hand. There was an umbrella in that drink, but then there were a whole bunch of those since Beck and his girlfriend, Kim, had a sense of whimsy when it came to engagement/going away parties. His future wife was also his old one. This would be their second wedding. Big things had been happening at McKay-Taggart the last six or so weeks. Kimberly Solomon had been located and retrieved. Tasha Taggart had been catfished by a CIA operative, and Big Tag was still bemoaning the fact that he hadn't been able to murder the dude because Kim had gotten there first.

Not that she'd been a part of that op. She'd been in her cube working tech for her friends and wondering why Kyle watched her but didn't approach since that night when they'd connected. He'd been polite and nice and standoffish, so she'd let herself be set up.

She'd also gotten herself a brand-new apartment. Without a roommate. She was inching toward whole-ass adult status, and it felt good. Even if rejection still hurt. There were more fish in the sea than Kyle Hawthorne.

She just wished they didn't remind her of guppies compared to Kyle's obvious shark.

"He was all right, but I don't think I'll see him again," she admitted. The lawyer had been her third blind date this month. It had also been her worst date, and it seemed like that story had already made the rounds. "He gave me a kind of creepy vibe and now he seems to always be around. He keeps calling and texting and showing up. Now Hutch wants me to take someone with me when I'm out of the office. It's annoying. I will not let a guy set me up again. Women have way better instincts on who's going to potentially murder us."

A brow rose over Kori's eyes. "Murder?"

She shrugged. "I'm being overly dramatic. It was just something about the guy."

"Yes, if we're going to talk about instinctively knowing which guy is potentially covering a dark past, we should discuss the way you watch Kyle Hawthorne walk by," Kori pointed out. "Because damn, girl, he's got *do not touch may explode* written all over him."

"I'm not touching Kyle. I barely know the guy." It was kind of a lie. She felt like she'd gotten to know the man that night in Tag's office. She'd opened herself up to him.

"That is not what I heard. I heard a tale of an epically annoyed Big Tag who had his booze and treats stash raided by young Kyle so he could woo you with criminally obtained luxury items."

Big Tag should have been a bard. "I had a bad night, and I couldn't go back to my place. He happened to be working late, and we sat in Big Tag's office and talked. That was all. His brother gave me a ride home, and we haven't said much more than *hi* since then. He's been training, and he went with Liam to New York when Erin couldn't go, and that was a two-week assignment. Since then I've been down in the bodyguard unit to fix stuff two or three times, and we briefly chatted about how his trip went. I asked him if he wanted to come to game night and he said he wasn't into those kinds of games."

Kori's eyes went wide. "Oh, and then the relationship was totally over."

She had been surprisingly disappointed. Since that night over a month before when they'd sat up late talking and drinking, he'd put a wall between them. From what she could tell he'd put a wall between himself and everyone. As far as she knew Kyle Hawthorne worked and went home to his brother's place and then got up and started it all over again. He ate lunch at his desk if he was in the building and worked out every day in the bodyguard gym. He didn't seem to have made friends. She'd seen him at Top when she'd gone on a Saturday night with Hutch and some of the subs from Sanctum. They'd gone in for dinner before heading to the club, and Kyle had been hanging out at the bar. When she'd asked if he wanted to join them, he'd suddenly remembered he was supposed to be somewhere else.

She got it. That night had been a one-off and they weren't going to be friends. The attraction was all one way.

So why did she catch him watching her?

Still, it wouldn't be a good idea to let the world know she thought of the gorgeous bodyguard way too much for her own good. "Yes. Any chance that man had with me was totally gone when he looked at me like I was some weirdo asking him to play *Chutes and Ladders*."

Kori snorted. "Yeah. He would soon discover how seriously you take board games." She sobered. "But honestly, I think that dude has got some shit to work through, if you know what I mean."

She felt the odd need to defend him. "He was in the Navy. He said he'd seen some things. He had an op go badly. I think he's also still dealing with the car accident that took his friend."

"That was a long time ago, but I suppose since he won't go to therapy, he could still be dealing with it." Kori waved as a couple of people they knew from Sanctum walked by.

MaeBe leaned in so no one would hear her. Dinner was over and there was a small dance floor and an open bar. She'd heard they'd already done a couple of weddings in this space, but Kim and Beck were planning on getting married in their new home in Bliss, Colorado. This was a way to say good-bye to a longtime employee and member of Sanctum, so there were lots of ears around. "I thought no one got into Sanctum without going through Kai or one of the other therapists."

The Ferguson Clinic was next door to Sanctum. It provided an array of mental health services, and Kai Ferguson and his partners also evaluated anyone who wanted to play at Sanctum.

Kori nodded. "Yes, but they'll accept another therapist's eval. Kyle sat down with the therapist attached to The Club, where his actual membership is going to be. He's only training at Sanctum because The Club doesn't have a training program right now. They send all their people to us. So Leo Meyer cleared Kyle for play. He's starting the program soon. We've got an interesting group coming in. Besides Kyle, there are a couple of doctors and a chemist. I don't even know exactly what she does with chemicals, but she sounds smart."

Would that incredibly smart woman end up being Kyle's partner? There would be at least a couple of nights he would spend playing at Sanctum as part of his class. She would get the schedule and avoid those nights. It wouldn't be hard. Mistress Lea ran the class, and MaeBe always came in and did the maintenance on the computers in the club. She made sure the Mistress's system was running at optimal speed, and in exchange she pretty much got away with murder.

It could be handy to be seen as harmless and helpful.

Sometimes it was hard to be the only person around who wasn't a walking weapon. Oh, sure, some of the support staff at the office hadn't been in the military and/or intelligence agencies, but even the accountant Tag watched like a hawk had done his time in the Coast Guard.

It was pretty much her and Yasmin and Genny. There were actual protocols in place to protect the three of them in case of a paramilitary team invading the office. She was supposed to run and hide and not engage.

"She sounds like fun, but like I said, I don't have anything to do with Kyle. I hope he has a blast with training and enjoys The Club."

Kori stared at her like she was looking for a crack to shimmy through. "You know he watches you when you're not looking."

MaeBe didn't intend to leave any holes open. She knew how

gossip worked with this group. She loved watching the people around her get into all kinds of crazy adventures. But she wasn't one of them. "I know, but I don't think that's about being attracted to me."

"I think it is," Kori argued. "I think he's a scaredy cat and can't figure out how to go for it. Or if he should go for it. I've talked to him a little, and I've been married long enough to pick up some of my husband's skills. Kyle knows what he wants but he doesn't think he deserves it. It being you in this case."

She didn't buy it. Kyle seemed like a man who would go after what he wanted with ruthless will. "I don't know about that. I've been pretty open that I'm attracted to him, and he's brushed me off."

"And then when you're not looking he devours you with his eyes. He's one of those guys. I'm sure he's got a big bad past that makes him far too dangerous to ever come close to a beautiful, innocent woman."

"Oh, are we talking about Kyle?" Hutch had a plate from the dessert buffet in his hand. "Because that dude is like walking crack for women. They look at him and think they can fix him. My ex came up to throw my old laptop at me, and Katy took one look at him from afar and asked why I couldn't have been more like that guy. I asked her what part? The crazy eyes? Or the part that looks like it's going to commit murder at any moment?"

There was a reason Hutch and his girlfriend hadn't worked out, and she would do well to remember that. Katy also wasn't interested in board games or fantasy and science fiction. They hadn't had much in common beyond they'd both thought they were ready for a longer-term relationship. MaeBe had been Hutch's friend for over a year, and she'd only met Katy a handful of times. They'd been a mismatch.

Like she and Kyle Hawthorne were a mismatch.

Why did that make her sad? "She was a crazy person who did not deserve you, Hutch. I think you should let Charlotte set you up."

There was nothing more certain to get them off her love life than talking about Hutch's.

"There's a whole new crop of subs coming in," Kori teased. "I think you might like a couple of them. In a few short weeks they'll be released into the wilds of Sanctum where all the Doms will lick their chops."

Hutch frowned. "I don't have chops, and I do not need a girlfriend. I will murder the first person who suggests to Charlotte that I do. The last one broke all my dishes. I bought a house and I don't have any dishes to go in it. Or lots of other stuff. It turns out most of the stuff I had was actually hers."

Hutch was making the leap from apartment renter to actual homeowner. He'd bought Beck's three bedroom and called it an investment.

MaeBe had forks. Eight of them, and they matched the spoons and knives. She'd bought them as a set at Target, and she was weirdly proud of them. "I'll take you shopping. And I won't even mention it to Charlotte. I think it's time I headed out. I've got a yoga class in the morning."

"Hang on a minute and I'll walk with you," Hutch said as Deke walked up and a brow rose over his eyes.

The two men started talking, likely about something work related, and Kori had been pulled into another conversation.

The parking garage was well lit, and it wasn't too late. She didn't have to drag someone out of the party to walk her across the street.

She set down her glass and started for the door, glancing back and watching Beck and Kim dancing. Beck was a little stiff, but it didn't matter. They were obviously so in love.

Was she ever going to find something like that for herself? Or was she one of those people who moved through relationships, never finding anything permanent?

The night was cool against her skin as the door closed behind her, and she stepped away from the lights surrounding Top.

"Hey, MaeBe."

A shadow peeled away from the big tree right outside the parking garage.

Her bad-date lawyer was back, and she should have waited for Hutch.

* * * *

Kyle sat back as MaeBe walked by.

The impulse was right there. To join her. To walk beside her. To do something stupid like ask her to dance. He didn't dance. Not anymore. The dumbass college kid who hadn't cared what he looked like was long gone, and he didn't have anything to offer her so he'd stayed away.

But the impulse remained.

I have a game night if you want to come. It's pretty fun. We play all kinds of games and I usually make something tasty for dinner. It's every Thursday at my place. Since I now have a place.

He knew about her place. He'd checked it out, and the security was solid or he would have had a talk with his uncle about gently steering her away from it.

He still didn't have a place because something was wrong with his credit reports. And his bank accounts. Someone—likely Drake— had dumped a shit ton of cash into Kyle's personal accounts, and he couldn't spend a dime of it because he rather thought the money had once been Julia's. Julia's blood money.

Someone might come looking for it. Yet another reason to stay in his seat and not follow MaeBe out.

"That girl is going to get in trouble." Kori walked over to his table, shaking her head. "Did you see which way MaeBe went?"

"She just walked out the door. Why? Did she forget something?" He stood, all prior thoughts consigned to hell. If MaeBe had forgotten something then he would definitely be faster than Kori.

"Yes, she forgot that she's picked up a bit of a stalker and shouldn't be walking around alone," Kori said with a frown. "She had a date go bad a couple of weeks ago. A lawyer from your building a friend of hers set her up with. Mae was not impressed but the lawyer was, and he's been calling her and routinely is in the same elevator as her when she leaves work. It's gotten annoying enough that Hutch has been walking her down and making sure she's safely in her car."

That did not go far enough. "Hutch is walking her down? Does he know there's an actual trained bodyguard unit he could call on? I'll have a schedule for her tomorrow, and I'll catch her and let her know how this is going to work."

Kori stared at him like he'd grown an extra head. "Uhm, I think she's cool with Hutch handling things. They're friends. I don't know if she's going to want the bodyguard unit involved."

He shrugged. "Then she shouldn't have walked out without Hutch."

He jogged away before she could say another word because he wasn't about to argue with Kori about something like this. She might have a lot of sway at Sanctum and with Kai, but she was not the boss of MaeBe.

And it was becoming crystal clear that MaeBe needed a damn boss.

He was sure she would argue with him that she was a grown woman and didn't need a man treating her like a child. He wasn't. Most of the children he knew obeyed way better than MaeBe.

Not that he would tell her that. Normally he was a deeply forward-thinking guy. Mae brought out the caveman neanderthal in him.

He would never have thought twice about Julia walking to a parking garage by herself. It wouldn't have even occurred to him she might be in danger. Because she'd been the predator, and she knew damn well how to protect herself. She never did a single thing that didn't serve her own best interest.

Damn.

He took the route that brought him to the kitchens and raced through to the back door, ignoring the cooks and waitstaff who waved his way.

Had he picked Julia because she was so self-focused? Because she wouldn't do anything she didn't want to do, anything that didn't serve her purposes, so if she died on an op, he could know it wasn't his fault?

Was he still in that car watching his friend curse him as he died?

He pushed his way through the door and started for the sidewalk. The street was well lit but it was still dark, and there were definitely places a stalker could stand and watch his prey from.

He was about to round the building and make for the parking garage across the street when he heard it.

"I saw you post about being here tonight, and it sounded like fun," a deep voice was saying.

"I asked you not to follow me anymore." MaeBe sounded annoyed.

"I don't know what games you're playing, but I'm getting tired of them," the asshole replied. "You've played hard to get. Now it's time to stop. You play the whore for everyone else. You can do it for me, too."

Kyle barely registered any word beyond *whore*. He rounded the corner, his vision going practically red.

And then an arm wound around his waist and he was stopped, his fists impotent.

"Calm down, son," a familiar voice said. "I know how much you want to take him apart, but calm down. There's a better way to do this."

Sean. His stepdad was behind him, holding him back as Jamal approached MaeBe. Jamal was six foot seven inches of pure muscle.

The bad-date asshole had gone pale and was practically hiding behind MaeBe.

"Sir, I don't think you should put your hands on her," Sean said. "I can barely hold my stepson back as it is. The only reason he hasn't broken free and eviscerated you is that I'm family. MaeBe, you might want to come over here and calm Kyle down."

Sean's hold eased as MaeBe rushed over, and he found the arms he'd intended to use to kill the other man full of shaking gamer girl.

Damn, but it felt good to wrap them around her, to let his instincts lead him for once. She shuddered and put her head against his chest, nestling against him like she belonged there.

"Mr. Fellows," Jamal was saying. "I think we should sit down and have a chat. I know. You're looking between me and him and thinking maybe you could take him. He's roughly your height and weight, and you probably do some boxing workouts that make you think you can handle yourself. You can't handle him. He's a highly trained former Navy SEAL, and he's got a little crazy thrown in for good measure. You're threatening the woman he can't admit he wants right now because that kid needs therapy. Which do you think he would rather do? Sit down and talk this out or take your head off?"

"I'll stay away. I didn't understand that she was serious. She gives off some vibes, if you know what I mean," the lawyer began.

Kyle started to stiffen up again.

MaeBe's arms tightened around him and her head tilted up, those big gorgeous eyes kicking him right in the gut. "Please let Jamal handle him, Ma...Kyle." She seemed to realize something and started to step back. "I'm sorry. I'm flustered. I shouldn't..."

He pulled her close again. She was right. She needed him, and Jamal would scare the shit out of the lawyer in a way that didn't get anyone sued. But there were going to be rules.

And he knew what she'd almost called him.

Master.

She knew. He knew. They fit together, and the roles they could play were so easy and true. He hadn't gone through the training class yet, but he'd studied. After he'd found out David had gotten Master rights at The Club, he'd read some books, talked to some people, realized that he could use some control.

MaeBe would be a sweet sub, someone he cared about, her affection salve to the wounds he'd taken, the ones that hadn't healed yet.

All he had to do was stay with her.

All he had to do was give up fighting.

"I'll take you home. Come on." He shifted but kept his arm around her.

Leading her away as his stepdad and Jamal started to take care of the situation was the best thing he'd done in forever.

Then he saw her car. "I could pick this up. Maybe with one hand."

Her lips curled up. "You could not." She had her keys in hand and they jangled together, proving how nervous she was.

He was all about instinct tonight. He reached out and covered her shaking hand with both of his. He clasped that hand, hoping he could help her find her balance. "Hey, it's okay. I promise Jamal and Sean will put the fear of God in that man. And Ian will likely go to his boss in the morning. He works in the building, right?"

She nodded, her eyes shining with tears. "Yes. He's at the law firm that moved in last year."

Over the years they'd had several law firms rent floors in the building. His uncle often ran them off. "Yeah, I bet he won't have a job soon."

"It was one date, Kyle. One. I don't get it. We didn't get along. At least I thought we didn't. We have nothing in common. He said he liked games, but he was talking about sports. I listened to him talk about the Cowboys for four hours then he was surprised when I didn't invite him back to my place and he started blowing up my phone with texts."

He hated seeing her so scared, hated the fact that he hadn't been there.

He thought about this woman far too much for his own good. He wouldn't be here in six months or so. He would be back to work at his real job, and she would be…

Likely with someone else. She was a sweet sub looking for a Dom to top her, and he couldn't do that.

"And it wasn't like I didn't vet him," MaeBe continued.

He let her hand go but took the keys from her. "I'll take you home."

"But then how will you…"

Kyle sighed. "I won't. I'll sleep on your couch tonight. Someone is going to be walking you up to the office for a while. I don't like the idea of you going through the parking garage by yourself if he's still around. Now get in and tell me how thoroughly you vetted him."

She stopped, chin turning up so she looked him right in the eyes. "I don't think that's a good idea."

"Well, that tells me you probably weren't thorough at all, and that's a whole other lecture."

Her head shook slightly. "I mean you coming home with me."

"Because you don't trust me? Mae, I would never hurt you."

"You would never mean to," she corrected.

He was confused. "I'm trying to look out for you. I believe this guy will go away once he realizes you're protected, but he could also make some bad life decisions because some guys are assholes like that. Some people can't handle rejection."

Don't think this is over, Kyle. You're mine, and that won't ever change. Not even if you try to kill me.

His stomach rolled.

"I wasn't worried about the lawyer," she admitted. "I was never invested in him. Like I said it was one date, and I go on a lot of first dates. And I'm not worried that you would try to sneak into my bed if you stayed the night with me. I am worried that I might try to sneak into yours."

Fuck. His cock had gone hard. Like from nothing to ready to fuck in two point five seconds.

Oddly, it made him want to step back, to take all the words he'd said and find a way to unsay them because this was too deep for him.

She was the one who moved away. "I'm sorry. I didn't mean to offend you."

"You didn't offend me." He wasn't ready for her. He might never be ready for her. Up until this moment he'd thought she was a way to pass time. Not with her, of course. He was toxic and didn't have anything more than a night to give her. But what if she wanted that night? What if she wanted him enough that she would take the risk if she fully understood what the risk was? "MaeBe, I'm never going to be able to love you the way you should be loved. I'm not that guy. I'm not going to stay in this job for more than another couple of months. I hope you won't tell my uncle I said that, but you should know the truth. The military…not the military…things that happened to me while I was in the military fucked me up, and I'm not good for you. But I might be good for you in bed if that's all you want."

She chuckled, but the sound wasn't even close to amused. One hand wiped across her eyes. "Are you offering to be my booty call, Kyle?"

He didn't like the sound of that. "No. I was offering to spend time with you, but you would have to understand that it would only be sex. You said you wanted to climb into bed with me. Well, I want that with you, too. I've never wanted a woman the way I want you."

Not even the one he'd killed.

She sighed, a weary sound. "I want you, too. But I like myself, and I don't know that I would if I ignored all the red flags and threw myself into a storm I'm not ready for. Thank you for the warning. I truly do appreciate it. I think I'll take it and we can stay friendly."

That was not what he'd expected. "But we want each other."

Her head shook, the purple tresses gently caressing her face. "No. I don't think we do. Not really. I think you want a me that doesn't exist since you don't know me at all. Or you want someone who won't give you a hard time. If I had to bet, I would say one of the bad things that happened to you was a woman, probably one who was the exact opposite of me, and that's why you think it would be nice to spend time with me. She was likely a confident, take-charge kind of lady, and now you want a sub. A real sub. You might not have Master rights at Sanctum, but I'm sure you're aware of the lifestyle. Do you think you're the first top who decided I would be easier than his cast-iron ex? She probably wasn't, by the way. She was probably just a normal woman who knew how to ask for the things she wanted."

"You have no idea who she was." The words came out harsher than he'd intended.

She pointed his way. "I knew it."

He'd fumbled this. He'd seen a way in, a way he could have her and not feel like a shitbag when he left. "My ex isn't a part of this, but you should understand that she wasn't some sweet but assertive woman who meant well and I couldn't handle her being smarter than me. That wasn't the way it was."

"I'm a placeholder for her, Kyle. She hurt you and you want to hurt her back so you're going after someone who's her exact opposite."

"I can't hurt her. She's already dead, baby." Yes, there was the shitbag who lived inside him now, the toxic one who likely would have ripped the woman in front of him apart even though he wanted to protect her.

Her eyes went soft. "Then I'm sorry, but it doesn't change things. I would still be a placeholder for the woman you could love. I know there are women who would try to heal you, but I happen to know that never works. You have to heal yourself. Thanks for offering me a ride, but I'll be okay."

He'd utterly mishandled this, but then he wasn't sure what *this* was anymore. She'd said she wanted to go to bed with him. He'd offered and given her his parameters. "Do you require an offer of marriage from the men you sleep with?"

Her eyes narrowed. "No, but I don't sleep with men I don't have any possibility of a future with. Ask the lawyer."

"I am not like him." He huffed out of pure frustration. "I am not stalking you. I offered you what I have to give."

"And I turned you down because it's not enough for me," she countered. "Am I obligated to say yes because you asked? Because that does sound like the guy I just ran away from."

"I didn't mean to." Damn it. He used to be good at this. He used to be good at charming his way into a woman's bed. Years before he'd screwed up the world so brutally, he'd been that guy women slept with and then continued to hang out with.

She let a long moment pass. "It's okay. How about we agree to be people who work together and nothing more."

"Or we could be friends." He should take the out she was offering with gratitude. Drake would call him any day now, and he would be out of here. He wouldn't have to see her again with her big, gorgeous eyes and those lips he thought about way too much. With her saucy mouth that made him laugh even when she wasn't talking to him because he stopped and listened.

"I don't know that we're going to be friends, Kyle. We don't have much in common. That's another reason it's best you don't come home with me."

"Hey, you doing okay?" a deep voice asked.

Jamal was walking up the ramp they were on, his keys in hand.

Kyle took a deep breath because he liked the man and didn't want to be the next dude he had to warn off tonight. "I was thinking someone should drive Mae home and make sure she gets in okay, but it's late and I'm not sure the trains are still running. I don't want to get stuck."

"I'll follow her." Jamal moved in, standing next to MaeBe. He was at least a foot and a couple of inches taller than she was, taller than Kyle himself. "And you call me if you even halfway feel like something's off. I don't think that guy's going to come after you. He seemed to understand what Sean and I were telling him. But if he's going to try something it'll be in the next couple of weeks."

"I'll watch him." It was the one thing he might be able to offer her. "It's not like I have anything else to do with my time. I'll follow him for a couple of days to make sure. I have a job coming up. But it doesn't start until next week. I can do some background work on the guy."

Jamal's brow rose. "I didn't think you did background work. I kind of thought you were one of those guys who did as little desk work as possible."

Because none of the guys he worked with knew him beyond the fact that he was the boss's nephew and he was standoffish.

That was starting to get boring.

It had been far easier to hold back when he didn't give a crap about the people around him, when the people around him couldn't be trusted.

He could get soft again here. "I'll have something on your desk in the morning. I can do intel work, too."

Would his brother's laptop survive a deep dive into the Dark Web?

He handed MaeBe her keys and backed away. "Stay safe."

She nodded and then walked on with Jamal.

It was better this way. He would be more careful about staying away from her going forward.

Kyle took a deep breath and walked back to the restaurant, hoping his exile would end soon. Before his heart defrosted and started to ache again.

Chapter Four

Kyle finished the last few keystrokes and saw the light on Hutch's security alarm go from red to green and sighed in relief.

He hadn't lost his touch. He'd worried his skills had atrophied while he played down his talents here in Dallas, but he'd needed them tonight.

He was being smothered in this house in a way he hadn't when they'd been staying at Noelle LaVigne's. At Noelle's, it had all felt like work, like they were simply doing their jobs, but something had gone down tonight and he and Hutch had made the decision to move the client to a more secure location. Namely the house Hutch had bought from Beckett Kent when he'd moved to Colorado with Solo and their kid.

This house. It was bland and boring and cozy, and Kyle would never, never have it. He'd already seen Noelle looking around, a gleam in her eyes as she'd obviously thought about what she could do with this place. They'd only started the op a few days before and it was already a given that Noelle and Hutch would end up together.

It had only been a couple of weeks since Kyle and MaeBe had stood in the parking garage and he'd made a complete asshole of himself.

And then he'd tried to sleep and he'd had the dream again.

The one where he stood over Julia and she smiled at him and

held out a hand and he joined her.

It was a dream he'd been having since that terrible day in Singapore when he'd confronted her about working for The Consortium. He saw her lying there, blood staining her chest, and he knew he'd killed her. He could hear Drake shouting in the background and feel the heat from the fire that had started. In the dream he thought seriously about standing there and letting the fire take him. It would be easier than going forward. He wasn't good at this life thing. He fucked up and people died. His friends died. Julia died, and no matter what she'd done he hated that he'd been the one to pull the trigger. So he would stand there and let the flames take him. It was nothing more than what he deserved.

And then her eyes would open and the most malicious smile would spread across her pale face. Her hand would come out, and even though he was screaming inside he couldn't stop himself from taking it.

That was where he would normally wake up shouting and David would rush in and he would have to make up some excuse. Lately David just knocked and quietly asked if he was okay.

Not tonight. Tonight David wasn't here and the dream had been worse. This time when he'd taken Julia's hand he'd felt a tug at his other hand, and he'd turned and realized MaeBe Vaughn was standing in the flames, trying to haul him out, trying to save him. And he'd realized he was going to drag her down with him.

He'd also known a spark of hope. Somewhere in all the despair a voice had whispered to him.

What if she was strong enough to lead him through that fire? What if MaeBe was the one who could show him the way to the other side?

His hands were still shaking even as he reset the alarm and slipped outside. It would be easy to get back in now that he'd hacked the password. The great news was no one would think he could do that. It wouldn't occur to anyone that the latest bodyguard himbo could hack a system at all.

He reached for his phone and dialed the number he would have called earlier had the night not gone to hell.

The call picked up immediately, letting him know the guy on the other end of the line had been waiting for him. "Is everything all right?"

Drake. He'd called earlier, but this wasn't the kind of call he would answer until he was completely alone. Hutch was a smart guy. Despite his *aw-shucks* personality, he was always watching, always taking in everything around him.

Kyle was almost sure Hutch was watching him. "Hey, I'm sorry. This job is going sideways, and it kind of hit the fan tonight."

"Are you okay? Anyone hurt?" Despite the fact that Drake was on the outside, Kyle knew he cared about the people at McKay-Taggart. He'd worked with them many times before.

"No, but something's going on here and I don't like it. I don't like that MaeBe's involved. I want her off this case. At some point it's going to go bad. I think Jessica Layne is involved with The Consortium in some way." His every instinct was going off, but he worried his instincts were influenced by his growing feelings for MaeBe Vaughn. It didn't matter that he'd told himself to stay away—basically warned her away—he kept finding himself drawn to her. He couldn't stand the thought of her being hurt, but no one would listen to him.

"Most big tech companies are, whether they know it or not," Drake replied. "I've looked into Genedyne and while I think the CEO is into some sketchy shit, I don't think she's a formal part of the group. She's far too erratic and in the public eye for them to take her seriously."

"So you've been looking into it?" He'd known Drake would keep investigating the group his sister had worked for, but it was interesting that he'd done some research on the same company McKay-Taggart's op was about.

Drake was quiet for a moment.

"What's happening, Drake?"

He could practically see the look on his friend's face. It would have gone blank, and his head would shake slightly. "It's nothing. I had an op go wrong in Kraków, and I lost an asset. That's all."

Drake was normally a vault. The man did not talk about his feelings, but every now and then he broke down, and Kyle had figured out he was the only one Drake would talk to. "Do you think it was The Consortium?"

"I don't know, but I think I might have met a double agent,"

Drake explained. "I…I don't want to talk about what an idiot I was."

So Drake had met a woman and she'd turned out to be bad. He could relate. And the "I don't want to talk about it" was code for "I'm going to look stupid but I need help figuring this out." They'd only been friends for a couple of years, but they'd gotten close fast. When a man only had a few people he could be honest with, those friendships became tight. "You know the smartest man in the world can get derailed by his dick."

A deep chuckle came over the line. "Or the dumbest."

Such an ass. "Well, we all know that."

He was silent for a moment, and Kyle flattened his back against the side of the house as a car went by.

"I can't stop thinking about her," Drake said quietly. "I'm trying to forget it ever happened and forgive myself for being an idiot, but I seem to be an idiot a lot now. First Julia and then this."

He knew the hollow tone Drake was using. He'd used it himself for a long time. "Is she dead?"

Drake sighed over the line. "It doesn't matter, and you should forget we talked about this. It doesn't involve you and it shouldn't. I wanted to call because I haven't had a chance to follow up with those leads you sent me but I'm going to."

He'd been trying to piece together how long Julia had worked for The Consortium and what her possible other ties at the Agency were. He'd sent Drake those leads weeks before and now it suddenly didn't seem as important.

He felt for Drake. He knew how hard it was to shove his pain aside and get the job done. He wasn't sure how to advise his friend. When he'd found out Julia was a traitor, it had ended with her death. Julia had done everything she'd done for money. It could be different if this woman truly believed. If she'd been working against Drake because she wanted to help her people, there was some room for discussion. Julia had cared about no one but herself.

If he found MaeBe with a treasure trove of information she shouldn't have, he would ask her why she had it, what she intended to do with it. He wouldn't jump to the conclusion that she was the enemy. It was weird to trust someone again.

"Don't worry about it. I shouldn't have asked you to follow up." It was pretty much all he could do for his friend right now.

Drake wouldn't want to be pushed into talking about what had happened.

"I'm going to get it done. I think there are questions we need to answer," Drake replied. "I've put it off because I don't like thinking about Julia. Hell, I don't know what I do like thinking about anymore. I feel ripped up from the inside. I look normal, things feel normal, but inside I'm a fucking mess and I can't let anyone see it."

"Or you'll find yourself on sabbatical like me," Kyle pointed out.

"That wasn't punishment. You know you needed this time."

A sigh went through him. He'd been thinking a lot about this lately. The last few weeks had been a revelation. Becoming friends with Hutch was making him rethink a lot of things, and MaeBe was, of course, at the center of everything. "I think I might need more time."

"Good, because I don't think they're going to…" Another moment of quiet. "Are you telling me you don't want to come back?"

"Maybe."

Drake's chuckle now sounded entirely amused. "Oh, I definitely think this is about MaeBe Vaughn."

That woman was going to drive him crazy. "I like her. A lot. But I totally fucked things up. I told her I would go to bed with her but I couldn't ever feel for her the way she deserved."

"You did what?"

Yeah, he was certain everyone would have that reaction. "Well, it seemed like reality at the time. I don't know. I kind of thought she would either want the same thing or think she could save me, and then maybe she would save me. Turns out she believed me fully—as she should have because I wasn't lying at the time—and has a lot of self-esteem. She doesn't want anything to do with my toxic self. Except I pushed myself on her. She was supposed to be working tech on this job, and I dragged her into the thick of it. I told the target MaeBe was my girlfriend. I didn't intend to, but that woman was looking at me like I was a piece of meat, like…"

"Like Julia did," Drake prompted. "Like you were a possession, something that was due to her. I remember. Jessica Layne came on to you and you reached out to the woman you can't stop thinking about. How did she react?"

He would never forget what MaeBe had done. She hadn't even hesitated. "She put an arm around me and acted like a damn shield, and she's so fucking soft I can't stand the thought of her getting hurt, but I also can't stay away. I'm going through Dom kindergarten for her. I was going to tell my uncle I wasn't interested but MaeBe's in the lifestyle."

"I thought your membership was going to be at The Club," Drake pointed out.

His brother was already a member of the club owned by Julian Lodge because their...he wanted to throw up a little...mom played at Sanctum. "Mom and Sean play on Thursdays or Sundays. Never on Friday or Saturday. They're needed at the restaurant those nights. I'll have privileges at both. I don't know if I should go through with it. I'm still the same guy. I'm still not good for her."

"See, you saying you're not good for her like that means you'll never be good for her," Drake mused. "What you should be saying is you're not ready for her. You're more cautious now, and you need time to feel comfortable. I think she would give it to you if you asked for it."

"You think I need time?" He would like to believe this hollow feeling inside him wouldn't last forever.

"I think you're already coming out of it. If you're considering not coming back because you like your new job and like being close to your family, then you're halfway there, man. You're thinking about staying on a permanent basis, aren't you?"

This was why he felt so smothered. He didn't want to stay. He wanted the freedom of walking out into the world with no thought to anything but revenge.

The problem was he liked being around his brother. He liked hanging out at Top and farting around with the other bodyguards at the office. He liked playing video games with Luke and watching his sister date two guys at the same time right in front of Sean's nose and Sean didn't get it. Sean truly thought they were friends. It was fun to be part of a big, noisy, nosy family.

He liked being close to MaeBe, enjoyed the pretend relationship they had on this op. He liked the thought that he might get to a place where he could give her more than sex.

"I think I need more time." It was all he could say right now.

"Then you should take it."

The line went quiet again. "You didn't call me to ask if I'm coming home."

"I think you are home, Kyle." Drake's tone had gone deep, a sure sign he was either serious or getting emotional. "I think this time you're going to take will prove to you that DC was never home, and me and Julia were never your family. We were a blip on the radar of your life."

"That's not true."

"I hope it is for your sake," Drake replied. "I hope you wake up a year from now and barely remember what happened. You know you can trust MaeBe. I've done a deep dive on her."

"You investigated Mae?" He knew he shouldn't be surprised, but he didn't like the thought of anyone looking into MaeBe.

"I had to when I realized how close you were getting."

"We're not. That's the problem." But the words sounded like a lie. He felt close to her.

"Well, how close you're getting to one day actually asking her out," Drake said with a chuckle. "I thought I should make sure she's okay, though I was fairly certain given the fact that Big Tag vetted her. She's had a couple of brushes with bad guys, but she's never had a real problem. She's a white hat hacker. Anything she's done has been to try to help the greater good. I think you're safe with her."

"I thought I was safe with Julia."

A long sigh came over the line as though even hearing her name made Drake infinitely tired. "No, you didn't. That was part of her appeal. You know you never would have actually married her. You were already pulling away from her."

"Because I suspected something was wrong. I knew she was lying to me."

"Did you ever think I was lying to you?"

He considered his words. "Of course I thought about it, but then you came to me with the truth and I've trusted you ever since. You're right. I was thinking of breaking it off with her. I knew it wasn't going to work long term at the end. What happened between me and Julia was a hurricane. It was fast and adrenaline filled, and I was left wrecked by it. Mae thinks she's some kind of replacement for her."

"You talked to her about Julia?"

He couldn't talk to her about Julia. Not truly. So much of that time was classified, but he'd told her some truths. "Not in specifics, but yeah."

"Then you're further along than I thought, and I'm happy for you. But you have some decisions to make, brother."

About the money. The stupid money that had shown up in his account. "I want you to take it."

"I don't need it. I don't want it. I know it bugs you, but she wanted you to have it. I traced it back to an account I'm sure was hers."

About a month after Julia died, he'd realized there was more than a million dollars in his account that shouldn't have been there. It had come from an offshore bank, and he hadn't been able to trace it. It looked like Drake had more luck. Kyle had quickly opened his own offshore account and stuffed that almost certainly blood-stained cash in it.

"Why would someone move it to me?"

"I don't know. I suspect she was working with someone. An assistant of sorts. I've done some research on how I think the operatives function. I think Julia met with her Consortium handler several times over the course of the last year. I'm trying to pinpoint a location," Drake said.

Guilt swamped him. He should be working on this op, not following Hutch around. "Give me something to do. I can help you."

"Absolutely not. You need to stay out of this, but I want to ask you to keep the money. As a favor to me."

"You don't need the money." Kyle's gut tightened. "Or has something gone wrong?"

"I think if we have to go down a rabbit hole to get the whole story on Julia, we might need untraceable cash," Drake explained.

A million untraceable dollars would help if he needed to go on the run. They had no idea how The Consortium would handle it if they discovered they were being investigated. "You know where the account is, and you can easily access it. If you need it, I won't get rid of it, but I'm not going to touch that money. I'm honestly in a bind financially, but I'm not spending a dime that she earned by betraying us."

"All right. I just want to know it's there. Be careful. I think Jessica Layne could do some damage," Drake said. "And you should think about giving in. Tell MaeBe how you feel and what you need. It's easier that way. I wish I had the chance."

The line went dead and Kyle slipped his phone into the pocket of his pants and then eased out of the shadows and started to do the one thing that might help him get a decent night's sleep.

He started to run but wondered if it might not be time to stop.

* * * *

Every part of her body hurt. The trip from the bedroom to the kitchen shouldn't be such a terrible journey. Normally she skipped her way in when she woke up and smelled the coffee brewing because she'd bought a smart coffeemaker and always remembered to set it before she went to bed.

Except this time. She knew damn well she hadn't set the coffeemaker, so it had to be her new—unwanted—roommate.

Then there was the fact that she wasn't actually in her own house.

Sean and Grace Taggart had a pool house with a small bedroom and living area. She'd been told they used it as a guesthouse many times.

Now it was her recovery room.

"Careful," Kyle said as she walked into the living room where he was set up on the fold-out couch despite the fact that his mother had argued there was an extra bedroom for him. Grace had wanted her son in the main house, but Kyle was a stubborn asshole.

It had been three days since they'd been released from the hospital after the devastating night when Jessica Layne had used her to come after Noelle LaVigne.

That had also been the night she'd been absolutely sure Kyle Hawthorne was everything he claimed to be. He was dangerous. He was deadly.

He'd risked his life for her.

When Jessica Layne had told MaeBe she was going to use her

to get inside Sanctum, she'd laughed—that had hurt like hell because they'd worked her over by then—and told the woman no one would trade her for Noelle LaVigne. She'd known damn well Hutch wouldn't. Hutch was in love with Noelle. She'd been certain Kyle would do what he could to save her, but he wouldn't put the mission at risk.

She didn't think she would ever forget that moment when he'd opened the doors to Sanctum and walked out. It hadn't even taken long. There had been mere moments from the time Kyle had answered his phone to when he walked out. Like he'd run. She would definitely never forget the moment when that asshole had shot him.

She'd known in that moment that she was hopelessly in love with him and he was going to die. She'd crawled across the concrete to get to him and just as she was almost there, Layne's malicious guards had hauled her up with no thought to how much pain she was in.

"Let me get it for you." Somehow Kyle moved with grace though he was the one who'd gone through surgery. Both he and Hutch had taken fire during the op, but Noelle had come out unscathed and now Layne's company would be gone over by the Feds and sold to another big tech guru. She and Hutch should be able to prove that Layne had been selling early research to companies that wanted to squash the progress.

Layne had been willing to kill them all to keep her secrets. Now she was the one who was dead, and MaeBe had to deal with the fact that life was fragile and she was practically alone.

Her dad hadn't come to the hospital. He'd sent some flowers, but he was on a business trip, and naturally her stepmom couldn't be bothered to come see her. She didn't have anyone to take care of her outside of her work friends. She'd pretty much had the choice to stay in the hospital or go home with someone. Noelle and Hutch had offered, but Hutch was hurt, too.

Kyle hadn't allowed her to say no when his mom and stepdad offered to take her in.

"Hey, you went pale." Kyle had been acting like a mother hen since they'd been dropped off the night before. Grace Taggart had driven them over. She and Carys had tried to take care of her.

Kyle had pretty much chased everyone away.

"I'm fine. I didn't sleep. I need some coffee."

"Or you need to figure out how to get some rest." He loomed over her. "You're having bad dreams. I heard you crying last night but you didn't open the door when I knocked. Can we please talk about it?"

"About how I got my ass kicked? I went over all of this in the debrief. I brought Noelle some clothes when Big Tag put her and Hutch in lockdown at the club. They followed me. I suspect they put someone on me when the alarms went off. I wish we knew who stole Noelle's research."

It was the remaining mystery. Someone had set off those alarms, and it hadn't been her and Hutch. It had been a woman who'd worn some strange tech that made her face undefinable by the CCTV cams.

"You'll figure it out. But you didn't get your ass kicked. Someone brutalized you, and it wasn't your fault." He was so gorgeous standing over her. His hands came up to gently cup her shoulders. "None of this was your fault."

It had felt like her fault. "I led them right back to you. They followed me. Either from my place or Noelle's. I didn't see that I had a car following me. I didn't even look."

His head dropped down to hers. "Because you're not a field operative, baby. You're not trained for this, and there's zero reason you should be."

He'd gotten so affectionate since he'd taken a bullet.

The man had duct taped himself back together and come after her. The logical part of her brain told her he was simply doing his job, but when she'd seen him coming out of the shadows something had settled inside her. She'd known she would survive because Kyle was there and alive, and he wouldn't let anyone hurt her.

Further. He hadn't been there to stop the beating she'd taken, the one that reminded her she was so fucking fragile. Through all the pain, her greatest regret had been that she'd never kissed Kyle Hawthorne. It was stupid. She should have been thinking about all the things she hadn't done in her young life, and all that had been in her heart and soul had been him.

Nothing had changed. He still wasn't going to stay. He'd told her who he was, and she believed him.

At the time, she'd known she had to choose herself. She wasn't the woman who thought she could fix a man. A man was who he was. She'd known exactly what Kyle's real problem was—another woman had done him wrong—and it wasn't her job to make it right.

In that moment when she'd known she was going to die, it hadn't mattered. The surety of heartache had been nothing in the face of having a single moment to look back on. One moment of joy with Kyle would have been worth the pain.

"Well, I don't think Big Tag will be sending me out in the field again anytime soon since I got his nephew shot," she said, stepping back.

She hadn't taken his offer, and she would be shocked if he offered again.

"He doesn't blame you for that. My uncle can be an asshole, but he's fair, and he cares about you." He stared at her for a moment, and then his jaw tightened as he seemed to come to some inner decision. "Mae, I think we should talk."

He said the words with the gravity of a man on a mission. A potentially distasteful mission. She was confused since he was the one who'd insisted on pretending to be her boyfriend and then he'd been the one to take charge of her recovery.

Or had he? Had this been an idea of Big Tag's? So she didn't end up at his already full house? Big Tag would feel responsible for her. He was perfectly capable of feeling guilty, and she could see him trying to make sure she was okay. It hadn't made sense to send her with Hutch since he was hurt, too. This might have been the easiest place to watch over her since she didn't have family of her own and her friends were mostly single and worked a lot. Grace was already taking time off to watch over Kyle. Maybe she'd been pressed into double duty.

"I don't think we have to talk. It's cool. We ran an op and had a cover. I'm not misconstruing the way you're acting. I know I didn't prove myself out in the field, but I do know the difference between cover and reality. You don't have to worry that I'm going to be clingy. And I think I can take care of myself. I'm going to call a friend and have him bring my car out so I can head home this afternoon. It's sweet of your mom to offer to take care of me, but

I'm not the one who got shot. You should have the bed and all of her attention."

His eyes narrowed. "I don't think you understand the difference between cover and a desperate dude jumping at the first chance to stay close to you, and you definitely don't understand reality if you think I'm letting you move an inch out of this house before I decide you're healthy enough to take care of yourself. Even then I'll probably stick close."

She was confused. "Desperate dude?"

He sighed and his hand came out again, brushing down from her shoulder to her elbow. "Sit down and I'll get you some coffee and we can talk."

"I don't want to talk, Kyle. Look, if we're back to the not-so-friends-with-benefits thing, then I agree. Let's throw down. Nothing else has worked for me and honestly, I think about you more than I should. Let's give me some time to not look like an extra in a horror film and then we can scratch each other's itches until you leave."

"You are not an itch I want to scratch, MaeBe Vaughn," Kyle said, his eyes solemn on her. "You're a blanket I want to pull around me because I think you might be able to keep me warm for the rest of my life. Please sit down and let me take care of you. It's all I want to do for the next couple of days. Please."

It was the *please* that did it. Kyle Hawthorne wasn't a polite man. He was a lot like his uncle, though she knew they didn't share DNA. Some families didn't need DNA to share obnoxious traits. Sarcasm was Kyle's chosen language, and the fact that he was saying *please* meant something.

She moved to the couch he'd already folded up and turned into a sofa again, the only evidence that it was something else being the fluffy pillows on the chair beside her. He had something he wanted to say, and it was only right for her to listen. He likely wanted to tell her he'd changed his mind about the whole "let's go to bed and fuck each other out of our systems" thing.

He felt guilty, too. Kyle thought he'd gotten her caught in this and he was the reason she'd taken a beating. It wasn't true, but she wasn't sure she could make him believe it.

This was one conversation she was going to have to get through as quickly as possible. She would go back to her room, and it wasn't like he could actually stop her from leaving.

She accepted the coffee from him. It was the perfect color, a mix of the dark coffee and light-colored cream. When she sipped it, it was like she'd made it herself. "You put sugar and cream in. That was lucky for me. I forgot to tell you how I like it."

"I know how you like your coffee, MaeBe. Just enough cream to change the color and one spoon of sugar unless it's a dark roast and then you taste it and your nose wrinkles up and you put an extra one in. This is a lighter roast. You only need the one." He sat down beside her, twisting that big, gorgeous body of his with only the barest hint of the discomfort the motion must have cost him. He was in his recovery uniform, flannel pajama bottoms and a white V-neck undershirt that clung to all those muscles in his chest. He didn't wear socks, and she wished she thought his feet weren't sexy, but they were as hot as the rest of him. Something about sitting with him when he was barefoot felt way too intimate. Way too comfortable.

Especially as she sat here drinking perfectly made coffee. "Why would you know that?"

"Why do you think?" he asked, his eyes steady on her. "Because I like to watch you. Because sometimes getting to see you is the best part of my day, and the weird thing is I'm starting to have really good days. I'm starting to enjoy work and home in a way I didn't think was possible. I like my brother's place. I like hanging out with him even when he's grading papers. I like his cat. When did I become a cat person? I like seeing my mom and stepdad and having dinner with Carys and Luke. I went to his football game. I never thought I would do something so normal, and it felt good. I know I'm talking a lot, but what I'm trying to say is it means something that seeing you is the best part of my day because now I like my days."

He was not going to make her cry. "Then you're healing from losing your girlfriend. That's a good thing, Kyle. I'm happy for you."

"She wasn't my girlfriend. She was my fiancée, and I'm not ready to talk about her," he admitted. "I want to eventually, but I can't right now. What I can tell you is that before she died, I was getting ready to break up with her. Our relationship was toxic, and I had a part in that. Can you accept that I'm not ready to talk about her?"

He was a confusing man. "You don't have to talk to me about her at all."

"You are not a placeholder. I need you to understand that. You are special to me."

She shook her head. "You don't have to do this. I take back all the shit I said before. I thought I couldn't handle a short-term, all-sex relationship. Turns out nearly dying makes me think less about the future and more about the right now. You were right. We want each other. We should do it."

His brows formed a deep *V* over those green eyes. "I was wrong and you were right."

He was so frustrating. "So you don't want me."

"That's not what I'm saying." He reached out and put his hand over hers. "That's not what I'm saying at all. I'm saying I care about you in a way I've never cared about anyone. You are the light that's leading me out of a dark tunnel. Not just you. I'm not putting that responsibility on you, but you are a big part of why I want to get better."

That was the moment she realized he wasn't playing games. He wasn't trying to trick her into bed or get out of an uncomfortable position.

He was serious, and that meant she was serious, too. Tears pooled in her eyes as the intimacy of their situation washed over her. They had been through something traumatic, and she shouldn't trust this impulse of his, but she felt it, too. She'd felt like the world was going to end when she'd thought he was dead. She tightened her hand around his and he tugged her his way.

"Careful," he said as he gently started to bring her closer. "Sit on my lap. I want you close."

There was one problem with that. "You had surgery."

His gaze went steely. "And you'll be careful. I want you close, Mae. I need you close."

He was going to kill her. She set the coffee down and eased onto his lap, being careful of his injury. "Now I'm close."

"You're such a brat." His cheek rubbed against hers. "I want to move toward something real with you, but I need time. I need to ease into it. Can we try being friends?"

"This doesn't feel like friends, Kyle." There was something

hard under her thighs, and she didn't think he was carrying a gun in those pants of his. He wanted her, and she looked like hell.

He nuzzled her neck. "This is about how shitty it was to see you hurt. This is about reassuring myself that you're alive and here. I want you, Mae, but more than your body. I want the part of MaeBe Vaughn you don't share with anyone but the person who's closest in the world to you. I can't share that part of me yet, so sex is off the table."

"That doesn't sound promising. I told you I'll sleep with you."

His arm was around her waist, holding him to her. "I'll sleep with you whenever you want. But no sex until we're ready to be together. I don't want to be some guy you sleep with while you're waiting for the right one to come along."

This seemed so much worse than what he'd offered her before. Now he was being all obnoxious and mature. Serious. "You were the one who said you wouldn't stay."

"And now I'm saying I will," he whispered against her ear. "I think I want to."

"I don't know." It was perverse. He was saying he would give her what she wanted. Time. Time to be friends. Time to see if they could work before she put her whole heart on the line.

Except she was pretty sure it was already there.

"Then I'll change your mind," he promised. "I'm going to do something about my problems. I know I'm fucked up. I'll work on it. I want to work on being friends, too."

"Friends without benefits."

He leaned his head against hers. "For now. Until I'm ready and you're ready. Does that sound weird? I mean I know I should throw myself in because I know exactly what I want, but…"

"Is that what you did last time? Things went too fast?"

He was quiet for a moment, his hand gently rubbing over her hip. "Everything went fast back then. It was like the world sped up and I was suddenly made of adrenaline. The world was either brighter or harsher, and I didn't care which until the moment that I did. When I look back now, I don't recognize myself. I'm starting to remember who I used to be, the man I used to enjoy being. I want to find him again. If it's too much for you…"

He was trying, and that meant they had a chance.

"I like who I am when I'm around you, too. I've enjoyed pretending to be your girlfriend. In my heart it wasn't pretend." She leaned against him and suddenly she was tired. In a good way. Her bones were weary, but she knew if she went to sleep she wouldn't dream. "So we're friends for now?"

His lips brushed against her forehead. "We're working toward something. Something amazing. And we can tell anyone you want or we can keep it for ourselves. This thing between us, it's ours, and we don't have to define it or justify it to anyone else. I want a future with you but first I need a present. I guess what I'm asking…what I'm begging is please don't give up on me."

They needed time. He was asking her for it. He'd been honest before and he was being the same now.

It was enough.

"I'll make a deal with you. We don't give up on each other. Not even if it doesn't work. If it doesn't work then we'll be friends and we'll still have each other's back. No matter what."

He kissed her again, on her cheek. "No matter what. Now why don't I take you to bed and hold you and you can sleep and when you wake up, we're going to start this thing. Will I like game night? I might be bad at games. I'm really more of a shoot people kind of guy."

For the first time in days she laughed. And yawned. "I think you'll be great at them."

When she laid her head on his shoulder, she fell asleep, and all the pain seemed to slide away.

Chapter Five

"Come on," Yasmin begged. "You're dating him, right? You go to lunch with him at least once a week. I heard he's going to game night."

MaeBe looked up from her computer. It had been months since she and Kyle had made their bargain and while she was sexually frustrated, she was also pretty damn happy. And she kind of liked the mystery of their will-they-or-won't-they, circling-each-other relationship. It kept people on their toes. "We're friends."

They were. It was one of the oddest relationships of her life because while they were friends, there was always an underlying tension. She kind of worried about what would happen if it broke. When it broke.

He hadn't kissed her beyond the forehead or the cheek. Sometimes he stared at her like he wasn't sure what to do with her, but he damn straight wasn't letting her go.

She loved those moments.

Yasmin groaned. "Come on. I'm living vicariously through you. You can't tell me you're not playing around with that gorgeous man."

"I'm totally playing with him," she returned with a grin. "We've got a *Gloomhaven* game going. It's been on my dining room table for weeks because Big Tag keeps sending him on assignment. I was excited when he broke his foot because I could hold him down and finish the campaign."

Kyle had been attacked by a client's massive Louis Vuitton bag and broken his foot. He'd been the worst patient in the history of time. She was fairly certain Grace was going to murder her baby boy. He was once again recovering at his mom's place, though getting him there had been a miracle.

He'd wanted to stay at his brother's place. With all the stairs. When he was in a boot and not supposed to walk.

Frustrating man.

Yasmin's eyes rolled. "You are mean." The receptionist turned and started walking away. "If I was having a hot affair, I would talk to you about it."

"It's not a hot affair," MaeBe corrected. "More like a warm friendship."

With the hope of hotness when her damaged guy got his shit together. It was happening, but patience was the key when it came to Kyle Hawthorne.

"Morning, Mae." Hutch gave her that half grin that let her know he had something crappy to tell her. He also had a box in his hand. Macon's bakery.

He had something terrible he wanted to tell her. Or to ask her to do. "If this is about some overnight watch job, those better be chocolate croissants."

He winced. "And macarons. Also, they're not from me. They're from Kyle. You know how he was worried about his brother being in Argentina? Well, turns out they're pretty sure David got kidnapped and Big Tag and Sean are on their way down right now."

Her heart threatened to stop. "Is Kyle freaked out?" She started to grab her keys. "I'll go and sit with him. Grace must be a mess."

So many things seemed to be going wrong for that part of the family right now. Carys was in some kind of trouble over her relationship with Aidan O'Donnell and Tristan Dean-Miles. Luke had an accident. Something was going on at Top with inspections. It was a lot. Grace could probably use some help with her most annoying child.

"This is the part where you remember I'm easily moved to mischief." Hutch set the box down on the desk and backed up.

"Kyle convinced me to help smuggle him on the plane, and he's on his way down there, too. Sorry, MaeBe. He made me do it. I told him it was a bad idea and you would be mad, and he told me to tell you to take care of the cat."

Hutch hustled to his big office and closed the door.

That asshole. She was going to kill him.

* * * *

He was going to kill everyone, and this wasn't like the time when he heroically ignored his broken foot to go and save his brother from kidnappers. Nope. That was completely different.

MaeBe had been stabbed. Stabbed.

She was supposed to be safe behind her computer not out in the field where she could get hurt. She was supposed to guide trained agents.

He stood outside her hospital room. He wasn't allowed to even get close to her door because Michael Malone's client was in there. Hutch had been allowed in, but the man who cared about her most in the world had been told to sit on his freaking hands because he couldn't endanger Michael's op.

So here he was stuck in the damn waiting room while Michael played spy games with a former Hollywood actress.

Mae loved Vanessa Hale's movies. She was probably in there right now talking to the actress who might or might not be scamming Julian Lodge and asking her all kinds of questions about that horror movie she'd made him watch four times.

He was going to give her such a fucking lecture. When he got in.

"Should I sedate you, man? You look crazy right now. Security is going to show up any minute and take you to the floor where they soothe a dude with heavy meds," a deep voice said.

Excellent. His uncle was here, and Kyle had a couple of things to say to him, too. He stood and turned. "She is not supposed to be out in the damn field, Ian."

His uncle wore workout clothes and had likely come over from The Club where he had a weekly therapy group that masked itself as a basketball game. It was a bunch of old guys talking through their

89

shit while pretending they could still play.

Kyle had been invited. He found lots of ways to avoid that particular meeting.

His uncle shook his head and sat back in one of the seats. "It's always *Uncle* when he wants something and *Ian* when he's about to be unreasonable. You know she's an adult and can make choices and was not in any way forced to take this job, right?"

"She's also submissive and eager to please the only family she thinks she has."

Ian's eyes rolled. "She's not that submissive. Oh, I'm sure she would be in very specific places, but Mae can take charge when she needs to, and she doesn't hesitate to negotiate. She's been eager to do fieldwork, and this was an easy job."

"Then how did she get stabbed?"

"The same way she could have been stabbed on the train or walking down the street. She got stabbed because she saw something terrible about to happen and she intervened. She's a good person and she's not afraid to stand up when she sees an injustice," Ian said with a frown. "She's a lot like your mom and your aunt. I'm going to give you some advice. Don't smother her. If you can't love her for who she is and not who you think she should be, walk away now. And stop going behind her back trying to make decisions for her when you don't even have a real claim on her. Honestly, don't do that when you do have a claim on her. She might not know how to properly deball a man, but she has friends who would love to help her out. When you get in there, take care of her. Treat her like your friend and coworker and not some porcelain doll you need to protect. It'll go better for you in the long run."

He wasn't trying to smother her. He was trying to keep her healthy and whole. At some point he fully intended to convince her to go and work for Adam because Adam Miles would never send her out into the field to get her ass kicked. If she was working for Miles-Dean, Weston and Murdoch, she wouldn't be lying in a hospital bed. "How about you let me worry about my...about MaeBe."

Ian pointed his way, a gotcha look on his face. "You were going to say sub, but she's not wearing your collar. I knew you thought of her that way."

His uncle was so old-fashioned and a bit hypocritical. "There's more than one way to practice BDSM."

It seemed like every head in the room swiveled their way because he should have kept his voice down.

Ian sighed and sat back. "I worry you're not practicing anything but evasion."

"What is that supposed to mean?"

"It means you're never going to be ready for her if you don't confront what happened with Julia Ennis."

He paced, his voice going low. "I don't have to because it's over. I can utterly ignore it because she is no longer on this earth, and I can move on. I'm ready to move on. I do not get why you and all those people who run out of Kai's office feel the desperate need to live in the past, but I don't. I'm better. I'm happy. I'm not leaving."

"You are a powder keg who thinks he's suddenly a comfy couch, but you are going to blow up, nephew, and when you do that shrapnel of yours is going to go everywhere," Ian returned. "And she'll stand there and take it because she's far stronger than you're giving her credit for."

Kyle stopped and turned to his uncle, well aware they had an audience but unable to shut the conversation down. "I know how strong she is." Was he fucking this up, too? He didn't want to fight with his uncle. Ian wouldn't do anything to hurt him or Mae. He believed that. He couldn't have known how this would turn out. "But I don't think she's a field operative."

"I don't either. She would need an enormous amount of physical and mental training. But, Kyle, you can't keep her cooped up. She's going to want to test her skills, and that means working in the field from time to time. She was good today. The stabby part didn't have anything to do with the op. And it happened close to her yoga studio and the bakery. Are you going to try telling her she can't do those things anymore?"

He hated it, but there was a part of him that responded to logic. "No."

Ian relaxed back like he knew the worst had passed. "Then don't run in there like an angry, possessive bull. She didn't yell at you when you broke your foot, and that actually was part of the job."

"I didn't get stabbed. And she totally yelled at me when I got back from Argentina. Like psycho yelled at me. She's got some crazy eyes."

"You thought she was hot, didn't you?"

He felt his lips curl because he totally had. She'd given him hell but she'd been upfront about it, and it had been impossible not to see that tirade for what it was—caring, worry. "She might think I'm hot for yelling at her."

"You made the choice to put yourself in danger, asshole," his uncle pointed out. "She was walking down the street after she finished a non-dangerous job and tried to stop someone from being murdered. Don't be an ass. Go down to the shop and buy her flowers and promise to take care of her."

But he really wanted to yell.

He sighed because his uncle had a point.

When he finally made it into her room, it was with flowers in hand.

"Hey, spicy girl," he said when she held out a hand to him.

"Hey." Her eyes filled with tears, and he realized she'd held this emotion for him. She'd been smiling and holding it all in, playing her part in the op. Now he was here and they could be real with each other. "I was so scared."

He sat on the edge of her bed and leaned over, looking into those eyes and happy his uncle had kicked some sense into him. "I was, too. Don't get stabbed again."

He let his lips touch hers and knew it was almost time.

Chapter Six

Kyle could still hear her even an hour later. They'd been standing in the office of the BDSM club known as The Reef, and everything had seemed normal. Well, normal for them since they were on an op trying to figure out if a billionaire tech god was connected to the group called The Consortium. Up until that moment, he and MaeBe had been a-okay. They'd even made plans to take a brief vacation after this op was over. He was taking her to…he didn't want to think about it or talk about it because it was dumb and cutesy…Disneyland. She'd never been and they were here in LA, so he was indulging his sub.

Not quite his sub. Not yet, but after he'd spent a day indulging her inner child, he would spend that night right here in The Reef, and he'd already quietly reserved a privacy room.

And then they'd met with Kayla Summers. It was a pre-op meeting to let them go over what would happen when Deke Murphy and his client/ex-girlfriend/current bed buddy, Maddie Hill, brought the aforementioned billionaire, Nolan Byrne, and the mysterious Jane to the club.

Kyle didn't like Jane. Something was off about her, but he couldn't tell what. He would know more tonight, but he had bigger problems this afternoon.

MaeBe was pissed. Or hurt. Or both. Or she was just tired of waiting for him.

He shouldn't have to talk if he doesn't want to. And it's not right of her to make him. There are things that are personal and private.

He'd been talking about Deke and Maddie. Deke didn't want to discuss what had happened to him during his military days. He didn't want to focus on the past. Kyle understood that. The future was the only thing that mattered.

Not in a relationship there aren't, MaeBe had replied quietly, her eyes on him. *Or at least there shouldn't be. I'm sorry. I'm with Maddie. There shouldn't be secrets between people in love. There should be trust and intimacy. Your partner should be the only person in the world you tell everything to. The good. The bad. The ugly.*

And that was when he realized she might have mentioned Deke and Maddie, but she'd been talking about them. She was talking about the fact that he wouldn't open himself up and spill all his mistakes. She'd listened to Big Tag and only thought that purging every emotion he'd ever felt would make him happy and whole.

He had to show her she was the reason he was happy and whole, and they didn't need the past. They only needed the present and the future.

The past was over, and replaying it all again would do nothing but cause problems between the two of them. He wasn't the same man who'd made all those mistakes. He was better and she was the reason.

He thought he needed to make their first time together perfect, but he only needed to make it right, to show her how he felt.

He knocked on the door to the guest room she was using. She'd concentrated on work all afternoon, explaining she couldn't talk at the moment because she was monitoring what was happening at Maddie's office.

But now he knew Maddie had Deke to watch over her, and Drake had taken Boomer to a buffet for lunch, so they had hours and hours alone. And probably one restaurant owner in LA was about to go out of business as a sacrifice to his relationship with MaeBe.

The door opened and MaeBe stood there, a stubborn look on her face. Like she'd known exactly who was on the other side of the door. She wore her usual uniform of leggings and a dark T-shirt with some snarky saying on it, but she'd taken off her combat boots and her hair was down. The stubborn look quickly faded and she schooled her expression to as neutral as MaeBe could get. He could still tell she was irritated, but her lips formed an approximation of a smile. "Is the Boom man ready for dinner? Where are we heading? I have to get my bag. I figured with Deke watching Maddie we could get out of this place."

He followed her and closed the door, sliding the lock into place, though it was more of a warning than any kind of real deterrent to any of the people who might come through. "Boomer and Drake went to lunch, and then they're going back to the club. We'll order a pizza or something. We don't have to be at the club for hours. Until then, it's you and me."

She turned, and her eyes had gone wide. "What is that supposed to mean?"

The time for talking was over. They'd talked for months and months. If he hadn't been gone on assignment so much, they likely would be sleeping together and she wouldn't question why he didn't talk about unimportant things. They had needed time, but it was obvious to him not being together physically was starting to wear on them both.

He moved in, his hands going to cup her face and tilt her head up. "You can tell me no, MaeBe, and I'll back away, but I don't want to. I need you. I wanted to wait until I could make it perfect for you, but then you picked Disneyland and I realized perfection isn't happening."

She laughed, the sound so fucking magical to him. "Disney is perfect."

"It's not, baby." He adored this woman. She lightened his soul. She made him remember who he'd been all those years ago. "It's going to be full of kids, and I don't know how well I'm going to be able to fuck you if Mickey is watching."

She bit her bottom lip. "I think you'll manage, and besides, I thought we would also probably play at The Reef if Kay will let us. I might have mentioned I was going to seduce you while we're here in LA. And I talked to Hutch, and he approved my time off. Do you really want to take a vacation with me?"

It was time for some serious honesty. He needed to be real with her. "I want to take every vacation with you. I want to be with you all the time. When we're not together, I'm thinking about you. I'm going to tell my uncle I want to move into investigations so if I go into the field, I can take my tech with me. I don't want to be apart. I hate it when we're apart."

He kissed her.

He'd kissed her before, playful pecks and meaningful caresses over her cheeks and forehead. But he hadn't trusted himself to really kiss her, to let himself devour that gorgeous mouth of hers.

Now he was sure he'd been right because the minute her mouth softened, he couldn't help but dominate her. His tongue surged in, and he held her still so he could taste her, lose himself in her.

His whole body felt alive in a way it hadn't in forever.

"I shouldn't let you do this," she whispered, but her hands were already sliding under his shirt, the tips of her fingers brushing over his skin and making his cock jump.

He ran his tongue over that plump bottom lip of hers. Being close to her for so long and not touching her had been good for them but hell on his dick. He'd wanted her pretty much the moment he'd seen her, but he'd forced himself to get to know the real MaeBe Vaughn before letting sex muck up his thinking. Now he fully intended to revel in it. She might never get him off of her again. "I think you should let me do anything I want. I won't do a thing that you won't like, baby. I promise."

She let her head fall back as he kissed his way down her throat. "I'm not talking about sex. It's way past time we had sex. We've been together for a long time now. Even when we were working on our friendship, we were pretty much together."

She smelled so fucking good. The soap and body lotion she used was lavender, and he swore his dick perked up every time he caught the scent. Once he got those leggings off her, he would be able to smell the scent of her arousal, and he was fairly certain he would never stop craving it. The way he craved her. "We're going to be more together now." He lifted his head because she needed to understand a few things. "This is it, Mae. We're together after this. You're mine and I'm yours, and I do not want to hear about my caveman possessive instincts because you are every bit as bad as me."

"Am not." Her head was tilted up, those big eyes on him. "And I wasn't talking about that. I meant what I said. I've pretty much been yours since the night you asked me not to give up on you. The sex makes things easier because I hate not sleeping with you. I meant we still haven't talked about it. You said you wouldn't be ready until you could talk about it. And by it, I mean her."

He shook his head. "Please. I don't want her to ruin this. Haven't I done everything I possibly can to show you how much I care about you? Mae, I love you. I don't say that easily, but it's the truth. I love you, and I want to spend the rest of my life with you. You've got my future. Are you going to make me relive my past in order to have you?"

"I wasn't making this a transaction," she insisted.

He knew that. She would never do that to him. "I trust you, baby. I love you. Please let that be enough."

Her eyes softened and he knew he had her.

"It's enough. Of course, it's enough. I love you, too. I love you so much." She went on her toes and pressed her lips to his.

And he'd won. He picked her up, her legs wrapping around his waist as he walked her toward the bed. He'd been sleeping upstairs with Boomer, but he wasn't going to do that again. He was staying with her tonight and every other night.

This was the rest of his life. He kissed her as he tumbled them both on the bed. It was a full and too small for him, but he would cuddle her all night.

He somehow managed to twist his body so she was on top. "Take off your shirt and ditch that bra. We're going to set up some protocols when it comes to play time. Rule number one…"

"I'm naked," she finished, proving they were already in perfect synch. She sat up, dragging her shirt over her head. "They all told me it would be this way. Find a Dom and never wear clothes again."

She was such a cheeky brat. He was going to have fun spanking her. She had far more experience in the lifestyle than he did, but he was going to learn how to take care of the submissive side of her soul.

He was going to make a snarky comment about how red her ass could get, but she wasn't wearing a bra and her breasts were so perfect. And she had the prettiest nipple rings. She'd told him she'd had them done a couple of years back, but he hadn't expected them to be so fucking hot.

She frowned. "You don't like them?"

He was going to get rid of that insecurity. She was going to know how beautiful she was to him. "I fucking love them. My mind got fuzzy with all the things I can do with these rings." He reached out and traced one with his forefinger.

A shudder went through her, and the sweetest whimper.

He twisted the ring slightly, and that whimper became a gasp.

"Yes, you can definitely do that," she said, biting her bottom lip. Her hips were moving as though of their own volition, rubbing her pussy right over the hard length of his cock like she was in heat.

It was good because he was definitely hot for her. "Do you touch yourself, MaeBe? Do you ever play with these rings and wonder what it would be like to have hard hands on your body, twisting and pulling, putting a chain between the rings so you were always aware of your nipples?"

There was a gorgeous flush to her skin. "Yes, Kyle. It's always your hands. I can't even play with tops at Sanctum anymore because they aren't you. I canceled my sessions with Mistress Lea because it felt wrong to not be there with you."

He'd known she played with tops of all genders and preferences at Sanctum. He didn't care what or who she'd done before this moment. After was an entirely different story. "I promise I'll take care of you. We might get some play in tonight. If Byrne wants a demo, I promise I'll spank you."

She was brazenly riding his cock at this point, rubbing her clit over him through her leggings and his jeans. "Whatever my Dom wants."

She was going to kill him, and he would go down happy for her.

He flipped her over, wanting to take command again. He shrugged out of his shirt and kissed her, giving her his full weight until he pressed her down into the softness of the comforter. He palmed her breasts, tugging on the rings and making her squirm. He kissed his way down her body, stopping to play with the rings again before licking and nipping his way toward the apex of her thighs.

He dragged the leggings and the panties she was wearing off, tossing them to the floor and getting a good look at her for the first time. How often had he lain awake thinking about how gorgeous she would be once he got her clothes off? More than he would ever want to admit. But no fantasy could compete with the sight of her lying there, legs slightly spread and body flush, waiting for him to make good on all the promises he'd made with every kiss and caress, every long night spent learning the craziest board games or talking about her family.

He was going to be her family now.

"You are so fucking beautiful. Don't you ever forget that." He sank down and made a place for himself, spreading her legs wide.

He put his mouth on her and knew he'd found his way through the darkness.

He would spend the rest of his life in the light.

* * * *

MaeBe knew there was more to this sudden change of plans than Kyle simply needed to take her to bed or he would die, but it didn't matter. She couldn't deny this man.

It was time. The months and months of longing had led her to this, and it could be weeks before they stopped fucking like bunnies at every given opportunity.

She was going to love those months, too.

She got the feeling she would love almost anything as long as he was with her. This felt so right, and she was going with it.

Like she had a choice. She was fairly certain her body was in charge right now, and her body knew exactly what it wanted.

His mouth hovered over her pussy, and she gripped the comforter to keep from moving. They'd never played together, though she was well aware they'd been involved in a D/s light relationship most of the time they'd known each other.

Kyle was an indulgent top. He didn't have a ton of rules, and even those he did have, he rarely talked about. Instead he gently shifted her this way or that. It took her a while to realize what a sneaky bastard he could be. As all of his rules had to do with safety and her comfort, she didn't find them oppressive and went along with it.

Now that they were taking the next step, she wanted it all. She wanted to be his girlfriend with future wife options, and she definitely wanted to be his sub.

If someone had asked her a couple years before if she wanted kids, she would have said no. Now she realized her personal reasons had to do with her crappy family.

But if she had kids with Kyle, they would have a wonderful, supportive family. Her kids would be safe with this family.

"You are so fucking beautiful. Don't you ever forget that," he whispered right before he lowered his head and she couldn't breathe anymore.

His mouth was hot against her pussy, and she could feel how wet she was. The minute the man walked in a room her body responded. She softened and arousal poured through her. Her nipples still pulsed from him playing with her rings, and she knew he was going to be slightly sadistic about them.

She couldn't wait for that either.

She liked a pretty big bite of pain, and Kyle had a streak of sadism that she thought would work nicely on her.

But all those thoughts of funishment and happy aches flew away the minute he started to eat her pussy like a starving man. Pure sensation swamped her system, and she was utterly incapable of coming up with a single reason why they shouldn't do this.

He was right. The past didn't matter. It was only the future they needed to concern themselves with, and the future involved so much of this.

Waiting for Kyle Hawthorne had been the best decision she'd ever made.

His tongue worked her over, laving her clitoris with affection as his big fingers eased inside her pussy.

He stroked inside her, his tongue working her clit. She'd known it would be like this—incendiary and yet sweet. Like this was always supposed to happen.

Like they were meant to be.

Pleasure rose quick and wild and she came against his tongue as he held her hips, keeping her still so she could ride out the sensation.

She opened her eyes as she felt him slide off the bed, watched as he slid his jeans off after kicking his shoes to the side.

Damn that man was fine. She wasn't sure she was in his league when it came to Greek statue worthy bodies, but she didn't care. There was no room for insecurity here, only awe that she got to watch him, to know that body and soul of his somehow meshed with hers, and no one could keep them apart.

"Say it again." He climbed back on the bed, a predatory gleam in his eyes.

Her brain wasn't completely working because the sight of that man naked struck her hard. "Say what?"

His lips had curved up in that arrogant, oh-so-sexy smirk that would bug the hell out of her if he was actually an arrogant jerk. "You love me."

He wasn't. There was such a kind soul under all his pain. He loved his family, helped his friends, was patient with her. He'd opened himself up to the things she loved and asked very little of her in return. It was pretty much the easiest truth she'd ever said aloud. "I love you, Kyle."

He climbed between her legs, and she watched as he rolled a condom over his cock. That cock was a thing of beauty, too. She started to reach out but he shook his head.

"No, baby. I'll come in your hand, and I want to make this last as long as I can. Though you should know it's still going to be too fast. I haven't... Let's just say it's been over a year, and I think about you all the time. I haven't thought of anyone else since the minute we met."

She'd dated quite a bit in those first few months. "Kyle, you know I..."

"I don't care. I meant what I said. Whatever you did before doesn't matter. We made our deal, and I know neither of us has seen anyone since."

"No. I didn't want anyone else. I don't think I ever will."

"Oh, I intend to make sure you won't ever again. This is it for me, MaeBe Vaughn. You're my endgame. Always." He lowered himself on top of her, meshing their mouths together.

He kissed like a god, drugging her with the sensation of his tongue sliding along hers, his chest pressed tight. Soft skin covered all those muscles, and she couldn't stop touching him. She let her hands drift as they kissed, knowing when he got her in a club she would likely be tied up and held down in some way. She would love that, but she liked being able to touch him this first time.

She felt his cock tease at her pussy, rubbing over her clit and sending sparks of pleasure through her veins.

His forehead rested on hers as he started to move his hips. "You're going to feel so good. Do you have any idea how long I've been waiting for this?"

"As long as I have." She stroked back his hair. It had gotten longer over the months of their friendship, the hard military man softening over time.

"Longer. I was into you way before you were into me."

He was good at rewriting history. "It was a couple of weeks."

"Years," he whispered against her mouth. "Decades. But I'm not wasting another minute."

She gasped as he started to work his cock inside her. She adjusted, wrapping her legs around his waist and giving him all the access he could need. He pressed in, stretching her in the most delicious way.

She held on as he started to thrust inside, dragging that big cock out before filling her up again. She matched his rhythm, finding a perfect tempo.

He held her so tight as the second orgasm burst across her, even stronger than the first. She clutched him, letting her nails dig slightly into the skin of his back, loving the way he stiffened above her as he thrust in hard before he fell on her.

She loved the way it felt when he was all around her and there was not a stitch of clothes between them. There was nothing but the languor of after and the sweetness of the intimacy between them. There was no awkwardness, no wondering if the other person felt the same way. There was nothing but certainty that this was right and good and probably meant to be.

He nuzzled her cheek. "Yep. Knew that would be good. Expected it would be great. And then it still blew me away."

"I would definitely give that a ten out of ten. That gets a recommend from me."

He chuckled and rolled off her, but he quickly pulled her into his arms. "Oh, you should know we'll be doing that a lot. And I think you should take pity on your poor boyfriend and let him move in with you. It's way past time for me to get out and leave the newlyweds alone. I'm sick of hearing David and Tessa have sex. I want to make other people listen to you and me having sex. Lots of sex."

She'd already planned on doing that. At least until they could find a house. It was time for them to be actual adults and settle down. There were several houses for rent in his brother's neighborhood, and they wouldn't be far from his Uncle Theo. Still, she couldn't help but tease the man. "You wait until after sex to try to take half my place."

His arm tightened around her. "Only until we find a house. We should do adult things now."

They were so in synch. "I was just thinking that."

"There are a couple of places near…"

"David and Tessa," she finished. "I know. I already looked. I thought it would be nice because it's also pretty close to Theo and Erin."

"I don't have a ton of cash, but the good news is I also don't have any debt," Kyle began.

Oh, she needed to put that to rest right now. She rolled over and propped herself up on her elbow. "We'll be fine. We're a team, and we pool our resources. And you'll make more as an investigator. I think you'll like it. You're good at solving mysteries."

"Yeah. We should probably talk about the whole CIA thing," he began, his lips turning down. "I can't talk about most of my work there."

"I've always suspected you were Agency. I wouldn't have been able to prove it, of course, but I could have made an excellent case," she said quietly. "I'm pretty good at investigating, too."

His eyes narrowed. "You investigated me?" And then his expression cleared. "I would have, too. But I would think the Agency would be better at hiding things."

She sighed and relaxed. "Oh, if I didn't know better I would absolutely believed you were a normal, regular Navy SEAL. But I work where I work and I'm good at listening in on things. Also, I know how to read Agency bullshit."

"Well, I'm glad you've moved on from potentially working for the mob to just hacking military records," he quipped, proving he wasn't so bad himself.

She'd been young and embracing the intricacies of the Dark Web. "Yeah, that wasn't my shining moment. Lucky for me Hutch was investigating that syndicate at the time and gave me a heads-up, and later on a job. So when you think about it, it was a good thing."

"Because it led you here," he murmured and leaned over, brushing his lips against hers. "I will forever be grateful for that and to Hutch. I'll send him a candy basket for saving my girl before she was my girl."

"I think I might have always been your girl. You should know I've never felt this way about anyone else."

His hand came out to cup her face. "Me either. And that includes people I don't want to talk about. Only you, baby. Now come here and kiss me again. We only have a few hours until we go back to work. Let's not make a big announcement until we get home. I happen to know there's a betting pool, and I want to fuck my uncles over. They have this weekend. If we hold out until Monday, Alex McKay wins big."

They worked at the best place in the world. "I won't tell if you won't. As far as they'll know it was the excitement of being at Disneyland that did it."

He groaned but he kissed her again, and she got ready for the rest of her life.

Chapter Seven

"So how did you spend your afternoon off? Do I need to ask? You're practically glowing. Did she buy you a ring yet? Should I plan your bachelor party?" Drake asked, one brow raised.

They were secluded in Kayla Summers-Hunt's office at The Reef. Though her office was industrial chic like the rest of the club, there was no doubt that the works of art and furniture were expensive and luxurious. Kyle supposed that when one's husband was one of Hollywood's highest paid actors, one could decorate however one wanted.

Luckily his Mae mostly wanted storage for her board games and graphic novels, and a comfy seat in which to slaughter her enemies in virtual worlds. He had heard her talking about a virtual reality setup. That might set them back a couple grand.

"I think I'm going to tell my uncle I want to move upstairs."

Drake looked up from the laptop in front of him, a brow rising over his eyes. "First, way to evade. Second, that tells me everything I need to know. You're not coming back, and you're worried you don't make enough money for Mae. Don't ever tell her that. She'll do something mean to you."

"She's not mean," he replied. "And the money's more about making sure she's comfortable. Are they here yet?"

He was feeling pretty relaxed with the exception of this op.

Something about it felt off to him. He couldn't put his finger on it, but he was sure it had something to do with the woman named Jane.

Nolan Byrne—the man they were investigating—had requested an evening at The Reef for him and his girlfriend. Jane Adams was a consultant who regularly worked for some of the biggest corporations in the world. According to MaeBe, the woman spent almost all her time working. Maddie said her interest in BDSM came from taking back her power after a bad relationship.

The whole thing felt wrong to Kyle.

Drake glanced back down at the monitor he'd been watching. "No, but they still have a couple of minutes. Are you going to tell me what happened or not? Because something changed between you and MaeBe."

Drake was one of his closest friends, but he wanted to keep this to himself for a little while. "We're going to stay here in LA after the op. We're taking a week off and when we get back—if everything goes okay—I'm going to move in with her."

A smile broke out over Drake's face. "That's awesome, man. I'm happy for you." He sobered. "Have you thought about using the cash?"

The thought of the cash made his gut turn. It was still sitting there in its offshore account, Julia's blood money. "I haven't talked to Mae about Julia. I'm not about to buy us a new place with the money she made from treason. We'll be okay. Besides, I thought you might need it. I'll take that story anytime you're willing to tell it, by the way."

Drake had plenty of money, but untraceable cash would be helpful if he was going to do something he didn't want the Agency to know about.

"I'll tell you someday, but for now it's best you don't know," Drake replied, his eyes on the screen. "I want you to have plausible deniability if I actually go through with the op. I'd like to figure out if Jane Adams is a Consortium agent first. If we can catch her, we can question her. Then we'll have some information and if I have to disappear, at least I left something behind to help us find them. They're here. Unless someone else in this club drives a Bugatti. I don't think Kay's husband does."

And that was all he was going to get about whatever mysterious job Drake needed to do. Unless the guy got in trouble, and then Kyle might need the money to get himself out of jail because if Drake called him he would go no matter what the op was.

Kyle moved in behind him and saw the ridiculously expensive car glide into the parking garage that served the club. "Switch to the camera on the valet stand."

Drake hit a couple of keys and the camera view switched. The sleek blue and black sports car came to a stop at the valet stand.

His uncle didn't have a valet stand. His uncle would tell anyone who wouldn't park their own car to bite him and go to Julian's.

There was a difference between the old-money crowd and his uncle's working-class wealthy set.

He was going to have to work out a schedule with his stepdad because MaeBe loved Sanctum. He might suggest an old dudes night so he never had to see his relatives in leathers. Old dudes could have, say, Thursdays, and Fridays could be for the younger set so David and Tessa could play there, too.

Damn. It wasn't like he hadn't seen his brother in a set of leathers, but he'd been lucky enough to never be at The Club when he was playing. How did Ian and Sean manage it? He didn't want to listen to David and Tessa do it much less actually see it. He and Hamilton hunkered down when those sounds started up.

What would happen when his younger siblings got curious?

The whole club situation was starting to make him seriously nervous.

There were only two clubs. He had visions of running into family members in all states of undress.

"Dude, you went pale. Are you okay?" Drake asked.

That was a problem for another day. He'd heard Eric Vail often had private play parties for the people who worked at Top. Maybe he could sneak in there. Except his parents worked there.

So many mistakes had been made.

"It's nothing." He wasn't about to tell Drake he was suddenly worried all his BDSM dreams would go up in smoke if his mom showed up and gave him instructions on how to spank his sub. "All right. There's Byrne. He's a shitty top. He's letting security help his sub out of the car."

The big security guard held a hand out, and the woman in the passenger seat unfolded her slender body and stood.

"Is she wearing a mask?" Drake asked.

Kyle had heard a bit of the drama surrounding how Jane Adams wanted her night in The Reef to go. She'd apparently had a terrible Dom at some point, and this evening was about taking her power as a sub back. "She said she wanted to enter with the mask and when she feels comfortable with Byrne as her Dom, she'll take it off. The counselor here cleared her for play."

"In a virtual meeting," Drake murmured. "She couldn't find the time to actually come in. That's a red flag for me."

"Byrne didn't either." Kyle kept his eyes on the screen, and when the woman turned, he saw she was wearing a strapless dress, one that would be easy to get back into after a night's play. It wasn't the dress that made him stop, made the room suddenly go cold as an icy finger of suspicion climbed up his spine. "What is she wearing?"

Drake sent him a weird look. "I think it's called a dress."

"No. Around her neck. Is that what I think it is?" Every bit of his attention was on the black and gold charm around her neck, held there with a delicate gold chain.

Drake stared for a moment, and then his hands were working across the keyboard, freezing the image and enlarging it. "It's a coincidence."

Thank you, my darling. You knew exactly what I wanted.

Because you told me what to buy.

It had been their two-month anniversary, and Julia had made it perfectly plain that she required a gift and that gift should be a black Van Cleef and Arpels Alhambra necklace. Oh, she'd wanted a ten-thousand-dollar Cartier, but she'd settled for what he could afford.

She'd been wearing it when she died.

His Aunt Charlotte wore one. Hers was turquoise blue and every time he saw it, something tightened inside him.

For Christmas he'd gotten MaeBe a new set of dice that she'd wanted, and she'd been so happy she'd cried and hugged him tight.

He shook his head, unwilling to let it go. "It's not a coincidence. Jane Adams works for The Consortium, and she knows I'm here. That is a big old fuck you to me. We didn't consider this possibility. You think that The Consortium uses mostly women operatives. A sisterhood, of sorts. What if they figured out I was the one who took out their sister and they want revenge?"

"Or Jane Adams likes high-end jewelry. It's not all that high end, you know," Drake pointed out. "I mean it's expensive, but we're talking a couple grand. A lot of wealthy women wear those necklaces."

Nothing Drake was saying was wrong, but Kyle discounted it. He knew something was wrong, and it came down to that necklace. Deep down, he knew this wasn't some coincidence. That necklace was a neon sign flashing.

Danger. Danger. Danger.

Drake stood. "I know this is worrisome, but I need you to stay calm. There's no reason to think there's someone out there who would care enough about my sister to put themselves on the line to avenge her. Especially not a woman. You know how shitty she was to other women. She was quite awful."

It was true. Julia Ennis wasn't exactly a girls girl. She always saw other women as competition, and he'd never actually seen her make friends with...anyone. There was her family and her boyfriend, and the rest of the world was to be dominated and conquered.

Sometimes he wondered if that wasn't exactly why he'd fallen into her web. He hadn't wanted to care about anyone at the time. It hurt too much, and he'd been punishing himself. When he'd started to come out of it, he'd realized they couldn't work.

He stared at the woman in the picture. She wore a mask, but it didn't hide all of her features, and the woman obviously wasn't Julia.

Still, he couldn't stop the way his stomach turned. "I should go down to the locker room. I'll talk to Deke. I want to keep MaeBe close tonight. I know we want to get to know this woman, but I think she should steer clear. Kayla can handle her."

They would need MaeBe's talents tomorrow night when they intended to break into Nolan Byrne's personal system and take the data they needed. Although he'd greatly prefer Drake handle that part of the op, Deke was insistent on MaeBe being there since Drake was still Agency. Kyle trusted the man, but this was Deke's mission.

However, Mae was his, and he would make the decisions when it came to her. He wasn't going to let anyone put her in danger. Not even for the sake of an op.

He glanced back at the screen, but the woman was gone, likely already in the club.

The night was beginning. He had to get through it then they would go on their vacation and everything would be as it should be.

"Hey, are you worried about this?" Drake asked.

He was always worried about Julia. Even though she was dead, she still hung over his life like the sword of Damocles. She would show up as a ghost threatening everything. He just had to make MaeBe love him fully, wholly. Perhaps then she could handle mistakes he'd made with Julia. "I'm going to meet with Deke. I'll talk to him. There might be some worst-case scenarios we haven't played through yet. I'll feel better once I've been in a room with this Jane person and I know it's not Julia."

"How could it be Julia? You killed her."

"I shot her. I thought I killed her. I was sure I had. Now I wonder because we had to leave. That fire ensured we didn't find her body. What would she have done if she survived that night? What if she'd been wearing a vest? I didn't go for a head shot. I couldn't. I hit her in the chest, and I can't remember if there was blood. Her body fell and the fire was raging by then. I had minutes to get out."

The truth was that whole day was a blur. He remembered parts of it with brilliant clarity, but the rest was a mess in his head. He dreamed about it at night, and the dreams had woven in with reality, meshing into a nightmare where he couldn't tell truth from fiction. The one thing he'd known was that Julia was dead, and now even that was in question.

But now wasn't the time to confront the subject. He would do a deep dive into Jane Adams tomorrow. Tonight he would find Deke and keep Mae close.

"What else could have happened? I saw her. She's not..." Drake stopped, his face going pale. "You think she could have taken over someone's life. Someone vulnerable. Someone who wouldn't be missed. Damn it. We talked about this. Julia and I would have conversations about what would happen if we got burned. She said she had a couple of people on her radar if she needed a new life. I told her I did too. I would take over some Hollywood star's life."

"You were joking. She wasn't." His gut was suddenly in knots. "I'm not saying that's what happened. Mae looked into Jane's online presence and verified it."

"But that's what Julia would need. She would need someone with no family and very few friends. She would need someone with her basic build and facial structure so the plastic surgery wasn't too hard to get right." Drake's jaw was tight as he spoke, his shoulders a straight line. "You're right. We might have made the most rookie mistake of all. We didn't bury a body."

He couldn't even contemplate it. Julia wasn't in this building meeting Mae as they spoke. The good news was they were surrounded by people—smart, trained people. Kayla was with the women. If by some crazy twist of fate Julia had survived, tonight wouldn't be the night she tried to kill him. "I'm going to find Deke and join up with the women as fast as we can. You monitor the situation from here. If something goes sideways, you know what to do."

"No. I really don't."

"If that's Julia walking around this club, there's only one way out and that's for me to take myself off the playing board. If I'm alive, MaeBe's the pawn she goes after."

"Goes after?" Drake asked.

"It's all a game to Julia. She'll be pissed that I'm close to MaeBe." He couldn't believe he was actually considering the nightmare scenario. It couldn't be true, but he had to have it in the back of his head.

He hadn't seen her body after the fire, hadn't buried her so he knew one hundred percent that she was in the ground. She could have been wearing a vest. His shot could have been off and missed her heart. She could have had someone lurking in the background waiting to save her.

His brain was moving a million miles a minute, taking him to worse and worse destinations.

If I ever had to disappear, I wouldn't trust some Agency hack to make up a person. I would find some sad-sack asshole and take over their life. It would have to be someone without a family, without much contact with the outside world. I know that sounds hard, but these days it's pretty easy. The pandemic alone created an army of isolationists who live on social media. All I need is one who looks somewhat like me, and then I don't need faked documents. I would have the real thing.

They'd been lying in bed after some insanely nasty somewhat vicious sex and she'd posited the idea that every spy needed a way out. He'd said if things went to hell, he would call his uncle. She'd rolled her eyes and told him not everyone had a Taggart hotline.

He'd thought she'd been thinking out loud.

Had she been telling him her plan all along?

So many things had gone wrong over the course of the last few months.

"Kyle?"

Drake's voice cut through the cloud of panic that threatened to overtake him. He turned his way. "Huh?"

Drake's features were grave, as though he knew what had been going through Kyle's head, and the panic was threatening to take him, too. "It's time for the op. Deke's counting on us. I'm going to be watching. If anything goes wrong, you'll know what to do. If this goes to hell, you do what you have to do and meet me in LA. We'll figure out where to take you and Mae from there. I can find a place to stash you."

He shook his head. "No. If Julia's alive, I can't be. Mae has to think I'm dead. It's the only way to protect her."

Drake sighed. "It's not going to come to that."

It absolutely came to that.

* * * *

MaeBe looked up from packing her laptop to Boomer, who'd brought in a pack of pudding cups, hoping he could get her to eat something since she'd refused to eat the lunch the hospital kitchen had sent up. Vanilla. Like her life was going to be now.

"Look, Mae. I got the nurse to give us extras for the road." Boomer held up the package like he'd done something amazing.

He probably didn't even realize the nurse would have given him anything he asked for when he smiled at her. All the nurses had been talking about how hot Boomer was.

She'd been in the hospital overnight. It seemed like a theme in her life now. Lots of hospitals because she was the pawn everyone seemed to use. First Jessica Layne had used her to get to Noelle LaVigne. Then that asshole had stabbed her. Now she was a rag doll for Julia Ennis to throw around.

I feel sorry for you. He doesn't love you, you know. I'm afraid he's with you because you're not me. You're pretty much the opposite of me, and that's what attracted him to you. You're a reaction, not an actual relationship. Kyle needs a strong woman, one who can set him on his ass from time to time, and that's just not you. I would bet you don't even know the real Kyle Hawthorne.

Julia Ennis's words rolled through her head like some noxious poison that was also the truth. Oh, at the time MaeBe had found some courage and spat back that she knew him better, but now an uncomfortable revelation had settled deep inside her.

"I'm not hungry." She was ready to get out of here, to get back to her apartment and lock herself away for a few days.

"Come on, Mae. You know you have to eat. You can't feel better if you don't eat." Boomer was a glorious blond god of a man. He fit in with the Taggarts, but she always kind of thought of him as the human version of Groot from *Guardians of the Galaxy*. He was loyal and strong and amazing, and sometimes he didn't quite get the things that were going on around him.

If anyone was going to break the illusion Kyle was trying to spin, it was Boomer. The rest of the group was holding the line. "How about I eat when Kyle decides to be alive again."

Was that a sheen of tears in Boomer's blue eyes? "I'm so sorry, Mae. I'm sorry I couldn't save him."

Boomer had been the one to toss her broken body over his strong shoulder and haul them out of Nolan Byrne's mansion before Kyle had blown the whole place to hell. With himself inside. Or that's what he wanted everyone to believe.

She knew in her heart it wasn't true. She knew this was all one long setup to keep her out of the war that had begun. The war with Julia Ennis, who'd announced herself this evening by beating the crap out of MaeBe and trying to take the intel Byrne had wanted to trade for a place of power in The Consortium.

Though in the moment, she'd bought it all. In the moment she'd felt her soul split at the thought of Kyle dying. She'd known she wouldn't love another man, that he'd taken a piece of her with him.

She'd had to be dragged to the hospital and sedated so they could set her arm and see to her other injuries. When she'd woken up, grief had poured through her, a wild river she'd known she would drown in. That pain had been so much worse than the physical. It had been worse than the realization that her father loved keeping the peace more than he loved her, worse than that moment when she'd accepted her mother would die.

Losing Kyle had made her wish she'd been in that building with him so they could go together.

And then Kyle's tracker had come back online. Someone had made sure her phone was on the table beside her, and she'd had to look. She'd had to see that Kyle's tracker was dead to start to accept the loss. She monitored the trackers on all the operatives. Ian Taggart liked to tag his puppies, as he called them. More than once those locator devices had saved the day.

Kyle must have forgotten about it in the moment. She could understand. Things had moved quickly once Julia—who'd presented herself as Jane Adams—had killed the doctor who'd performed her earliest plastic surgery. That was the excuse she'd given for murdering the man. He'd been a member of The Reef, and Julia had worked her way to a position where she could take the doctor down and screw up her ex-boyfriend's life at the same time. So it was reasonable that Kyle had forgotten his uncle could literally track him.

Not that Ian wasn't in on it. He had to be since someone had gone in and made it look like the tracker had gone dead at the time when Kyle would have exploded. They'd erased the hours when she'd tracked him from Malibu to downtown LA, where the signal had suddenly been lost.

She wondered if Drake had been the one to tell him he was a dumbass and the world was still watching him or if he'd figured it out on his own.

Of course there was a darker scenario. Maybe Julia had pointed it out herself.

"Boomer, Kyle's alive." She was suddenly deeply concerned

that Boomer hadn't gotten the memo the rest of the group seemed to have received. Oh, they were all holding the line that she was sure Kyle wanted them to hold, but they couldn't fake the grief they obviously didn't feel. Yes, they were military dudes, and perhaps if she hadn't checked the monitor list, she might have bought it, but she had.

Boomer frowned. "I don't see how."

She reached out and held his hand. Boomer was the best guy in the world. He'd been in the room the first time she'd had this argument with Tag, but he might have only heard his boss telling her Kyle was dead and he'd ID'd the body himself. "He faked it because his ex-girlfriend is alive and he either thinks he's protecting me or he's going back to her."

When she thought about it, it was a novel way to get out of a relationship that didn't work for him. The sex might not have been as good for him as it was for her.

Or she was exactly what she'd feared she'd been all along. A placeholder. The sanctuary in the storm of his real epic love story.

She could put on fishnet leggings and dye her hair purple, but deep down she was just a normal, boring girl. How was she supposed to compete with the Charlotte Taggarts of the world?

And what was Julia Ennis if she wasn't Charlotte Taggart gone wrong? Even a bad Charlotte would be more exciting than a boring MaeBe. Even her fucking name was dull. It literally meant someone who couldn't make up her mind. Maybe.

Kyle might think he could fix Julia and then he would have the gorgeous, dangerous lover of his dreams.

He hadn't even topped MaeBe.

"I don't think he would go back to her. I don't think he liked her much," Boomer said.

"I know he didn't." Ian Taggart stood in the doorway, his massive, muscular body taking up most of the space. Hutch was behind him, going on his tiptoes to get a glimpse into the room.

Well, that explained how they'd changed the records. Hutch was excellent with code, and he would have all of Kyle's potential problems erased as soon as they identified them.

Hutch was in on it, too. They all were.

Did they know Kyle had fucked her once and then decided she

wasn't strong enough to fight beside him?

Or he'd fucked her once and decided she wasn't worth fighting with at all.

"One of you better put Boomer out of his misery. He still thinks Kyle's dead," she said, unwilling to leave Boomer on the outside even though she knew she would be. She didn't need company. It wasn't like she was going to stay around.

Every muscle in her body ached. Her head still throbbed despite all the pain killers they'd given her.

"Ian, why don't you talk to Boomer, and I'll check in on Mae," Hutch began.

Ian's head shook. "No, I think I'll leave the Boom man to you. You two go and have lunch. There's not a big enough kitchen on the jet to handle Boomer. I need to talk to Mae about her training schedule."

I know Taggart trains you all, but not the way I was trained. Trust me. Taggart is a preschool teacher compared to my handlers. And I bet Kyle protects you so you don't ever have to fight for your life. That's your fault. Don't ever expect a man to protect you. When he says he will, he's lying, and what he really wants is for you to be weaker than him.

She'd agreed to stay on with McKay-Taggart if and only if Ian would train her. Not to simply protect herself but to become the baddest of the badasses.

She wasn't going to be weak again.

Boomer wrapped her up in a gentle hug and whispered in her ear. "I know what I'm supposed to know. But I am sorry I couldn't fix it for you. Please don't leave us."

Tears sprang, quick and bittersweet. She loved these people. Did she have to lose everything because she'd been a fool? "I won't."

She wouldn't until she had the training she needed. No one could prepare her for the fight that was to come the way Ian Taggart could. She stepped back and Boomer and Hutch disappeared out the door, talking about where they could find a buffet.

"All right. I need one more agreement from you." Big Tag stood there, towering over her. There was a weariness to him that tugged at her. He'd been through a lot in the last twenty-four hours, and she hadn't made it easy for him. "Can we agree there's a wall between us when it comes to Kyle?"

"Like you insist he's dead when I know damn well he's alive?"

"You can't be sure."

She stared at him for a moment and then he cursed.

"You checked his tracker?"

How did she want to play this? Did she want to be the woman who constantly reminded everyone of how she'd been hurt? Or did she take the punch to the gut and learn how to not get punched again? Did she constantly cry about the why or did she simply move forward? "Do you want the wall, Ian? Or not?"

Ian's eyes closed, and she wondered how hard it was for him. If he genuinely cared about her, then she was asking him to choose between his nephew and her. Kyle had already put him in that position. Was she going to do the same thing? He'd been kind to her, stepping in when her family failed her.

"Ian, Kyle is dead and I won't ever say anything different, and I don't want you to say anything different to me, either. This is not a fight between the two of us. I thank you for everything you've done for me, for what you're willing to do for me."

Ian looked at her, his relief plain. "And I thank you for being the most reasonable of my... I don't know what to call you anymore. You're not merely an employee."

"And I'm not quite family. I'm something in between, and I have to stay that way because he is family."

"I can honor my family and still treat the others in my life with the love and respect they deserve."

He needed the same love and respect. And she would give it to him. "In the future if things change, I can't promise I wouldn't need to find another situation."

Ian's hands went to his pockets, big shoulders shrugging. "We'll deal with that, if it comes to it. And you should understand, the Agency fully believes that this is now in their hands, and I'm going to stay out of anything to do with Julia Ennis."

So Kyle wanted them all out of it, not simply her. Did he understand his uncle at all? "Well, you're known for being a good boy, boss."

His lips quirked up in an approximation of a smile. "I was

thinking you might like to work with Adam and Chelsea to see what you can find out about our opponent. Part of protecting yourself is having all the intel you can find on the enemy. I know that Kyle wanted to keep you out of everything. He was worried about how delicate you are."

"And his solution was to hide me away. But that's not yours. Or mine."

"No, it is not," Ian agreed. "If Julia Ennis wants a fight, we'll give her one. So what is rule number one in the Taggart family rules of war?"

She knew that one. "We don't fight fair."

"No, we do not. And we don't play by anyone's rules but our own, and Kyle should have remembered that before he blew his ass up," Ian vowed. "So, you up for this, Mae?"

For the first time since that building had gone up, she was. This was what she needed. Not to be treated like a damsel in distress. She needed to be treated like she could handle this, like she could win.

"I'm ready."

She walked out of the hospital with an aching body and heart.

And a real purpose. She wouldn't be weak again. Not for anyone.

Definitely not for Kyle Hawthorne.

Part Two

Here

Chapter Eight

MaeBe looked down at the man she'd just kicked in the balls and wondered where her sympathy had gone. It—like many things in her life—had fled with Kyle Hawthorne's "death."

Things like her dignity. Her open heart. Her confidence—though she'd pretty much gotten that back.

Still, she should feel for the guy. She'd been excellent at what Tag called Ball Breaking 101. And she'd learned the proper way to punch a chick in the tit.

She holstered her gun as the door came open and West Rycroft came through, Glock in hand. She preferred her SIG P238, but she'd left it in her laptop bag. It fit her hand properly and was easy to conceal. She'd gone to the gun range with Erin and Charlotte and tried pretty much every handgun possible. The two women had argued about what would work best while MaeBe had shot at a big picture of some man's lower half. The SIG had been the easiest to blow away the crotch with, and now she and Wanda were besties.

And yes, she'd named her gun after the Scarlet Witch because she could make men magically disappear when she brought it out. Drinking in bars was so much more fun with Wanda in her life.

"What the hell is going on? Hey, show me your hands or I'll shoot." West might be new to the job, but he took it seriously. He'd been her constant guard the last few weeks. He'd been willing to spar with her after she'd proven she could take him down, but he still consistently held back, so she preferred sparring with Erin. They'd gotten along quite well. So well, she'd wished she could work off her stress in a different way. West had gently hinted he wouldn't mind guarding her more personally.

If she could force herself to do it. If she could get over the asshole on the floor long enough to get her sex life back. Not that she'd had much of one before.

She wondered if Ian would get her a sex tutor. He probably would. The big guy was surprisingly open about those kinds of topics.

"It's me," Kyle groaned. "And I can't show you my fucking hands because they're the only things keeping my balls on my body right now. Fuck, Mae. Did you have to do that?"

She sighed and looked to West. "West, Kyle's back. In my defense, I thought he was a ghost since he's supposed to be dead. I certainly would never hurt a poor alive guy by ensuring he'll never have sex again."

West frowned and stood down, seeming to understand the world wasn't about to explode. "I thought he was dead too. I thought that was why you're so sad all the time. Wasn't he your boyfriend?"

"No," she said.

"Yes," Kyle replied at the same time. He managed to get to his knees. He used one hand to balance himself as he stood. "And she obviously knows I'm not dead. I was pretty sure that was the worst-kept secret in the world. Now, if you'll give us some privacy, I would appreciate it."

"We do not need privacy." She wasn't about to be alone with the man. She'd gotten over him. Mostly. "What he needs to do is call his uncle or his mom and have someone pick him up. Unless you have a car now. Also, don't try this again. I'll change my alarm code."

"And I'll figure it out again." Kyle managed to stand up straight with the merest of grimaces. His eyes narrowed as he turned to West. "I suggest you walk out of this room right now. Go and do what you should do and call your brother and brief him on the situation."

"You are not his boss." God, the man was still so arrogant it hurt. Once she'd thought it was a kind of sexy trait. Now she saw it for what it was. Kyle believed he was the center of the universe, and for some reason he wanted something from her. Likely information of some kind. She was almost certain something had gone down a few days before because Grace and Sean had come into the office and Grace had looked worried.

She stayed far away from any information concerning Kyle.

Julia Ennis was another story entirely, and she knew damn well something had happened with Julia's family in the past couple of days. She hadn't figured out if the incident in London had been a normal tragedy or if it fit into the bigger picture she'd spent months putting together.

But Kyle couldn't know the information she'd gathered on his ex-fiancée and her family, including Kyle's bestest bestie, Drake Radcliffe. He couldn't possibly know that she'd been tracking Drake's father because she'd begun to suspect he might have had ties to The Consortium before his death. She hadn't even told Big Tag that yet. Adam knew she had some suspicions, but they'd decided not to accuse the man before they had proof.

"No, but Wade is," Kyle said in an annoyingly calm tone. "And the fact that the situation has changed means West here should call his supervisor."

"I don't see how the situation has changed except that MaeBe kicked your ass. Well, your balls." West had an arrogant smirk of his own. He was a handsome man with sandy blond hair, green eyes, and a muscular, lean body that should have had her panting if her libido had been functional. "I'm not worried at all about that little darling taking care of you."

Kyle moved almost faster than her eye could track. One minute he was standing by the bed she'd once hoped they would share, and the next he had a gun to West's head.

West's gun.

She had to remember Kyle Hawthorne wasn't the funny, strangely sweet bodyguard she'd fallen madly in love with. That was a mask he'd worn. Kyle was one of the Agency's best killers, and here was the proof of it.

"I should definitely give my brother a call." West didn't move an inch, and his tone was even, proving he'd learned a lot in the last couple of months. He'd certainly learned how to deal with a predator who had his teeth on his throat.

Kyle backed off, offering West his gun back. "Yes, you should, and consider yourself fired, you dumbass. I heard you were thinking of taking her to Coachella or Burning Man or something. What the fuck kind of bodyguard are you?"

West's shoulders straightened, and his jaw went tight. "The type who knows she can't hide forever. She's a vibrant young woman, and she needs to have a life. I'm not going to hold her down because you weren't smart enough to care about her."

"I care about her enough to not want her dead," Kyle argued. "There is a woman out there who wants to kill her."

"And I believe that she'll find Mae way harder to kill than she ever imagined. After all, she took you down pretty easy, from what I can tell." West's tone was hard and though he wasn't moving, she was pretty sure he was steeling himself for something.

The testosterone was flowing now.

"She took me by surprise," Kyle corrected. "It won't happen again. Besides, I have no intentions of hurting her. I don't care about you. From what I can tell you've let her run wild."

"How would you know what he's done or didn't do?" She'd made a deal with Tag that she wouldn't ever ask him about Kyle. He was like Schrödinger's Cat to MaeBe. Schrödinger's Kyle. She wasn't opening that box, so the state of his aliveness or deadness didn't matter. He could be both for all she cared.

Had Tag been talking to Kyle about her? That hurt more than she would have thought possible, but then she'd imagined Tag would show her the same courtesy he'd shown Kyle.

Blood, it seemed, was still thicker than any water.

Kyle's expression softened. "I kept up with you, baby. Did you think I would just walk away?"

"Yes. Mostly because that's exactly what you did. *Walk* is not the right word. You probably ran since that explosion damn near took me and Boomer out, but you weren't thinking of us, were you? You were only thinking of making a big bang for Julia."

"I thought Deke would move faster." Kyle took a step toward her, one hand coming out. "I would never have hurt you. Baby, you can't imagine how I felt when I found out what she'd done to you.

You shouldn't have fought her. You should have waited for the team to save you. She wouldn't have broken your arm if you'd complied."

Her arm still ached when the weather changed. She'd been told it likely always would. That ache was a reminder that she'd been weak. She moved back so he didn't touch her. "So it was my fault? I should have done what the kidnapper told me to do and the world would have been a better place?"

West whistled. "Now you stepped in it."

Kyle's eyes practically blazed fire. "I mean it. Step out now, Rycroft, or I'll kick you out. This is between me and Mae, and you don't have a say in it."

"She does," West replied. "I'll leave when she tells me to, but even then I won't go far. You're right. My brother is also my boss, and until he tells me to stand down, I'm not leaving her for anything but a bullet through my heart."

"That can be arranged," Kyle swore.

They were staring each other down like angry bulls.

Testosterone. It made the world an angrier place. It fueled so much boy drama.

This was why she enjoyed life online. If this was happening online, she could tap out and let them play their boy games. She wouldn't be forced to deal with them. She could be online right now. There was a raid on a castle scheduled in about half an hour. She could slide her headset on and then these two could do whatever they liked and she could talk to Kraven, who was the only dude in the world who seemed to get her these days. She kind of pictured him as some fifty-plus dad of four who was trying to get away from his life as an accountant. He gave her sound dad advice.

Play it safe. Always be careful.

Are you sure you're ready to date? You should give yourself plenty of time. There's no reason for you to push yourself.

And she often took his advice because she was pretty sure he was involved with another man. He never talked about a woman in his life, but a couple of times she'd heard a man yelling at him to get off that computer and join him for whatever unintelligible words he would say at that point because Kraven knew how to mute a mic.

She wondered if he was online. She could ask him how he would handle two guys who didn't care about her but were acting like they did because they were assholes.

She wasn't being fair. Not to West, at least.

"You're barely able to protect yourself," Kyle was growling.

"You have no idea what I'm capable of," West growled right back. "But I could be convinced to show you."

She needed a beer.

Mae started down the hall, leaving the boys behind. Oh, she was absolutely certain that in her past life she would have thrown herself between those two overgrown toddlers and begged them not to fight. She would have pleaded for them to understand each other, and couldn't they all sit down and talk this out?

Yeah, she did not have time for that now. If they wrecked her room, she would have some balls hanging from Tiny's rearview mirror come tomorrow, though. She'd just gotten back to her own room in her own apartment.

And she'd already been assaulted by a hundred memories of nights Kyle had spent here. They'd sat at her game table and played for hours and hours. Sometimes with friends. Sometimes alone together.

He'd burned place-and-bake cookies in her kitchen once because he'd found out she had a sweet tooth and Noelle had made baking sound fun.

He'd sat beside her on her couch and let her lean on him while watching *Stranger Things* for the tenth time because she'd found out on social media that her father had thrown a huge sweet sixteen for her stepsister and she'd been left out again.

She could have handled him walking away if all they'd done was have sex. But they'd had months and months of building what she'd thought was a genuine friendship, a strong foundation for a real relationship.

The fact that he could walk away from that meant there was no hope for them.

She made it to the kitchen and opened the fridge, praising Hutch's name because there was a six-pack of Shiner sitting there. It had been months since she'd been allowed in her apartment. She'd gone from guest room to guest room, staying at friend's places while she was training to be able to protect herself. So when she'd finally been cleared to head home—with a guard in tow—Hutch and his wife, Noelle, had been kind enough to make sure she didn't come home to an empty fridge.

Her eyes caught on the bottle of Sriracha. It had been sitting there in the middle of her kitchen island like someone had left it as a present. She loved it, put it on pretty much everything she could. When they'd been together Kyle had made fun of her because he couldn't stand it. But he'd always made sure she had it. So much so that he'd carried a small bottle in the backpack he used. Once they'd been in a fancy restaurant where the waiter had looked at her like she was crazy to ask for the condiment. Kyle had pulled it out and she'd made that pasta as spicy as she'd liked.

Hutch hadn't left that bottle for her. He would have put it in the pantry. He wouldn't have carefully placed it on the middle of the island where the light would shine down on it, announcing the arrival of spice back in her life.

She reached for the beer because that thought had come from the old MaeBe. From the MaeBe who'd thought because a guy was overly protective and possessive, that meant he loved her.

She wasn't letting the old Mae take over ever again.

"Hey, why did you walk away?" Kyle was suddenly in her kitchen, and West wasn't far behind.

She popped the top on her beer and did not offer the men one. They had testosterone to fuel them. They didn't need precious beer. "You two were having a moment. I didn't want to interrupt."

Kyle seemed to consider her words and took a deep breath before turning to West. "I believe she's telling us we're acting like idiots and she's not going to have a part of that. She's right. At least about me. I'm sorry. I care about that woman more than you can understand, and I'm fucking things up. Would you please give me a moment with her? I promise I'm fully trained and usually in control of my own damn emotions. You should call your brother so he can panic call my uncle and the wheels to get us out of this awkward situation can be put in motion."

Ah, reasonable Kyle had shown up. He was a mask, of course. The arrogant ass was the real man. She tipped back her beer, taking a long swig because she knew what would happen next. West would be impressed by Kyle's apology and forget that the dude had been holding his own gun to his head not five minutes before.

Women did not forget that shit. Oh, women could smile and get along and not ruin the world, but no woman would have truly accepted an apology after that.

West gave Kyle an aw-shucks grin and held out a hand. "It's okay. Welcome back, man. I would probably be on edge if I'd gone through what you had."

Poor Kyle. He'd gone through so much. She took another long swig as West and Kyle became best friends and shit and West promised to do exactly what Kyle had said to do because it obviously now made sense to call his brother. Yadda fucking yadda.

It was weird. She'd thought about this a lot, sat up at night going through all the scenarios about what would happen when she saw Kyle Hawthorne again. She'd wondered if he would show up one day with Julia on his arm, all shiny and new because his love had healed her psychotic brain. She'd dreamed about him getting on his knees and begging her to take him back. In some, he'd utterly ignored her as he took his place in his family and she was frozen out.

In all of those scenarios, she'd thought she would feel something. Something other than this awful numbness that had come over her a few weeks after he'd blown up their world. Sometime between Kyle's "funeral"—which she hadn't attended—and the beginning of her hardcore training, she'd gone cold.

"Mae? Baby, please can we talk?"

They were alone now, though she doubted West would go far unless his brother for some reason decided to pull him off the assignment. Then she could be alone, and that would be nice for once. "I can't seem to stop you. So talk. Get it off your chest." A thought occurred. "Did you manage to kill your ex-honey?"

It would be the only truly acceptable reason for him to show up in her apartment. He'd broken them utterly, and he couldn't possibly think she would welcome him with open arms, but if he told her she was free of his murder-minded ex, then she might actually give him a beer. She'd kick him out after, but she would pass him that beer.

He hesitated for the first time, his arrogance fleeing, and for a moment he looked like the Kyle she'd loved, the one only she got to see.

The mask he'd used to lure her in.

"No. In fact, I think what happened in London a few days ago might have given her even more power."

That info made Mae put down her beer, the bottle slapping against the granite with a thud. She'd kept up with the Radcliffes since they seemed to be at the center of everything. "Holy shit. The news reported it as a robbery gone wrong."

The week before, the senator, Samantha Radcliffe—mother of both Drake and the daughter from her first marriage, Julia Ennis— had been attending a conference in London. Her husband had been found dead in their suite. It had been a minor story, quickly overtaken by some Hollywood starlet's encounter with a stalkerish fan. An old man dying wouldn't have made the papers at all except for his wife's job.

Kyle's palms were flat on the countertop as he stared at her. "There's a lot to the story. I don't know how much I should tell you. I want to keep you out of this as much as I can. It's for your protection."

Yeah, she'd heard that before. She ignored him, getting to the good stuff. "Did The Consortium kill him? Were you there?" Her stomach took a dive, proving to her she still could feel some compassion. "Oh, please tell me Drake wasn't forced to kill his father."

She wasn't crazy about the man, but she wouldn't wish that on anyone. She knew what it was like to have problems with a dad.

Kyle's jaw had dropped slightly, and he took a moment before he replied. "Why do you think Drake would kill his father?"

Oh, had he thought she would sit in her appointed room like a good girl? He'd given up all access to her good girl side when he'd walked away. His face had gone from that momentary surprise to a damn fine poker face. Like he wasn't going to give anything away. He didn't have to. She already knew. "Because I think Don Radcliffe is a member of The Consortium. I don't have absolute proof, but there's a pattern of behavior especially in his financials that can't be denied."

If there was one place where she might be willing to spend time with him, it was work. The case was everything to her, and she would put aside her pride to take Julia Ennis down.

"What the fuck has my uncle been letting you do?"

"Letting? Ian doesn't let me do anything." She'd been an idiot to think Kyle would want to talk about the case with her. She was also being foolish to try to discuss this with him. "What are you doing here?"

"How deep have you gone? I need to know which system you used to do your research. Is it your primary system? Or one you leave at the office?" He moved into the living room, going for her laptop bag.

"Hey, I didn't say you could touch that."

"Is it this system, Mae?" His voice had gone cold.

What was going on with him? "Kyle, it doesn't matter what system I'm on. I'm smart. No one can trace me. I know you think I'm some idiotic damsel in distress, but I do know what I'm doing when it comes to this."

"You have no idea what Julia can do and what kind of resources she has at her fingertips." Kyle reached into her bag and pulled out her sleek laptop. "Was it this system?"

"I've used several systems. What exactly do you think is going to happen?" She wasn't going to explain the exhaustive protocols she went through to make sure no one could find her. And she'd only hacked a couple of systems. Four or five. Ten at most.

The lights suddenly went out.

"Get down!" Kyle yelled as a red dot showed up, a vivid splash of color against his white shirt.

She heard glass break as her body hit the floor.

* * * *

Kyle's whole system flooded with pure adrenaline as he covered MaeBe with his body. He had his chest over her head, that luscious ass of hers up against his pelvis and her head nestled under his chin. She'd gone still, and he was thankful that she wasn't fighting him.

Or simply kicking him in the balls again because it was obvious to him that Mae had some issues she wanted to work through.

But that would have to wait because she'd basically told Julia she was ready for their war to begin.

"Hey, are you all right?" West's voice came from behind him to the right.

"Yes. Stay behind that wall," Kyle ordered. "I assure you that whoever is on the other end of that rifle knows you're there and they're watching. They won't hesitate to take you out."

"Is it Julia?" Mae asked quietly.

At least now she might believe him. "Not her personally. She's actually not a good sniper. She's much better up close, but I'm sure The Consortium will provide. I'm going to roll to the side and you're going to carefully move back. Slide on your belly and keep your head down. I have no idea what kind of tech they're using. Hopefully they're far enough away they can't use heat scanners to detect movement."

"There's nothing that strong on the…" She sighed. "I was going to say on the market, but that doesn't matter. If The Consortium can dream it, they can probably build it. All right. I'll move back to West. How do you want to play this? Call the cops?"

"They'll own at least a few of them." He'd expected her to show some fear but she was completely steady. "I'm moving now. Go slow. Don't stand up until you get to West, and then we'll move out of here. Leave that fucking laptop behind, Mae."

He could practically hear that brat's eyes rolling. "Like I need the laptop. I can use any laptop. My car's downstairs in the garage. We can make a run for it."

"I assure you it's probably already been fitted with a tracker. And that's the best-case scenario." He eased to one side, letting her move from under him.

Her head turned and her eyes were wide. "You don't think they'd blow up Tiny, do you?"

It would be the smallest bomb anyone had ever made. That freaking car of hers. He'd always meant to buy something they could both comfortably fit in. Not that he would replace hers. She loved that environmentally conscious teeny monstrosity. "We have to leave everything, Mae. I'm making a call and then I'm dumping my cell. You do the same, and make sure West doesn't have anything on him that they could follow."

"You mean like the tracker in your arm that somehow got blown all the way from Malibu into LA before it died?"

Fuck. He should have known she would find out about that. Hutch hadn't been able to tell if she'd been on the system during the time he'd completely forgotten that his uncle had implanted a device in his bicep. "Yes. Like that."

"I don't have one yet. I'm supposed to go in next week," West said quietly. "She can't find me that way. A little bit more, darlin', and then you get behind me. There's a pistol in my boot. You take it."

He hated West Rycroft. He'd played nice once he'd realized how pissed off MaeBe was, but he hated how that man talked to Mae. Like they were friends when he knew damn well that wasn't what was going through that cowboy's head.

Her head. God, that had been a kick in the gut. She'd always worn her hair with vibrant colors. In the time he'd known her she'd had purple and pink hair, and she'd been talking about going Little Mermaid red in honor of their upcoming trip to Disney. It was brown now. It was pretty, but it wasn't Mae. It wasn't his vivacious, bright woman, the one who smiled and the world seemed to light up.

She hadn't smiled at him once.

"She's safely back," West said. "Do you want me to take her out of here?"

"Don't you fucking dare." Kyle moved quickly, backing up like he knew the place by heart. Which he did. He'd planned on living here once. He'd basically spent all his time here with her. He'd been an idiot because he'd wasted all that time he could have spent in her bed, and then they likely wouldn't be in the situation they were in.

He made it to the hallway wall where West and MaeBe were huddled together. She had a small pistol in her hand, and West that Glock he'd gotten hold of so easily. The young man needed way more training.

Kyle quickly slid his cell out of his pocket and sent a single text. He'd programmed it in with the full belief that he wouldn't need it because everything was going to be okay. He'd known that MaeBe would cry and she would be angry with him and she would also trust him. They were meant to be.

She would go with him to the safe house he'd found for them, and after spending a night together she would get on the plane for Loa Mali in the morning with the full knowledge that it would only be a few more weeks before they could be together forever.

It was obvious he'd made a miscalculation.

Things had not gone as well as he'd hoped, and Drake was going to give him such hell.

He was going to have to take that lecture because he couldn't get Mae to the safe house without him.

"Drake will meet us downstairs." He reached for the gun at the small of his back. He hadn't expected he would need to use it. He'd been so careful. When he'd left, he hadn't even told Drake what he was doing or where he was going until he'd ensured that he was safely in Dallas.

This wasn't about him. No one had followed him.

They'd followed MaeBe, and he would bet a lot they'd followed her because of her reckless investigation. He'd walked away to get her out of his war with Julia, and she'd gone right back on the battlefield and waved a damn flag.

They would be talking about that later. For now, he wanted to get her safely out of the building because he was certain that sniper wasn't Julia's only soldier on the field.

They would likely face a fight getting out of here. What he needed was some chaos.

He wouldn't call the cops, but he could call someone else, and he'd come prepared. He opened the door to the small closet where Mae kept her coats and sweaters. He'd slid his bag in here earlier knowing it was warm outside and she wouldn't be opening that door when she'd come home. He shrugged the bag over his shoulders and pulled out a small device that would give him some cover.

"Is that what I think it is?" Mae asked with a frown.

"It depends on what you think it is." He set the timer and nodded West's way. "You go first. Expect trouble. The stairs will be on your left. Move quickly but keep your eyes and ears open. We're going to meet Drake on the west side of the building."

"What are you doing with that?" West asked, his brows coming together.

"It's a flash-bang." MaeBe looked weirdly hot with a small pistol in her hands. She carried it like she knew what she was doing.

"Sort of. It's mostly smoke." He pulled his second cell, a burner phone. He dialed the only number he ever would on this one. 911. "There's a fire at the Monroe Apartments on Oak Street. Please hurry."

He hung up the phone. He would dump it once they were far from Mae's building.

It wouldn't matter. He had ten more exactly like it.

And one in case his enemy called.

He nodded toward West. "Let's go. Mae, don't you dare move from in between us. I don't care what my uncle's taught you. You are not to engage."

She didn't even look back at him, simply followed West.

He was fucking this up, but now wasn't the time to gently explain to her that he dreamed about losing her at night. That when he closed his eyes his nightmare was looking down at her dead body and knowing there was no reason for him to go on.

Time and space had done nothing to change his feelings for MaeBe Vaughn. Except to make them stronger. He knew once and for all that she was the one. She was the woman he would go to his grave loving, and she seemed to not feel the same way.

He was fairly certain his therapist would give him a whole list of reasons why he wasn't being fair to the woman he loved and that his unwillingness to allow her to be a full partner in this current mission had undermined the trust they'd had. Yes, that's what Angie would say.

Her wife, Sandra, would merely slap him upside the head and tell him to be less of an asshole.

West eased out of the apartment and nodded back, letting Kyle know the hall was clear.

It wouldn't stay that way.

When he was through MaeBe's door, he rolled the modified flash-bang down the long hallway. The timer went off and smoke billowed from the small device.

"They'll likely think it's the Harwood boys," he said quietly.

"Great, blame a couple of sweet high school kids," MaeBe replied under her breath.

They weren't sweet. They were minor criminal geniuses, and they would weather the accusations well. After all, they'd managed to get out of any number of pranks they had actually committed.

They slipped inside the door that led to the stairs as the elevator opened and someone cursed.

There was the crackling sound of a radio. "The fire department is on its way. Pull back."

He eased the door shut behind him. It had worked.

They wouldn't start a firefight in such a public place. The last thing Julia wanted was attention. She couldn't buy everyone.

"Keep moving. I don't think they're going to attack at this point." He could hear a siren in the distance. "But now we need to leave before the fire department gets here. When we get to the ground floor, go straight out the back. Drake will be waiting. Don't hesitate. I want her in that car two seconds after we open the back door."

They moved down the stairs as quietly as they could with West wearing cowboy boots. He wanted to lecture the dude on why it's not smart to wear cowboy gear when bodyguarding, but he rather thought MaeBe would take West's side in that argument. Likely any argument. He could probably say the sky was blue and she would argue with him.

He'd been trying to protect her, damn it. Why was she looking at him like he was worse than Julia?

And why the hell had she put herself in the line of fire?

Damn. Had she been trying to protect him? Trying to find a way to free him from his past mistakes?

How did he handle this?

He glanced behind him, and the stairwell was silent.

"I think we're in the clear," MaeBe whispered. "They were coming up in the elevator and the smoke scared them off."

"Or made them change their plans and they're waiting for us outside the building." West proved he'd had at least some amount of training. The ability to think through worst-case scenarios was invaluable to a bodyguard.

"I doubt it," Mae replied. "And even if they are, what are they going to do? Shoot me in the lobby? There are cameras everywhere."

"Which they've probably taken over," Kyle pointed out. Mae needed way more paranoia.

"Well, if someone hadn't left my laptop behind, I might have been able to fix that problem," she muttered under her breath.

He was not going to argue with her about this. Not now. There would be plenty of time later. They reached the bottom of the stairs.

He looked to West because it was time for him to take the lead. "You keep her here until I make sure the lobby is safe."

It wasn't a long trek to where Drake would be waiting, but he wasn't taking any chances.

He eased out of the stairwell and checked both ways. The lobby was quiet at this time of night. There was only one security guard on watch, and he was fairly certain the old guy napped most of the night. It was one of the reasons he'd intended to talk MaeBe into finding a small house they could afford. Somewhere in the suburbs with a backyard where they could get a dog to go with the cat they would absolutely be adopting. It had to have at least three bedrooms because she would want to turn one of them into a game room. They could host game nights and he could barbecue, and they would be boring and normal.

He'd been planning a life and a family with her and he might have fucked it all up, but then he'd done that a long time ago.

"All right, buddy, don't move. I've got you dead to rights."

Fuck. He held up his hands. The guy from the elevator must have waited down here, hoping he could pick off MaeBe before the fire department arrived. He didn't drop the gun though. "I've already called 911. Unless you want to explain what you're doing here, you should leave."

"I will once I secure the girl," the deep voice said. "You're just a bodyguard, man. You don't want to die for this chick."

They thought he was Wade. That meant Julia didn't know he was in Dallas, or he would be a target, too. There would be no "just walk away" speeches for him. Julia's mercenaries would have been ordered to take him into custody along with MaeBe.

What the hell did Julia want with Mae if she didn't want to kill her? If Julia wasn't trying to punish him, then she was likely ready to make a big move and thought having MaeBe in her custody would be leverage to get him to do anything she wanted.

But if she knew he was in Dallas, she would move heaven and earth to kill them both if she could.

"Sure, man." He had to believe West was listening in and would move MaeBe. "She's up in her apartment. Feel free to go get her."

"Drop the gun and turn around."

He was going to do neither. "I don't want to see your face. If I don't see your face, then I can't say anything. You should hurry or you're going to miss her. I told her to meet me down here in five minutes. She'll be easier to catch if you're waiting on her floor when she comes out."

"Drop the fucking gun or I'll take you out here and now," the man vowed.

He was going to have to move and quickly.

A shot rang out and for a second he was absolutely certain he was a dead man. He turned and watched in shock as MaeBe stepped forward, her gun in hand.

"We should take the body with us and move quickly. The fire department won't be more than a few minutes away. West, take his feet. I'll deal with the blood." MaeBe had shot the man, and she'd done a damn fine job of it. Her brow arched as she stared at Kyle. "You should take the arms."

He hesitated.

"He was going to kill you. Or he was going to figure out who you are and bring Julia down on all our heads. Hurry and we'll discuss why she's making a move now. But we can't do that if we're all in custody."

His head was reeling. MaeBe had shot a man. His sweet Mae had taken down a bad guy.

Because she hadn't wanted the bad guy to shoot him.

She frowned his way as though she could read his mind. "It doesn't mean anything."

She didn't want him dead. She'd made a split-second decision and that had been to save him.

Not wanting him murdered wasn't exactly a declaration of love, but it was better than the alternative.

"What's happening?" a feminine voice asked, and Taylor Cline made her way into the lobby. Drake Radcliffe's girlfriend was one of the Agency's smartest operatives and one Kyle felt comfortable watching his back. "We need to...are we taking that with us? Is he one of Julia's?"

MaeBe walked to the door, stopping to nod Taylor's way. "I think it's safe to assume he's one of Julia's, and she's decided it's time to bring me in. I killed him because I don't want anyone to know Kyle's here, and he would have talked. Or perhaps not since he was about to kill Kyle and he wouldn't want to admit that to the big boss. Now that I think about it, I might have acted hastily. Anyway, where's the car? In my family the women do the assassinating and the men clean up. At least that's what Charlotte's always promised me."

She and Taylor walked out.

And Kyle got to cleaning up.

"Dude, she is pissed at you," West said, taking his half of the body.

"And you are excellent at stating the obvious." Kyle moved. He could hear sirens coming in hot.

His night wasn't going at all the way he'd planned.

Chapter Nine

"You're home for less than one hour and you bring me a dead body." Ian Taggart stood in the parking lot of Sanctum, his hands in fists at his hips as he stared down at the trunk of Drake Radcliffe's rental vehicle.

Oh, Kyle had heard all about how expensive it was going to be to clean up that rental car. Drake had complained about it incessantly as they'd driven around Dallas making sure they didn't have a tail. Drake had become a complaining old man since he'd settled into a relationship.

Kyle wanted to be a complaining old man. It sounded fun. Complaining old men complained because they had a good life, and anything outside of that happy bubble was something to be complained about. He didn't complain about dead bodies because his life was actually livened up by them. For a good at least half a year, he'd almost made complaining old-man status because he'd been with MaeBe and everything except MaeBe's world annoyed him. The last couple of months had been spent hiding and plotting and doing a surprising amount of dishes because the woman who'd been willing to hide him didn't believe in free rides.

He'd also learned how to work a commercial fryer. If he made MaeBe some truly delicious fried food, would she smile his way?

"Yes, I was rather surprised myself since he knows damn well this is a rental," Drake huffed.

Yup. That was what he'd dealt with the entire time they were driving, waiting for his uncle to tell him where they should meet. Taylor had tried to soothe Drake. No one had tried to soothe Kyle, and he was the one who'd nearly gotten shot. "You're a freaking spy. You should know to get the insurance."

"I told him," Taylor said with a shrug. "We should have gotten the one with the trunk liner. Body storage and cleanup is so much easier with a good trunk liner."

"Mr. Taggart, I assure you it was a necessary kill." West had been standing at attention like he was in the Army or something. "There was no other way out of the situation."

The asshole had also taken the seat next to MaeBe in the car. The cowboy had been damn quick to slide in beside her, and those sirens had been too close for Kyle to force the issue. MaeBe hadn't said a word since she'd boldly told Taylor the men would do the cleanup. She'd nodded Drake's way and then sat in the back seat like someone was taking her to prison.

He needed to get her alone. He needed to get his arms around her, and apparently he definitely needed to do some fast talking because she'd misunderstood what he'd done. Or rather why he'd done it.

He loved her so much. That love had been the only thing that kept him going—even when he'd accepted he might never see her again.

He'd also gotten his uncle up in the middle of the night to deal with a dead body. "I'm sorry."

A grin spread over Ian's face. "You mistake me, nephew. I was saying no one ever brings me dead bodies to deal with and here you are like a cat with a mouse in his mouth not an hour after hitting town. This is a treat. I've got some decisions to make. Fun ones. Do I use the acid I've been wanting to try, or bury it somewhere on Julian Lodge's property and give that old man something to think about? There's no wrong way to go. Hence my delight. Oh, and I'm glad you're all okay."

"It wasn't Kyle, sir. It was MaeBe." West just had to spit that truth out.

His uncle's grin turned to a full-fledged smile. "Seriously?

Because that looks like a complete blindside. That bullet went straight through his back and into his heart. You obviously didn't warn him."

"We don't play fair," she said quietly.

But Mae always played fair. Always. Even in stupid fantasy games, she made sure she knew the rules and carefully followed them all because she believed in fair play.

What the fuck had she gone through while he'd been away?

His uncle's smile muted, and he walked right up to Mae and wrapped her in the bear hug the man reserved for his closest friends and family. Ian Taggart was a massive ass much of the time, but Kyle had quickly figured out that was a façade that hid a nosy, meddling, loving grandmother who wanted all of her kids to be happy.

"You okay?" Ian asked as MaeBe hugged him back. "You did what you had to do. I know you know that, but it's hard the first time."

She sniffled, the first sign of emotion she'd displayed since she'd kicked him in the balls. "I'm okay. He was going to kill Kyle. I thought about letting him, but I figured Kyle would be heavier to carry. He's got at least a hundred pounds on that guy."

"Well, Kyle's gotten tubby because he's been working at a bar that serves nothing but burgers and fries," Ian replied.

"I have not gotten tubby. And Sandra serves salads." Not often, since she ran a bar in the middle of rural Wyoming, but he felt the need to defend himself.

Ian snorted and stepped back, putting his hands on Mae's shoulders. "You go upstairs and settle in for the night. I know you wanted to be out of this place, but it's the best I can do for tonight. We'll talk to these guys in the morning and get things sorted out."

"I have a safe house and a plan." Sure his plans up to now had gone to hell, but that didn't mean he was changing the rest of them. He needed his uncle's help with the body, but if he let things go, Ian would take over. Ian would call his stepdad and then his mom would be involved and his brothers and sister would show up, and he wasn't ready for that.

MaeBe simply walked into the club, West following behind her.

"Hey, she doesn't need you anymore," Kyle called out. "You

can go home."

West didn't look back, but his arm came up and so did his middle finger.

"He's fitting in well. I was worried about that idiot for a while, but he's coming along nicely," his uncle said with a nod, and then those blue eyes were arctic. "You are another story altogether. What the hell are you doing here, Kyle? Besides dropping dead bodies off. Should I bother trying to ID this one? He doesn't look like John Smith, but dead bodies are weird things. Yours didn't look like you at all."

And his uncle was right back to being an asshole. It had probably been his idea to throw the fake funeral that Kyle had been promised included a blow-up doll and all of his hard-earned gaming systems. He'd loved that Xbox. "It's not John Smith. Although we're sure that's not his real name."

They didn't know much about the man who'd taken the identity of John Smith from Colorado. He wasn't even sure he'd taken an identity the way Julia had or if his ID was simply fake.

"The intel we have placed the man known as John Smith in Europe last week. MI6 had picked him up for questioning. He was brought to DC," Drake explained. "And somewhere along the way, a prisoner switch was made. The man in custody in DC was not the same John Smith who worked with Julia. He looked similar, but the facial recognition doesn't match. After some talk the man admitted he wasn't Smith, but he wouldn't give us more than that. And then he was found dead in his cell. Poison."

"So he's in the wind, or more than likely, he's back with Julia," his uncle mused. "Unless he's the one pulling the strings tonight."

"I assure you, no one is pulling the strings except Julia." Of that he was certain. A car began to pull into the lot and Kyle recognized Alex McKay's big SUV. "I asked you to keep this quiet. Have you already called my parents?"

"Alex is the soul of discretion," Ian assured them all. "And no, I didn't call your parents. You're going to do that before we have our debrief tomorrow."

He intended to be out of Texas tomorrow. He certainly wasn't planning a family reunion. They'd had one of those in Wyoming when his mother had shown up completely uninvited. Not because he didn't want to see her. He missed the hell out of his family, but it was dangerous to be around him right now.

If Mae was in the same situation, would you accept her doing what you did?

Angie's question had been asked while they'd been making apple hand pies. He'd barely realized it was therapy because the sneaky lady had built their "talks" around work. And she hadn't required an answer from him. Merely smiled and said it was "something to consider."

If his mother was a bomb waiting to go off, would Sean be satisfied with staying at a safe distance?

If someone was coming after MaeBe and she couldn't stand the thought of him being hurt, would he accept being left behind?

At first he'd told himself it was a dumb question. He was trained and she wasn't. Now he had to consider the fact that she might have loved him enough to take the risk, and if he didn't let her make the decision he was...what was the word Angie used...marginalizing her.

Yeah, he missed his mom. His mom might be able to talk him through this if he wasn't such a stubborn asshole.

"We're supposed to leave in the morning," Drake pointed out.

Taylor glanced her boyfriend's way. "You know it wouldn't hurt to have backup. We can't use Agency resources on this."

"It'll take more than Agency resources to get MaeBe on a plane to Loa Mali," his uncle said with an arrogant grin.

"How do you know about that?" Kyle hadn't told anyone what he'd arranged. No one but Drake and Taylor knew, and they wouldn't have told his uncle. That wasn't exactly true. The king, Kashmir Kamdar, had been informed.

"Who do you think trained the guards at the palace? Who vets anyone coming through?" his uncle asked.

"I did a favor for the king a couple of years back. I thought he would repay me by not immediately snitching to my uncle," he admitted.

"I don't know if it was immediate or if he took some time before he called me, but I assure you Kash owes me more." Ian held up a hand as Alex slid out of the SUV.

Alex was a big dude in sweats and a T-shirt, his hair rumpled as though he'd rolled out of bed to make this meeting. Which he probably had. "All right, I'm here and I brought a shovel. This better be a practical joke and not a real..." He sighed as he caught sight of Kyle and Drake. "Fucking Agency. How many bodies are we dealing with, and don't you guys have your own cleaners?"

Ian leaned against his own big-ass SUV. His uncle drove a Navigator that proved that Ian Taggart did not eat nails for breakfast. Oh, he might look like it on the outside, but the man liked luxury. The Nav used to be Charlotte's, but she'd exchanged it for what she called the cutest Volvo ever. "The young ones have gone rogue, apparently. They can't use Agency resources."

"Ah, so they've come to the old guys," Alex said with a shake of his head. "What's the plan? Not for the body. We'll deal with the body, and no, we are not burying it in Julian's backyard. And no, you're not using acid. We're putting this asshole on ice until we can ID him, and once things go back to normal Drake will deal with it."

"Where are you going to store a body? It sounds like you know exactly what you're going to do and where you're going to put it. Has this been going on for a long time?" He had the weirdest family. "Does Aunt Charlotte know?"

His aunt joked a lot about proper cleaning techniques when it came to bodies. At least he'd always thought she was joking. He knew she'd once been a mafia assassin, but he'd thought those days were over.

"It's fine, Kyle. You don't have to worry about it. That's why you called me. Alex and I will get what we need to ID this asshole and then stash him until you're in a place where you can take care of things. You bring everyone by the office in the morning, and we want the whole story. I mean everything." Ian stood up straight and looked to his best friend of over thirty years. "You want head or tails?"

"I want to be home in bed with my wife. My cleaning days are supposed to be over," Alex complained.

"Come on, man. It'll be fun. Open your trunk," Ian countered.

Alex's head shook. "Absolutely not. We're not using my car."

Ian slapped a hand on his Nav. "This baby is a Black Label. My children know that if they so much as sneeze on her they are disinherited. Yours still smells like curdled milk from seven years ago. Why do you think I called you? Li went middle-aged crazy and bought that Porsche. A living body barely fits into it. Jake drives a truck, and while that guy won't care about being exposed to the elements, there are lots of cameras that will find him deeply interesting. I would call Erin. Her SUV is pretty bad, but she gets cranky when she doesn't get a full eight hours."

"So do I," Alex growled back but then he laughed. "All right, but you're buying the waffles. It's a rule. Waffles come after body clean up."

They were practically a comedy duo, but he did not have time for that, and his uncle needed to understand that he had a plan in place. The fact that Ian knew some of it didn't change what he needed to do. "We're going to be on a plane to Loa Mali in a few hours. I will be more than happy to teleconference with you and bring you up to date."

"It wouldn't be terrible to bring Damon Knight and even Tennessee Smith in if they're willing to help," Drake said. "I'm not sure exactly where we're going to be, but I know we'll be in Europe and possibly Asia."

"Sure. I'll have MaeBe set it all up," his uncle said. "That girl can teleconference like no one else. And now she shoots people, so my job here is done."

He ignored the sarcasm. It was a talent he'd been forced to develop over the years. "You're going to have to have Hutch do it. Mae is going to be on that plane."

"Is she?" his uncle asked.

"I bet she's not," Alex offered. "I got a hundred that says she does not get on that plane."

"I am not taking that bet," Ian replied. "I would bet a grand that Kyle's going to get his balls kicked in."

Alex's head shook. "Nah, see that's a bet I wouldn't take the opposite side of."

"I think that already happened." Drake gave him an apologetic frown. "You're walking a little bowlegged, man."

"She did?" Taylor was shaking her head. "I thought she was a civvie. The way Kyle talks about her she's barely able to protect herself from bees. He describes her like a fainting damsel in distress."

"Not anymore," Ian said.

"I never described her like that." Disappointment twisted his gut. And his balls still hurt. "MaeBe is smart and capable, but not all strength comes from muscle. She doesn't have to be some ball buster to deserve respect."

"No. She needs to be a ball buster to survive Julia Ennis and feel somewhat safe," his uncle countered. "I'm going to give you some advice, and you can take it or you can continue to fuck up. Don't treat her like a doll you cuddle at night and put in a glass case when you don't want her to get dirty. If you love that woman, get on your damn knees and beg her forgiveness because you were wrong. People in love discuss their problems. Dumbasses fake their deaths. You want to talk to one? Call your Aunt Charlotte. You know what she did when she came back? Apologized and got on her knees."

"Do not talk about that blow job," Alex said with a sigh. "We don't need to hear about it again."

His uncle had zero discretion. "I promise I'm going to make it all up to her, but after she's safe. Drake, Taylor, and I have to travel for a bit, and we kicked the hornet's nest, as proven tonight. Julia's not going to stay away from MaeBe any longer. Loa Mali is safe. She'll be secure, and we'll handle everything when I come back."

If he came back.

"It'll be too late, but I can't convince you of that." Ian gestured to the rental. "If you have a brain cell left in your head, you'll bring her to the office tomorrow morning at ten and we'll strategize. If not, well, I would watch your balls, nephew. Drake, you have more sense than he does. You want my people to help, be there at ten."

He and Alex had that body in the back of Alex's SUV in quick time, and then they were taking off for wherever the hell they kept a freezer big enough to keep a body in.

"We need them," Drake said, a grim expression on his face.

He wasn't wrong. "Then Taylor can escort Mae, and she can meet us when we figure out where we should look for the intel."

"You okay with that, baby?" Drake asked the question carefully, as though he wasn't at all sure of the answer.

Taylor's lips curled up, and she winked her boyfriend's way. "Sure. I'll get MaeBe where she needs to go. You two handle Taggart."

At least one of the women in his life was reasonable.

It was time to deal with the one who wasn't.

* * * *

And she was back in the car again.

That was how she felt. Like that scene from *Jurassic Park* where they managed to get out of the car that was stuck in the massive tree only to have the car fall on them and they were right back where they'd started.

And she had a T-Rex after her. Julia might not appreciate the comparison, but Mae wasn't feeling particularly fair right now.

"You okay?" West had followed her inside and had spent the last couple of minutes talking to the guards Big Tag had dragged out of bed to watch over her. Again. West had two small bags in his hands.

She knew what those were. The group used Sanctum as a safe house often enough that they kept toiletry bags available for the refugees who sought sanctuary here. They usually didn't have time to pack a bag.

That had been the nice part about the first time around. She'd at least had a bag of her clothes and her computers and some of her things. Naturally Kyle Hawthorne was back and she'd lost everything again.

Also not fair, but she didn't care in the moment.

"I'm fine." She sank down on the lounge chair. It might be smarter to go up to the third floor where the privacy rooms would serve as their bedrooms, but it would merely put off the inevitable. Kyle would find a way to get inside whatever door she locked, and she would rather have it out here and now. "Thanks for picking that up for me. I'm going to sit down here and deal with Kyle."

"I can sit down here, too. I think Kyle might be hard to deal with."

She sighed at the thought. She was too wired to sleep. Kyle might give her another chance to kick him in the balls. That would be worth it. Besides, she had to figure out what his plan to get rid of her was so she could get around it. "If you stay down here, you and Kyle will turn into four-year-olds fighting over a toy."

West sat down across from her. "I'm sorry about that. I guess I didn't like him walking in and acting like he owns you."

"So you had to act like you own me?"

His lips kicked up in a heart-stopping grin. "I know I don't own you, girl, but I reacted like I did. I'm sorry. I kind of have a thing for you, but we're never going to be more than friends, are we?"

"Are we going to be friends? Some guys can't be friendly with women who've turned them down."

He outright laughed at that. "I wouldn't have any women friends at all then." He sat back and sobered. "I'm sorry. I'm joking and I shouldn't be. My sister-in-law was in a bad relationship for years and I have another sister-in-law who is more than willing to educate me on how hard it is to be a woman. I like you, MaeBe Vaughn. I can handle it if you don't like me in a romantic fashion, but I won't stop trying to be your friend because I think your friendship is valuable."

He'd never really come on to her. There had been a moment in the beginning but when she'd gently rebuffed him, he hadn't missed a step. He'd been a good friend when she'd needed one. All of her friends were settled down and married, and she was the third wheel. It had been fun to hang with West.

"Of course we're friends. And that's why I'm going to ask you to let me talk to Kyle on my own. Ian wouldn't have sent us back here if he wasn't sure we're safe."

"Hutch's wife wasn't safe here, from what I've heard."

"Only because I was dumb enough to get caught by Jessica Layne's henchmen." She didn't like the fact that she'd gotten her ass kicked at the orders of not one but two boss bitches. At least Julia had done the beating herself. Layne had delegated. "She used me to get Kyle to open the door. Hutch wouldn't have."

He would have tried to save her, but he wouldn't have opened that door. He would have protected Noelle.

Kyle had practically run to the door and thrown it open and gotten shot.

She didn't want to think about that tonight, didn't want to play that memory through her head.

"You don't think this Julia person would try that?" West asked.

She'd done as thorough a study on the woman known as Julia

Ennis as she possibly could. She'd gone deep and found material she was sure Kyle had no idea existed. Of course finding that material had been dangerous as hell, but she didn't care. "No. She could have tried to take me any time in the last few months. I've been going in and out of the office. I've had a guard on me at all times, but I haven't been in hiding. So something happened recently that changed the status quo, and she tried to take me out. Or pick me up."

"I think the sniper thought I was West. We're roughly the same height. In the low light we could be mistaken for one another," a deep, familiar voice said. "You could be right about that. You're definitely right about the timing."

"Julia's timing?"

"Yes," Kyle replied, easing behind the bar. He glanced West's way. "I'm sorry about how the evening has gone. Can you give us some time?"

West stood. "Yeah. I'll take first pick of the rooms. She prefers The Ménage Mahal. Because it's the biggest."

"It's got the nicest bed, and only Jake and Adam and Serena ever use it for ménage. Well, for permanent ménages. I'm pretty sure it's been a pit stop for a lot of people." She wasn't going to apologize. It was a great privacy room, and it was fine for two people as well. It simply had multiple sets of devices in case a Dom or Domme had several subs.

"It's the nicest one, but I also like The Cunniloungus. All the surfaces are perfect for... Well, it's all in the name isn't it?" Kyle grabbed a martini glass from the display overhead. "We could go there and talk."

And remember how she hadn't had sex in years except that one mind-blowing time with him. "I've been in there a lot lately. I think we can stay down here."

"And I'll be leaving now." West started for the stairs. "Good luck, you two. Call me if something goes terribly wrong."

"That hurt," Kyle said as he opened the fridge. "But I can't blame anyone but myself. I've been staying at a club, too, but I didn't play. I did a lot of dishes and learned how to work a fryer. Did you know the oil can actually get into your skin? I used to love the smell of French fries. Now they make me want to shower."

"No stomping around asking who touched your property?"

"You're not property, baby. I'm an idiot. A jealous idiot. If you had a relationship or casual sex while I was gone, then that is your right. And now I'm going to take care of you, and hopefully you won't want anyone else. I meant what I said, Mae. There's no one but you."

"And Julia."

"Until very recently, I hadn't set eyes on Julia since the day I thought I killed her. I saw her at The Reef that night but it was through a monitor, and I wasn't sure it was her until...I let her take you."

"You didn't let her take me." She believed him when he said he hadn't known Jane Adams was Julia until she'd murdered the doctor. "But you could have tried to save me. I think about that, sometimes. I was thinking about it not ten minutes ago. When Jessica Layne kidnapped me, you walked right into what you knew was an ambush to save me. When Julia did it, you nearly killed me to try to get at her. I always wonder what changed in those months. I wonder if it was the sex. If the sex wasn't as good for you as it was for me, and if that made the difference. It would have been nicer to break up with me."

His whole body had gone still, color leaching from his face. "You can't believe that."

She wasn't sure why not. "It happened. I nearly died in that explosion. Since you didn't, then I have to assume you set it on a timer and you knew you would get out."

"I knew Boomer had you when I started the timer. I knew you would get out. I wouldn't... Do you honestly believe I would risk your life? The minute I knew it was Julia and that she had you, I knew what I had to do. Can't you see this whole thing has been about saving you? MaeBe, I love you. I know you're mad at me and that we should have sat down and talked about it, but there wasn't time. You can't know what she's capable of."

"I do, though. I know she probably set a bomb off in a small factory in Vietnam, killing fifty children to cover up the fact that one of her high-end employers was using child labor to manufacture cheap goods," she explained. The numbness was starting to feel tight around her, like if she didn't pierce it, it might never go away. "I know she poisoned a reservoir in France to make a rival company look like they were flouting environmental regulations there. The company got shut down and a Consortium corporation moved right in. I have a whole list of her sins. I know what she is capable of. She probably kicks a puppy every morning when she rolls out of bed."

After all, Julia had kicked the shit out of her and she'd pretty much been a puppy. Without thinking about it her right hand moved to massage her left, a soothing habit she had now. Especially when it rained.

"Does it still hurt?" His voice had gone quiet. "I broke my leg during an op once and it still aches from time to time."

"How do you know she broke my arm? Did you call up Deke and Boomer and get a debrief? Or was it Ian?"

"Ian didn't talk about you with the singular exception to tell me you were happy with West as your bodyguard and that you were back at Sanctum."

She'd been back at Sanctum because Ian had ordered her to stay there for the week while he was gone somewhere he didn't want to talk about. "Did he come to see you?"

Kyle nodded and picked up a cocktail shaker. Sanctum was quiet around them, so the sound of ice sliding into the shaker sort of echoed. Usually she ordered a drink and all she could hear was the thud of music. Now she could hear every movement he made. Like they were the only two people in the world.

It was a dangerous thought because immediately after came another one.

Would it be so bad to use him the way he'd used her? She might not feel so fucking cold if his hands were on her. It didn't have to mean anything beyond she needed to get this man out of her system so she could move on. She was a different person. This MaeBe wasn't about to fall for him again.

"I was in Wyoming with Sandra Croft. She owns a bar there. I went the morning after Julia came back."

He poured a healthy amount of tequila, and she realized what he was making. Kyle didn't do craft cocktails. He drank beer and whiskey. That was it. He was making what he liked to call a Sriracha martini. It was pretty much a tequila sunrise with her favorite condiment. He'd turned her on to them, and he always insisted on making them for her. When they went to Top, he would slide behind the bar and ensure it was made exactly the way she liked it.

It hadn't been terrible being Kyle's…whatever they'd been. Well, it hadn't been terrible until he'd left her behind.

"I hope you were comfortable there. Are you going back? Or are you planning on heading to DC after you talk with Ian in the morning?" She didn't bother to tell him she wasn't about to go with him or to hide wherever he would want her to hide. She would continue her investigation into Julia and The Consortium right here in Dallas. Though she might be stuck in Sanctum again.

Thanks, Kyle.

He rimmed the glass with the spicy salt she liked. "I'm not going back to Wyoming. The whole point of hanging out at Sandra's was to let Julia know you weren't involved in this war of ours. It's recently been pointed out to me that I can't keep you out of this by leaving you here."

"You can't keep me out of it at all."

"I can, and I have a plan that will keep you safe while Drake and I put an end to this," he vowed as he poured the drink into the glass and slid it her way. "Please don't throw that in my face. There's enough Sriracha in there to blind me."

She wasn't about to waste that drink. She hadn't had one since he'd left and likely wouldn't have one again. He had some weird magic touch. She took it from him and had a sip, forcing herself not to sigh. She'd missed it, missed how he would show up at her place before game night and make a big batch of them because Noelle would drink them, too. They would order pizza and Noelle would bring whatever she'd baked that week and Boomer would eat everything in sight.

She hadn't been able to spend much time with Boomer's girlfriend. She'd barely met the woman and only because she'd been staying at Boomer's place when she'd come into his life.

When would it be over? When would she get some part of her life back?

"And I'm not going to DC when this is over. I'm coming home, MaeBe." Kyle pulled a beer out of the fridge and popped the cap off. "I'm coming back to you, and I'm going to prove to you that everything I've done was with you in mind. I panicked. It might

151

have been pointed out to me recently that I overreact."

"Really? Was it Sandra who told you that truth?" She'd only met Sandra Croft once. By the time she'd hired on at McKay-Taggart, Sandra had moved to Wyoming to be with her daughter and son-in-law and grandkids. But oh, she'd heard the stories. Sandra could rival Big Tag for her level of sarcasm and honesty.

"No." Kyle took a long drink and then set the bottle on the bar. "It was a guy I was working with. He died. Some of Julia's coworkers killed him, but not before he pretty much put me in my place. He accused me of creating chaos and drama when I should have been patient, and I think now that he might be right. I was so panicked that night. All I could think about was the fact that she would hurt you to get to me."

"Oh, that was pretty much her plan. I think she was going to use me to make you do what she wanted." She sipped her drink. The events of that day still wore on her. Between those dredged up memories and the fact that she'd killed a man, her carefully placed walls were starting to shake. She forced her hand to stay still because a fine tremble threatened. "She claimed I was a long-term project. I think she might have liked to see if she could turn me. The funny thing was she made some sense."

"Julia was always good at sounding sane. She's not."

"I don't know about that. I think she's perfectly sane. She's simply lacking any empathy for others. She's a sociopath, but she doesn't understand that. Like most malignant narcissists, she believes she's better than others, that hers is a superior mind. She doesn't think there's anything wrong with what she does. She thinks what she feels for you is love."

Kyle's head shook. "It's not."

"Of course it's not. It's possession, but that's how the narcissist views love. Throw in probably watching too many epic love stories, and she's built you up in her mind as some god of a man."

"She doesn't know me. Not the way you do."

"You asked her to marry you, Kyle. How long was the relationship before you did that?" She wanted to know, and this wasn't in the hacked files she'd managed to obtain.

"We worked together off and on for about six months before we formed a team. And then it was very quick," he admitted. "We slept together the first night we were sent on an assignment by ourselves. I asked her to marry me six weeks after we were placed on a permanent team together. I knew fairly quickly that it was a mistake. We spent most of our time fighting. That was part of the attraction in the beginning."

She held a hand up. "I don't need the whole story. I was curious. You took so much time before you would even sleep with me. It makes sense. I was the opposite of her. She pointed that out to me, too."

"I did not fall in love with you because you were her opposite. I fell in love with you because you're half my damn soul, Mae. When I met her I was in a bad place."

"I'm pretty sure the same can be said of meeting me."

"It's not the same at all. Meeting you was the best thing that ever happened to me. Meeting you made me want to live again. The only reason I came home last year was to spend some time with my family while the Agency forced me to take time off. I was going to do my time and then rejoin Drake, and I wasn't coming back again. I was going to work until it killed me, and you changed that."

It was an easy thing for him to say. Words meant little to her. His actions had proven the truth. "You walked away from me very quickly. Look, I don't want to talk about this. I'm tired and disappointed because I thought I was finally getting some freedom back and now it's gone again. It could be months before I get out of this freaking club. I used to love it here. Now all I see are walls to my cage, and all I feel is how deeply stupid I've been."

"You weren't stupid." He set the beer down and moved around the bar. "Baby, you didn't do anything wrong. I reacted poorly. My only thought was to get as far away from you as possible. I know how Julia works. I needed her to understand I wasn't going to bring you into this. I thought I could buy myself some time to kill her and make sure you were safe."

"But you intended to leave me. You intended to never see me again. You faked your own death in a way that could have led to your actual death. You didn't talk to me or leave me a nice note explaining the situation and asking me to stay safe and wait for you." In so many ways she was glad he hadn't because she knew what would have happened. "I would have done it. I would have patiently waited and not given any trouble to the people guarding me. If you'd wanted me to go into hiding, I would have gone and never argued. I wouldn't have trained or changed my lifestyle in any way. I would have forgotten everything that woman told me."

"I don't think you should believe anything Julia says," Kyle pointed out.

"But she told me the truth. The truth about myself. The truth about you." She took another sip of her drink and turned to Kyle, feeling so much older than she had this morning. This morning she'd been halfway excited about the week. She'd been ready to start game nights again, ready to go out for a girls night with Noelle and Maddie. Oh, they would have had to drag a couple of bodyguards with them, but she could have felt halfway normal.

She thought she might be able to get a piece of herself back, some tiny spark she might be able to grow into a flame.

Then Kyle had come back and she'd killed a man, and now she was fairly certain Kyle was going to try to ship her off somewhere and she was so fucking tired. Tired of the awful juxtaposition her life had become. Months of boredom broken up by moments of complete terror.

She kind of wanted the fight so it could all be over, and she or Julia would be dead and they could all get on with their lives.

He moved into her space, looming over her because he had a foot on her and despite the muscle she'd put on, he still had at least seventy-five pounds more of it. How big and strong he was had been part of his appeal. He'd found a beautiful balance between protective and funny. Between making her feel safe and bringing a spark to her world that made her feel alive.

It was still there. She was everything Julia had said she was because there was a part of her that wanted to put her hands on Kyle's waist and tilt her head up so he would kiss her. If he kissed her, she could forget everything and have a couple of hours where she pretended they could work.

"She can't begin to comprehend the truth about us." Kyle's expression had gone perfectly earnest as he stood there, mere inches between their bodies. "Baby, you might never forgive me, but do not think for a single second that this was some way to get you out of my life. You are my life. My only thought in those moments was to save you. My head went back to a bad place, a place I thought I'd left behind. I didn't think. I acted out of pure panic."

"And then you had months to correct the situation. Months to call me and let me help you."

"I can't. I can't expose you to her again. She tortured you."

"I wouldn't call it torture. We fought. She won. She won't find me so easy to deal with this time. This time I'm taking her down, and I'm going to do it for me. Not you."

Now his hands came up, cupping her shoulders. "You are not getting close to her. I won't let that happen."

Adrenaline rushed through her system as she reacted exactly the way Big Tag and Erin had taught her. It was second nature now to bring her arms up and out, breaking his hold on her. She turned as she brought her elbow back and caught Kyle in the solar plexus.

She heard a satisfying gasp as he tried to drag air into his lungs. She started to turn so she could explain to Kyle that this wasn't going to go the way he wanted, but before she could begin to pivot, he was on her. One big arm wrapped around her, and she was dragged back against his chest. She could feel the hard length of his cock right against her ass.

"Yeah, baby. You damn near took the thing off me not an hour ago. It still aches but I'm ready to use it on you because you are the only woman in the world I want." His mouth was warm against her ear. "I don't care how many men you've had since I've been gone. Let me show you why I'm the only one for you. Let me."

She brought her foot down on his toe, but he didn't let go.

"Let me, baby. You know you need this. You haven't cried. You need to cry."

After everything she'd been through, yes, she did, but it couldn't be soft and sweet. She was neither of those things any longer. But it didn't mean she couldn't get what she needed. When she thought about it, he owed her.

"Hey, are you two okay?" Drake and his girlfriend were standing by the bar. Drake frowned as though he thought he would have to step in.

She needed to prove something to all of these people.

"We're fine. You don't..." Kyle's statement was cut short as she managed to get enough leverage that she flipped him over her shoulder and he landed with a hard thud on the carpet of the lounge, his handsome face screwed up in a startled expression as he gazed up at her.

That felt good. She turned to Drake and Taylor. "We're fine. I think I can handle him. You two should find a room and bed down for the night. Kyle can sleep on one of these lounge chairs. He likes to keep watch."

Kyle flipped himself up like he was in a martial arts movie, and damn, but she wished that didn't do something for her.

Then she wished she'd been a bit more careful because he moved in, and before she could counter, she found herself tossed over his shoulder like she weighed nothing.

"We'll be fine, Drake. Trust me. She's got a safe word. She knows how to use it but I'm betting she doesn't, and if she does I'll be sleeping outside her door. You two take the room marked Paradise City. We'll be in the one across the hall. Don't worry. They're all soundproof."

She tried to kick him, but his big arm held her legs tight. She used her fists on his back, but the bastard merely chuckled as he started toward the stairs.

"We're going to work some things out," Kyle tossed over his shoulder.

She growled and wriggled against him.

But she didn't say her safe word. She didn't even come close.

Chapter Ten

Kyle wasn't sure if he was making a terrible mistake, but he couldn't simply walk away from her. She needed him even if she wasn't willing to make things easy on him.

"Put me down, Kyle." Her fist beat on his back as he started up the stairs.

"Say your safe word, Mae. We're in the club. You know how to make this stop." He knew exactly what she was doing, but it was good to get the rules of engagement out on the board.

She groaned and struggled again. But that safe word did not come out of her mouth.

Perhaps this was the only way she could deal with him tonight. He'd put her in a corner, and she had her pride. He'd been a fool to think she would melt for him. He'd put her in this situation, and he had to help her find a way out.

MaeBe was a longtime sub. She knew the rules and understood that all she had to say to make him walk away was to spit out the word she'd selected that would stop any top she was playing with. It would absolutely stop him, and then he would do what he'd promised. He would sleep on the floor outside her door and make sure no one could hurt her.

He opened the door marked Ménage Mahal. It was the largest of the privacy rooms and was lushly decorated. They wouldn't need the multiples of each toy and binding, but he appreciated the space because it seemed like Mae wanted to beat on him. He could handle it.

Besides, some of the other rooms had cages, and he wouldn't put it past her to lock him in one.

He closed the door behind them and set her on the floor. "Do you want to do this here, or we can go down to the dungeon. I can chase you if you want."

He could let her fight him in a safe way. She could beat those fists against him all she liked and maybe she would feel better.

Her eyes narrowed as she stared up at him. "You think I'm going to play with you?"

"I think you need a release, and you can't let me do it sweet and slow. I think you need to have the illusion of me forcing you to push past the wall you've built up," he explained. "But it *is* an illusion. I love you. I won't ever force you to do anything."

"Except mourn you."

He had no pithy reply to that. "I thought it was for the best. I thought I was saving you. Honestly, I think I was also punishing myself. I hated myself so much in that moment, hated that I'd fallen for her. I was ashamed."

"I don't care. I meant what I said. I stopped loving you when you left me behind in the cruelest way. But you're right. I need something tonight. I just don't need it from you."

It made his gut twist, but he'd put them in this position. "Who have you been playing with? I'll call him or her and get them up here if that's what you need. I'll make it happen."

That made her stop. "You'll bring in someone to fuck me?"

"I wasn't thinking it would go that far," he admitted, and he could feel bile rise. What the hell could he do? How far was she willing to push this? "I didn't think I would fuck you, baby. I thought I would spank you until you cry. I...I don't know that I can stand outside while you're with someone else. Do you want to hurt me that badly?"

He wasn't sure what he'd do if she said yes. It would be so far from his Mae that he would have to accept she might be changed forever.

She softened slightly. "I don't want to hurt you at all. I never did. And I was lying. I didn't play with anyone. I haven't, but I want to. I want to get to the point that I can have that part of myself back. I used to walk into this club and pick a top for the night and I would play. Sometimes it was for fun. Sometimes it was because I'd had a rough week and I needed a cry."

She struggled to cry, but a good spanking could open the door for her. She would sleep so well after a cry. At least that's what she'd told him.

"Let me help you, baby. You can stop me any time you want. Don't make me call in someone who doesn't matter."

Her eyes were sad as she looked up at him. "You don't matter anymore."

He tried not to let her see how much that hurt. "Then it shouldn't mean anything that I'm the one giving you what you need. You had a terrible day. You were so out of control, and now you can't let go and do what you need to do. If I don't matter, then I'm nothing but a hard hand on your ass and a commanding voice to guide you on the path."

He wanted to be so much more, but he didn't have room to argue with her. If he survived the upcoming battle with Julia, they would have time to reconcile. He would spend the rest of his life making it all up to her, and he could start with giving her everything she needed with no strings attached.

MaeBe stepped forward and put a hand on his chest, pressing him back. "Fuck you, Kyle."

He held his ground. She didn't want his tenderness, couldn't handle this being soft and sweet.

So he would give her his roughness, his dominance.

He reached out and tangled his fingers in her hair. "I wished we'd played. I wish I knew exactly what you like and what you don't."

"I can say the words *yellow* and *red*. Unless you don't remember your training. It's not like you put it into practice. You were far too busy keeping your hands to yourself." She was taunting him, pushing him back and behaving like the worst brat in the world. "You wasted it, you know. I don't even know why you bothered to take that class."

Oh, she wanted to be mad at him. He could give her so many

more reasons for anger. He meant to be honest with her this time around. About most things. Definitely about this. He tightened his hold, bringing her up on her toes and watching as her eyes went wide and her pupils dilated. "I didn't just take the class at Sanctum. Baby, I've been working at The Club one night a week since I came home. I've taken private training with Julian Lodge, and I've practiced hard."

"I thought you were working late. That was the excuse you always gave." She swiped a hand at him but he held her off. "More lies."

"I'm full of them," he admitted, his cock tightening. His cock was an optimistic idiot because there was zero way she let him get inside her tonight. Unless he was really, really good at what he was about to do. Unless he brought her so much pleasure she forgot everything but her next orgasm. He couldn't help it. His mind went there. They were alone in a room together, a room filled with toys he'd dreamed of using on her. A room for the fantasies they could play out.

Like the fantasy where he'd never left Dallas and had been waiting here when she'd shown up. The fantasy where he was good enough for her.

"Was she your sub?" Mae asked, a challenge in her voice. "She said she'd had a bad Dom in her past."

Oh, they weren't going to play this game.

He picked her up again and carried her to the big bench where he sat down and dragged her over his lap. He was gentle with her, but he wasn't about to let her go. If she wanted out, she knew what to do. Until then, he was in charge.

"I told you. I started training when I got home and met this gorgeous brat who fucking rocked my world and who needs this." He felt one of her hands grip his ankle. She knew exactly what she was doing, and she was absolutely manipulating him. What she didn't understand was how far he'd go to stay close to her. "I wasn't interested in any of this until I met you, until I realized how deep you were in, and I knew I better learn how to swim."

He brought the flat of his hand down on her ass, once then twice and again.

"You can have a D/s relationship without ever playing and you know it." She seemed determined to push him.

He gave her a stronger slap and then found the waistband of her leggings, starting to drag them down, exposing that gorgeous ass of hers. "No. A D/s relationship must be talked about, must be consented to, and not merely at the beginning. Every single day. Sometimes minute by minute. What you're asking is if I was the asshole who abused Julia and made her a monster."

She went still beneath him. "I didn't... Kyle, I didn't mean it that way."

But deep down she had. Deep down she wanted to blame him for everything, and she was right to. He didn't want to talk about this, wanted to keep her as far away from his past as he possibly could. "I didn't top her."

"But you did top me, and we didn't have a contract."

"Yeah, I topped you so hard, baby. You did pretty much whatever you wanted and got into all kinds of trouble. I never wanted you out in the field. If I was topping you, I would have made damn sure you were safe." Another volley of slaps and her ass was starting to get pink.

"I was never going to allow you to decide how and when I work. But the rest of it... We had a D/s relationship and you broke it. We might not have had a fucking contract, but I deferred to you when you needed it. I let you lead me in so many ways and then you were gone."

"I didn't want to leave you. I never wanted to leave you." He slapped her ass, punctuating each word. "I was willing to risk my life to keep you safe."

She went quiet as he brought his hand down again and again. He watched as her body quivered and shook, going stiff and then relaxing time and time again.

But she didn't cry.

No, something else was happening. Something that had his cock as hard as a rock.

He peppered her ass with little slaps, the scent of her arousal filling the air around him.

If his hand wasn't working, then he could try something else. "Get naked and stand by the bench."

She slid off his lap and onto her knees since her leggings

trapped her neatly. "I'm not getting naked for you."

He had a button he could push with her. "Then say your safe word."

Her middle finger came up.

Then they would do it the hard way.

He reached down and ripped the blouse open, buttons scattering across the floor. "If you want to keep the rest of your clothes, you'll take them off."

Her eyes were wide, and her mouth slightly open. "You asshole."

"Do you want to start the spanking again? I assure you I can slap your ass and then I'll rip the leggings off your body and go after your underwear. Don't worry. I've already asked Noelle to bring you more in the morning."

"You have no right."

"I have every right while we're in this club and you haven't said your safe word. Get naked, Mae Beatrice."

She was frowning as she shrugged out of what was left of her shirt. "Fuck you, Kyle."

He could only hope. He watched as she kicked out of her boots and fumbled her way out of the leggings, her soaking wet panties coming with them. "You won't want to wear those again anyway."

She got to her feet and unhooked her bra.

His breath nearly stopped in his chest. "You are so fucking gorgeous."

"I don't want to hear it, Kyle."

"But you are. You are the most beautiful woman in the whole fucking world."

"I'm close to saying my safe word."

She wouldn't take anything from him. No sweet words. No kindness at all. No love when he had so damn much love for her. It was pathetic, but he would take whatever he could get. He might not be able to say it again, but she was gorgeous. He missed her vibrant hair but only because it was so familiar. Her natural hair was brown with threads of gold and red, and it spilled past her shoulders down her back. She'd gained muscle where she'd been soft. She looked fit and stunning, but then she'd been stunning before. She always would be to him. "I told you to go to the bench. When you get there, place your palms on the seat and spread your legs. I want that ass high in the air."

"It won't mean anything," she said, her voice hollow. "If you give me an orgasm, it'll be purely physical. It won't mean anything beyond I want an orgasm."

Oh, but it would mean everything to him. "I am meaningless. Got it."

She turned and walked to the bench.

And he prayed that meant he had a chance.

* * * *

MaeBe made it to the bench, cursing her weakness when it came to this man. She couldn't resist. Even when she knew damn well she should walk away. She leaned over, placing her palms on the padded bench.

She'd never played in this room. It was meant for ménage, so when they had to pick a room, she'd selected this one because she'd never once fantasized about playing with Kyle here. Kyle wasn't the ménage type. She'd been absolutely certain this wasn't a man who would ask her to join him and his wife in a little play, and if she'd been the wife, it wouldn't even have been a thought in his head.

Of course she'd thought she'd known the man. Now she knew that everything she'd built with him before was based on lies.

Yet here she was, her whole body pulsing with need, and it was all about him. Months and months she'd felt nothing, and the minute he'd shown up her libido had come back online.

Her ass ached slightly, but she wanted more.

"Eyes closed," he ordered.

Bastard didn't want her to know what was coming. He wanted her to stand here and squirm in anticipation.

Of course that was part of the fun.

She closed her eyes and tried to be in the moment because she'd missed this.

She'd missed him.

MaeBe shoved that thought away. It was the play she'd missed, and they'd never played. He'd put her off, telling her he wasn't ready for that yet. He was never ready until he was, and then he'd been gone.

A crack split the air and sweet pain brought her out of her thoughts and back into her body. Heat spread through her, and she realized he'd gone and grabbed a crop.

Fuck, she loved the crop.

"Can I tell you your ass looks pretty with a pink mark on it? Or will that scare you off?"

Such an ass. "It's fine, Sir."

Yes, that was good. If she called him Sir and didn't look directly at him, he could be any Dom in the world. He could be a complete stranger.

"Way to deflect," he muttered, but he brought the crop down again. "Whatever you call me, your ass is still the prettiest pink right now." The crop struck once more, this time to the crease where her ass sloped to her legs. It was a tender spot, and the pain made her shiver.

She wasn't sure why she loved this, but her whole body responded to the pain—the willingly taken pain, the asked for pain.

She knew the difference. Pain was different when the person giving it wasn't careful. Then it was just hate on her skin. This was something else. This was caring, a song that lulled her into comfort. She breathed through the pain and let it morph into something warm and lovely.

He used the crop on her ass and thighs. Whoever had trained him had done a spectacular job because he knew exactly where to hit her for maximum sensation and minimal possible injury.

Then something warm caressed her, and she felt a shudder of pleasure go through her. His hand. She loved his hands. They were callused and warm, and she'd always felt safe when he'd put them on her. Was she going to turn him away tonight? Wasn't tomorrow soon enough to tell him to fuck off?

Her pride was rapidly losing to her horniness.

When his fingers teased at her pussy, her safe word wasn't even close to the tip of her tongue.

"You respond so well to a good spanking."

She thought about being a brat. Questioning his use of the word good *was* on the tip of her tongue, but it wasn't true. It was stubbornness and would do nothing but lead her to hurt him in a way she didn't want to.

She didn't want to hurt him at all. At least that was what she was telling herself. She just wanted the world to be normal again.

His fingers teased against her pussy. Her embarrassingly wet and hot pussy.

"You know there's another way to release this tension. When you've had a terrible day, one way to let off steam is to have a string of orgasms." His voice had gone deep. She remembered that tone so well. She still dreamed about it at night.

A single big finger slid across her clitoris, and she could barely breathe.

She needed to say that word, the one that would make him stop because if she didn't, she was going to end up in bed with him, and she'd promised herself she wouldn't do that.

Or had she? She'd only truly promised herself that she wouldn't fall in love with the man again. He didn't matter. He was basically a warm vibrator, and why shouldn't she enjoy him?

It would only be a bad idea if she was worried about her feelings for him. She didn't have those anymore. So it was all right to take what he offered.

The pad of his finger started to work over her clitoris, rubbing and teasing and pushing her higher and higher.

When she thought about it, fucking Kyle could be the natural step to getting back into the dating scene. Closure. It was what she'd been waiting for. Sweet closure.

"I want to put my mouth on you, MaeBe."

Suddenly she couldn't think of why that would be a bad idea. She simply nodded. Saying yes would be too much, but then she didn't need to say yes to him in this room. That was a given. He had her consent until she withdrew it.

D/s was something she could handle. There didn't have to be emotions in a pure D/s relationship. It could be compartmentalized. She didn't have to be devastated when he left again.

Because no matter what he said, he would leave again. He would lie again. She would be alone again.

"Don't. Don't think," he implored. "Just feel. Just for the next hour. Let all the rest of it go and know this is real between us."

This part could be real. This part she could accept. When he picked her up and cradled her to his chest, she didn't resist. She let her body go soft and submissive. This was the only place where she could indulge that part of herself, where she could stop fighting her instincts and simply be.

She needed to get back to this place, and without Kyle.

He laid her down on the bed and spread her legs wide. She let him because she couldn't work up the will to stop.

As long as he was in town, she would play with him, and then it would be done. Then she could move on with her life.

Of course he might not want to play with her when he realized she was going to kill his ex.

"You know this is what my uncle told me to do." Kyle had gotten to his knees, and his mouth hovered right over her pussy.

She was going to ask him what he'd meant by that, but then her brain went on the fritz as he licked her. His tongue dragged along her flesh, and she felt her whole body seem to go liquid. It had been so long since she'd used her body as anything but a tool. She'd trained it and ignored all her other needs, but it had been there boiling under the surface, waiting to be fulfilled.

He licked and sucked, drawing one side of her labia into his mouth and then the other. He worked a big finger deep inside her. "You still taste so fucking sweet. I've never been able to forget how good you taste."

He'd been able to forget so many other things though.

She let the thought drift away as he tongued her clit. Fire licked across her, and she hadn't realized how cold she'd been.

He worked another finger inside her, curling them up so he could stroke her sweet spot.

The world seemed to float away as she let all the sensations take over her senses. Her backside ached in the sweetest way. Kyle's fingers pierced her, thrust carefully in and out as he sucked at her clit.

The orgasm burst across her, making her every limb stiffen. She pressed herself against his tongue, not wanting to let go of the pleasure that coursed through her. Nothing else mattered, and the moment seemed to lengthen, swallowing her whole world until there was only him.

She relaxed, every muscle loose and limber.

Yes. That was exactly what she'd needed.

Kyle's head came up and then he was kissing his way up her body. "I can do this all night long. Let me stay here with you. Let me hold you, Mae."

He moved until he was lying beside her, his hand on her belly.

She was so tired, and she couldn't think of anything nicer than not sleeping alone tonight. "Kiss me."

A look of pure relief crossed his face as he leaned over and his lips met hers.

It wouldn't feel the same. It could still simply be sex. They could keep it to this room since she was sure he would be gone in the morning after he'd attempted to stash her somewhere and gotten whatever intel he needed from his uncle.

One night wouldn't make a difference.

The memory of how it felt to be loved by him rushed over her as he kissed her. He rolled on top of her, pressing her down. Her arms wound around him and something softened inside her. This might be the only night they had together.

She'd wanted so much more from him. She'd ached with the need to be with him, and it oddly felt good to ache again.

"Baby, you won't regret it." He stared down at her with those gorgeous green eyes of his. He looked so earnest, so deeply into her.

She was fairly certain no one had ever looked at her the way Kyle Hawthorne did.

"I already do." But she lifted her head to kiss him again. She was falling off the wagon tonight, and tomorrow she would face reality. "But I can't help myself."

"Because we belong together," he said solemnly.

She shook her head. "Don't talk. This is going to work so much better if you just kiss me."

He grinned and lowered his head. "All right. But you have to admit, this is so much better than a raid."

His mouth covered hers and his tongue found her own. He drugged her with kisses, and her body started to warm up again. Her breasts were pressed against his chest, and she resented the fact that he was wearing a shirt. She wanted to feel his skin against hers.

She wanted to feel his body driving into hers. If he fucked her hard enough, she would be able to feel him all day tomorrow. It would make it easier to get through…

Raid? Why would he use the word raid?

"What did you mean?" She forced herself to say the words because it would be way too easy to let him work his way down her body again.

He already had a hand on her breast, and his mouth was close to the other one. "I was just saying how happy I am you changed your mind." He licked her nipple, tonguing the ring there, and her spine bowed at the sensation. "This is far more than I dreamed of."

She shook her head and gritted her teeth as he nipped at her. One nipple was trapped by his fingers and the other caught gently between his lips. "Raid. You said raid. Why would use the word raid?"

He stopped as though someone had flipped a switch and turned him off and he was trapped in the moment.

Which told her one thing. He'd been caught and he was going to try to find a way out because he was Kyle freaking Hawthorne and he was made of lies.

His head came up. "It's only a word…fuck." He rolled off her and laid back, staring up at the ceiling. "I'm not doing this to you again. I'm going to be honest. You can't believe me when I tell you I love you if I'm keeping the truth from you about other things."

She was confused. She pushed off the bed, all the relaxation gone now as she grabbed one of the robes. Usually there were two. Not so in the ménage room. There were five of those suckers, and she'd managed to pick up the largest one. It didn't matter. She wrapped it around her body. "What did you mean? Have you been playing something online?"

He didn't join her when she played massive multiplayer online role-playing games. He loved video games—especially war games and shooters—and he'd seemed to be starting to enjoy board games, but he never wanted to play the group online games she loved.

He sat up, looking at her. "I couldn't stand not feeling close to you so I joined your guild. I wanted to be there for you in some way. Any way I could."

All the heat she'd felt for him turned icy cold in an instant. "You joined my guild?"

She played a medieval game that felt like dungeons and dragons online. She enjoyed the camaraderie, and she'd played so much more lately because she'd needed the escape. The people she played with online didn't know how dumb she'd been. She could be someone else online. She'd only gotten close to...

"I'm Kraven," Kyle said, his expression grim. "Like I said, I wanted to be there for you."

Anger raced through her. "Then you should have picked up the phone. Or written me an email, asshole. Get out."

"I know you're mad because it feels like I tricked you, but I think it proves something, too. You were getting close to me. You didn't know who I was, but you were drawn to me."

Oh, she had news for him. "Because I thought you were a forty-something dude with a husband and a couple of kids. I thought you were older and smarter than me. I thought you could actually tell me something meaningful. I wasn't attracted to Kraven. I felt comfortable with him."

"You flirted with me."

"You think everyone is flirting with you."

"No, I don't," he countered. "I barely notice other women. Since the day I met you all I see is you."

"Then you shouldn't have walked away." It was always going to come back to this. She wasn't sure what she'd been thinking. "And you definitely shouldn't have lied. I trusted Kraven. He felt like he cared about me."

"Because he loves you."

She didn't want to hear that. He was right. She couldn't believe a word he said, and she never would again. "Get out."

"MaeBe, you don't mean that. I'm sorry. I couldn't stay away from you. Honestly, being able to play that game with you kept me sane."

If she let him talk, she would end up in bed with him again, and she couldn't do that now because the storm was coming. She could feel it. She hadn't cried at the pain from his hand and the crop, but this felt like betrayal.

And she'd killed a man.

She couldn't even think about that.

Tears were building, and she wasn't going to do that in front of him. He didn't get her emotion anymore.

"Meeple." It was a dumb safe word. It was what board gamers called the wooden pieces some games used as markers. She always played green, and Kyle had somehow ended up with blue. She often made their meeples kiss like she was a preteen with a crush.

His face fell. "That is not fair. This conversation isn't about D/s. You can't safe word out of a relationship."

"Meeple." It was all she was going to say to him. In this place a person absolutely could safe word out of a relationship. She could also simply *no* her way out.

He stopped, and she could see that he was trying to figure out how to fix this.

"Meeple." She needed him to leave because her calm demeanor was a mask that was rapidly disintegrating.

He grabbed one of the many pillows off the bed. "I meant what I said. I'm going to be right outside."

He strode out, and she was alone.

She waited for the tears. She'd felt them building, but now they seemed stuck like the pin had been pushed back into the grenade right before the strike lever released.

The explosion was still there. It wrapped around her gut and heart, squeezing tight because she couldn't do what she needed to let it go.

She'd touched it for a moment when it had felt like she could at least have Kyle while the op was on and he was here in Dallas. And then it was gone and she was numb again.

She moved back to the bed but knew she wouldn't get any sleep.

Chapter Eleven

$\mathbf{M}$aeBe opened the door, ready to deal with whatever fresh hell the day would bring, and nearly tripped over the big body that lay across the doorframe.

Kyle. His eyes had come open, and he stared up at her for a moment. "Everything okay?"

He was asking her that? She'd spent most of the night trying to figure out how to avoid whatever trap Kyle was planning on springing on her. Somehow she didn't think he would take no for an answer. He would be all about safety and forget the definition of the word *consent*. "Everything's great. I need to get to work."

He moved just enough that it would be hard for her to step over him. "We need to talk about that."

"We don't need to talk at all. Let's go to the office and get to work," she insisted. She might feel better when she was back at her desk, behind the computer she knew so well. Her friends would be there. She could joke with Hutch and have lunch with Yasmin and life would feel normal, or at least as normal as it could be.

Before he could answer, the door down the hall came open.

"Where did your uncle get a life-sized painting of Axl Rose done in pure Elvis black velvet style?" Drake asked as he walked toward them. "It was disturbing. I think its eyes glow in the dark."

"Charlotte had it done a couple of years back. It was a birthday present." Kyle straightened up like his spine no longer functioned properly, but then that was what he got for being a dumbass. There were plenty of comfy couches on the second floor. He could have pulled one of them in front of the stairs and guarded her that way, but no, he had to make a point.

He was the most stubborn person she knew, and she was close to Erin Taggart, so that meant something.

She was dressed in yesterday's clothes with the exception of a too big for her Sanctum T-shirt she'd found in one of the closets. She'd left off the underwear since there was no saving those. They were nothing but a reminder that her pussy did not have any pride when it came to Kyle Hawthorne. Her pussy was a traitor.

Or maybe your pussy is rational and reasonable and understands that this time she should take everything she wants from this man and shove him out the door when she's done with him. Maybe your pussy is vengeance itself.

Her brain was excellent at justification.

"I liked it." Taylor looked beyond perfection. Of course she had a whole suitcase to rely on since she'd known she was going on a trip.

MaeBe sized the other woman up. Taylor was gorgeous with shoulder-length auburn hair done in a sleek bob. Her clothing was fashionable, but in a functional way. The slacks she wore would be easy to move in and the blouse wouldn't inhibit her in any way. MaeBe was fairly certain that was the intended effect.

Taylor Cline dressed like the well-trained CIA operative she was.

She didn't know much about Taylor except she was an experienced agent and obviously with the guys.

She would need to do a deep dive on Taylor Cline before she made any real decisions about how to handle her. If she got the chance. She wasn't sure Kyle wouldn't simply toss her over his shoulder and shove her in a cage somewhere. For her own good, of course.

"It had a whole rock and roll vibe, but from another era," Taylor explained. "And the eyes did not glow in the dark. Drake was a little freaked out when he realized a couple of Big Tag's kids were probably conceived in that room."

"In that bed," Drake said with a shake of his head. "And it has a big jukebox, but there's only Guns N' Roses on it, and when I tried to play any song it was 'Sweet Child o' Mine.' Like 'November Rain'? You're shit out of luck because 'Sweet Child o' Mine' is playing. Want to select 'Mr. Brownstone'? Nope. You're going to get 'Sweet Child.' And what the hell is the Adam Miles Memorial Princess Castle? Did Adam die? I talked to him last week."

Ah, that was more Big Tag assholery. She was going to miss the hell out of it if she had to leave and find another job. "He put that in last year as a prank. Like spent a ton of money on it and everything. It's a two-story playroom with a princess theme. It's the pinkest room I've ever seen and filled with tiaras and tulle and a weird amount of poufs. You know those ball things that some people sit on."

Kyle forced himself up, stretching out his mangled spine. "I don't think Ian understood how versatile those things are. In a BDSM setting. Nor did he get how popular the room would be."

"How would you know?" Drake asked, a brow rising.

"Guys talk. A lot. There was a whole discussion about how much time Erin and Theo spend in there and who wears the tiara. I thought it was rude to suggest that because Erin is tough she doesn't like being feminine and because Theo can be nurturing he's the one in the princess crown, but guys are assholes. Bodyguards as a set of men do not rank high on the thoughtful scale, and now I realize I shouldn't say men because my sister-in-law pretty much started the whole thing. And she's a woman who dresses up as Queen Elizabeth from time to time and lets my brother make that whole virgin queen thing a moot point. Why am I in this family?"

He was so stinking cute sometimes. She needed to remember that he was a liar and a manipulator, and he'd fooled her for the last time. "The point is what started as a Big Tag prank ended in Sanctum history. And it's memorial because Big Tag said Adam's dignity died in there. Serena has some very specific fantasies, and they require costumes. And an unholy amount of glitter. Adam should have changed before he went out to get a drink. It's Big Tag 101."

"My uncle is an asshole." Kyle hid a yawn behind his hand. "But he's serious about a schedule. We should get going. He wants a debrief this morning. He'll do whatever he can to help us, but this will go so much easier if we respect his wishes and bring him up to speed."

She would also like to be brought up to speed.

She wasn't sure how she was going to sit in that conference room with him. She'd been up half the night, and none of her tension was gone. Her gut was in a knot, and she was waiting for the next shoe to fall and likely hit her right in the head.

It was stupid but she was angry with him for admitting he'd tricked her again. Almost angrier about that than the actual manipulation. If he'd kept his damn sensual mouth shut, he likely would have been in bed with her this morning. They would have fucked all night, and she wouldn't have this hollow place inside her.

"You said Noelle was bringing me clothes." She was not going back to the office in mostly the same clothes she'd worn the day before. There was an actual code for *Walk of Shame* that would make its way through the office, and inevitably someone would bring by a box of condoms and she would want to kill them. It wasn't her fault she'd had to flee her apartment two minutes after she'd gotten back into it.

It was Kyle's.

Mostly. And the underwear was all his freaking fault, and she hadn't gotten the barest hint of the pleasure those soaked undies had promised.

"I'll go check and see if she dropped them off yet. Then we should talk. I know you're upset with me, but Julia won't care about your feelings, and last night proves you're in danger." Kyle gave her a grim look before he ran down the stairs.

The door to the castle room opened, and West stepped out. He was in what looked like clean clothes. Jeans and a plain black *T*, though it was slightly large on him and the belt was buckled tight. He yawned as he looked around, and then a flush went over his skin. "It's actually pretty comfortable in there."

"Sure it is, Princess," Drake shot back.

Drake did not understand how Sanctum worked. "That is the plushest room of all. There's a reason it's still standing a year after it was supposed to become a seedy hotel playroom. Though I've had to clean some of those fuzzy blankets, and it can get gross."

The idea of leaving Sanctum made her infinitely sad. Or at least it should. The emotion was there. She could sense it, but she couldn't quite tap into it. Sanctum had become her home. Why couldn't she panic at the thought of leaving it? Leaving her friends who were her only real family?

Was she starting to think it was better to be alone? To not risk getting hurt again? Was it better to not feel anything at all?

West's hands came up. "Nothing got gross last night. I even snuck down to the locker room and took a shower before I slid between those satin sheets. Those are nice. And I like all the pillows. When the lights are out, it doesn't matter that everything is some weird shade of pink. I don't think that room is an accurate representation of royalty."

She was pretty sure Big Tag had let Bella Rycroft point at her favorite things in a princess catalog. And then he'd dusted every surface with glitter, some of which clung to West's well-trimmed beard.

"You and Kyle okay?" West turned serious. "I noticed only three of the rooms were occupied last night."

He must have gone to bed before she kicked Kyle out. "Kyle and I are fine. We're exactly the way we were before he decided to be alive again."

"He started out being in there with her, but he slept on the floor in front of her room," Taylor pointed out. "I went downstairs to grab a bottle of water and he looked like a puppy who'd been left outside by mistake."

"It wasn't a mistake. He explained to me that he's been cyberstalking me and I asked him to leave." She felt stupid even explaining it. How had she not known?

"I'm surprised he offered that up. I told him he should never tell you that." Drake yawned behind his hand. "Though you should know he spent pretty much every day waiting for the moment when he could get online and see you."

"Or he could have called. He could have seen or talked to me every day. We have these things called cell phones." It was obvious Drake was one hundred percent Team Kyle. It would mean his girlfriend was too, and MaeBe should remember that.

"Yes, those things my sister can track," Drake replied. "I'm sure she has been tracking yours, and I'm not talking about duping your phone or anything a normal hacker can do. I know you're excellent at your job and you think you would be able to tell if someone was tracking you, but she's not even playing the same game. The telecom company that provides your cell service could be one of The Consortium companies. If they are, then she could be using them to track you and listen in on calls. How do you think she knew where you were last night? Why do you think I wanted you to leave your cell behind?"

"We're working off burners," Taylor explained. "I'll get a set for you. They were purchased under different names, and there's no way to connect them to us. The same with laptops. If they're registered with a company, we have to consider them potentially dangerous."

The device itself wouldn't be, but once it was connected to a user, the company could track it. "I can get a clean system from Hutch. We're not tourists, you know. Cybersecurity is literally my job."

"Then you should understand why he couldn't call you," Drake shot back.

"Or I could know all the ways he could have made it work." She wasn't listening to Drake plead Kyle's case. "Now that we've established I'm involved in this op, could someone explain what the op entails?"

She was going to be bold. Perhaps if she dug her heels in, Kyle would understand she wasn't the same timid girl he'd left behind.

"No one has said you're involved," Drake hedged.

"She got shot at last night," Taylor argued. "I think that's the definition of involved."

She hadn't expected Taylor to take her side.

"If you don't bring her into this, she'll do it on her own." West proved he'd learned something vital about her. "She's been researching all kinds of crazy stuff."

Nor had she expected West to turn on her.

"Like what?" Drake lasered in on West.

"None of your business if I'm not involved with the op." If they didn't want her help, she wasn't giving it to them. She would lay it all out for Big Tag. He was her boss, not Kyle Hawthorne. When she was sure she had something, she would give it to Big Tag and he could decide what to pass on.

Walls. There were walls between them now, and she had to place her loyalties on the proper side.

Kyle jogged back up the stairs, a bag in his hand. "Hutch and Noelle dropped this off earlier. Hutch went by your place last night to make sure it was secure. He says we're in the clear with the authorities. All anyone knows about is the smoke bomb. They suspect nothing but a prank played by some kids. He has a report he's going to send to you, but know that he's taking care of things and will continue to do so until you can come back."

Here it was. She'd known they would end up right here. Anger bubbled up. It might be the only emotion she was capable of anymore. "Come back? From where, Kyle?"

His face turned grim as he passed her the bag. "Could I have a moment alone with MaeBe?"

"I don't..." West began.

"Your brother is waiting downstairs. He's giving us a ride to the office," Kyle explained. "Please go down and introduce Drake and Taylor to him."

"I'm not going to leave her," West argued.

She wasn't bringing West into this. Now she had to consider that Ian could side with his nephew for the sake of his family, and that could get West in trouble.

She was on her own. "You should head into the office. I promise I won't leave here by myself. I suspect our time together is over, and I'm about to be moved to a new location. Go talk to Wade. He'll know what's happening."

"All right, but you should remember that no one can make you do something you don't want to do." West turned and jogged down the stairs.

But they could. They could trick her, manipulate her. She was fairly certain Kyle wasn't above kidnapping her if he thought it would make the job of tracking down his ex easier.

"Be gentle with her," Drake said under his breath as he and Taylor followed West.

She didn't intend to go anywhere. If Big Tag sided with Kyle, she would be on her own and she could finally concentrate on the op she needed to work on. It would be easier to work with them, but it was obvious that wasn't going to happen. "Where am I being shipped off to now? I suspect you don't want me to stay here at Sanctum."

"We were safe last night, but this is one of the first places she'll look." Kyle was studying her as though trying to figure out what game she was playing. "I don't want to put this place in her cross hairs for more than a day or two. She is completely capable of blowing it up or burning it down to get to me. I've worked hard so she doesn't come after the people I love."

She'd figured out long ago that the only way to win this particular game was to not play at all. And he was right to not want the members of Sanctum involved in this. It was precisely why she was thinking about getting out altogether. "All right. So you've decided on a place where she can't find me?"

She had to ask because according to Kyle, Julia was all seeing and all knowing. She was the alpha predator taking down everyone she wanted to with ease.

"Loa Mali."

She barely managed to not roll her eyes. "You're going to put me on a twenty-hour plane ride by myself? What if I manage to get a parachute and escape? Do you think Julia would be waiting for me on the ground?"

His eyes narrowed, a sure sign he didn't appreciate her sarcasm. "I'm going with you, and we're using the company jet. We've got a plan so Julia will have a hard time tracking us. We fly into London and then change planes without leaving the private airport. The logs will show your fake ID. You're going to look like a British environmental consultant who's being flown in to meet with the king and queen."

It was good to know he had a plan. "And I'm staying there for how long?"

"I don't know. Until we can solve the problem."

Until they could catch or kill Julia Ennis. There was only one problem with that. "And if that takes years? Am I supposed to live in Loa Mali now?"

"It won't be years. I promise I will come and get you the minute I can. When you get to Loa Mali you'll have a dedicated guard, but you won't need to leave the palace often. I've ensured you have a whole apartment to yourself, and you'll be treated like a valued guest. Their oldest daughter is interested in coding. You could tutor her. You've always wanted to mentor girls."

Yes, she'd wanted to encourage more young women to get into coding, but she hadn't thought she would travel halfway around the world to do it. Still, there was nothing she could say to sway him, and she wasn't about to argue when there was nothing to win. She needed to figure out how to work her way around him. If he realized she wasn't going to be easy to deal with, he would probably never leave her alone.

"I should get dressed then. When are we going to the airport?"

He stared at her for a moment. "I thought you would argue with me."

"Could I win an argument with you?"

"That's not fair." His tone had softened, and he had that little boy lost look in his eyes.

"Neither is sending me halfway around the world. We're not dealing in fairness here. When do we leave?" She needed to know the particulars of the plan so she could thwart it. There were places she could go. She still had friends who had nothing to do with her work, friends she'd made when she'd been a hacktivist. They knew what it meant to be on the run.

It could be the best way to handle things. She didn't want to put her friends at risk either. If somehow Julia got her hands on Noelle or Yasmin or Maddie or Vanessa Malone, there was no way MaeBe didn't walk into that trap. She wouldn't have another choice.

"I have to go to the office. I'm taking Drake with me. We need backup and logistics from my uncle. You'll stay here until it's time to go to the airport. Taylor's going to drive you there, and we'll meet up after we're done with the briefing," Kyle explained like she was a piece he was moving around the board. "We'll fly to London with you and from there a guard will escort you to Loa Mali. Damon Knight's men will handle that part of the journey. I'll come for you when I can."

"No need. Just give me a call when I can have a life again." She turned away to go back into her room. She needed to change and figure out how hard it was going to be to get away from Taylor Cline.

The good news was she knew the club far better than the other woman.

Kyle reached out, grabbing her elbow and turning her around. "I'm not doing this to hurt you. I'm doing this because I love you."

"Then let me come on your op. Let me decide for myself what I'm willing to risk. Value me as something more than a romantic partner."

He hesitated and she realized if he said yes, she would try again. If he could change, she would give him a shot, and that was such a dumb thing to do. But deep down, she loved this man.

Again, not an emotion she was able to tap, but if he said yes, maybe the wall would crumble and she would be able to feel again.

"I can't. I do value you, but I can't risk it." His face had fallen as though he realized he'd lost it all.

She moved to the door. "Then when the op is done, don't come for me. Give me a call and let me know it's safe. I don't want to see you again."

His expression went tight as though he could feel in a way she couldn't, and he was having a hard time containing his emotions. "This is exactly what Julia wants."

"I don't care. This isn't about giving Julia something or taking something away from her. It's about you and me, and we're done. Don't try to track me online again. I'll give up games. I'll give up whatever it takes to be free of whatever this is."

"You make me sound like the bad guy."

She simply walked into the room and locked the door behind her. She got dressed and ready to deal with whatever happened next.

If she went to Loa Mali, she might be able to continue the work she needed to do. Or the king would want nothing to do with it and she might put the whole royal family at risk.

She walked down the stairs, bag in hand as she worked her way through the problem because there were definite downsides to running away on her own.

If she did run, would Ian use valuable time and resources to track her down? Probably. Would she be putting more people in danger if she walked away? Probably.

Would Kyle come after her or let her go? That was a question she could likely answer. He would come after her—if only out of pride—and that put the entire op at risk.

Finding Julia Ennis was important, and so was bringing down The Consortium.

Why was she the only one who seemed called on to sacrifice? She'd sacrificed the most important relationship of her life, her freedom, her naïveté. She would likely have to give up her job and her friends because she wouldn't be able to work with Kyle when he returned. And no matter what he said, he wouldn't leave his family forever. She would have to give up Sanctum.

She'd had to become a different person. She wasn't sure she liked the person she'd become.

"So, the guys are expecting us at the airport at noon." Taylor stood in the lounge section of the club, working the coffeemaker.

How many times had she fantasized about sitting in the lounge with Kyle? She'd dreamed of long nights spent in the club, and they would come here after they'd played. She would sit on his lap and let her head rest on his shoulder while he talked to his friends, and she would feel so safe. "All right."

She had some time to decide what she wanted to do. Could she take Taylor in a fight if she decided to run?

Taylor pushed the button to start the coffee. "So the guys told me I'm supposed to take you to the airport. Do you want to go to the airport?"

MaeBe hesitated. Was this some kind of a trick? "No."

"Okay," Taylor replied like they were talking about whether to go shopping or not. "Where do you want to go?"

"I want to go to the office."

"Cool. Should we have breakfast first? I'm always cranky until I've fueled up," Taylor admitted. "I saw a pancake place a couple of blocks back. If someone tries to assassinate us, at least we had pancakes, you know?"

MaeBe wasn't sure what was going on. "Are you being serious? You're not going to force me to go to the airport?"

She shrugged. "I'm not going to force another woman to do anything. I know the guys think I'm here to do their bidding, but I'm really here to be their conscience. They don't think straight when it comes to Julia. I have to make sure Drake doesn't do something he can't forgive himself for and that Kyle doesn't wreck the rest of his life, starting with this morning's debacle. And when I think about it, I only promised I would get you where you needed to go. Where do you need to go, Mae?"

Could Taylor be an ally? "To the office. I need to go to the office. I have some information on my system there that might be helpful. But pancakes sound great."

Taylor passed her a mug of coffee. "Excellent. Now let's talk because I've put together some things the guys seemed to gloss over. You've been researching The Consortium, haven't you? That's what West was talking about. What do you know? I'll tell you what I know, too. You need to be brought up to speed on the last couple of months."

Oh, Taylor was definitely an ally. "Kyle will try to ship me off again."

"Then he can go through me," Taylor vowed. "I'm not joking, Mae. I think you should be a part of this for several reasons, not the least of which is how much stake you have in this particular game. He's wrong for shutting you out, but I don't know how to convince him. I can only explain to Drake that I won't have any part in kidnapping you. Because that's what he's talking about. He doesn't see it that way, but it's the truth. I also think if Kyle's going to have a shot at being with you at the end of this, you need to come with us."

She shook her head. "If you're doing this because you think I'll forgive Kyle, I won't."

"Then there's nothing for you to worry about. If you can watch him work this op and not feel for him, then nothing can change your mind. But I suspect he's never told you the real story and you don't understand why he's so tied up in knots over this."

"He never talked about her. Not in any real or valuable way. Most of what I learned I discovered on my own or through talking to Big Tag." Kyle never wanted to talk about her until she'd come back from the dead, and now she was the only thing he wanted to talk about. Now she was the most important thing in the world.

It was weird but somehow in her head Kyle's deep belief that Julia was the greatest evil ever known almost made her jealous. Almost.

Great. The other emotion she could feel was jealousy. Awesome.

"I'll talk about her." Taylor took a sip of her own coffee. "You'll find I'm an open fucking book when it comes to her. She killed my father."

Oh, there was a spark of sympathy. "I'm sorry to hear that."

"Let me tell you a bit about her and then we'll grab breakfast to fortify ourselves against the fight we're going to get when we show up at the office," Taylor said. "Do you think Charlotte Taggart will be there? I might fangirl over her. Her CIA records are amazing. And she was kind of the bad guy then."

MaeBe knew Charlotte had never truly been the bad guy. She'd been used by her mobster father, who'd tried to twist her into something evil and useful to him.

Although if she thought about it and her instincts and research were right, wasn't that what had happened to Julia Ennis, too?

"I'll introduce you. She's one of the best people I know." Charlotte hadn't allowed herself to be twisted.

It was obvious that Julia had.

This might be Taylor's way of disarming her, of getting her to open up and tell her what she knew right before she shoved her on an airplane.

She'd given up trusting in anything at all.

She couldn't keep living this way. She had to take some steps to get back that piece of herself that loved. She talked about the people she loved, but it was an academic thing now because she couldn't trust anyone.

"All right. Let's talk." MaeBe drank the coffee that probably didn't have a sedative in it and decided to roll the dice on Taylor Cline.

* * * *

Kyle sat down, the familiar conference room bringing back a thousand memories of MaeBe. How many times had they sat in here listening to client overviews and arguing about how best to deal with a job? He always wanted to drag her over and make her sit on his lap while the meeting went on and on.

Drake seemed determined to go over every minute detail about what had happened since the last time he'd talked to Tag. Kyle had lived it so he didn't think he needed to pay too much attention.

He'd called the pilot his uncle had approved and made sure he understood what was going to happen. He'd made sure there would be plenty of Sriracha and Mae's favorite beer and chocolate chip cookies. The woman who ran the palace had assured him Mae would be given a laptop to use that would be as untraceable as it could be.

She hadn't even seemed to care that he was sending her away. He'd expected a fight, been ready for it, and it had been so much worse.

He hated how shut down she was. MaeBe had always been an open book, every emotion she felt clear on her face. He could read her so well. He'd made a study of her, and he knew what she was feeling by her expression. A cocked brow meant he was a dumbass. The left side of her mouth curving up meant she had a secret and she was eager to share. When she cried, she didn't hold back.

She hadn't cried. She'd been forced to kill a man and she hadn't cried.

MaeBe cried when she watched rom coms and when she read books. She got super emotional over fictional characters, and he would have told anyone who asked that he would think that was weird. On MaeBe it was lovely and quirky, and he missed it.

"Is there somewhere else you would rather be? Because I can call you an Uber." His uncle's sarcastic voice broke through his reverie.

He forced himself to sit up straight. "Sorry. I'm thinking about everything we need to do before we head to the airport."

"I've already had Yasmin and Genny go to the store to get you everything you might need," his uncle explained.

"I don't need anything, but MaeBe will." He wanted her to be as comfortable as possible. Perhaps if she enjoyed her time in Loa Mali, she might start to forgive him. "Noelle and Hutch brought her a couple of days' worth of clothes, but she needs more."

"They're picking up some toiletries for her, but I sent Hutch out to get the most important thing for you," his uncle explained.

"I'm good. My go-bag is well stocked." It was sad but he had a whole bag packed in case he needed to… Well, in case he needed to fake his own death and leave everything he loved behind.

"Does it have a cup?" Ian asked.

He kept a collapsible cup with him along with anything he might need to purify water in case they were out in a rural area. "Of course."

"He means a protective cup." Adam was sitting in on this meeting. "Like for when MaeBe kicks you in the ball sac."

"Oh, she already did that." Charlotte sat in the chair next to his uncle's. She'd walked in and immediately dialed a number and put the phone on speaker so the person she'd called could listen in.

"Good for MaeBe."

His mom. Yep. His mom was happy he'd gotten kicked in the balls. He was absolutely the bad guy to all the women of his world. "Hope you don't expect grandkids."

His dick still ached, though not really from the kick. It was from the brutal cockblocking he'd given himself. He'd always meant to tell her, but he'd thought she would find it charming. Or at least flattering.

No wonder he'd gotten kicked out of the CIA. He was clueless.

"I'm sure your sperm still works. Trust me. I've heard lots of stories of Sean's time in the military, and he still managed to produce two kids. One after his vasectomy." His mom was in New York with his stepdad, who was filming for some cooking show. It was lucky they weren't in town or he was sure they would be sitting right at this table. Sean likely would have shown up last night and had to help deal with a dead body.

Oh, shit. He'd figured out where they'd put the body. He turned to his uncle. It would be just like him to leave his brother a present, and the dudes who worked there would likely shrug at a dead body and wonder who'd pissed off Chef. What they wouldn't do was call the police.

"Please tell me you didn't leave the present I gave you last night at Top. Please."

His uncle's lips curved up in the most devilish expression.

"Present?" His mom asked. "What present? Why would you store a… Ian, there better not be a body in that freezer. You know Carys is working at Top on weekends. I do not want my daughter walking into the freezer and finding someone her brother killed. Kyle, I taught you better than this. Were you raised by wolves?"

Lately, yes. The Taggarts were absolutely a predatory clan. "That asshole was working for Julia, and I didn't kill him. MaeBe did because he was about to kill me."

"Did she do that before or after she busted your balls?" his mother asked.

He wanted to grab that phone and hang up on his mom, but he was fairly certain Charlotte knew where to kick a dude, too. "After. And they're not busted."

He could have used them on her the night before if he hadn't been an idiot.

"So she saved your life even when she was mad," his mother mused. "That's interesting."

"I thought so, too, Grace," Charlotte said. "It's a good sign."

"Or MaeBe's simply a nice woman who defends innocent... You're right," Ian agreed. "I've taught her well. She should be able to let an asshole die, so we have to work on the assumption that this relationship is salvageable."

It was sad that he kind of clung to the fact that she hadn't let him die. "Shouldn't we get back to the debrief?"

Adam waved that off. "Drake's father turned out to be working with The Consortium for years and years. We figured that out weeks ago. Julia killed him to save you. John Smith is probably back with her, and you're looking for them both but you can't involve the Agency because you don't know who was working with the dad, so you need us. Cool. Let's get back to how MaeBe took off your balls. What technique did she use? Did you need a doctor?"

"You figured out my father was evil weeks ago?" Drake was suddenly interested. "You could have given me a heads-up."

"It was a theory," Adam admitted, his face flushing slightly. Adam was shameable. "And one I wasn't sure she was right about, so no, I wasn't going to ruin your relationship with your dad and possibly wreck his reputation on a gamble. Now can we talk about the fact that Kyle managed to make it into MaeBe's bedroom last night but got himself kicked to the curb."

Not all that shameable.

"It was the hall not the curb." Sometimes he understood why his uncle gave Adam such hell. "Did West talk? You know he spent some time in your memorial castle last night."

Adam shrugged. "Because it's comfortable. You know it wasn't my dignity that died in there. It was my lower back pain, and I'm fine with it."

"Wait," his mother said over the phone. "Kyle slept with MaeBe?"

"There was no sleeping involved," he corrected.

"Also, I don't think there was sex involved," Drake said. "Can I see the information you've collected on my father? We're actually looking for something of his."

"Did you talk to her?" Aunt Charlotte asked.

"No, I topped her and then she said we could sleep together and then I told her I was Kraven," he explained. "I didn't mean to tell her. It kind of came out."

There was an audible group sigh.

"Dumbass," his uncle groaned. "I told you that would get you in trouble. That is the kind of thing you tell her after you've saddled her with five kids and she can't get away."

"Oh, I could get away if I wanted to," Charlotte said with a grin.

"Of course. I'll get you what I have." Adam was talking to Drake. He leaned over and said something about asking "her" if she was okay sharing the data.

"But she let you get close." His mom's tone had gone to that gentle place that let him know she was about to get emotional.

What the hell was he doing? He was supposed to be giving a short debrief and then moving on. He was not supposed to be telling his mother about his love life. He didn't talk about his love life.

Except he did once. Once it felt normal and natural to talk to his brother about his relationships. Once he would have asked for his mom's advice.

He was well on his way to finding those pieces of himself again, and Mae was the one who'd led him here.

And he was the one who'd shattered her utterly.

He turned to Adam. "You're the one who encouraged her to do this."

"She came to me asking for some advice. I was intrigued so yes, I helped her. She's excellent. I mean, it was truly superlative work. Chelsea checked her work and we both agree that Mae's fabulous," Adam explained. "You know if you two break up, it's going to be uncomfortable with you working at the same company. Mae can come down to MDWM."

Ian pointed a finger Adam's way. "Don't you poach my employees."

Kyle sat back and cursed inwardly. How deep had she gone? What had she found out? How much did she know?

How much did she blame him for?

His gut tightened, awash with shame and guilt and a whole bunch of other emotions he'd hoped he'd gotten over.

"I'm just saying it might be awkward for the two of them to work together, and you know how much shit he gives her when she tries to do her job," Adam replied.

"I don't give her shit. I'm trying to keep her safe." But the words... He was hearing the words that were coming out of his mouth and they didn't ring true. He was trying to keep her safe, but what if she didn't want to be safe? What if she wanted to take some risks?

"No, you're trying to make your life easier," his aunt shot back. "And you do give her shit. You go behind her back and tell her coworkers what she will and won't do."

"See, I'm going to have him blocked from coming into my office when MaeBe starts working for me." Adam pushed back from the conference table. "He won't have a chance to undermine her."

"You would put her in the field?" He wasn't surprised Adam was throwing him under the bus that seemed to chase him everywhere these days.

Adam stood. "In a heartbeat."

"Because *I* trained her." His uncle's eyes had narrowed. "Erin and I turned her into a badass. I don't think you should reap the benefits of all our hard work. You can take Kyle."

Adam's head shook. "Thanks but no thanks. He disappears too often. Drake, I think we're getting to the emotional part of this conference. You know the one where everyone goes off the rails and someone special has to talk the idiot dude off the cliff his ego has led him to."

Drake frowned. "What makes you think that? I thought we were arguing over who had to take Kyle once all of this is over."

Adam picked up his tablet. "Nah. Grace went super quiet. She's about to ask for some time alone with her baby boy. I think we should get some coffee and wait for MaeBe to show up."

"MaeBe's on her way to the airport," Kyle said, realizing Adam was right. His mom had gone quiet, and that wasn't a good sign.

"Is she?" Adam asked with a mysterious smile.

Ian's eyes flared. "Dude, who did you leave her with?"

Drake pulled out his phone and then sighed. "I can't track them because if I did Julia might be able to track us. She's with Taylor. And now that I think about it, Taylor never said she would take her to the airport. She said she would take her where she needed to go."

Panic flared and he stood. "I'm going to find them. Does she have a tracker?"

His uncle sighed. "Grace, would you like a moment with your son?"

"Yes, I think we should talk," his mother said. "Could we have the room?"

"I can't. If MaeBe is out there," he began.

"She's with a woman you trusted enough to leave her with," his mom countered. "Ian, I assume you've met this woman? Would you trust her to protect MaeBe?"

"She's a highly trained CIA operative, and she's beyond suspicion." His uncle was on his feet, hand reaching out to Charlotte, who let him help her up. "But I should point out that MaeBe can handle herself now. And Kyle, if you don't chill, she'll take off on her own. You've got one shot at this. Don't fuck it up. When she shows up at this office, and I have no doubt she will, you let her sit in this conference room and explain what she's discovered like the professional she is. You treat her with respect and not like a toy you're afraid of losing."

"Ian." The name was a warning from his mom.

"You know he's right, Grace," Charlotte replied. "We'll go and get some coffee and restart this meeting when everyone is actually here." Her voice went low as she passed him. "Do not give your mother hell. She's been through enough."

Drake clapped a hand on his shoulder and gave him a nod as he left the room.

And he was alone with his mom, who was miles and miles away, and yet he could feel her judgment. "Say what you need to say, Mom."

He would listen to her and then he would figure out where MaeBe was. He would track her down and she would get on that plane and go to Loa Mali and be safe.

"I might not like how he says it, but your uncle is right. You're screwing this up."

"What am I supposed to do?" This was what he genuinely didn't understand. "What would Sean do if he was in my position? I know damn well he's sent you into hiding before. Do you think I don't remember what happened when Charlotte's uncle was after her? He sent you away."

"Because he had to watch his brother's back. Also, I had Carys at the time. I wasn't trained the way MaeBe is, and I didn't ask him to take me with him. I wouldn't have because I had to protect Carys, but I also knew Sean would come home to me. He did not fake his own death and leave me mourning him. He explained everything that he needed to do and why he needed to do it. He called me often, and I knew where he was. I worried like crazy, but I was still a part of his life."

He didn't like the way his mother's words made his skin feel too tight. "Charlotte's uncle wasn't directly after you."

"Stop. Kyle, I love you but you're not being fair to this young woman. You left her. You don't get to come back into her life and start bossing her around. You left her and she built a new life and you're not a part of it. That was your choice."

"I didn't have a choice."

"Yes, you did. You could have talked to her."

Frustration welled inside him. "When should I have done that? Before Julia broke her arm? Or should I have waited until Julia shot her and we could have another talk in a hospital? You know it wasn't the first time Julia put her in a hospital. It wasn't even the first time she'd put a member of my family there."

"You can't be sure she caused Lucas's accident."

A few months back his youngest brother had a freak accident in a training gym. His leg had broken, but it could have been much worse. "He was the only one scheduled to use that machine at that time. It would have been easy for her to get that information, and you know damn well she was behind the fake social media account that outed Carys."

It had been one of the first of Julia's nasty pranks. He'd put it together during the long days spent in Wyoming. When he wasn't working at Sandra's bar, he was researching and mapping out all the ways he was fucked. He'd traced it back to eighteen months before when Carys's relationship with Tristan Dean-Miles and Aidan O'Donnell had been "featured" on a gossip social media platform.

Then there had been Lucas's accident. Kyle's credit rating had been ruined in a way that didn't make sense. His stepfather's restaurant had a bunch of nasty reviews and was scheduled for several nuisance inspections.

Then MaeBe had been stabbed. At first they'd thought it was a random robbery, but he knew Julia had sent her boy toy to do the dirty work.

He should know. That used to be his job.

"I understand that this woman is dangerous," his mother began.

"She's deadly. She tried to kill MaeBe two seconds after I showed back up in her life." That was where he'd made his mistake. He'd let a single conversation with a man push him into forgetting how deadly Julia was. He'd felt stupid after Brad Perry had told him he was an overly dramatic narcissist who didn't think of anyone else.

All he did was think about MaeBe and his family.

"I understand that, too. But I know she should have a choice, and you're not giving her one."

"Apparently Taylor is," he said, bitterness dripping. "I would bet Taylor talked her into it because she was perfectly reasonable this morning. She understood."

His mother sighed, a weary sound. "That's not good."

"Her being reasonable isn't good?"

"I've spent some time with MaeBe since you've been gone," she admitted. "I wanted to see if I could salvage anything for you. She's changed. What you did to her… Kyle, you let her believe you were dead. I know you told me and Sean, and I appreciate that, but it's not the act of a loving partner. If she seemed reasonable to you this morning, it's because she's done fighting with you. She's put you in a room and locked the door, and she'll do what she needs to do the minute you're gone."

He'd felt that door between them. For a brief moment it had felt like MaeBe had unlocked it, peeked around and thought about throwing it open, but then he'd fucked up again. "Things will be fine once I take care of Julia. I'm going to make this up to her. I love her. I've made that plain."

"I'm sure her father did, too. I'm sure she felt incredibly secure that she had a dad who loved her, and then the world changed and he was gone." His mom proved she'd spent time with MaeBe because she didn't tell that story to everyone. Most of the time she simply explained that her mom had passed and her dad didn't live close. He did but she lied so she didn't have to get into it. He would bet his mom had put her at ease and gotten the truth.

How many times had her dad made plans and then flaked out on her, choosing her stepmom each time. It might have been different if MaeBe had a part in forcing him to choose, but she'd never done anything but ask if she could have a relationship with him. "It's not the same."

"I bet it feels the same to her. I bet it was hard for her to trust you the first time around. When you think about it, faking your own death is kind of the ultimate rejection. She knows what it means to actually lose someone, someone who loved her, who didn't want to leave her. And she knows what it means to be abandoned. Which camp do you think she puts you in?"

The words made him ache. "I was trying to protect her. Why can't anyone understand that?"

"Because you hurt her. You might have protected her from Julia Ennis, but who protected her from you? I know this is going to surprise you but a part of MaeBe died when she realized you left her behind. I think a part of her thinks you chose Julia. I don't know what that woman said to her, but it was poison and it's still in her system. I tell you that, but I don't want you to focus on what Julia did or might do. You have to make a choice, and you need to make it now."

"There's no choice between Julia and Mae. I love Mae. What I feel for Julia is the furthest thing from love."

"Oh, baby, that's not true," his mother argued. "Hate isn't the opposite of love. They're two sides of the same coin. Tell me you haven't spent as much time thinking about Julia as you do Mae lately."

"It's not like I want to think about her. I have to. She's going to try to kill me. She already tried to take out MaeBe. Are you sure Carys and Luke are safe?"

"They're here with us. They're doing online school for a few weeks while Sean is filming," his mom explained. "And I assure you we have a McKay-Taggart bodyguard. David came up with her so he could do some research."

So Tessa and David were with the rest of the family. Tessa would take care of things, and David followed her lead when it came to security. His brother had learned how competent his wife was long before they got married.

Would David hide Tessa away if someone was coming for him? Or would he have sat down with her and asked for her advice. Would they have worked out as a couple what to do?

If he'd sat down with MaeBe and asked her to go into hiding for his sake, she would have done it. She would have hugged him and told him she loved him and been waiting for him.

"I panicked. When I found out Julia was alive, I was so angry. I didn't behave like the trained operative I am. I lost my shit and went to the absolute worst place. I couldn't see a world where Julia lived and I got to have a happy life. All I knew in that moment was if she thought for a second I wasn't willing to give up MaeBe, she would kill her. So I did it. I thought I was being unselfish. I thought I was saving her."

"And she thought you were abandoning her. You're using the wrong word, Kyle. You weren't angry."

His eyes went watery because he knew she was right, but he didn't like to admit it. Even to himself. "I don't know. I was pretty pissed at her."

"You cannot face the truth of this if you can't put a name to the feeling. This is what I've been talking to your uncle about. And your Aunt Charlotte. They understand what you're going through. They couldn't move on until they accepted what happened and why they had done what they did to each other. It starts with naming what you feel."

"Afraid." He brushed that obnoxious watery proof of his emotional state away. "I was afraid. I was afraid of everything she could do to me. I was afraid if MaeBe had to learn the truth, she wouldn't love me anymore."

"Yes," his mom said with a sigh that sounded like relief.

He looked up and MaeBe was walking through the door. She was in utilitarian jeans and a plain T-shirt, her hair covered with a baseball cap she'd likely had to borrow from someone because she was not into sports.

She looked so unlike the vibrant woman he'd fallen for. He'd brought her to this place.

"Should I walk away, Mom? Should I apologize and promise to stay away from her?"

"Do you love her?"

"So much I ache with it. I hate the fact that I ever thought about another woman."

"That's ridiculous and more about you than her. I assure you she doesn't think you should have come into her life as some virginal sacrifice who's held off for the right woman. She's practical and understands the world far more than you're giving her credit for."

MaeBe's head turned and then she stopped in the middle of the hall, her face going stony. The conference room had floor-to-ceiling windows that his uncle often closed the blinds to, but not today. Perhaps because they didn't have a media presentation. Or it was fate that he was staring at her.

She stared back at him, practically begging him to show his true colors.

What were they? What was he feeling if he took Julia out of the equation? How would he feel if he was just Kyle and not some combination Kyle and the mess having a relationship with Julia Ennis had turned him into?

He would be happy that she had walked in a room. His heart softened at the sight of her, and if he took his fear and shame out, he would simply love her.

He felt the freaking tear roll down his face, but he didn't wipe it away. He was talking to one of the two women in the world who got his emotion, and he was looking at the other. If he was lucky, he would someday have a daughter and he wouldn't ever want her to think her father couldn't cry.

He smiled her way and held a hand up in greeting.

Her whole body seemed to soften. She waved to him and for a second he could see the MaeBe she'd been.

The one she could be again.

And then she walked away. But he'd seen it. He'd been open and she'd responded.

"Mom, what should I do?"

He sat back and stopped reacting. It was time to stop being the man Julia had turned him into and think and act like the one he wanted to be. The one MaeBe Vaughn deserved.

Chapter Twelve

He'd been crying.

Kyle Hawthorne had stood in the conference room with a phone to his ear and tears rolling down his cheeks, and her whole fucking soul had responded.

Her first impulse had been to run into that room and wrap her arms around him and tell him it would all be okay. She would do whatever he needed her to if it meant wiping those tears away.

Kyle didn't cry. His emotions were joy or anger, and the joy was kind of muted because he was a manly man.

Vulnerable Kyle was so fucking dangerous.

Thank god Taylor had been behind her. They'd had a great talk at breakfast, and she felt comfortable with the woman. Perhaps she should still be suspicious, but she was starting to trust Taylor Cline.

She walked toward her cubicle as the door across the hall came open and a familiar figure walked out.

Erin Taggart's normally taciturn face lit up. Erin was one of those women born with resting bitch face, but her active bitch face was so much scarier. And when she was happy, the woman could light up a room.

"Hey, you're here. I heard a rumor you were getting shipped off by a Taggart-adjacent scaredy cat. I'm surprised to see you."

She walked up and gave Erin the quick hug they always gave

each other after they hadn't seen the other for a couple of days. "Well, I told him what I thought of his plan and now I'm here. Have you met my friend Taylor Cline?"

Erin turned Taylor's way. "No, but her reputation precedes her. Hey, I'm Erin Taggart. It's nice to meet you. I think I worked with your dad on a couple of occasions. I was intelligence in the Army. Mr. Black comes off totally different with a thick Russian accent."

Taylor's face split into a big grin, and she shook Erin's hand. "My dad loved working with military intelligence. So much more than his Agency contacts. It's nice to meet you. And our girl here has decided she doesn't want to go to Loa Mali. She's had enough sun. I think she should come with us on our op."

Erin laughed. "Holy shit. Did the boys think you would do their bidding?"

"I didn't lie. But I'm also not sending a sister where she doesn't want to go." Taylor glanced around the office, taking it in. "Have you seen my boyfriend? He'll be the one who's ticked off I didn't do as I was told. We should get this fight out of the way."

"No fighting, baby." Drake rounded the corner with Adam Miles behind him. "I don't know what I was thinking. *Chicks before dicks* is your favorite phrase. I should have taken that as a warning." He moved in and put a hand on Taylor's hip, gently urging her close so he could press his lips to hers. "Did you two have a good plotting session? I would like to point out that this was Kyle's plan. Not mine. So any plotting should be strictly against him."

"We had pancakes," Taylor replied with a smile. "Only a little plotting."

They'd mostly talked about the case. It had been odd to listen to Taylor going over the horrors of what had happened to them in London. Taylor had been trying to go undercover, to become a Consortium agent so she could map the organization from the inside much like certain FBI agents had done with mafia organizations.

Though Julia Ennis hadn't been her original contact, she'd been the Consortium agent Taylor had met with that night in London. Her first assignment—the one that would prove her willingness to work for the group—had been to assassinate Drake Radcliffe's mother. Senator Samantha Radcliffe had no idea her daughter was still alive. She'd been mourning her, and now she had to mourn her husband as well. Don Radcliffe had been a double agent for years, working for the Agency at the highest levels, all the while holding a place with The Consortium and bringing his daughter in.

According to Taylor, Julia had killed her stepfather because he'd had Kyle in his crosshairs. Rather than allowing Kyle to die, she'd taken out the man who'd raised her.

She'd sat there and listened and realized Kyle was right about how far this woman would go to have him, and she'd felt...nothing.

She'd felt nothing until she'd walked in and seen Kyle talking on the phone to someone, tears rolling down his cheeks, and she'd waited for him to turn angry. He was good at getting mad. She'd known that he would be mad at her for catching him in such a vulnerable moment. He was definitely not good at being vulnerable.

He'd simply raised a hand and greeted her, doing nothing to hide the pain he was in.

How much pain was Kyle Hawthorne in and how had that affected the choices he'd made?

Yes, there it was again, that thawing of the ice she'd built up. She shoved it away because it was better to feel numb than let herself rip open that wound again.

"We're pretty much through with the debrief. Adam was taking me downstairs to show me what he and MaeBe have been working on," Drake was saying.

"MaeBe can join us." Adam was wearing his typical dark suit with a white shirt and colorful tie she was sure Serena had picked for him. Adam was a bit more formal since he'd become the head of a company. "Most of this was her work."

Miles-Dean, Weston, and Murdoch specialized in missing persons and identifying and tracking known security threats. She hadn't thought about it until now, but they'd also been brought in by Drake's mother when his sister had "gone missing."

"I'd like to read the Samantha Radcliffe file."

Adam's jaw went tight. "Mae, you know some of my files require security clearance."

"She can read it," Drake said. "I can call my mother and have her give you the go-ahead to allow MaeBe to be brought in as a consultant. She knows what's at stake."

Adam nodded. "Then I'll send you the file. I'm going to go tell

Ian you're here, though he likely already knows. The man has freaking eyes everywhere."

"I'm sorry your mom had to go through that." She said the words because she knew she was supposed to.

"Me, too." Drake's arm went around Taylor's waist, and she leaned into him, offering him her support.

"So how is this going to work?" It was better to face the problems at hand than to stew about what had made Kyle cry. It didn't matter. He didn't matter, with the exception of how much trouble he could cause for her. "Is someone going to throw me over their shoulder and tie me to the chair of the private jet?"

"I won't." Drake's head shook. "Like I said, I'm with Taylor. Kyle is…he's not thinking straight. It's hard to when my sister is in the mix, but I have someone who grounds me so I'm better at it. I can talk to him if you like, but I think his mom is trying to be the voice of reason right now."

He was talking to Grace. Grace, who'd checked in on her even after her son was gone. Grace, who'd treated her like she was part of the family even though she wasn't and wouldn't be.

Grace, who she'd been somewhat standoffish with because she represented so much of the life she'd lost when Kyle had walked away.

She was self-aware enough to know that part of her attraction to Kyle was how much she adored his family. That was all. A big part of her attraction. When she thought about it, they were pretty much opposites.

And opposites attract. They work beautifully when both partners are willing to bend. Kyle didn't walk into the relationship playing games every Thursday night. He'd been closed off and solitary, and he'd done things he wasn't sure he'd enjoy because you enjoyed them. And you wouldn't even watch a football game with him.

"Are you willing to share that data with us?" The curiosity in Drake's tone made her wonder if she'd lost track of time while she'd been thinking about Kyle.

"Data?" She needed to focus on the case. Kyle would be gone soon anyway, and her life could get back to the shitty normal she'd found. "It's more than data, but I'll share everything I have."

"Do you want to go down to MDWM with us?" Drake asked.

"Or we can do this in the conference room and not leave anyone out this time," a familiar voice said. Kyle stood behind her, and she wondered how long he'd been there. "I think you'll find my uncle is setting up to start again. We can exchange information, and I have some thoughts about how to move forward, if you can forgive me long enough to work with me."

She had not expected that reaction. It took her off guard, and she found herself nodding and following him into the conference room where Adam, Charlotte, and Ian were taking their seats.

Kyle took a seat across from her, the careful way he moved letting her know he was giving her space.

Or was he lulling her into a false confidence? This would be an excellent way to get all her information right before he had her hauled off.

"Uncle, could you please explain to MaeBe what you'll do to me if I force her to go to Loa Mali against her will?" Kyle's eyes were on her as if he could read her mind. Which he had.

"I'll show you how I taught MaeBe to kick a man in the balls. You can get up close and personal with the technique." Ian settled his big body into the chair at the head of the table.

He was being a bit of a hypocrite. "You know you told me once you would lock me up if I didn't do what you wanted."

Ian shrugged. "What I wanted was to make sure you could protect yourself. Now you can, and you've earned the right to be a moron and run headlong into danger if you choose. You should have read your employment contract. It's got a moron clause in it. Only morons who can fight are allowed to."

Charlotte winced. "Mitch always tries to take that out."

She hadn't actually read the contract, but it would be exactly like Big Tag to put in some weird clause he couldn't legally enforce. It was one of the reasons she loved working here. It was constantly amusing.

"So I'm not going to be kidnapped?" MaeBe asked.

Kyle leaned forward. He looked tired, his eyes slightly red and that normally well-kept hair of his messy. Like he was a guy who hadn't slept well in a long time. "I'm sorry. I'm afraid of a lot of things, but I don't have the right to tell you what to do. I'm going to ask you to take the threat seriously and protect yourself. She will come after you again."

"Are we certain Julia intended to kill MaeBe?" Charlotte asked. "Or did the sniper she sent think he was taking out West? You said something in your report about the man who attacked you last night saying he was going to bring her in."

"It's entirely possible that the object of the attack was to take out her bodyguard and make it easier for the operative to grab her," Kyle said. "Did you find anything out about him?"

Ian sighed, and his eyes rolled slightly. "Well, he was packing some fake ID that says he's Ed Jones from Topeka, Kansas."

"He's not," Adam corrected. "We got lucky with this guy. He has a record. They tried to cover it up, but I'm awfully good at finding the stuff they thought they erased. He is…or rather was…Jeremy Harris from Oklahoma. He was thirty-four and a small-time dirt bag. He did some time for assault. I'm not sure if he made his connections in prison, but shortly after he was released on bail, he disappeared and shows up again as Ed Jones, and there was serious cash behind his new identity. I'm still working on figuring out his movements. I think he's probably excellent at evading security cameras."

"We all know if he's Consortium, he would have had access to tech that is not available to the general public." MaeBe had first become aware of that high-level facial imaging evasion tech during the Jessica Layne case. Julia had been wearing a pair of glasses that warped the light around her face and made it impossible to get a photo when she'd made her first appearance in Mae's life. "Did he have anything like that on him?"

They hadn't gone through the guy's pockets. They'd had to move quickly and then they'd handed him over to Ian and Alex.

"He did not," Ian replied. "But he did have a potent sedative. It was in the same device Julia Ennis used on the doctor. It was hidden on his arm. We know it was a sedative because my dumbass brother nicked himself on it and fell straight asleep in the middle of stashing the body."

Taylor's eyes went wide. "Is he okay?"

Charlotte grinned. "Theo met them at the stash site. He said it was the best sleep he's had in years, so hopefully that hits the market soon."

The idea of Theo Taggart meeting his brother and Alex McKay to stash a body and ending up taking a long nap because he picked up the body in the wrong place made the corners of her lips curl up. He would never stop catching hell from the group.

"So he was definitely trying to kidnap MaeBe." Kyle wasn't even close to smiling.

"It's what all the cool kids are doing these days." The snarky remark was out of her mouth before she could stop it.

Ian snorted. "That's the first time I've heard you sound like Mae in months."

"This is serious," Kyle countered. "If Julia wanted MaeBe brought in, then she was doing it to manipulate me. She knows I'll do anything if she's got MaeBe."

"Why would she think that? You dropped me fast enough." She was sick of hearing that excuse.

"Kyle knew what he had to do," Drake said quietly. "Julia has what I like to call *rules of engagement*. If he took you off the board, you would be out of the game. At least until she was backed into a corner and she needs something. She surprised me at my parents' country club a few days before we went to London and told me as much. She told me as long as Kyle wasn't pursuing you, she would leave you alone. I'm afraid my sister has some delusions. In a way she thinks you were a distraction for Kyle. She believes they're soul mates."

Kyle had gone pale. "She fixated on me early on. She's determined I'm her perfect mate and that all I'm doing is being difficult in order to get a better position in our relationship."

"Then none of this makes sense. You said she knew you would do anything to save me. If she doesn't believe you care about me, why would you do that?" Julia had said as much to her when she'd spent time in the woman's company.

"She believes Kyle has a strong streak of morality that she needs to break," Drake replied. "She knows he's got a conscience. Deep down she knows he cares about you. Her narcissism simply won't allow her to believe he could love anyone the way he loved her."

She watched Kyle, saw the way his eyes had found the file in front of him.

What was he thinking? Feeling?

How much had he loved Julia Ennis? Sometimes it felt like he was every bit as obsessed with her as she was with him. He'd changed their whole lives for her.

"What do you think she wants from you?" Ian asked, bringing her out of her thoughts. He was looking at his nephew.

Kyle's head came back up, and his expression was blank again. "It could be that she wants the money she sent to me after she died. It's a little over a million. We've never been able to figure out why it was put in there except to make me look guilty. I talked to Drake. We traced it back to one of her accounts. At the time we didn't realize it had to have been Julia herself moving that money."

"And where is it now?" If Charlotte was surprised, she didn't show it.

"It's in an account in the Caymans that both Drake and I can access," Kyle replied. "I did not touch that money even when I needed it."

"There's another explanation," Drake added. "She might want the money back, or she wants something far more important. Information. When my father died, he left a power vacuum in The Consortium. I'm sure my sister would like to fill it, but she would need leverage. Likely the same leverage my father had."

MaeBe sat up straighter. "He had a burn folder, didn't he?"

She'd known damn well that a man like the one she thought Don Radcliffe might be would have an escape plan if he needed it, and there was only one currency the man understood.

Intelligence.

Now Kyle was looking at her, a frown on his face. "Yes, that's what we think. Why do you think that?"

"Because she's been investigating your father for a few months now," Adam explained. "She came to me for some help with hacking a couple of sensitive sites."

"You know you could have told her…" Kyle began and then settled back. "She would have done it on her own. Thank you for helping her. As she's not in jail or Agency custody, I take it the hack went smoothly."

"Without a hitch," Adam agreed. "Though we also had some

help from Chelsea."

Chelsea Weston was a badass who'd taught her a thing or two. While Ian and Erin had trained her on how to protect herself, Adam and Chelsea had tutored her in some new hacking techniques. She'd been able to find the information she'd needed, but putting all the puzzle pieces together had been a challenge. "Drake, I don't know what Adam's told you, but I suspected that your father was involved with The Consortium for a while."

Drake's expression didn't change, but there was an oddly charged air around him. "And why was that? I'm a seasoned CIA agent and I didn't suspect my father of anything but being a bit cold and emotionally unavailable."

It was time to come clean on everything. "Oh, I investigated all of you. Your whole family."

The faintest hint of a flush was the only sign that Drake had a reaction to that news. "I suppose that makes sense. So you knew she was my sister."

"I knew her name, so it wasn't hard to find out."

"I should have told you," Kyle said quietly. "That was a mistake. I should have laid it all out for you the minute I knew we were serious, but I thought I could hide it. I thought you would never need to know how stupid and reckless I'd been, and then it was too late. By the time we knew she was alive, she had you."

"As I've said before, that would have been a good time to send me a note. A carrier pigeon, perhaps. She might not be able to trace a pigeon."

That actually got a chuckle out of him. "Yeah, I'm beginning to understand there might have been something more than logic behind that decision."

She wasn't sure what logic had to do with it. Kyle was a man who moved on instinct, and his first had been to push her away. "So you believe Julia's after her father's leverage. Do you have any idea what that would be? I'm going to assume given his connections he could prove some powerful people have done bad shit. My research puts him knowing most of the world's best known CEOs."

"Yes, but he did run in some influential circles when he was younger," Drake said. "He's spent most of his time at home the last few years. The most he's done is take some golf trips with friends.

He doesn't…didn't travel much anymore. I was surprised when he came to London with my mother."

She felt for Drake. Or rather she understood his problems. He was still processing the loss of his father and the truth of his life. But she didn't have the luxury of coddling him. "Adam, do you have a system I can use?"

Adam flipped open his laptop. "If you want to pull up the surveillance, I can do it for you."

Within a few keystrokes Adam had the photos she needed up on the conference room screen, easily using the wireless connections built into the office.

"From what I've learned your father's golf trips were usually covers for meetings with suspected Consortium members." The picture showed what looked like a normal group of wealthy men indulging in a harmless hobby. The photos she'd pulled showed Don Radcliffe meeting with a group of men she'd identified as the CEOs of major energy companies.

"That's from an exclusive country club outside of Hilton Head," Drake said with a frown. "How did you get surveillance photos? They're supposed to protect the privacy of their members."

"Oh, you sweet summer child," Big Tag said.

But MaeBe understood. "He's not naïve. He's still in shock." She turned Drake's way, a bit of sympathy welling up inside her. "I'm sorry, but there's always a way around whatever security a site says they have. In this case, I connected with a black hat hacker who I suspect is actually a foreign intelligence operative. The country club scrubs their system, but the hacker picked it up in real time. I had some information they wanted, so we made a swap."

Kyle's spine had straightened, and he looked at her like she'd grown a whole extra head. "You did what?"

Ian held up a hand as though he could ward off the impending explosion. "She worked with Adam and Hutch and Chelsea. She was perfectly safe. I can assure you my sister-in-law knows how to deal with shady characters."

Chelsea Weston had once been the world's greatest information broker. When she'd wanted to investigate Julia's shadowy world, she'd gone straight to Chelsea.

"Chelsea's been out of the game for a decade. She's a mom

now." Kyle seemed intent on arguing.

Charlotte leaned forward, the constantly amused expression on her face replaced with a stillness that MaeBe found disconcerting. "I assure you, nephew, we will never forget how to play this game. We played it from a young age and when we are old, we will still be the queens."

Charlotte spoke perfect English with no hint of an accent, but she'd let her Russian accent flow with those words—a reminder of where she'd come from. She'd been dragged into her father's world, into a world of mobsters and criminals, and she'd fought her way out with blood and sacrifice.

Kyle sat back, his eyes wide. "Okay, Aunt Charlotte. Now I get why everyone says they never worry about Uncle Ian. It's always you they're truly afraid of."

Ian frowned, a genuine expression of shock. "I am very scary. See, this is what happens when you get married and your wife won't let you beat the employees anymore. Or stab a couple of them. I'm telling you once you've murdered one for being an asshole, the others fall in line."

She often thought Ian Taggart would have been an excellent pirate. It was kind of his perfect life. Living the life of a dude who got to stab people and sail the wild ocean. Scurvy might be a problem, but he wouldn't care because he would be chasing booty all the time. And then he would find a lady pirate who stole his heart and probably his ship.

MaeBe shook her head. That was the first time in forever that her mind had wandered into ridiculous territory. Sometimes she saw the world like that, fun stories that played out in her head. She hadn't for the longest time. It was like her creativity had died when Kyle had.

"See, that reminds me of what it was like in the old days." Adam Miles smiled wistfully. "We had no money, and when Ian would set out a box of office supplies, we would *Hunger Games* the hell out of it. I've got serious scars from taking those pens from Liam."

"Yes, it's terrible for all of us." Charlotte was right back to her normal chic perfection. "Now you two pull each other's hair over who gets to use the private jet."

Ian grinned her way, a devilish expression. "It wasn't the hair on his head."

"Asshole," Adam replied and then shook his head and turned back to Drake, sobering. "I'm sorry we didn't tell you. You have to understand the position we were in."

"You couldn't be sure I wasn't part of it," Drake replied. "I do understand that."

"He better," Taylor said under her breath.

He brought her hand to his lips. "I assure you, I do. I learned my lessons, but I hope the group can consider me above reproach at this point."

"Someone could have mentioned it to me," Kyle grumbled.

She didn't like the guilt she felt. "The majority of this was gathered by me. I didn't send it to Ian until it was too late to warn you. I needed to be sure. I didn't want to ruin a whole family if I was wrong. I also didn't honestly think Drake was involved. I knew how I would feel if someone I loved was accused like that without irrefutable proof. I didn't understand that things were moving forward the way they were or I would have said something."

"Yes, this is a case of the left hand not knowing what the right hand is doing," Ian began, "mostly because the right hand cut itself off and ran away."

"What Ian is saying in his extremely non-helpful way is we didn't have the information we needed to make that call," Charlotte explained. "That needs to stop."

"This is no longer an Agency operation." Drake's hand was firmly in his girlfriends as he spoke, their fingers tangled together. "I have no idea who I can trust at the Agency."

"I have a list of most of the Agency employees who either visited your father in the last several months or he visited them." This was what she'd done since Kyle had been gone. She'd devoted it to figuring out how to get to Julia Ennis and fallen down the rabbit hole Don Radcliffe represented. "I've managed to piece together the last six months of your father's life. I have a question I haven't been able to answer though. According to the records, Julia went missing in Hong Kong. Three weeks after, your father bought a ticket to Hong Kong but he was a no show at the airport that day. I believe instead of the commercial flight he told everyone he was going on, he took a private jet owned by a billionaire real estate developer we think is a member of The Consortium. That jet went to Singapore and two days later made its way back to DC after a stop in Los Angeles."

Kyle's face flushed and Drake cursed.

She'd known it had something to do with Julia. "Did he tell you he was going to search for her?"

"He convinced my mother not to go to Hong Kong with him," Drake said with a tight expression. "She didn't go until Julia had been missing for three months."

"So we have to assume that your father brought Julia back and perhaps put her in touch with the plastic surgeon." She'd wondered about that. She'd known one of Julia's early plastic surgeries had taken place with Dr. Blumenthall—the man she'd murdered at The Reef on the night she'd kidnapped MaeBe. "Though I wouldn't think a nose job would be the first of her surgeries and while the doctor was known primarily for that, his only other expertise was with burn victims."

"There was a fire," Kyle admitted. "It was precisely why I didn't bury her body. The building we were in caught fire. I shot her. The roof started to come down and Drake and I left. The fire was pretty intense. It was a chemical company's test site. From the reports on the accident, the fire burned at over 700 degrees Fahrenheit. More than enough to burn human bones."

How hard had that been on Kyle? She'd known he'd been the one to take the shot at Julia, but listening to the hollow tone in his voice it hit her how terrible that moment must have been. How much had he loved Julia? How hard had that betrayal cut him? Had it been such a blow he could never truly come back from it?

"It's why we weren't surprised they didn't find her body." Drake took a sip from the water bottle he'd brought with him. Julia was his sister. She'd betrayed him and then he'd discovered his father had betrayed him, too. Yet his voice was steady as he spoke. "It's why we've been walking around thinking everything was fine. I would like to see any information you have on my father and to talk to you about where you think he might have stored data he considered highly valuable but also dangerous. I've looked over every place I can think of in DC, but it appears I never knew the man at all, so I might not be good at this."

Drake had support. He let the woman he loved lend him her strength. She would bet Drake didn't shove her in a cell to protect her. He would want Taylor to watch his back.

"What you need is an outsider." Charlotte looked thoughtful, as though she was playing through the scenario in her head. "Someone who's studied your father from a distance. Someone smart who knows how to dig up information other people can't access."

"Obviously we need MaeBe." Kyle wasn't going to play the game. He turned his attention directly her way. "All right. MaeBe, can you work with me? Can you help me find what I need to finally take this whole organization down?"

If only he'd asked her months ago. Things would be so different, but her answer hadn't changed. "Yes."

She started to explain what she'd discovered and tried her hardest not to think about the man sitting across from her.

* * * *

An hour later MaeBe finally closed her borrowed laptop. She'd given them everything she had, and there was a part of her that was grateful to be done. She was almost certain that now Kyle would thank her and he and Drake and Taylor would go catch that airplane they'd intended for her.

He might come back one day, but she would know it wasn't about love. She'd thought about their relationship a lot and come to the conclusion that Kyle still viewed her as the opposite of Julia Ennis, and she couldn't be that.

The truth was she and Julia had something in common now. She could see the world through Julia's eyes, and she didn't like her place in it.

She'd been prey, and now she had to be the predator.

Big Tag closed his notebook and sat back. "All that sounds like an excellent start. What do you want to do with that information?"

"I'd like to have MaeBe discuss everything she knows about my father. It might help us figure out where he might have kept his personal files." Drake had been solemn all morning, listening to the rundown of his father's crimes.

She could do that from the comfort of her cubicle. "Of course."

"And when we decide on a couple of locations that might work as a place for him to have stashed the intel, the four of us will go and hopefully find the data we need." Kyle sat up straight and stretched, moving one muscled arm over his chest. "Mae can act as our analyst and tech when we're in the field. I'm going to raid the storeroom for some equipment and then I'll set up a couple of desks for us so we can work from here, if that's all right."

Why had he said four of them? Who else was he taking?

Charlotte stopped Ian, who looked like he was about to protest. "Take whatever you need. I think you'll find we're pretty well stocked here. Your uncle likes his toys."

"Yes, and I tend to like to keep them." Ian didn't move when Charlotte stood and gathered her things. "He better not touch my flamethrower."

"What do you mean *act as your tech*?" MaeBe asked. He couldn't have said anything that would have surprised her more. Kyle didn't want her to work. She'd always gotten the feeling he would be so much happier if she'd stayed home and waited for him. Like some pathetic doll. "You want me in your ear?"

It was something she'd done many times before for ops, but almost never for Kyle. He mostly did bodyguard work, and MaeBe worked tech for investigators.

"You're the only one I would trust. I want Taylor ready to come in if she has to." He pushed back and stood. "She'll stay with you and help with tech, but if you're there then we can be assured we'll still have someone in an overwatch position."

Now she understood. She could easily do that job from here. It would be good to keep an eye on what was going on. "Sure. We'll need to coordinate and make certain we've got a secure link from here to wherever we end up."

She was thinking DC. It was where Don spent most of his time. He'd lived there for forty years and was well established in the area.

"Here?" Kyle moved for the door. "This is not a remote job. I don't want to use anything that requires long-range contact. You're coming with us. I've decided that's the best way to keep you alive. It's what I should have done in the first place. I should have faked both our deaths and then you could have learned how to run a fryer, too. We still might have to do it. Think about how you want to fake die. I'm going to grab some lunch. I saw the pizza guy dropping off a bunch of pies. Is Boomer here?"

"Boomer took the day off to go to his daughter's science fair," Charlotte said as she started out the door. "I ordered the pizza because I thought it would be easier for you guys to eat here."

"Come on, babe." Taylor took Drake's hand. "Let's get you some lunch and then we'll figure out where we're staying tonight. I have to admit, I'm intrigued by the princess castle. I think you'll look good with some glitter."

She'd expected to be stuck at Sanctum for the time being, but she hadn't counted on having roommates. She'd honestly expected him to lose his shit and storm out when he realized she wasn't going to fall in line.

Instead he moved into her space, one hand coming up to brush her cheek. "I want you to think about letting me stay with you tonight. I'll be a good boy and not kidnap you, but I will sleep outside your door if you don't let me in. I meant what I said. I made a mistake and I'll do anything I can to fix it. Can I kiss you? It's been an awful couple of days, and all I want to do is kiss you."

Her wall of ice threatened to melt completely, and she stepped back, shaking her head.

She didn't owe him anything. Not one single thing. Not comfort. Not a kiss. Nothing. He'd left her alone and he had to deal with the consequences.

"Okay." He looked so sad, his shoulders curved slightly inward. "I'll go get some lunch and then I'll get to work." He turned and started out the door as a familiar man walked in. "Hope there's some sleeping bags at the club."

Kai Ferguson did a double take as Kyle walked by. "Hey, welcome back from the dead, man." Kai was Sanctum's resident therapist. He also ran the Ferguson Clinic which was housed in the building next to Sanctum. "And if you need a sleeping bag, check the second-floor closet. Also, there are still some nap mats in the kid's room."

She tried to envision Kyle napping on mats meant for toddlers. He would need at least three of them.

Was he going to sleep outside her door again? What would he

do when they were out in the field?

The idea of being in the field sent a thrill through her. She could do something active to bring down her tormentor. She didn't have to sit and hide and feel utterly helpless.

If he was telling her the truth.

She started for the door. She wasn't hungry, but she would force herself to eat something. She would take it to her desk because sitting around a table with Kyle and Drake and Taylor would make her feel too much like a part of the team when she knew damn well she wasn't. Kyle needed her technical expertise. That was all.

"MaeBe, could I have a minute of your time?" Ian asked.

She turned and realized he hadn't moved an inch. Kai shut the door behind him, closing the three of them in.

Suspicion played along her brain. "What's going on?"

Was she about to get a lecture on why she shouldn't go on this op? Or worse. Was Ian going to find a way to gently tell her she needed to find a new job because Kyle was coming back?

"I want to talk to you, and I'm hoping you'll listen," Big Tag said.

She would do almost anything this man asked of her. Even leave if he needed her to. She wasn't actually family. He'd done everything he could to help her, but his family had to come first. "Of course. Did you need to bring in Kai? I'm not going to lose my mind because you let me go. I'll be fine."

"Let you go?" Ian's head shook. "I was serious. I'm not letting Adam poach my employees. I know you think it's nice down there, but only if you like the smell of lemongrass and douchebaggery. You won't get any adrenaline rush working for Adam. I thought you wanted to go into the field. He does not have a field."

"Ian, she thinks you're going to bring Kyle back and let her go." Kai had taken a position on Ian's right side.

Ian snorted. "Yeah, like I'm going to pick Kyle over her. Let's see. Kyle lies a lot and has so much fucking baggage he needs his own private jet to carry it all. And he randomly dies and comes back. It's obnoxious." Ian sobered. "But he's also a great guy who will someday make someone special an amazing..." He sighed. "I can't say that with a straight face. He's such a bag of cats, but he's my nephew and I have to try."

"Try?" MaeBe asked, feeling odd standing there.

"To talk you into giving him another chance," Ian said with all seriousness.

"I'm here to translate." Kai wore what she liked to think of as his daytime uniform—slacks and a button-down shirt, his long hair in a neat man bun. "He's bad at this."

"I'm excellent at everything," Ian countered. "Now, let's get this part over with so I can sneak some of that meat lovers pizza my wife thinks will be bad for me."

Ian and Charlotte were almost always in synch, with the exception of his diet. He wanted to eat like he was still twenty-two, and Charlotte steered him toward a salad every now and then.

She'd wanted that for herself and Kyle. When she thought about it, Ian and Charlotte were her relationship goals. But it turned out Kyle wasn't his uncle, and she damn straight wasn't Charlotte. "Kyle and I aren't together. I don't think we ever were. We were friends."

"So the two of you never took the relationship past friendship? All this angst has been over two buddies who like to hang but never bang?" Ian asked, the answer patently obvious.

She wanted to tell the man it wasn't any of his business. But it was. He'd made it his business when he'd taken care of her, taken the time to teach her how to protect herself. He'd put in the work and that meant she had to be honest with him. "I thought it was more. I thought we were working toward something special. I've given it a lot of thought and we kind of fell into a part-time D/s relationship. I submitted to him a lot of the time."

"Were you submitting to him when you volunteered to be Michael's backup in the field?" Tag asked.

"That was part of my job," she returned.

"I could have gotten a dozen others to do that job," Tag countered. "You wanted it. You asked me for it. Did you know Kyle would want you to stay in the office?"

"He doesn't get to tell me what to do with my career." She'd known Kyle would be upset, but she wasn't about to let that man put her in a corner.

"I believe Ian is trying to point out that you weren't and aren't all that submissive in your daily life." Kai added his two cents.

"Like most of the women at Sanctum. I think it's healthy to indulge both sides of your personality. So you were submissive in your intimate life."

She had to laugh at that. "Intimate life? He wouldn't sleep with me until the day he decided to blow his own ass up."

Ian's eyes didn't leave her, but one hand came out and patted Kai's arm. She would bet a lot that the gesture was his way of saying, *see, look, I was right.*

"Did you think the two were connected?" Kai ignored him, adjusting his glasses and getting that therapist vibe going.

She'd resisted his attempts to get her to come in for a session. She didn't need therapy. Training had been her therapy. "Well, it makes a girl think."

"MaeBe, do you believe Kyle used the fact that Julia was alive to get out of sleeping with you again?" Kai asked, his tone going soft with sympathy.

She did not want to be here, but it might do her some good to face the facts of their relationship. If she was actually going to work with Kyle, she needed to be able to function in his presence. "Logic tells me no. I don't believe he knew she was alive when he decided he was ready to move our relationship forward. But logic isn't the same as instinct."

"Hah." Ian said the word with an almost excited air. Like he'd made a discovery. "Let's talk about instincts and how some dumbasses shouldn't trust theirs because shit happened to them. I think you are not considering a couple of good points. The first is that my nephew has lost his fucking mind."

Kai held up a hand. "What Ian is trying to say is that men process trauma in different ways, and it can look very different than what we typically think given that most of our mainstream media focuses on female trauma. Mostly because of all the traumatized women out there, but men experience it as well."

So they were talking about Kyle's instincts. "I understand that. I'm sure that last day was awful for him, but I can't forgive what he put me through."

"It's not just about that last day. It's about several episodes he doesn't like to talk about because he's a good man and good men shove that shit down deep," Ian replied. "I'm proud of him for ignoring all that emotional shit."

"Ian's worried that despite Kyle's loving upbringing, he was still affected by societal ideals of how men should behave. He wants Kyle to talk about what happened and also about the incident that led to him ending up in the CIA and vulnerable to a predatory woman like Julia Ennis. The word *vulnerable* makes Ian throw up, but I think words are important."

Ian shuddered. "I just did. I think only the taste of pizza might erase it."

She ignored Ian because she knew who she was really talking to. "I thought he was in a car accident and his friend died. That's all he's ever told me. He doesn't like to talk about the past."

It had worked for them before, but now she understood if they didn't deal with his past, they couldn't have a future. Didn't have a future. Unlike most people, his past had fangs and claws and a vendetta against her.

Ian nodded. "I'm sure he put it exactly like that, but I think there's far more. He's a moron who can't understand that shit happens and there's not a lot you can do about it."

"Kyle blames himself for the accident, and that one moment sent him into a spiral," Kai explained. "Since he was young and lost his father in a similar way, Kyle has difficulty feeling like the world is a safe place. He was a kid when he lost his father, then he lost his friend, and the mind can make odd connections. Illogical connections."

"Dumbass connections that cause him to act like a damn fool," Ian insisted.

"We think Kyle..." Kai began.

But she had this one. "You think I should forgive him because he's had to deal with so much loss that the idea of losing me made him do something he wouldn't normally do. I understand that. And I understand that men have trouble processing trauma, especially when it has to do with relationships. But I can't change how he made me feel. I don't know that I can feel safe with him again."

Ian groaned. "I married a mob princess who faked her own death and left me hanging for five years. Safety is negotiable. Unless you have some unprocessed trauma of your own."

"I believe Ian is pointing out the fact that you are one of the most forgiving and kind people he knows. You have one button and Kyle pushed it," Kai said.

"A button?" She shook her head. It wasn't a hard leap to know what they were talking about. She'd lost her mom, but she'd worked through that. Her mother hadn't wanted to leave her. "I know Kyle isn't my father."

They both stared at her.

And she really thought about it. Did she know Kyle wasn't her dad? It was one thing to acknowledge that a person or event hurt her. It was another to dig into that pain and figure out how it affected the rest of her relationships. Her father had chosen another woman over her. Other children.

Wasn't that what Kyle had done? Julia Ennis walked back into his life and he was done with you. He was biding his time until someone better came along. Just like your dad. He never loved you. Only your mom. The minute she was gone he was out the door. No one is going to...

"Damn it." She sat down. "I hate it when I have to be self-reflective."

Ian slapped at the conference table. "It's the worst. It's so much better to ignore it all."

She sighed because there were those tears again. She hadn't felt them in months and months, and now they seemed to well up. Now they seemed like a temptation she couldn't afford.

"Mae, you're traumatized, too, and you won't talk about it," Kai said quietly. "Neither one of you will talk about it. She nearly killed you."

"It wasn't that bad." It was only a broken arm.

That wasn't all she broke. She broke you, and you aren't willing to do the work to heal yourself. You would rather ignore it because healing yourself means opening yourself up to that pain again.

Are you willing to spend the rest of your life encased in ice?

She called it anger and practicality, but wasn't it fear?

"See, I told you it was fine," Big Tag agreed. "She's great. She's happy and acting completely normal, and she's not going to let this affect the rest of her life. Kyle was a dumbass and he hurt her, and he gets what he deserves."

"Fuck you, Ian. That's not fair." Her chest felt too tight.

"But isn't that right?" Ian's expression had softened. "Don't we get what we deserve?"

Wasn't that what her dad had told her? She got the grades she deserved. Later they'd found out she couldn't see the chalkboard and needed glasses, but the lesson had been learned. When she got robbed a few years back, her stepmom had asked her why she'd been walking alone at night. What had she been wearing? If she didn't get a job, it was because she hadn't worked hard enough. The world told her time and time again.

Julia Ennis had told her. Julia Ennis believed she deserved Kyle because she was the strongest and the smartest.

How many times had some asshole thought they deserved sex with her because they'd bought dinner? How many times had some guy thought because she'd been nice to him that he deserved a relationship with her?

Vulnerable. She'd always felt vulnerable around those types of men. She'd never considered the fact that there were also those types of women.

Men were vulnerable, too. Men were vulnerable to women who felt entitled to what they wanted, who burned down lives to get it.

Was that voice in her head a product of that world?

She sat down as the first tear started to fall. "I did not deserve what she did to me and neither did he."

Kai sat as well, reaching out a hand to cover hers. "I am so glad to hear you say that. Let's talk."

Ian stood, one big hand slapping his perfectly tight stomach. "My work here is done. It's pizza time."

The father figure of her world strode out, and she honored him and herself by finally opening up.

Chapter Thirteen

Kyle looked up from his laptop at the sound of the knock. "Hey."

MaeBe stood in the doorway, her bag in hand. "Hey. I'm surprised you were in your uncle's office. I thought you might be downstairs at your desk once you figured out it's still open. They cleaned it out, but all of your things are in a box. I could get that for you if you like."

"I didn't have that much anyway." He wasn't like the other bodyguards who had evidence of a life outside of work on their desks. There had been no family photos or bobbleheads of sports figures. None of the Funko pop figurines that decorated MaeBe's desk. She had tons of tchotchkes around her cubicle office. "My uncle left early to go do something at the club, and I thought I could work in here without the whole world coming up to tell me what an idiot I am."

He'd snuck into Ian's office for a couple of reasons, the most important being he knew she'd come looking for him, and he wanted privacy. He wanted to be alone with her for a few minutes.

The conversation he'd had with his mother had played around his brain all day.

He had to shove down his fear and show this woman she could trust him.

"You weren't an idiot. You were doing what you thought best."

She walked in and sank onto one of the chairs across from the big desk Kyle had been sitting at. "Tell me something. Were you avoiding your old desk because you didn't want to see your former coworkers? Or was there another reason?"

If she wanted to talk, he could at least be honest. "I was happy here. I liked working here. So much more than I thought I would. So I didn't want to get comfortable. I didn't want to sit at that desk and pretend I wouldn't have to leave it again."

She seemed to think about that for a moment. "I suppose that's one of the reasons I'm not sure I want to get close to you again. Even when I know it's not a forever thing."

"I would like for it to be. I know you're not ready to talk about it, but I hope over the course of the next few weeks you'll feel more comfortable with me. I hope I can make you trust me again."

"I spent most of the afternoon talking to Kai." She sighed and sat back. "I know you're not my father, but I think my relationship with him is affecting how I reacted to you leaving me behind. I knew quickly that you weren't dead, so I had to try to process all of it in a very short period of time. The fact that Julia was alive and I didn't understand your relationship with her, the kidnapping, the building blowing up—it was all so much. I didn't even mourn you. I was in shock and then I realized it was all a trick."

The fact that she saw the situation that way made his heart ache. "It wasn't supposed to be a trick on you."

"It's hard for me to believe that it didn't have anything to do with me."

"I never said that," Kyle corrected. "It had everything to do with you. If you hadn't been there, if you hadn't been in my life, I wouldn't have done it. If I'd been single, I would have turned to my uncle and put a whole lot of this in his lap. I'm thinking about doing it now. I think the thing I did wrong was I immediately decided to play by her rules. It was an instinct."

She snorted slightly, the first sign of emotion since she'd walked in. "Yeah, well don't talk to your uncle or Kai about our instincts. They think we're all fucked up and in need of therapy."

"I've kind of been in therapy," he admitted. "It was a weird form of therapy, and I didn't get it until I figured out that Sandra's wife, in addition to being incredibly creative with a fryer, is a licensed therapist. And I wondered why my stepdad and uncle thought Sandra's would be a great place to go. I hate therapists. I hate it when they don't actually say anything at all and suddenly you're talking about your childhood trauma. Angie was good at that. She was good at getting me to see I wasn't fair to you or anyone in my life. I thought I was being unselfish, but I was acting on a selfish impulse. I didn't want to worry about you. I wanted some distance between us because I was so fucking afraid of being the reason you died."

"Because you were the reason your friend died?" MaeBe asked quietly.

His stomach took a deep dive, but he had to talk to her. About everything. If there was one truth his mother had pointed out it was the fact that they couldn't be a couple if he held back from her.

"I don't talk about it a lot. We were stuck in the car together for…" It had felt like forever. At night he could still hear the way Ken had labored to breathe. "I think it was about twenty minutes before they got us out. He wasn't dead on impact. He died from blood loss, and he blamed me the whole time. I know that he was in pain and angry because I was supposed to drive. It should have been me, but no I had to have a couple of drinks so I would feel confident enough to talk to this woman I liked."

It was getting easier to talk, almost pleasant in a way. Like a slow letting off of steam that had pressurized his life for so long.

Those hours spent with Angie had done something to him, had opened up some part of himself he'd long denied. A little piece of the Kyle he'd been.

A glimpse of the Kyle he wanted to be.

"That wasn't your fault."

"And yet in a way it was," Kyle said. "Like my father. I didn't mean to get sick in the middle of the night during a bad storm. I didn't mean to have a fever that sent my dad out when no one should have been driving. But I did."

"And I'm sure your mom thinks if only she'd made sure she had Ibuprofen," MaeBe argued, sympathy plain in her voice.

"Probably," he admitted. "She told me later on that it wasn't my fault but it's buried deep inside me. It's a weed that grew when Kenny died. A weed that started to strangle me. I went into the military because the people around me worried that if I didn't find something to center and focus me, I would end up in a very bad way. I was self-destructive."

"But the Navy didn't work the way they wanted it to, did it?" MaeBe asked, but she probably already knew the answer.

"I think if I'd stayed strictly in the Navy, it might have. But I didn't. I went Special Forces, and within two years I was working intelligence and I met Ms. White."

"Julia?"

He nodded. It wasn't a surprise that MaeBe knew about the Agency use of what he thought of as Crayon names. He'd been Mr. Black, Mr. White, Mr. Brown. Julia had preferred Ms. White. "I think one of the reasons I've never told you this story is the fact that I don't exactly come out of it looking great. Or stable. I didn't find my stability until I came home and started working here."

She sat back, her expression softening. "You don't have to tell me about it now."

He knew later wouldn't make the situation better. "Do you want to hear it?"

"Will you be honest?"

"With you? Absolutely. With myself? I don't know. I don't know where I am with that."

She paused, staring at him as though making a decision. "Did you love her?"

He let a moment pass before he answered, thinking about the question carefully so he could give the woman he did love as much truth as possible. "I thought I did. What she was excellent at doing was making me forget who I was, who I wanted to be. When I was with Julia, I was someone else. Especially in the beginning. I was freaking James Bond, and I didn't have to worry about anything but the next mission. I liked intelligence work so much more than running ops in the Navy. When we were in the field, we were in charge. We made decisions. We treated the people around us like chess pieces, and it was great because I didn't have to care about a chess piece. In a lot of ways, I didn't have to care about Julia."

"What is that supposed to mean? You asked the woman to marry you. You intended to bring her home to your family."

"Did I?" It was hard to think about himself during those crazy

221

days. "She was dangerous. She lived on the knife's edge, and it was intoxicating. It was more about the adrenaline high I got from being around her. There were no normal days between Julia and I. There weren't game nights and movie watching. Life was one long and deadly game, and for a time I enjoyed playing it. I didn't have to think about my family or the ghosts that seemed to chase me during those days. They all faded away because the mission was all that mattered. Sex with her was different than anything I'd had in my life before. It was intense and sometimes almost violent, and I hated it in the end. I hated how there was nothing soft about it. I asked her to marry me because she pushed me to do it. By that time I was thoroughly invested in my job, and I didn't see a way out. I didn't think. She said it was time and I didn't want to fight. Because the fights… I hated who I became in those days."

"I think I might have had a similar experience, though it wasn't with another person." She tucked a lock of hair behind her left ear. She wasn't wearing the normal three earrings she typically wore. Just a pair of gold studs he'd given her for her birthday. "I've told you how I got into some trouble when I was a kid with hacking. Well, I never really gave it up. I treated it like a diet. I had to stay away from certain places and I would be safe. After my mom died and I was going through things with my dad, I fell off that wagon."

"This was when Hutch found you?"

She nodded. "Yep. I know he thinks I was being a good hacktivist, but there was a part of me that knew I was getting in deep. I knew it wasn't as innocent as it seemed, and the thought of being recruited by the bad guys…intrigued me. I think I was acting out. Angry with the world and the fact that I had zero control over the most important things in my life. Now I realize I would probably be in jail if Hutch hadn't made that contact. So I understand the whole living on the knife's edge thing."

"It gets old." He needed her to understand he wasn't interested in that life again. He loved the life he'd found with her. "At the time I wanted to be away from my family because I didn't think I deserved them at first, and then because I didn't want them to know all the things I'd done. The most shameful being allowing Julia to manipulate me into doing things that went counter to my morals and my job."

Her eyes went wide. "What?"

"I didn't realize it at the time, but she sometimes used me to further her Consortium work. She held a higher rank than me. She was on the same footing as Drake, and so I didn't question it when she gave me orders. I read what she put in front of me, and I did my job like the good soldier I was. That was how I ended up figuring it out. I thought I was taking out the bomb maker for a certain terrorist group. It was only by chance that I was going through an Internet news site that covered the man's murder. He wasn't a bomb maker. He was a landowner in Vietnam who happened to own a long stretch of property a hotel group had been trying to build a resort on for years. When I assassinated him, his son took over and immediately sold the land."

"Kyle," she began.

He felt sick laying out the truth of his life. "That's who I am, MaeBe. That's why I don't talk about my past. I've killed eight people I'm sure of. A few of them in self-defense. One was a mass murdering dictator. There were a couple I can verify were dangerous enemies. I feel okay about those. But that man... He should be alive and living on his land with his grandkids. I didn't bother to verify anything."

She leaned toward him. "Your CIA handler gave you an assignment. I suspect she also gave you a doctored file that you read."

"Of course."

"That was your verification. If I'm your tech and I tell you there's someone coming up behind you, are you going to verify the intel or act on it?"

"It's not the same, but I do understand. I feel like I keep making the same mistakes, and I don't know how to stop." He was so tired. "I love you. I've never loved anyone the way I love you, and I do not feel worthy of you. I feel like if I'm not careful, I'm going to lose you, and I won't survive that. If she kills you, I'll lie down beside you and I won't get up. It doesn't matter if you can't love me. It's just the truth."

Her eyes were shiny with tears, and Kyle felt no small amount of relief. She was starting to feel, starting to come out of the shocked, shut-down state she'd been in.

"I don't know if I can trust in your love. If you'd asked me to go with you, I would have dumped my life and done anything you wanted," she admitted. "I was so in love with you. I was ready to start my life with you, and I would have done it on the run if I had to. But that wasn't what happened. I worry if we try now, I'll spend the rest of my life waiting for you to disappear."

He'd opened a wound he wasn't sure he could close again. "I can only give you my word. I can only promise you that I'm working on the problem and I will fight my every instinct. I think my real instinct is to always pick misery because I'm punishing myself. I want to stop. I want a life, a real life with you, but my past is trying to drag me back. It feels like I've been swimming in deep waters and every time I manage to get to the surface, she drags me back under. I don't think she'll stop until one of us is dead."

"Then you make sure it's not you." MaeBe wiped the tears from her cheeks, obviously steeling herself. "You need to ensure that she's gone this time and that no one can use you or anyone else like that again. Whatever Radcliffe put in that file has to be something we can use to take The Consortium apart."

He believed that, too. But the thought of MaeBe getting involved… He forced the fear aside. "Are you ready for this?"

She nodded. "I am. I've been preparing for this the whole time you've been gone. Your uncle thinks I'm ready. If you need me to…"

He wasn't about to make her prove anything. "No. I don't need proof. I trust you. But I need you to understand that you're the junior operative. You have to follow my instructions in the field."

"I get that. And I also get that I'll be behind a computer most of the time." For once she sounded excited.

There was a knock on the door and Yasmin stuck her head in.

"Hey, I heard you were in here," Yasmin said. "Uhm, there's a woman on the line looking for you. I thought no one was supposed to know where you are."

A chill went up his spine.

"Yasmin, I'm going to need you to try to trace the caller. Hutch has protocols in place." MaeBe stood and looked cool and competent. "Tell her you're transferring her."

What was Mae doing? "Or she could say I'm not here."

MaeBe shook her head. "Julia knows exactly where you are. I don't want to lose a chance to get a possible location for her. I want to know if she's here in Dallas. If you wonder how you can start making me feel safe around you, start trusting me. Start by letting me have a say in this."

He didn't want to. He hated the fact that she knew his shame. The last thing he wanted was to have her listen to him talk to Julia. "She told Drake I should expect a call from her and that I better answer. I haven't been in a place where she could get hold of me. I suspect that's why she tried to hurt you. It was a message to me. See."

That brat's eyes actually rolled. "Yes, you control the world and everyone in it. When did you become such a broody boy? I always thought I would love a broody vampire. Now I realize how obnoxious that would be. Thanks for ruining paranormal romance for me. Yas, we'll take the call in here, and don't forget to start that program."

Yasmin hurried back to her desk.

And Kyle got ready to face his biggest mistake.

* * * *

The landline on Ian's desk buzzed, and a weird thrill went through MaeBe.

She'd been wanting to face this particular bad guy for a long time. That was where that excitement was coming from. It had nothing to do with the fact that she was going to be working with Kyle, and he seemed to actually be trying.

She'd listened to his story and realized they had a lot in common. Neither of them had really gotten over what happened in the past.

Could they work through it together?

Did she even want to try?

Kyle's jaw was tight as he reached out to push the button that connected the call to the speaker. "This is Hawthorne."

A sigh came over the line. "Do you have any idea how good it is to hear your voice?"

The woman sounded like this was an ordinary call between two

225

people in a relationship.

She needed to stop thinking about Kyle as the asshole who hurt her and start thinking about the fact that he'd been in an abusive relationship, one where his partner had manipulated him into doing things he would regret for the rest of his life.

And yet he'd never questioned MaeBe. He'd never worried she was doing something she shouldn't. He'd been a complete freak about her getting potentially hurt, but he hadn't watched her carefully.

"I wish we could say the same," MaeBe replied because she wasn't going to let Kyle deal with her. She remembered well how he'd handled that damn lawyer asshole. He wouldn't have sat by and forced her to negotiate with him. "What do you want, Julia?"

There was a pause before Julia answered, all the sweetness stripped from her tone. "Well, we could start with you leaving so I can talk to my fiancé."

Kyle stood and started to pace, a blank expression on his face.

"Not happening, and just so we're all clear on this, he is not your fiancé. He is my boyfriend, and I'm going to ask you to leave him alone."

A low chuckle came over the line. "Did kitty finally decide to sharpen her claws?"

She hoped Hutch's program was working its magic. "I took your advice and got some training."

"Well you didn't take all of it. I do believe I told you to stay away from my fiancé," Julia pointed out.

"I did for a long time, but he came back and now he assures me I can't get rid of him even if I want to. I did kick him in the balls though."

"You hurt him?" Julia made the question an accusation.

"I made myself plain. Now we have an agreement. He doesn't tell me what to do and he gets to keep his balls intact. I'm going to ask again, what do you want, Julia? Besides me dead. I figured that one out when your loving employees took their shot last night."

"Well, in my defense, they weren't supposed to kill you," Julia admitted. "They were supposed to take out your boy toy bodyguard and bring you to me since Kyle has refused to take my calls. Now I think I will kill you because I've put up with this nonsense long enough. Tell me something, Kyle, did you have fun killing Ed?"

"Oh, we both know that wasn't his name," MaeBe replied. "He was a dirtbag named Jeremy Harris, and I killed him. You need to train your boys better. He was about to kill Kyle."

"Well Kyle wasn't supposed to be there," Julia snarled back. "Kyle was supposed to be staying away from you. Babe, have you decided to put her on the playing field and see how she fares against me? Is that how you want to play this? You want to put her in between us?"

Kyle shuddered. "Absolutely not. I wanted to keep her out of this, but it has been pointed out to me that if I want a relationship with the woman I love, I have to stop treating her like she's a delicate piece of china."

"I assure you, I'm going to break her," Julia vowed.

"I'm sure you'll try," Kyle replied.

"This isn't going to work. I know you're angry with me." Julia's voice had gone low again. "I had hoped that choosing you over my father would have softened your attitude a bit. He gave me everything, but I knew who I had to pick in that moment."

Kyle's head shook. "You should have let him kill me because I'm not coming back to you."

"All right. You're still angry," Julia conceded. "I can understand that. I can even understand punishing me with that ridiculous little girl."

"Ridiculous little woman, please." She had her standards. And she wasn't all that ridiculous. Was it silly to enjoy board games and coloring her hair? Life was short. Why should she spend all of it plotting and planning and worrying?

Julia ignored her. "It's not like I've been faithful. I understand physical needs, Kyle, but you can't push me much further."

She was a legit crazy person.

She felt better talking to this woman now. Had she imagined that Julia was some demon who'd tormented her? She was a kind of sad chick who didn't know when to let go. "Why don't you tell us what you want from Kyle and I'll explain to you how you're not going to get it."

"I think I'll get whatever I want because if I have to, I'll start killing people," Julia said in a husky tone, as though the very idea of killing was sexy to her.

These were the games she played with Kyle. Sick games that she thought were foreplay.

"Just tell me what you want," Kyle said, moving toward the desk.

"I want the files my father left behind." Julia finally got to the point. "Drake has to know where they are."

"Why would Drake know where your father hid burn files? He didn't even know your father was a double agent." Kyle pointed out the simple truth.

"He knows my dad better than anyone but me. And he still has contact with our mom. I can't exactly ask her advice since I did try to kill her," Julia said. "I've looked in the places I think he might have kept it and it's not there. I want you and Drake to find it for me. Bring it to me and I might not hurt your family the way you've hurt me. When you bring me what I need, I will have an unassailable place in the organization and that will be good for all of us. For you and me and Drake. You don't have to work if you don't want to. I'll have more than enough money for all of us."

"You want to make Kyle a house husband?" She tried to envision it. And couldn't.

"I want to take care of the man I love," Julia shot back. "And you, little girl, better walk away now. I'll get you one way or another if you don't."

"And my little dog, too?" She couldn't not poke the bear it seemed.

"I mean it, bitch." Julia sounded like a pressure cooker ready to explode. "Get me what I want or I'll go after the kiddos. Do you think Kyle's sister can handle me? Or his youngest brother? How about his mom?"

"I think you're truly psychotic, but so far you've also been practical and that's why I'm going to explain a few truths to you. Don't threaten his family again. Right now we're keeping this whole thing quiet because none of us is interested in causing a huge scene and bringing the authorities in. Ian has stayed in the background. I assure you if you lay a hand on his family, we will all come for you. Every single one of us. We will take all of the resources McKay-Taggart has collected over the years and turn it on you. We won't care about the business. We won't care about profits. We will have one goal and one goal only—killing Julia Ennis in the most painful way possible. Imagine how helpful you will be to your Consortium overlords when twenty or thirty of the world's best-trained operatives and assassins and hackers are focusing all their energy on you. If you so much as mildly inconvenience one of the kids, we will take this war to an entirely different level, and you cannot win."

"I think you're underestimating me," Julia countered. "I have resources you can't imagine."

MaeBe needed to point out some more truth to this woman. "Only as long as you're valuable to them. What happens when you can't work anymore because you're being hunted? You won't be able to settle in and work over your target because you'll always be on the run. And don't think you can simply leave the States. We've got an office in Europe, and Tennessee Smith handles our African branch. We have a couple of people who know Asia well. We'll hunt you down wherever you go. Or you can back the fuck off."

"I want that data," Julia insisted.

"Then you should hurry up and find it." If the program hadn't run its course by now it never would. She was done with Julia Ennis. She wasn't going to give her another second of Kyle's time.

MaeBe hung up on her.

Kyle was staring at her, his jaw open a bit.

"Well, you've seen me deal with the electric company and Ticketmaster. Did you think I would be nice to the woman who wants to kill me? I want to know what her appeal is."

Kyle shrugged. "I was going through a self-destructive phase."

Yasmin ran in the room, pushing the door back. "She's in London. I've got all the data."

"Excellent. Why don't you go and give that to Drake and Taylor? I need to talk to Kyle. And send Ian a text letting him know Julia Ennis contacted us and I will send him a report shortly."

Yasmin nodded and walked out of the office.

MaeBe turned to Kyle. That woman was toxic, and she'd infected Kyle's life. If Kyle had been attracted to her because she was the polar opposite of Julia, then she wasn't sure why that was a bad thing.

He wasn't in love with Julia. That wasn't why he didn't talk about her, wasn't why he'd run the minute she'd shown up in his life again.

He was ashamed of her, ashamed that he'd let himself get in deep.

"Who are you?" Kyle asked with a huff. "Because that was pretty badass. It actually made sense. I have to warn my mom, but I'm pretty sure you made Julia think twice about fucking with us."

"We need to be vigilant, but I gave her something to think about." She moved so she was standing in front of him. "Now it's time to give you something to think about. I am not the same person you fell in love with."

A hint of a smile hit his lips. "You are. Deep down. People do not stay the same all their lives. They grow and change, and sometimes we get off the right path because some terrible thing made us veer away. But we can get back on the right path. I have to believe that. I have to believe that the person I want to be is in here somewhere, and I can find him. You're wrong about one thing, though. You think I'm in love with the woman you were, but I'm in awe of the woman you are right now. I want you happy, baby. I miss your crazy hair not because I think you're hotter with it. I miss it because you loved it. But do not doubt that the MaeBe who stands before me and takes out everyone who acts like an asshole is a woman I can love."

Every word went straight to her heart, but she wasn't ready. "I don't know how to forgive you."

"You don't have to. Not right away. Let me work for it."

"I don't even know if I want to." She wasn't sure she wanted to put herself in that position again.

What position? The one where you have a chance at love and a family? What are you going to do, Mae? Skip the whole part of your life where you might be happy because there's a chance you get your heart broken?

But it had broken so brutally.

Was she going to let Kyle's fear break them, too?

"Give me the chance to show you why you should," Kyle prompted. "I'm willing to take the chance that you never forgive me, that you use me for sex and walk away. I'm willing to take the chance because I'm going to do things right this time. I let you tug the tiger's tail. I kept my mouth shut and let you deal with her when all I wanted to do was hang up and go on the run."

"That's no way to live a life." She had to get out of the limbo she found herself in. They couldn't go on this way.

"Am I doing the right thing?" His head came down to rest against her forehead. "I stayed away because I worried I wasn't ready, that I was toxic. I know it was my relationship with her that was toxic, but it infected me. I don't want it to infect you. I love you."

Julia was a virus, and he was worried he would pass on the pain to her. "I have to think about it. But I can do this."

She wrapped her arms around his chest and felt a shudder go through him.

He'd run from more than her. He'd run from anyone who could give him comfort, who could hold him and show him the world wasn't completely trash. She'd been surrounded by friends and family—his family. He'd been alone.

"You're a dumbass," she whispered.

He held her tighter. "I know."

There was another knock and Kyle stepped back, taking a long steadying breath. "That should be reinforcements. I know I upended your life, but I swear I'm going to make it right. Starting tonight. We might be in lockdown, but that doesn't mean we can't have fun. Come on in."

The door opened and Hutch and Noelle were there. Hutch had the big bag he used to cart around board games. Noelle was carrying a tote bag that likely contained whatever she'd baked this week.

"We brought game night to you," Hutch announced. "I'm planning on leaving *Cards Against Humanity* cards tucked away all over this office so Big Tag can find some of the most rancid phrases he's ever seen at random times."

"And I'm going to leave him lemon tea cakes as an apology," Noelle explained.

A big blond god of a man walked in, carrying way too many pizza boxes. Well, it would be too many if he wasn't here.

"Boomer." She hadn't seen him in a couple of days, and she'd missed the big guy.

"Hey, Mae. Lou won first place at her science fair. I'm

supposed to thank you for all the help." Boomer nodded Kyle's way. "Dude, I thought you were still alive. Your funeral was fun. Sad you missed it. Welcome back, man."

Kyle leaned over. "I'm going to go and help Drake and Taylor, but I thought you would enjoy a game night. Sorry about the pizza. It's kind of the easiest food to get when you're hiding from assassins. Also when you have to feed a Boomer."

"You're not staying?"

"I want you to have fun. I want you to forget about all the crap for a while, and I don't think you can do that with me around."

Maybe it was the talk with Kai earlier or finally facing Julia and realizing that while she was dangerous, she was also pathetic. She wasn't some glamorous force of nature. She was a woman who'd been manipulated by her father and twisted into something vile. Julia had probably been born a narcissist, and if she'd been raised normally, she would have been a crappy mom and wife and that would have been the end of it. What her stepfather had done had taken that deep-down instinct to always center herself and turned it malignant.

Kyle was a dumbass who should have gone into therapy but instead he'd fallen into a toxic relationship and there but for the grace of god…

"Why don't we take a night off?" She couldn't pretend like things were normal if he wasn't here. "Go and ask Drake and Taylor if they want to play. Do we have anything that will play seven?"

Hutch started pulling out his games. "Maddie and Deke will be by soon, so it's nine. I thought we could split up and play two. Deke is bringing beer. He's excited about pranking Big Tag's office too. We're never allowed in here alone. It's like we're in Dad's bedroom."

"Especially given how Ian and Charlotte spend so much of their time in here," Noelle said with a shake of her head. "I was up here once waiting on Hutch and I was going to bring Ian some cupcakes I'd made. I should not have opened that door."

Maybe Ian and Charlotte should still be her relationship goals.

"Are you sure?" Kyle asked, but there was an eager expression on his face.

Suddenly she was surrounded by friends, and the world didn't seem so dark. It might be a mistake, but it was time to start making those again.

It was time to start living again.

"I'm sure. And Boomer, there better be some veggies on those pizzas."

Kyle went off to invite their new friends. And for the first time since he'd left, she felt a bit like herself again.

It felt damn good.

Chapter Fourteen

Two hours later Julia was still pissed, still staring at the phone and wishing she wasn't a continent away.

The little bitch had hung up on her.

It was obvious that Mae Beatrice Vaughn had not heeded her warnings. She remembered how good it had felt to break that sad girl's arm when she'd doubled down on defiance. She'd been fucking with Mae since the moment she'd realized Kyle was using her as a replacement. She wanted to use the word *placeholder*, but it was time to get real with herself.

Kyle was scared, and that fear of her was coming out as anger. He wasn't playing games. He was serious, and that meant it was time to get serious about the woman who was standing in her way.

The question was how. How seriously should she take the threat? The Taggarts wouldn't want to lose their business over what was basically a lover's spat.

Sometimes in life one had to bluff, and sometimes that bluff had to be called.

She picked up her cell and called the only man in the damn world she could actually count on. Well, mostly. He'd fucked up the first plan, but then they hadn't realized at the time that Kyle would be there. Had she merely been protected by that West Rycroft person, MaeBe Vaughn wouldn't be so arrogant. She would be all tortured, and Kyle would likely be on his way to "saving" her.

It might be time to simply take what she wanted. The question was how to bait the trap. He wouldn't walk into it for nothing, and she couldn't risk Kyle getting hurt.

"This is John."

"How many men do you have left? You lost one, right?" She'd sort of read the report he'd sent. She'd had other things to worry about. It wasn't like she didn't have a job. Chasing after Kyle was merely a hobby, and since that day when she'd been forced to kill her father, her position was a tenuous one.

She had to prove herself all over again and that rankled.

"I still have three mercenaries. I lost the other John," he stated flatly.

Johns stuck together, apparently. Bros before hos and all that. "Is there a problem?"

A long sigh came over the line. "No. Of course not. He was sloppy. I just wish we hadn't lost him on a side job, that's all."

"You know why it's important. It's not all about Kyle." She had to balance a careful line with him. John had been servicing her physical needs for a long time now. It was inevitable he would get jealous. "It's about finding those files my father left behind. It's about taking back my place in the group. Once I find that intel of my father's, I'll be in a position to move forward with the board."

If what she suspected was in that file, she might be able to take over the whole fucking thing. Her father had been a cautious man. He'd kept the data as leverage in case someone decided to push him out.

She intended to be bolder. She intended to take over. That would be good for John.

Until she killed him because he knew too much. He'd been an excellent assistant/guard/living vibrator, but all good things came to an end and when Kyle was back in his place she didn't intend to dishonor the vows they'd made when he'd asked her to marry him. She would forgive him the pudgy hacker and in return she would get rid of John so Kyle never had to worry that she might cheat.

But she needed him for now.

"I understand," came the half-hearted reply. "You think your brother is going to find it first, and you need something to ensure that he turns it over to you instead. MaeBe Vaughn is a much better target than Taylor Cline."

Her brother's girlfriend was a lying bitch who was also quite capable of handling herself in a fight. Taylor had been working a years' long op to infiltrate The Consortium that would have worked if Julia hadn't been involved. At least that was the way Julia had presented it to the board. "No, I don't particularly want to tangle with her in a personal sense. If you need to kill her, do it from a distance. It would be better to do it after we get the files. I think my brother could prove vengeful if something happened before. Are they all together? I know Kyle is at his uncle's office."

A pause came over the line. "Did you call him?"

"I needed for him to hear my voice, to know I'm serious." She was sure John hated the fact that she'd called Kyle, but he simply had to deal with it. She wasn't about to tell him that Kyle had let his whore talk for him. "Are they all at McKay-Taggart?"

"Yes." John was watching Kyle's office for her. The Consortium had rented out an apartment across from the building where they could watch who came in and out. After the McKay-Taggart firm had gotten involved in their cases one too many times, the board had decided to allow her to monitor the group. "She and Kyle are up there, and I suspect she's not spending the evening alone. Your brother and Taylor have been there since this morning."

"Who else is in the building?" She didn't think they could get through actual building security, but she had a plant in the garage. She would have preferred to place her own man there, a Consortium-trained agent, but she'd had no luck getting through the hiring process. So she'd improvised. One of the long-term parking garage attendants had a little boy with cancer, and wouldn't you know it? She could get him in a clinical trial. But only if he played ball. As far as she knew Timmy was still a living cancer warrior, and it was time for his pops to pay up.

"They've shut down for the day, but Greg Hutchins and his wife and Brian Ward showed up a couple of hours ago. Since then Deke and Maddie Murphy also joined them. So they're surrounded by well-trained agents. I don't think we're getting close tonight."

Oh, he of little faith. "You never know. They think they're safe while they're in the building. I think everyone who comes in after hours is required to sign in. Let's see if I can tempt one of the rabbits to come downstairs. If I can do that, you can use the rabbit to get MaeBe to come down. I want her taken into custody, and then we'll open negotiations with my brother and Kyle. Drake will know where to look. I haven't been able to figure it out at all."

"And what am I supposed to do with the rabbit?"

She would prefer killing whichever woman she managed to catch. Noelle Hutchins and Maddie Murphy had caused her no end of trouble, but their dead bodies would likely cause more. Still, Kyle would take the threat to MaeBe more seriously if there was a dead body. The question was how much did she honestly believe Taggart and his people would care about a woman who was merely an employee? There was also the fact that she still had a card to play with Kyle. If Taggart truly loved his sister-in-law's son, he would back off once he realized the power she had over him.

She'd played nice up until now. It was all MaeBe's fault that one of her friends was about to die.

"Kill her and take MaeBe to the safe house. I'll meet you once we know where my brother thinks we should go," she said, her decision made.

She hung up and grabbed her laptop. The intelligence she'd gathered on the people around Kyle was there. All it would take was the right temptation and her trap would be set.

* * * *

MaeBe took a swig of her beer and sat back, feeling more relaxed than she had in forever. She glanced over at the opposite end of the conference table where Kyle was playing *Wingspan* with Deke, Hutch, and Drake. Boomer had chosen to join the ladies. She, Taylor, Maddie, and Noelle had decided on *Dead of Winter*. Surviving a zombie attack with friends was exactly what she needed.

It made her feel almost like she could survive whatever attack Julia Ennis came up with next—because there would absolutely be a next. She'd tried to give the woman something to think about, but she didn't doubt that Julia would come back and likely hard.

"It doesn't look like the guys are close to being done." Noelle yawned and stretched before reaching for her cane. She'd been in an accident as a teen and relied on the cane. "I think I could use some tea."

Boomer stood, pushing his chair back. "I think I'll see what's left in the fridge. I could eat."

Boomer could always eat. Luckily he'd turned out to also be a good cook. She'd liked living with Boomer and was so happy to see him settled down with his new wife and stepdaughter.

Maddie chuckled. "I brought some sandwiches in case we ran late. See. I know what to do when I'm on Boomer duty. Come on. I think there's some hot chocolate in the break room, too."

Noelle was already on her feet, and she walked over to where her husband sat, leaning over to kiss the top of his head. "You want some hot chocolate? I know. It's a silly question."

Hutch smiled up at his wife. "With lots of marshmallows."

"I can help," MaeBe began.

Boomer waved her off. "We've got it. You get to pack up. I hate packing up. I always feel like a giant trying to get those tiny pieces in the baggies."

Hutch was an organized board gamer. His cards were all in plastic sleeves, and there were different bags for the pieces. "Will do. And I will take a hot tea. I think there's some green tea in there."

"Same for me." Taylor started to gather the cards. "How about we wait for the guys to be done and then we could play some *Monikers*? It's my favorite."

Monikers was a party game and one MaeBe usually was slightly drunk for, but she could compromise. She loved watching Kyle try to figure out how to act out the game's odd prompts. She should make up a deck of McKay-Taggart prompts. Over the last couple of days she could come up with a few that would be fun to work out. Alex's Malodourous Murder Mobile. Kyle's Swollen Ball Sac. She could easily act that one out.

"So are you two okay?" Taylor kept her voice down but there was music playing and the conference table was big enough that she wasn't worried Kyle would hear them.

He had his head down, studying the board. He'd been reluctant at first, but his competitive nature had taken over and now he was incredibly serious about games.

He'd bent so much for her. Shouldn't his actions count for

something?

"I don't know." She'd had a great talk with Taylor this morning, but they'd stuck to work-related topics. Taylor had talked about her previous work with the Agency and how she'd specialized in building online personas so real, one of them had been recruited by The Consortium. But how deep did she want to get with her new friend? "I'm still processing the fact that he catfished me for months."

Taylor grimaced. "Yeah. That was actually pretty pathetic. He spent all his time trying to make sure he could be ready to go online. He planned his whole day around it. And if you canceled on him… That boy can get morose."

She wasn't sure if she was supposed to be flattered by that. "He could have called."

"I think in some ways he was sure he wasn't going to be able to come home. I didn't talk to him much about it, but I would bet he thought he was doing the right thing by you," Taylor said quietly. "I was kind of a victim of Julia's wrath, too, though I didn't meet her until over a year later. I spent some time with Drake shortly after they discovered what Julia had been doing. We got stuck in a safe house together." A smile came over her face, her short auburn hair brushing along her jaw. "It was not long before we decided to give a relationship a try. We made all these plans and roughly three minutes after we slept together the first time the Agency hauled me away because they thought my father was a double agent and Drake did nothing."

That was hard to believe because Drake seemed to never take his eyes off his girlfriend. She'd known Drake for a while, and she would never have guessed he would be such a huge fan of holding hands. "Nothing?"

Taylor shrugged. "There was a lot of talk about how he'd planned to bust me out eventually, but I'm not sure how serious he was about that. I decided a long time ago that it doesn't matter. I understand why he reacted the way he did. His sister had turned out to be the bad guy. It was a world-changing thing for him. He'd always known she could be a bit ruthless, but the idea that she was completely amoral was a shock. Was it that surprising that I might be, too?"

That hadn't been their problem. "Kyle never thought I was a bad guy."

"No. He thought you were the best part of him, and he had to protect you." Taylor sat back, her well-manicured hand toying with the beer bottle in front of her. "I spent time with him, and you have no idea how he can talk about you. You are the sun in his sky, but it's not the kind of thing where he doesn't get you're not perfect. Some guys can put a woman on a pedestal and inevitably she'll fall off and hard. Kyle spent lots of time talking about how stubborn you can be. There was a lot of talk of getting yourself stabbed."

MaeBe rolled her eyes. "I certainly did not."

Taylor shrugged. "You would not know it from Kyle. I'm just saying he knows your imperfections and is crazy about you anyway. Even when he thought he could be bad for you, he made you the center of his world."

She glanced over to make sure Kyle wasn't looking her way. He was arguing a rule with Drake while Hutch paged through the rule book. "I've accepted his reasons for leaving me. I do understand them. The question at this point is how do I forgive him?"

"You don't owe him forgiveness. You know you could live with the man for the rest of your life and still be a little mad at him for something he did in the past. I don't think there's such a thing as perfect contentment. Unless you don't think you can be happy without wholly forgiving him. That's a whole different thing, and worse when you think about it. Because then you can't live with him and you can't live without him, and you're miserable either way."

That sounded terrible, but she was right. "So you forgave Drake for letting them take you away?"

"Mostly," she said, wrinkling her nose. "But the person I really forgave was myself for loving him anyway. Honestly, that's the hard part. Julia fucks up everyone she touches. Think about it. Her father's dead. Her mother...Samantha is lost sometimes. She doesn't understand what went wrong and wonders if it's her fault. Drake...she was his sister. I use the past tense because she's not the same person he grew up with. I think Kyle has it worst because in some ways she did show him who she was, and he fell for it briefly. I understand how that kind of mistake can make a person view the world differently. So I had to step back and decide if I could live with loving him."

That was a good way to put it. One of the things she'd figured out when she'd talked to Kai was that having her view of herself shaken so wildly had contributed to her anger with Kyle. Her world had been tilted on its side, and she'd had to work hard to right it. "How did you do that?"

"I talked to him. I let him top me because I wanted the sex and convinced myself that this time I could take what I wanted and walk away. It was silly, of course. It was my conscious self making excuses for what I needed deep down. I kind of lived day by day with him at my side. We decided that as long as the op was ongoing, we didn't have to make decisions about the future. We could live in the present, and by the time I got to the other side, I couldn't imagine that future without him." She frowned. "Almost watching him die had an effect, too. That was a shitty, crazy night. You know we almost lost Kyle."

"I know Julia said something about being forced to choose between her father and Kyle." She hadn't asked him about it. He'd seemed so wound up after that conversation, and now he was relaxed. She didn't want him to think about Julia Ennis again tonight. They had spent the day narrowing down places to search, and when they were ready they would be heading to Washington DC first, and they would always be watching their backs. They needed this time when they felt fairly safe.

When they were out in the field, would she be able to sleep without him? Would she force him to stay on whatever couch was around? Or would she do what Taylor had done and bargain with herself?

Taylor nodded. "Yes. It was pretty awful. Mr. Radcliffe was aiming at Kyle, and there was no way he was going to miss. Even the Royal Suite is tight when it comes to a gunfight. To be honest, I'm surprised Kyle survived at all. John Smith was there and he had a couple of excellent shots at Kyle, but all he got was his shoulder. Kyle was lucky as hell that night."

He could have died, and she wouldn't have known until someone thought to tell her. She wasn't his next of kin. The police wouldn't call her. They would have called Grace and Grace would have told her, but it seemed wrong that she wouldn't have known first. It was weird, but the idea that there would be hours or days when she didn't know caught in her brain and rambled around her head.

"He was okay. John was obviously okay since he somehow managed to get away," Taylor said. "You know we were supposed to go to DC to interrogate him. We changed our flight at the last minute because Kyle wanted us here. Not for him. For you. Turned out to be a good thing since we would have been staring at his replacement's dead body, but still. Kyle was utterly insistent that we back him up when it came to getting you to safety. He didn't want to bring his relatives in, and he didn't trust anyone but us. We're an odd little family. I don't have much of one, so I take it seriously. I know we don't know each other, but I feel like I know you because for Kyle it's like you were always beside him."

"It didn't feel that way to me." She'd felt so alone, left behind again. "I worry that part of me wants him back simply because I could lose the family I have if I'm not with him. I've come to view his uncle and aunt as my family, and I don't know what happens if I'm no longer his girlfriend. I'm sure he wouldn't want that to be the reason I gave him a second chance."

"You would be surprised at what I would do for another chance with you."

She felt hands come down on her shoulders and realized the game going on at the end of the table had broken up.

Taylor winced. "Sorry. He moved in quick." She stood. "I will help them change out the games."

Kyle knelt behind her as Taylor moved away. He leaned in, and she could feel the heat of his body. "I will take any reason you give me, and then I'll work to make it better. I promise. If all you want from me is sex, I'll give it to you. I'll give it to you until you either love me again or tell me to go away. And even then I wouldn't ever take this family away from you. Never. They like you better anyway."

His arms wound around her waist and for a moment she let herself breathe him in. His warmth. The smell of the soap he'd used. The feel of his rough cheek against hers because it was long after five o'clock and that beard was trying to come in.

"Taylor thinks I should use you for the time being." That wasn't what she'd meant. "She thinks me using you would be a way to slide back into a relationship."

"Only if you want one. If you don't, I promise I'll stay away. I'll let you live your life."

"I could move down to MDWM."

"My uncle would kill me," Kyle assured her. "I can find somewhere else to work. Hell, after everything comes out, my uncle might not want me here anyway. Maybe I'll go back and finish my grad degree and find a job where I don't have to shoot anyone."

They'd had so many plans for the future. Was she willing to give them all away? Was there anything to be won by making the decision tonight? Or should she do exactly what Taylor said. Should she take what she needed from him? "If we slept together, it wouldn't mean anything."

He nestled his head against hers. "Not if you don't want it to."

There it was. He was bending again because she knew his instinct was to argue.

Or was it? Had his instincts been thrown in a bowl and mixed up with trauma, endlessly cycling until he wasn't sure what was what?

Weren't those her instincts, too?

This was a compromise between the MaeBe who wanted the world to be a shiny, happy place and the one who'd been left by her father. Between the one who'd loved the Kyle who'd never fucked up and the one who understood that love would be hard.

She could float for a while.

"I think I want you to kiss me, but this is not forever."

"I meant what I said. I'll take any time you're willing to give me and then I'll wait around to see if you ever need me again."

She didn't have to walk away for now. She might later. But for now, she could simply be.

She tilted her head up.

"Hey, I've got an alarm going off." Hutch stood, his cell in hand. "I set the locks from the outside, so it has to be someone leaving. Was anyone else here working late?"

In the distance, MaeBe heard the sound of her desk phone going off. It was clearly hers because no one else had programmed their lines to ring using the Dr. Who theme song.

Why would someone be calling her this late?

"I'm going to grab that." She got up, looking at Kyle. "You figure out who left."

"Hot chocolate for everyone," Maddie said as she walked in with Boomer. She held a big tray in her hand. "And a couple of teas. I found some honey, too. That is a well-stocked break room."

Boomer had a big bag in his hand. "Hey, Noelle got a work call. She'll be right back."

Hutch frowned as MaeBe walked by and toward the door. "Did she walk out into the hall?"

"I think she was going down to get something from your car," Boomer was saying. "Something about reports."

Noelle was constantly running experiments. It wouldn't be the first time something had gone wrong with a machine that was supposed to be running overnight and Noelle had to talk the tech through fixing it and getting the experiment back on track.

They were still talking behind her, but she made her way toward her desk.

"Who would call you this late?" Kyle was hard on her heels.

"Well, anyone who can't get me by cell phone," she replied. "Which is everyone because you made me leave it behind. It's probably someone looking for tech help. Alex, Li, and Erin always call me if they have problems with their laptops. Shockingly Ian never calls. He has one of the girls fix it. I swear those three Taggart girls could hack the world if they wanted to. Lou's been teaching them how to code, too."

She was proud of Ian and Charlotte's daughters. They didn't let anything hold them back. Sometimes she was scared of them. She picked up the receiver. "This is MaeBe."

"I have your friend Noelle, and if you let anyone know you're talking to me, I'll kill her here and now. Am I understood?" Julia's voice sounded husky as if she found the current conversation slightly sexual in nature. Not strange for a deeply deranged woman. "Is Kyle with you?"

That hadn't taken her long. If she didn't know that he was standing beside her, she didn't have eyes on them. Not that putting eyes in the office would be easy. Big Tag was hella paranoid, and they had some amazing security around their systems, including the cameras. "He's in the conference room. I'm in my office. Where is Noelle?"

Kyle went stiff but didn't make a sound. She turned the receiver out so he could hear.

"My men have her, and they'll trade her for you," Julia offered. "And don't think you can call in the calvary and catch me. I'm not there. I'm not foolish. My men are armed and well trained. John won't hurt you. He'll simply bring you to a safe house, and then my brother and I are going to discuss where my father's files are. I think Kyle will help him work faster if he knows we have you."

She would bet Julia believed that. "Don't hurt Noelle. Please don't hurt her."

She made her voice breathy and desperate, finding a piece of the MaeBe she'd been before. Although she was probably being hard on that version of herself. It wasn't like she'd been some shrinking violet. She'd stood up to everyone who'd tried to hurt her. She'd had a backbone.

She just hadn't taken the time to learn how to protect herself. It was an odd moment to have a big revelation, but here it was. The old MaeBe hadn't been weak in any area of her life beyond her actual muscular frame. She had fought for what she wanted.

The old MaeBe should have found out where Kyle was and gone and given him the talking to of a lifetime. She'd gotten her heart hurt, but her heart was the strongest thing about her.

"Oh, there's the MaeBe I remember." Julia practically purred over the line. It was something that would have made her stomach turn a few days ago, but now she felt a little sorry for this woman.

She was going to be so easy to fool. MaeBe sniffled. "Noelle is innocent in all of this. Hold on." She halfway put a hand over the receiver. Halfway because she wanted the other woman to hear this. "I'll be a minute, guys. It's my dad. He's got computer problems. Y'all start without me."

Kyle's jaw was tight, but he leaned over and kissed the top of her head before quietly walking back toward the conference room. As he got far enough away, he looked back. "Don't take too long."

He would inform the rest of the group.

He was trusting her to handle Julia, to get the information they needed to save Noelle.

"You know you're not going to be able to keep him," Julia said. "You're not enough for him."

MaeBe forced another sniffle, willing the woman to view her as a crying, self-sacrificial pawn. "It doesn't matter. Noelle does. Tell me where she is."

"Someone is waiting to take you into custody in the parking garage," Julia explained. "Go there now. Noelle doesn't have long. And if my men get a hint that you're not alone, they'll put a bullet in her and she won't need that cane anymore."

The phone disconnected and MaeBe turned. It looked like her fun night was over.

It was time to go to work.

Chapter Fifteen

Kyle's heart was threatening to beat out of his chest as he forced himself to walk away from MaeBe. He'd done what he needed to do. He'd given credence to MaeBe's ruse. She obviously didn't believe there was any way Julia could have taken over their inner security cameras. Mae knew the security system and the protocols around it as well as anyone in the company. So much better than he did. If she thought Julia would be shut out and couldn't have eyes on them, then they had the upper hand. He had to do anything he could to sell that fake out.

If he could keep Hutch from losing his shit.

He walked toward the conference room, but Hutch was already walking out.

"I'm going to…" Hutch began.

Kyle held up a fist, a sign to anyone who'd spent the amount of time they had in the military that it was time for quiet.

Hutch's expression went tight, and his hand went to the small of his back.

Boomer seemed to have gotten the message, too. He was suddenly beside Hutch, and he had a gun in his hand.

"Where is my wife?" Hutch breathed the question. "I track her smart watch and her heartrate spiked about three minutes ago. I was about to go down to find her."

He knew exactly why Hutch tracked Noelle. She had been

attacked once and while Hutch had chilled about how vulnerable she could be physically, he still felt the need to watch over her. Conversely, he happened to know Noelle could track Hutch, too.

The women seemed to be starting to understand that something was going wrong. Maddie and Taylor were staring out at him, Taylor saying something to Drake that had him on his feet.

Kyle glanced back, and MaeBe was still on the phone. "Julia called, and she claims she's got Noelle."

Hutch paled. "She's in the parking garage. At least her watch is. I have to go to her."

He understood. "I know this is the most unfair, hypocritical thing I've ever said to you, but I need you to stay calm. First, we need to know how many assholes we're working with. Can you pull up the parking garage cameras?"

Hutch took a deep breath and seemed to get himself under control. "Of course. You have to understand that I'm going to kill any fucker who puts his hands on her."

But not completely under control. "I'd like to keep at least one of the fuckers alive so we can question him."

Julia would be more dangerous when she learned this plot of hers hadn't worked.

"What's happening?" Drake asked quietly.

Hutch had his cell out, pulling up what they needed to see. "The guard's at the desk. The second guard might be doing rounds or they might have taken him out. I'm not showing… Fuck me. The guard let them in. They wouldn't be able to sneak in without an alarm going off. There's not a note in the log that they let someone in after hours. It would be there unless they didn't want me to know. She's got someone on the inside."

"I assure you she found some way to force them to help her." He knew exactly how Julia worked. He'd watched her do it and ignored the way her methods raked against his conscience because he'd told himself American lives were worth more than his morality. Then he'd realized she didn't give a shit about any life but her own.

"Noelle's being held in the parking garage." MaeBe was cool and collected as she walked up. "I'm supposed to go down to the second level using the west elevators. Hutch, do you have eyes on Noelle?"

"I'm looking." Hutch was working his way through the security cameras.

"Wouldn't she take out the cams?" Deke had Maddie's hand in his. "That would be the first thing I would do."

"That would have immediately set off an alarm," Hutch replied. "So would anyone taking over the cameras or piggybacking on them. I have that set up for the whole building."

"But if she's got one of those two guards, they can tell her whatever she wants to know," Drake continued. "And they can't know that Hutch gets an alert when internal doors are opened after hours. They don't understand how paranoid Big Tag is."

MaeBe redid her ponytail and set her gun on the table. "It's Carl. I'm sure of it. His son recently got into a clinical trial that he shouldn't have been able to get into. It was full. He called it a miracle, but now I know what it likely was. The pharmaceutical company is on a list of suspected Consortium members. Don't blame him. His son was dying."

"And I'm sure my sister told him she would only need a favor down the line." Drake sounded bitter.

He knew exactly what had happened. "This is one of her reactionary, poorly thought out plans. MaeBe pissed her off earlier, and Julia wants to punish her."

"She wants her father's files," MaeBe replied. "And you. I'm not going to risk Noelle. I'm going down. You come up with a plan that's not poorly thought out." She went on her toes and brushed her lips against his. "Think fast, babe."

"Wait, you're not..."

MaeBe shook her head as she walked toward the front of the office. "This is who I am, Kyle. Take me or leave me. I'm never going to leave a friend hanging when I can stop it. And if they take me into custody, then Julia better be ready for me to bust out." She opened the door. "But I suspect you guys aren't going to let that happen."

She was going to kill him.

And she was right. This was exactly who MaeBe Vaughn was and would always be. She would always try to save her friends, always use any strength she had to help others. He didn't want her any other way. It was why he'd fallen in love with her.

It was time to stop putting her in a box and start being her actual partner.

Boomer followed her. "I'm going to work my way to the service elevator. Can you start a loop on every camera but the one on the west elevator?"

Hutch nodded, his eyes on the screen as his thumbs moved. "Yep."

"You can do that?" Taylor was watching over Hutch's shoulder.

"I have protocols in place in case we need to get out of the building without anyone seeing," Hutch admitted. "I have full control of this building and every security system in it. They don't know it yet, but those gates aren't going to open, and Kyle's ex won't be able to see anything but what I want her to see. She doesn't get to come into my house and hurt my wife."

"I'm going with Boomer." Deke squeezed his wife's hand. "Lock yourself in Tag's office. Give him a call to let him know what's going on. And don't come out until I give you the all clear."

Maddie nodded. "I will. Should I call the cops? That's a dumb question."

The cops wouldn't let him interrogate whoever they caught in the manner he would like. In his world, his uncle was the ultimate authority. "I'm going straight down and walking in behind MaeBe. Hutch, you come with me. Drake and Taylor, use the east elevator and come in from behind. That way we have them on three sides."

He made it to the outer office in time to watch MaeBe disappear into the elevator.

This was his nightmare. His first instinct was to call Julia and tell her to take him instead, offer her anything in order to get her to leave MaeBe alone.

Did he want a life with MaeBe or did he want to sacrifice himself so he didn't have to worry about her? She was worth the worry. His mother had tried to tell him that this was a bad time and it would pass, and one day he wouldn't have this aching pit in his soul that told him he was cursed. One day he would forgive himself for making mistakes, for hurting people he'd never meant to hurt.

He wanted that day, longed for it.

"All the cameras with the exception of the one on MaeBe are in a loop. We can go down," Hutch said. "They've got Noelle next to a van in the back of the garage. They're going to kill her. They want to be as far as they can from any possible interference."

"MaeBe will buy us some time, and we won't need much," Kyle promised. But in his head he could see so many other possibilities. He could see those assholes Julia hired blowing both women away.

He'd been wrong. This wouldn't have happened if he hadn't come back into her life. He'd been right the first time around. This was his fault.

That voice in his head wouldn't go away easily.

"Hey, isn't this the guy you had me look into a couple of months back? The one even Adam couldn't get a real ID on?" Hutch turned the cell phone his way and proved that though he'd looped the cameras for the security guards, he could still see everything.

There were four men, each dressed in all black. Three wore ski masks, except the man he knew as John Smith. His face was out in the open. He had a hand on Noelle's arm and a gun at her side. He leaned over and whispered something in her ear. Noelle's head nodded slightly.

"That's him. He's Julia's main Consortium assistant. He does her dirty work." He might not know anything about the actual man, but Taylor had learned a lot about his function in the group when she'd dealt with him and Julia.

John had been the reason Julia had gotten away in London. They'd had her basically pinned down, but he'd found a way out. If not for that bastard, the problem would have been solved by now.

The elevator doors opened, and they strode in. Kyle checked his gun, ensuring the safety was off and the magazine loaded. "We bring him in, and this time we won't take our eyes off the bastard. I have no idea how he got out of Agency custody and here so fucking fast."

It didn't make sense. Did Julia still have contacts on the inside of the CIA?

All questions John Smith could answer. After he'd let Hutch take a couple of shots at him. He figured the guy could take some pain.

The elevator began to descend. "MaeBe's on the ground."

Hutch had switched to the camera on the elevator. MaeBe

stepped out but turned and looked up at the monitors that showed what floor each of the two elevators were on. She hesitated, likely to give them time.

Or she was worried about the noise. He winced because he hadn't thought about what he was doing. They'd taken the elevator that tended to slam shut, and that sound could echo through the parking garage.

She was frowning at the camera, pure judgment in her eyes.

He knew exactly what she was thinking. She was mentally calling him a dumbass for not taking the elevator they knew damn well wouldn't alert the bad guys another one had arrived.

"Tag is already pinging me," Hutch announced. "He's on his way in. Drake and Taylor made it to their elevator. Boomer and Deke are already on the ground floor. They'll have to sneak around to the front of the garage and take out the guard."

"Don't kill him. He was trying to save his kid, and I know all too well how Julia can convince a person to do something terrible." His gut was in a knot. He couldn't lose her. He couldn't be the reason Hutch lost his wife. If either one of the women got hurt because he was a dumbass who didn't think…

The elevator doors opened quietly, and MaeBe rolled her eyes his way.

That was when the solution became clear. He reached out and pushed the button to hold the damn doors open.

Panic was not his friend. He had to stop. He had to trust that he had a team around him. Hutch wasn't Julia.

MaeBe wasn't Julia.

He didn't have to watch his back. He did have to watch hers.

MaeBe would never be happy spending the rest of her life behind a computer. She would want to be out in the field. There would be nothing safe about life with this woman. Except she would never turn on him, never betray him.

She sighed and turned and started walking away. "Noelle? Noelle, are you here?"

Of course if they had a D/s contract, at least he could spank that sweet ass when she got reckless. That would make him feel better. He could have one place where he was in control because otherwise, he would simply be at her side.

He let her get past the first row of parking slots, almost around the corner where they would be able to see her. He nodded to Hutch, and they silently moved across the concrete. Hutch had shoved his cell in his pocket and had a doublehanded hold on the gun in his hand.

Kyle could feel his heart thudding in his chest as MaeBe held up her hands and disappeared behind the wall.

"MaeBe?" Noelle's voice floated through the parking garage. "Get down!"

The last two words were shouted, and then there was a sound that damn near stopped Kyle in his tracks. Three pings.

A suppressor.

Kyle took off, all thoughts of stealth long gone as he ran around the corner, Hutch hard on his heels.

In his mind's eye he could see Mae on the ground, blood starting to surround her body. He would lie down beside her. He would be true to his promise to her.

"Put down the gun!" Drake was shouting in the distance.

MaeBe was standing in the middle of the parking garage, her hands on her hips and three bodies in an arc in front of her.

"I will put down the gun." John Smith had one hand up, the other around Noelle's waist. "But someone needs to help Mrs. Hutchins. She rolled her ankle when these idiots scared her, and she doesn't have her cane. Ma'am, would you mind asking your husband not to kill me?"

MaeBe turned to Kyle, gesturing to the bodies around her. "He shot these guys. And I think he was protecting Noelle."

"I don't care. I need a better reason than that not to kill that fucker." Kyle stepped in front of MaeBe because Smith was still holding a gun in one hand.

This could be Julia's plan. Something worse was about to happen.

Hutch rushed in and picked up his wife, carrying her away as quickly as he could.

Drake and Taylor moved into position, and from the side, he heard Deke and Boomer running in to surround the man.

John Smith placed his gun on the ground. "Then let me give you one, Mr. Hawthorne. I'm Canadian Intelligence."

MaeBe's hand found his, squeezing.

Murder was going to have to wait.

Forty minutes later his uncle sat behind his desk and doubled over laughing. "I just…can you say it again? I need to hear it again…it's the best…"

His uncle was a massive ass sometimes. "He says he's Canadian Intelligence."

Ian slapped the desk, and his laughter boomed through the office. "Charlie, baby. Can you record that? I want to play it back any time I get sad. He said Canadian and intelligence like they went together."

His aunt looked more casual than she normally did. Likely because he'd gotten her out of bed. She wore yoga pants and a sweatshirt, her strawberry blonde hair in a messy pile on her head. She'd been pacing at the back of the office, her phone to her ear. "Ian, be nice."

"Don't take offense. He does this to pretty much everyone." MaeBe looked absolutely none the worse for the wear. "You should only get worried when he gets quiet. As long as he's laughing, he won't hurt anyone."

"I'm not laughing." Drake was watching the man like a hawk. He and Taylor were the only ones left from their truncated game night.

The man he'd known as John Smith shrugged it all off. "I've heard worse. Trust me. I've been undercover with The Consortium for two years now. I've been called every name in the book. They aren't particularly kind to employees. And we're not even allowed to unionize. Also, I've been Canadian all my life. I know Americans are assholes."

John Smith had explained that his real name was Joseph Caulder, and he was originally from the suburbs of Toronto. They hadn't gotten much further than that, and Charlotte was checking out his story with some Canadian contacts.

Big Tag pointed Joseph's way. "He's not Canadian. He cursed. Shoot him." Big Tag kind of wheezed the words out. "No. Don't. I can't do it. I love him for that joke alone."

His aunt and uncle had gotten to the office very quickly. Ian had dealt with the guard, who'd cried a lot, and then left Boomer and Deke to deal with the bodies. He hoped there was room in that freezer.

His stepdad was going to kill him.

"When you interrogate a subject, do you force-feed them your weird bacon? Is that how you do it?" his uncle was asking.

It was blatantly obvious he was going to have to take control of this situation. He turned to the other man. "Why should I believe you?"

"Mrs. Hutchins explained to you that she was never in any real danger." Joseph glanced around as though looking for threats—which proved he had a brain in his head because they were all threats. "I never let her out of my sight."

"She had to be carried out of here." Kyle was fairly certain she would have been fine with her cane, but Hutch wasn't letting her go anywhere without him. He'd apparently decided the best way to keep track of his wife was to carry her around everywhere.

"I am sorry about that. When Julia sent me here, she hired those mercenaries. They weren't exactly careful," he explained. "She twisted her ankle when she tried to run. I kept her close to me after that. I knew damn well Ms. Vaughn wouldn't come down alone. She's far smarter than that, so all I had to do was bide my time."

"What was Julia thinking?" His uncle suddenly sounded slightly serious.

"She wasn't. From what I can tell she talked with Ms. Vaughn earlier this evening and it sent her into a rage. She'd intended to talk to your nephew," Joseph explained.

"How did she know I was here?" After the events in London, he'd left the hospital without telling anyone where he was going. He'd made his way to Dallas and planned how to protect MaeBe. He'd only called in Drake and Taylor when he had it all in place.

"It was a good bet that you would come back here. She sent me out when she realized you'd gotten out of London." Joseph turned to Drake. "I'm sorry that my replacement won't give you much intel. I would bet he doesn't know much. They likely picked him strictly because he looked enough like me he could fool a casual guard."

"He's dead," Drake said flatly.

Joseph's expression went blank. "I suppose I should have expected that." He seemed to shake it off. "Anyway, Julia has a brilliant if wicked mind. However she is running on emotion now, and that's when she's both vulnerable and at her deadliest. You can't trust her to make a logical decision, as you've seen this evening. I would have tried to talk her out of it, but she wasn't going to budge. I went along to ensure no one got hurt."

Kyle studied the other man, his mind going over their every encounter. "I've tangled with you several times now, and tonight is the first time you've ever helped us out. I think you realized we had you cornered and came up with this plan to stay alive."

"Haven't helped you?" Joseph turned MaeBe's way. "How many organs did you lose, love? When you were stabbed a few months ago?"

Kyle started to see red. He'd thought Julia might have had something to do with that, but if this fucker had done it, he was about to get stabbed, too. Kyle had knives. He never went anywhere without them. He could see exactly how he would do it. He could slowly open the guy's gut and force him to watch as his bowels slid out.

"Kyle." Ian was suddenly serious again. "Do not kill the Canadian dude in here."

"Tarp," his aunt said sharply before turning back to her call.

MaeBe's eyes rolled again. "He's not killing anyone. We talked about this. You yourself said he was either really bad at stabbing or really good at it."

"Good at it." Joseph leaned against the back wall of the office, as if he wanted to make sure no one could come up behind him. "The key is going for the upper left quadrant. Not a lot there. You have to go low enough that you don't hit a lung and far enough over you don't nick the pancreas. Neither of which I did, and she did not make it easy on me. She moved a lot."

"Well, I was trying to avoid getting stabbed altogether. So you weren't trying to lift Vanessa's handbag." MaeBe was taking the news with her usual aplomb.

He was not. "No, he was trying to hurt you."

"I was trying to fulfill the requests of my employer, who is also my target," Joseph replied. "Trust me. She's made a study of you,

Ms. Vaughn."

"You can call me Mae or MaeBe," MaeBe offered.

"Ms. Vaughn works great." He didn't like the way Joseph looked at her. It hadn't escaped him that the other man was roughly their age and beyond fit. He actually looked a bit like Kyle himself, which was probably Julia's attraction to him.

Joseph ignored him completely. "Most of that study was based on my work. When Julia wanted to send a message, I planned it out. I had been shadowing you for a couple of days and realized this was going to be your first time doing something physical for an op. I took into account that you would take note of me. That's precisely why I followed Ms. Hale into that alley. I knew you would be worried and follow me."

"That was a ridiculous gamble." The man obviously had no idea what he was doing. "She could have left early. She could have gone a different way. She could have ignored the situation entirely."

Joseph's head shook. "No. She was always going to make sure Vanessa was safe. It's who she is. She couldn't have made a different choice."

He felt a low growl threaten to begin. Perhaps he didn't need a knife. He could rip the man apart with his bare hands, and then Joseph would know not to shadow his girl.

The man needed to understand that just because they had a few things in common didn't mean they needed to share anything. Including the earth they were both walking on at this moment.

"There's one problem with this scenario. Canada doesn't have a foreign intelligence agency." Taylor watched the man warily.

"Not one we recognize in the public." Joseph had been polite the whole time. "I know we have a reputation as the naïve children of the world, but don't think we won't protect our country. We know how good we have it, and we won't allow ourselves to be stepped on. A few years back we realized the US wasn't as stable as we'd once believed, and that relying on the CIA for our foreign intelligence was a mistake. I was one of the first agents recruited. Someday we'll have a formally recognized agency. I'm going to build it on the back of the work I've done here. I'm going to take down The Consortium, and they'll hand the reins over to me."

"Will they pay you in maple donuts?" His uncle was grinning

again.

"Only if I'm lucky." Joseph gave his uncle a thumbs-up.

Kyle was planning on taking this guy seriously. He was either lying or he wasn't, and either way they had problems. "Taking down The Consortium is your mission?"

"A few years back my government realized that certain companies were colluding to keep prices high. They used the pandemic to destabilize markets and send corporate profits soaring. Beyond that, these companies are manipulating politicians and attempting to set policy that is favorable to them, not to the public. They use their media conglomerates to spread disinformation and keep the public on edge so they don't see what's actually happening. My country wants it stopped," Joseph explained.

"Everyone wants it stopped." Drake sat down on the couch, keeping his eyes on Joseph.

"Do they? Has the Agency made it a top priority? Or are they all playing the stock market?" For the first time, Joseph sounded a bit savage.

"Don't question my motives," Drake retorted.

"Hey, you know he's right." Ian sat back in his chair. "There are forces in the Agency that would rather see the stock market rise than ensure it's being done fairly. You've spent your whole life in politics and intelligence." Ian chuckled. "See, I did it, too. Put together two words that do not match. Just like you, buddy."

Joseph's lips curled up slightly. "You're not what I expected. When they talk about you, they make you seem larger than life and twice as deadly."

"Yeah, they always forget how funny I can be." Ian shoved his chair back as Charlotte moved in. Without missing a beat, she gracefully eased onto his lap.

"He checks out," Charlotte said, draping an arm around her husband's neck. "My contact with the Canadian Security Intelligence Service verifies his identity. But only after putting me through a bunch of hoops, so they're serious about his cover."

Ian snorted, his arm around his wife's waist. "What does the CSIS do these days?"

"Mostly keep watch on Quebec separatists." MaeBe proved she was a smarty pants once again.

Ian started laughing again. Charlotte gently slapped his chest. He shook his head. "I can't help it. They all speak French. What would the uprising look like? Is there cheese and wine?" He looked to Joseph. "Hey, did you guys invent poutine so you could force-feed it to prisoners and make them talk?"

MaeBe frowned. "I think it's delicious."

Joseph smiled her way and gave her a wink. "It is, indeed. See, we Canadians don't care what the alpha holes of the world think. We're pretty confident in ourselves."

"Hah. See he put alpha male and asshole together. Those totally go together. All the dudes out there on the Internet who call themselves alphas are really assholes." Ian turned his chin up, looking at his wife. "He's funny. I think we should keep him. He's way funnier than the other sad sacks who've come through. He can say Canadian things and make me laugh."

"Could you be serious for five seconds?" Kyle'd had enough of his uncle. "This man shot me."

His uncle shrugged. "Lots of people have shot you. Can't kill them all."

"I shot you in the shoulder," Joseph countered. "That was intentional. I'm an excellent shot. I could have hit your heart, but I barely grazed you. Did the same to Deke Murphy several months back. You're welcome. I've done everything I can to keep you safe and out of her hands because I'm not sure what she'll do with you if she gets what she wants. Right now she can fool herself that once you're back with her, you'll see the light. Once you spit some bile her way, she'll likely slit your throat and I'll have to bury you. You look heavy. Save my lower back. Stay away until I get what I need and take her down myself."

"What exactly are you looking for?" MaeBe asked.

"I've been attempting to do exactly what Ms. Cline was trying to do." Joseph finally moved to the couch, and the fucker took a seat right next to MaeBe. "I'm trying to map The Consortium from the inside."

"Well, I wasn't going to sleep with Julia to do it," Taylor admitted with a shudder.

"I'll admit there are parts of my job that I find distasteful," Joseph said. "But it was necessary to make her believe I am who she thinks I am. Actually, a great deal of this job is to make Julia not think of me at all. I'm a useful tool. No one worries about their hammer. It sits there until you want to use it. That's what I am to her."

"How far have you gotten?" Drake asked.

"It's hard to get concrete proof." Joseph answered Drake but his eyes were on MaeBe. "There is some incredible anti-surveillance tech they have that isn't close to being on the market yet. I can't get any of it on camera, and I have to be careful. I'm not the first agent we sent in. She was made, and the police found her body in a dumpster. That was when we decided to try to send a man in. They view males differently. We're far more expendable than the women. They're better trained and more invested in the group. Conversely, we're also ignored more. I've worked hard to get Julia to view me as nothing more than a convenient handyman/fuck buddy."

MaeBe had turned all soft and sympathetic. "I'm sorry you had to do that. I know men are supposed to always want sex and not care how they get it, but it must make you feel used."

Joseph leaned in. "It does. She's not entirely sane, and she doesn't mind taking that out on me. I can't tell you the amount of times she's made me pretend to be Kyle."

Ian huffed another laugh out. "You're going to find out what it's like to be in Kyle's belly if you don't stop hitting on his girl."

Charlotte laid her head on his shoulder. "Is she his girl? I kind of thought no, and if not then the Canadian is attractive."

Kyle was so fucking happy his relatives were having fun.

MaeBe stood, and her eyes narrowed on the couple. "You two are bad people. Now hush. We're working things out."

MaeBe turned and then was lowering herself onto his lap.

The world seemed less shitty than it had two seconds before. He didn't give a fuck that this was supposed to be a meeting. His uncle and aunt had the right idea. It was better to be connected. He wrapped his arm around her waist and brought her close. If she didn't want him to do weird things, she should have picked another dude because he liked smelling her hair. Only hers.

He could feel his blood pressure go down.

"Can we talk now? Without looking like you're going to kill our guest?" MaeBe's lips curled up in the sweetest smile.

"Probably." This was why his uncle had many a meeting with his wife sitting on his lap. There were men who could handle the shittiness of the world and men who couldn't without some help. They were those men. He let his free hand find her knee so she was completely in his arms. Then he could deal with Joseph. "I suspect you think her father's files would go a long way in helping you take down The Consortium."

"I think they're the key to everything." Joseph suddenly seemed professional again. "They're certainly her obsession right now. What happened in London hurt her with the organization. They wanted her mother dead so they could replace her seat in the senate with a more friendly senator. Not only did she fail, but her father died during the op."

"Do they know she's the one who killed him?" Drake asked.

Joseph's head shook. "Absolutely not. I was given the story she wanted to tell, and I haven't deviated from it. You have to understand that if Julia loses her position, they don't merely move me to another operative. They fire me, and permanently. Julia's fuckups are my fuckups. So I have to support her on this. According to the reports we filed, Drake killed his father."

"Of course I did," Drake said with a bitter twist of his lips.

Taylor leaned against her boyfriend. "Everyone who counts knows the truth."

"They don't realize he had records, do they?" Now that Kyle's inner caveman was satisfied no one was taking his woman away he could think better. "Did Julia?"

"She would have known something about it." Drake seemed calmer, too. "Our father taught us to keep intelligence on the people around us. Especially the ones with power. What have you figured out about how high up my father's placement went?"

"I did not spend much time with your father. I was brought in shortly before the incident that led to Julia's transformation," Joseph began.

"You mean right before Kyle tried to unalive her?" his uncle asked.

Kyle had always been curious about this. "I was sure I'd hit her heart."

"No." Joseph clasped his hands together. "You missed, and the fire I started managed to get you to leave."

"You got her out." That shook his calm.

MaeBe smoothed back his hair. "She was his only way into The Consortium. You would have done the same thing in his place."

"She's right. I would have been blamed for losing a valuable asset," Joseph agreed. "If The Consortium didn't kill me, I suspect her father would have. He would have worried anyone close to Julia might have known his secret. By that time I did know he was involved at the highest levels, despite the fact I did not spend time with him. After I got Julia away, I called my contacts, and it was your father who made the arrangements to move her. First to Mexico and then to Los Angeles. Every operative has what we call a doppelganger. They have to find someone in the world whose identity they can take over in case of emergency."

"I made up my own." Taylor brushed back her hair. "I knew I would have to ID someone if I got in. It's kind of creepy. You have to find someone with your basic height and bone structure. Someone vulnerable, with no real family or friends. It's surprisingly easy to do in the age of social media. People can isolate and still feel like they have a foot in the world when they really don't."

"It was easy for her to take over Jane Adams's life." Joseph crossed one leg over the other, sitting back, though he kept that watchful energy around him.

"Did you kill her?" Kyle had to ask the question.

A hint of a smile crossed his lips. "Julia thinks so. Being able to save Jane is one of the good things I've done in the last several years. We staged her death so Julia had the proof she needed, and she's living under the protection of the CSIS. She has a job with them that I've been told she enjoys, and she's got real friends there. I don't know if she'll go back to her former life after we're done with the op." He glanced up at the clock. "I need to get going because Julia will want a report. I told her we would need a communications blackout until I got back to the safe house, but she'll be getting anxious."

"What exactly are you going to tell her?" Kyle was curious. He wasn't completely convinced.

"That there was a firefight, and we lost the others." Joseph stood, straightening the dark shirt he wore. "She won't care about that. She'll only care that Kyle Hawthorne is alive and that I managed to get out with Mae."

The room seemed to still.

MaeBe's hands found the sides of his face, and she forced him to look at her and only her. "Babe, I need you to stay calm and hear him out."

He stood, picking her up as he did. Hutch was right. "I'm going to kill him and then we won't have a problem anymore."

She groaned. "It makes sense." Her arms locked around his neck. "I'm not going to let you kill him. Think about what I can do if I'm behind the scenes, so to speak. I can gather so much information, and if Joseph helps me, I can get that to you easily. It keeps Joseph in the game, too. He can't walk back in with nothing."

"He can die and then we don't have to worry about him anymore." It was simple. It was a perfect plan.

"Kyle, agree with her." Big Tag had stood, Charlotte standing beside him. "Tell her she's smart and she can handle any situation she gets into."

"She is," Joseph insisted. "And I'll be there to make sure nothing bad happens to her."

Joseph could say that all he liked, but Julia was volatile. She'd proven it tonight. It had been stupid for her to move on MaeBe in this fashion. There had been not an ounce of logic to this plan. It had been driven by Julia's emotional state and her ego. She'd broken MaeBe's arm when she'd been cool and calm. There was no way of knowing what she could do when she was unhinged.

Joseph would honor his mission. He might want to save MaeBe, but he would also allow her to take some damage if it served his country's needs.

His uncle moved in, and Kyle put MaeBe down. He would need both hands to crush that fucker's windpipe.

"Do it, nephew. Do it now." Ian's jaw was a tight line as he put his will behind those words.

What the hell was his uncle doing? Was this some kind of play he was making?

He trusted his uncle. His uncle wouldn't ask him to go against his every instinct unless he had a plan or his instincts were utterly wrong.

He'd felt so alone in the world, but he'd had this man in his corner since the day his mom had married Sean. He'd had Sean and Ian, and then their brothers and sisters, even the ones who didn't share an ounce of blood.

He'd searched the world trying to find what he needed to feel whole, and it had been here all the while. Here with his family.

He was a dumbass, but he could be something more.

He stared down at Mae. "Do you need to do this?"

It would make him sick inside, but if she needed it, he would have to back her up.

MaeBe returned his gaze, the truth in her eyes. "I need to get this woman out of our lives to make sure we have a chance."

He looked over at Joseph. Charlotte was slowly moving around the living space. Was she going to open the damn door and send them on their way? What were they doing? This was some play his aunt and uncle were making, and he needed to perform the part Ian had assigned to him. Charlotte was using the fact that she was a gorgeous, soft-looking woman to come in behind a trained operative.

He was supposed to do his part to distract the man. "If you get her killed, I swear I'll hunt you down."

Joseph gave him an earnest look. "I promise you. I will protect her. I'll do everything I can."

"What you'll do is unlock your cell, call that psychotic asshole, and hand my husband the phone." Charlotte emphasized the words by putting a gun to the back of Joseph's head.

"What?" MaeBe gasped because Ian suddenly had a gun in his hand, too.

"Try anything and I won't care what my wife will do to me because I didn't put down a tarp," Ian promised.

"It was time to redecorate anyway," Charlotte conceded.

"What the hell is going on?" Joseph had his hands up in the air.

"Yeah, I'd like to know that, too." MaeBe frowned Ian's way.

"I think we're about to get to watch the OGs work." If Taylor was worried about all the guns being drawn or the sudden turn of events, she didn't show it. She merely sat back and looked ready to watch the show about to play out.

"I'm not joking." Charlotte didn't move an inch. "I want that phone connected and in my husband's hands in ten seconds or I will blow you away. You should understand that I already laid the groundwork with my Canadian contacts. You'll find I told them you were acting erratically. I might have made it sound like we caught you after you initiated a gunfight. You know a lot of spies go bad. You think we sent Hutch home, but he's set up downstairs with my sister, who assures me she can make you look as bad as we need you to. You might know her name. Chelsea Weston."

Ah, Chelsea Weston. A name that should strike fear in the heart of anyone who knew something about the Dark Web. She'd once been the queen of information on the dark corners of the Internet, and she still did specialty work for intelligence agencies across the globe. If anyone could frame an operative and get away with it, it was Chelsea Weston, and Hutch would do his best to help her after what had happened to his wife this evening.

"You are killing my years' long operation." Joseph's words were even, but there was a tightness to his stance that worried Kyle.

"No, I'm saving your life," his uncle corrected. "Because I need you to understand that there is no way I allow you to put MaeBe at risk like that. Kyle has to back her. He's her partner, hopefully her husband someday. I'm not. I'm as close as she's got to a father, and I get to lay down the fucking law and not give a damn about the repercussions of her feminism."

"And her mom isn't here with us," Charlotte said. "So I get to represent her feminism by telling you if you tried this with one of my sons, the result would be the same. I would have a gun to your head, and you would get to decide if you want to allow the parameters of your operation to change or if you want to die. We've got an extra-large freezer. There's space for you."

"But we should all agree that I'm not old enough to be MaeBe's father. It's a metaphor," Big Tag insisted.

Charlotte shook her head. "Nah, he's old. There's plenty of room there."

"This is not fair." MaeBe totally sounded like one of the Taggart girls. "I can do this job."

"She can. You made sure of it, Uncle Ian." He had been given a massive gift, and he intended to use it to its fullest. "You trained her. Trust her now."

Ian didn't look his way, but there was a slight curling of one side of his mouth—a smirk that let him know he was proud of the assholish way Kyle was taking advantage.

MaeBe's eyes rolled. "Like I believe that but fine. Fine. Ian, why won't you let me go in? And you are a couple of years older than my dad. He got started young. So, Pops, why can't I go undercover and get us all out of this problem?"

"Because this isn't a simple op. That woman's emotions are involved, and he can't protect you from her." Ian proved that great minds truly did think alike. "And you are her poison. She'll enjoy torturing you, and I can't trust a foreign operative to choose you over his mission. I know I wouldn't have when I was working for the Agency. I would have told myself the mission was more important. Kyle can't make this choice because he would be taking something away from you and you could resent him for it. I can make it because I don't care if I piss you off. I want you alive."

"Beyond that, we don't want the Canadian operative's death on our consciences," Charlotte continued. "You've been here too long. It won't work. You can't walk back into your safe house and tell her you lost all the men but managed to get MaeBe. If you go back on your own, it will be suspicious that you're perfectly fine but everyone else died."

Kyle had figured out an option no one else had. "We could brutally injure him. Putting him in the hospital would be an excellent cover."

He would volunteer.

"That might work," Drake agreed. "What was it he said about the upper left quadrant? We could start there."

"He'll need a couple of bullet holes, too." Kyle could see the entire thing play out in his head, and he felt good about it. He would need some tarp, though. Or they could do it down in the bodyguard gym. That was an easy to clean surface.

"You are not shooting him." MaeBe frowned fiercely up at him. "If anything I get to do it. I'm the one who got stabbed."

Thank god she was on board. It had probably been the whole dad thing that did it. It was funny how those relationships worked.

"Fine. Fine. Tank my whole career." Joseph pulled his phone out and unlocked it. "You're probably right. I think she's on the edge right now. She could kill me without a thought. I take it you want to tell her I'm dead, or do you want to trade me for what? I assure you she won't care about me."

"Then you're welcome." Ian took the cell and in a moment he had found the number and put it on speaker. The ringing sound filled the space.

"John? Do you have her? I want to hear her."

"I'm here," MaeBe said in a small voice.

"Listen up, Mae. If you're a good girl, I might think about letting you live through this," Julia began.

"John is dead," Ian said flatly. "This is Ian Taggart, and I would tell you to stay away from my nephew, but you're not going to do that, are you?"

Joseph sighed and sank down to the couch beside Drake. His shoulders slumped, but he didn't say a word.

"Kyle? Kyle, are you there?" Julia didn't sound so confident now.

"You don't get to hear his voice," MaeBe replied without moving away. "He's not going to engage with you in any way. He's busy burying the men you sent. Don't send anyone else or we'll kill them, too."

"Well, that's interesting." Julia proved it wasn't easy to dissuade her. "I wonder what the police will think about that. Perhaps someone should call them."

"Feel free," Ian replied. "I assure you I'm excellent at cleaning up messes. You send the cops here and I'll explain exactly what happened. I'll open my files and you'll have some new surgery in your future. Or maybe I can do it anyway and be done with you because we both know there won't be any surgery for you. You fuck up and get made and there's not even a coffin."

"You won't do that because if you do, I'll bring Kyle down with me," she vowed. "Has he told you all the things he's done? All the people he killed for me? He was good, Taggart. He was as good at murder as he was in bed."

Shame washed over him. He had done both. He'd killed for her. Slept with her in what now felt like a mockery of everything love had come to mean to him. He'd sought out that life because he'd believed he'd deserved it. His past had pushed him to recklessness, and now it might cost him a future with MaeBe.

"He was working for the CIA." MaeBe moved in beside him. "He was following orders. No one is going to blame him for that."

"I can prove he wasn't." A long sigh came over the line. "Mr. Taggart, if you move on me, I assure you I can make your nephew's life a living hell. I have everything I need to do it. You've been surprisingly good at avoiding getting entangled with my group in a business sense, but I can find something on you, too. Stay in your lane and I'll stay in mine. And Kyle, I know you're there. I'm not done with you. Not even close, baby. I'll see you soon. We'll talk then."

"You won't see him at all. I meant what I said. He will not answer your call again." Ian hung up.

"Drake's father helped her put money in your account." Joseph looked oddly relaxed now that it was over. "She has all the information on the fake assignments she sent you on. She intended to use it to force you to her side."

"What?" Drake sat up. "I know about the money, but what do you mean by fake assignments?"

He hadn't told Drake, hadn't wanted to let his friend know how bad it had gotten.

"Not tonight." MaeBe put a hand in his. "He's had enough tonight. So are we heading to Sanctum or are we staying here? Ian, you should know that Kyle and I have decided to go at it hard while we're working this op, so that will happen wherever you decide it's going to happen."

What was she doing? "Mae, we should…"

She turned to him, her face set in frustrated lines. "No. We shouldn't. I'm done with debriefs for the day, and I can't stand another confession. I have had the shittiest day. I want to play. I want to have someone spank me and tie me up and let me forget for a few hours. If that's not going to be you, let me know."

Joseph held up a hand. "I've had a terrible day, too, sweetheart. And now that I'm unemployed, I have some time on my hands."

"My office is a sacred space. No one except for me is having sex in here." His uncle's hold on that big gun had gotten tighter.

"Then we should get these guys to Sanctum." Charlotte was right back to her charming self, putting a hand on her husband's shoulder. "No one would ever do that in here. They know how much you love this space. Why don't you go and tell Hutch he can stand down, and let's get everyone where they need to go so we can go back to bed."

"We'll talk in the morning about how to handle whatever she has on you. Unless you fuck up my private space, and then I will eat you, nephew." Ian walked out, grumbling.

"We're never going to tell him what Adam did in here. Never." Charlotte put on a bright smile. "So, let's go to Sanctum. Joseph, welcome to the team. I suspect you'll be hanging out with us for a while. I hope you like glitter."

She turned and followed Ian out.

"What is that supposed to mean? Also, I'm not into sex clubs," Joseph complained. "I could find a nice hotel."

"Let's go, Joe. There's a great bar there, and we can play with the lights and stuff," Taylor promised.

MaeBe took Kyle's hand as Drake stood and moved in front of him.

He got ready for whatever judgment was about to be passed. Drake would be pissed that he'd kept something from him, angry that he'd only given him half the story. Drake would be disappointed that he'd been so fucking dumb.

Drake put a hand on his shoulder. "Whatever it is, we'll fix it. I promise. I'll stand by you. We all will. Okay?"

He was not going to break down. He simply nodded.

Drake walked out, and MaeBe started to follow.

He couldn't let that happen. Not right this second.

One of the things he'd learned that he should start doing was give in to the impulses he thought might be unmanly. Fuck that.

He dragged her back and hugged her, putting all of his soul into that embrace. She was home to him, and he wanted so badly to return home. He'd thought he didn't belong, thought he didn't deserve it.

But home wasn't something one earned. It was a gift given with no thought to reciprocation.

She didn't hesitate. She wrapped her arms around him and opened that magnificent heart of hers.

They stood there for the longest time.

Chapter Sixteen

Julia realized time had passed but she wasn't sure how much. That fucker had hung up on her, and she'd seen red.

It was a thing that had happened a few times in her life. Someone would push her too far and when she was herself again, the world had changed. Like that time when she was twelve and that boy had made fun of her and then he'd suddenly been at the bottom of the stairs.

Her father had taken care of that. He'd cleaned everything up and sat her down and explained that there was a better way to deal with the rage that burned through her all the time. He'd taught her to focus it and refine it, and he was gone now.

The only fucking time in her life she'd felt good was when she'd been with Kyle. Kyle had made her feel normal.

She had been chasing that feeling from the moment they'd met.

She looked around the small flat she'd been hiding out in. It was owned by the group. A one bedroom in an inauspicious part of the city. Nice, but not too nice. The building was known for short-term rentals. It was exactly the kind of space The Consortium used as a safe house.

She'd pretty much destroyed it.

She'd managed to break the table and the big mirror over the couch. She thrown her phone into it, and she apparently hadn't stopped there. In her rage, she'd trashed the kitchen, too.

When she'd calmed down enough to be back in actual reality, she'd been sitting with her back against a wall, surrounded by broken things. Rather like she was in real life.

She'd lost everything. Even fucking John, who was a somewhat competent assistant. She certainly hadn't cared about him, but she'd needed him and now he was gone and that fucker Taggart had done it to her.

There was a knock on her door. Likely because she'd been loud in her rage.

She took a deep breath and forced herself to stand, forced herself to move to the door and explain to her neighbor that she'd accidently dropped something and it had broken. The nosy fucker shrugged and shuffled back off to bed.

Julia closed the door and realized how bad this was going to get for her.

When she filed the report of John's death, she would have to admit what she'd been doing. She'd been warned to stay away from Kyle. She could dress it up and say she was doing something else, but one of her fellow operatives would be sent to investigate since she was still on probation.

Everyone was against her.

When one got fired from The Consortium, there was no severance pay. There was the severance of one's head from one's body.

Unless she could find the intel her father had left her. Her. Not Drake. She'd been his true daughter. All her father and Drake had shared was DNA. She'd been the one he'd brought into his real life.

That information belonged to her.

The problem was Drake was likely the one who could find it.

How could she force Drake to give it to her when he found it? She wasn't sure she could look for it herself. It would be too dangerous to show her face around DC at this point. She needed someone to do the dirty work for her, and her brother was the best candidate.

She sat down in front of her computer. She needed leverage, and it obviously wouldn't be Kyle.

But it could be. It was all about finding the right leverage. She'd thought it would be that crybaby of his, but maybe she should go younger.

After all, she'd accrued an enormous amount of information about Kyle's family and extended family. It had been a long-term project. Up to this point, she'd used the information for minor annoyances. It had been fun to give the Taggarts some hell. She'd caused some social discomfort for Carys Taggart after finding out about her teenaged threesome. She'd fiddled with some gym equipment and put Luke Taggart in a cast. That had been fun. She'd fucked around with Top's reputation. But now she needed something serious.

She would go after his brother, but the wife was surprisingly well trained and kept an eye on her prized professor. Kyle's younger siblings were with their parents and a whole lot of security. His primary family was out of reach.

But there were others. One silly girl who thought she was smarter than everyone else.

One dumb girl who thought she was a spy. She was excellent at sneaking out of her parents' house to meet a boy at his house once a week. Always on Saturday night when her parents were at their club. This week she just might have to meet the girl along the way.

Taggart could fuck himself. If he wanted to play, she could play. He'd promised to take her down. She believed him. What he didn't understand was that if she was going down, she would try to take them all with her.

It was time to go to war.

* * * *

"Okay. As prisons go, this isn't so bad." Joseph stood in the lounge looking out over the quiet dungeon. He had a whiskey sour in his hand.

MaeBe wasn't worried about the Canadian fitting in. He seemed to have taken his early retirement with something close to relief. She'd overheard him talking to his superior back in Toronto. They were shifting his focus to working with Drake and Kyle. Drake had already promised Joseph they would share any intelligence they found in his father's work that impacted Canadian interests.

Drake had also spent a decent amount of time on the phone with the head of CSIS.

"Don't think of it as a prison." Taylor was busy playing bartender. "It's right there in the name. Sanctum. It's a sanctuary from Julia's evil."

"So I can leave?" Joseph's brow rose as though challenging Taylor to give him a different answer than the one they all knew was correct.

"Of course not." MaeBe wasn't going to mince words with him. "We don't completely trust you. You could go right back to Julia and tell her everything you know about us, including where we're going next."

"She knows you're going to DC." Joseph sank down on one of the comfortable chairs. "It's the best bet as to where he hid the data."

Where had Kyle gotten off to? Since he'd pulled her into his arms and she'd felt how much he genuinely needed her, he'd been quiet. Though she wouldn't call him withdrawn. Drake had driven them over while Big Tag and Charlotte had brought over Joseph, likely discussing how they would work together going forward. Kyle had been quiet, his hand in hers. When they'd gotten here, he'd gone to talk to the security guards and he hadn't come back yet.

"If she shows up, we'll deal with it." Taylor sent MaeBe a look that told her that was all they should say about that.

Collaboration would only go so far with this man. They'd talked about it in the car on the way over. She'd identified a couple of places around town where Drake's father might have left sensitive data—the most important being with the law firm he'd used for many years. Drake had explained he'd talked to them and there was nothing left in the estate to deal with, but she wasn't so sure.

"She could be harder to handle than you expect," Joseph mused. "Right now she doesn't want her bosses to know there could be information out there. If she gets desperate, she could play that card with them, and they will open up the armory, so to speak. Especially without me there. She'll get another John, you know. She'll have one in a few hours. It's not like she'll sit around mourning me."

"Do you honestly believe you could have walked back in

without her suspecting a thing?" Taylor asked.

"I think it would have been easier if I brought MaeBe in with me," he admitted. "But apparently she has a daddy."

It was the first bit of bitterness she'd heard from the man. She felt none of it. In the moment she'd wanted to do the job. She'd wanted it over with so she could move on with her life.

Now she kind of didn't feel the same need. She knew she should be upset. A man had pulled a runaround on her and she was pushed to the side again. So why did this time feel different?

Even though she knew damn well Kyle had been following Big Tag's lead, it had felt good to have him back her up. And it had felt good to have Big Tag and Charlotte ride in like the parents she'd always wished she'd had. Her mom had been lovely, but she would have nodded and told her to make the decision on her own. Her father did whatever the woman in his life told him to do. Even as a whole-ass grown woman, it was good to know there was a safety net. That's what parents were—these people who didn't let you fall through the cracks, who did what was best for you even when it could cost them.

She and Kyle had that safety net. They had Ian and Charlotte and Sean and Grace as role models, as mentors. They had Hutch and Noelle and Deke and Maddie as friends they went through all of this bad stuff with, friends they held on to.

"I would say he could be my daddy but that would get me in trouble with a whole bunch of people," Taylor said with a smirk.

"Ewww." MaeBe understood Ian Taggart was an attractive man from an aesthetic point of view, but pretty much from the beginning he'd been a father figure.

Taylor did not have that problem. She shrugged. "That man is hot, and he is not even close to old."

Drake walked into the lounge area, a fierce frown on his face. "Seriously?"

"If it helps, I feel the same way about Charlotte. That woman does not age." Taylor sent her boyfriend a wink.

"She was awfully hot with a gun," Drake admitted.

"Well, I couldn't see her, so I'll never know," Joseph groused. "Now can we all sit down and discuss what we know? The sooner we find that intel the faster I can get back to my life."

Drake looked out over the dungeon floor. "I think that's going to have to wait."

She followed Drake's line of sight, and then her heart threatened to skip more than a few beats.

Kyle was walking toward her, but he wasn't the same Kyle who'd gotten out of the car. That had been a slightly tentative, careful man who sweetly held her hand. She loved that Kyle.

This one could be her daddy anytime. A different kind of daddy, but one who absolutely told her what to do.

He wore leather pants that hit him right at the notches of his hips. He'd left off the vest that most Doms wore around the club, but she was fine with that. His chest was muscled perfection, and that included the scars on his body. She didn't merely mind them. She liked to trace them, to brush her fingertips over them right before she pressed her lips down.

He was her walking Dom dream.

"Is there a reason Hawthorne's dressed like a porn star?" Joseph managed to look slightly horrified.

"He's dressed like a Dom." He'd taken her request seriously, but now she worried if he was ready for this. He'd seemed so quiet when they were in the car. Then there was the fact that she was still in her day clothes. It wasn't like Sanctum was formally open, but she'd never played in the dungeon without fet wear.

"This is the stuff Julia's been going on and on about. She's been studying all this weird crap since she found out Hawthorne joined a club." Joseph knocked back the rest of his whiskey.

"Do not mention her name when we're in this space." She couldn't take her eyes off Kyle while he stalked toward her. He must have changed in the locker room and then used the elevator around the security desk to sneak up on her.

Or to set up a scene in one of the spaces at the back of the dungeon.

"Well, it's hard since we're supposed to be working," Joseph complained.

Taylor moved in as Kyle stepped into the lounge. "Let's get you settled in. We'll find the room upstairs that scares you the least. I hope you don't mind sleeping near an insane amount of lube."

Joseph was asking questions as they walked off with Drake in tow.

"Greet me."

It was all Kyle said. He stared down, his eyes practically burning through her.

They should probably talk. "Kyle, I know I said…"

She didn't get another word out before he leaned down and tossed her over his shoulder.

Joseph was halfway up the steps when he turned and stopped. "Uhm, should we do something about that?"

"Not unless you want to make your fake death a real thing, man," Drake advised.

"I'm fine." She gave Joseph a thumbs-up. "He's overstimulated. Everything is fine."

A hard hand slapped on her ass.

"I thought we were trying to keep Ms. Vaughn from being tortured," Joseph argued.

"I like this torture. Don't be a judgmental vanilla asshole," MaeBe called out.

"What does vanilla have to do with anything?" Joseph asked.

Then Kyle was striding past the hamster wheel that lit up when a sub was running on it. It was not her favorite funishment. Not even close.

He was exactly what she'd said he was. Overstimulated. That was why he'd been so quiet. The whole damn day had been one crisis after another, forcing him to pivot and change plans and go against those faulty instincts of his. He needed to be in control for a while. She could give that to him the way he'd given it to her the night before.

Were they ready for this?

The question floated through her head, but she let it go. They didn't have to decide anything tonight. Taylor was right about that. She felt his pull, knew this man was special. That was all she needed to know.

He walked past the main stage and past several spaces that were rigged for suspension play. He stopped at one of the smaller play areas. A plain space with a massage-style bed and a table with a kit laid out. She didn't get a chance to see what was in the kit because Kyle set her on her feet and then crowded her space.

"Have you changed your mind about sex tonight? I can let you go but I'll sleep outside your room again because it would be hard to keep my hands off you this evening." He was staring down at her, intensity in his eyes.

There was no way she was letting him sleep outside her door. "I haven't changed my mind. About anything. Not yet."

One big hand sank into her hair and twisted lightly. She had to force herself not to freaking melt. This was what she needed. He'd been reluctant the night before, but there was no such hesitancy now. He tugged her head back and loomed over her—the big bad Dom ready to eat her up. "Then greet me and do it properly."

They had never gone over protocol surrounding their D/s relationship, but she thought she knew what he wanted. She hadn't needed to worry about fet wear since this had been his plan all along. He wanted her naked and on her knees.

She stepped back and undressed in quick, efficient movements. She folded her jeans and shirt then stacked on her bra and undies and turned to the man she knew she would love whether they were together or not. She'd loved him even when she'd been enraged with him, even when he'd dulled her shine by walking away.

She set the clothes on the table and tried not to think about the many toys Kyle had lain out, including a plug that probably would fit. Might. With a lot of lube. Of course the straps would make sure that sucker stayed inside no matter how he eventually twisted and turned her body.

Her Dom was clearly planning on making a statement she would feel all through the next day.

Well, she had been kind of a brat.

She moved in front of him, feeling more confident than she had in months and months. Maybe ever since she was a different version of herself. She was different than she'd been when they'd first met. Different than she'd been when she'd woken up this morning. Today she'd begun to build a bridge between her selves, between the MaeBe who'd been blindly optimistic and the one who could handle herself.

There was a happy medium between the two that combined the best of both MaeBes.

Content in her own skin, she sank to her knees in front of him, giving her Dom the deference he deserved in this space. She spread her knees wide and let her head lower submissively. This was the place she'd longed to be in all day. She'd fought it because somewhere deep inside she'd thought she didn't deserve it. She hadn't feared it. This place was happy and relaxed. This place was a second home to her, where she could rest and find pleasure and joy.

One big hand came out to cover her head. "I'm so glad you didn't change your mind, baby. I know I said I could handle it, and I would have, but I need you so fucking much tonight. You have no idea what I felt when I thought they'd shot you."

She brought her head up because that was bullshit. "I once watched the house you were in explode, Kyle."

"Fair, but not the place." He leaned over and brushed his lips against her forehead. "I'll let you rail at me for hours and hours tomorrow. And when we leave for DC on Sunday, you and Taylor can drink wine and complain bitterly about how dumbass your boyfriends are."

That was news to her. Apparently he and Drake had found some time to talk. "We're leaving for DC Sunday?" There was only one real reason to do that. "Drake thinks he knows where it is?"

"He looked at your list of possible places and found an account he didn't recognize. He has two keys from his father's things he hasn't been able to match up with a lock. One of them is for a safety deposit box. We need to wait until Sunday because his mom is out of the country, and he knows Julia will be watching the house. The senator has agreed to meet with us on Monday and hand over that key. Until then, we're going to keep working, and you have to make everything look normal to the Canadian."

That was a great lead, but she was still dismayed. "We're leaving Joseph behind?"

"Absofuckinglutely." He stepped back. "Have I told you how gorgeous you are? Those rings...I think about them all the time."

She knew because his eyes were often on her breasts. She dreamed about being comfortable enough as a couple that he would corner her in the middle of the day and play with them, twisting until she was creamy and wet and ready for a quickie.

But they should also think about other things.

"Have you thought about..." She began because Joseph seemed

to be a legitimate intelligence agent. Charlotte had checked him out and then ruined his op even after they'd discovered he was legit. She understood why, but they could bend a little, couldn't they?

He held a hand out. "Stand."

Oh, that command sounded super irritated. She put her hand in his and let him help her up. "All I'm saying is…"

"Do you need a gag, love? Because this is not a workspace, and you damn well know it."

She hated gags. Drooly things. And she did understand it wasn't a workspace, but she knew what was going to happen. "You're going to keep my mouth occupied all night and probably the next few days, and I'll be on that plane before I can make my point."

"Oh, then let's make your point right now, brat. As long as you want to talk, I can spank. Turn around. Hands flat on the table, and spread your legs wide."

He was going to make her pay for being the logical, reasonable one. She turned and put her palms flat on the padded table. Well, it wasn't like he wouldn't have found a reason. It was part of the play. He got to spank her. She got to have her ass slapped in just the right way. She got to feel powerful and complete. She probably wasn't going to win this argument.

"He's been working this case for a long time," she began and then gasped because his hand came down on her ass.

Pain bloomed, but she was ready for it and let herself ride the wave of heat until it crashed into something like pleasure.

"He probably knows the target better than any of us." She was careful not to use Julia's name. That woman didn't get to be here in this space with them.

Three quick slaps this time had her panting. Was he going to argue his point? Or was the discipline his point?

"We need to keep good relations with Canada or they might not send us anymore syrup, and I don't want to be completely dependent on Vermont." If he wasn't going to argue then she would go for the silly.

A nasty smack hit her ass and he held his hand there, forcing the heat on her skin. "Do you have any idea how much I love it when you tease me? When you're weird and funny? When you walk in a room, it gets brighter for me. I find you so sexy it hurts."

She could take care of that ache for him. She rolled her hips, pressing her backside against his hand. "I haven't had a lot of reason to glow lately, Sir."

Another three hard smacks and she bit back a groan.

"I promise to give you a reason. You're the sun in my sky. I know I hurt you, but I won't do it again," he promised. "I learned my lesson. I trust you, and I won't shove you aside again. I did it out of fear and guilt and yes, there was love in there, too, because I've never loved anyone the way I love you. It's new, and I'm so scared I'll lose you."

He settled in to spank her, ten and then twenty more times, the sound of his hand striking her ass making a symphony of arousal. She could feel herself getting soft and wet. She held on to the sides of the table, letting the sensations roll over her in waves.

He'd been scared. His past had wrongly taught him he was cursed. She'd thought the same from time to time, but then she would look at the world through different eyes. That was what she'd forgotten to do while he'd been gone. She'd forgotten there was often another side even to bad events. His fear had forced him to push her away, but she hadn't been alone. She'd had her friends. Her father had left her behind, but Ian Taggart hadn't. Charlotte Taggart wouldn't. Hutch and Noelle and Maddie and Deke and Boomer and Daphne wouldn't leave her behind.

She was strong enough.

She *was* enough.

The tears began then, a welling of emotion that nothing to this point had been able to spur.

Kyle kept it up until she sobbed, until her body went limp with the relief that came from releasing all that toxic emotion.

He stopped, hauling her around and pulling her into his arms. "Baby."

She hugged him, but she was already starting to normalize, like she'd needed that cry to finally expel the end of her anger and fear. She didn't want this intimacy between them to end. She wanted everything she'd said to Ian. Her ass ached in the best way as she tilted her head up. "I'm okay. I needed that, but I'm okay."

His big hands came up and brushed her tears away, cradling her face in his hands. "It's all I want. I want you to be okay. I want you to be happy. I want you to have everything you want in life even if that doesn't include me."

They needed more time before she could commit, but she knew what she wanted right now. "It does for tonight. For tomorrow."

"Even though I have no intention of taking the Canadian with us?"

She could bend, too. They knew very little about Joseph. Kyle was trusting her information-gathering skills. She had to trust that he knew what to do in the field, and sometimes that meant carefully picking the team. "We'll share what we find with him?"

"I suspect we'll share what we find with the world, so giving him a preview won't be too hard. I promise," he vowed. "And I promise not to do anything stupid. We're going to find the intel and get right back here, and then I'm dumping this whole problem on my uncle's lap. I've been informed he hasn't had anyone assassinated lately and he looks forward to the project. I think my aunt might do it. She's a little bloodthirsty."

But she did it with style. "I hope they have fun." He was offering to give up control so he could stay with her. He would keep her safe by keeping her by his side. "Then let's have a nice night because I suspect we won't be staying in such cool places when we get to DC. Kiss me. Play with me."

He lowered his mouth to hers. "Don't think all this sweetness from you is going to stop me. I'm going to plug that pretty ass of yours and then fuck your pussy. I want you to feel me everywhere tonight."

Then his lips were on hers and she gave over to him. His tongue surged in, dominating hers. He devoured her mouth, his hands moving over her shoulders and down to her waist. He pulled her against his chest, and her nipples brushed against the fine hair there. She could feel the hard length of his cock against her belly, and it sent her arousal rocketing.

His big palms cupped her ass, making her hiss. She would feel that spanking all day tomorrow and remember how he'd given it to her. That familiar sweet ache would remind her who her Dom was.

She knew they were going into danger, but she wasn't worried because they would be together. They could face anything if they trusted one another.

He stepped back. "Turn around."

They didn't need the plug. "It's okay. I am willing to admit I might have been a little bratty."

His hand came up, circling her throat. His lips curled in a sadistic smirk. "A little? I want you to think carefully about the next words that come out of that sweet mouth of yours. I set up this scene. I know we haven't played much, and that was my fault because I wasn't ready before. So I'm giving you a choice. You can have the me who is still filled with guilt and worry or you can have the top who is going to forget all of that shit for a night. We can go back to our room, and I'll give you whatever you want. You stay here and we do this my way, all the way, and that includes a plug up your pretty ass that's getting bigger every second we stand here. We can start talking about exotic lubes as well. I've got a water based one right now. How do you feel about ginger?"

She loved it on food. Not so much up her asshole.

And there was no decision to be made. She wanted this man in all of his iterations. She adored the man who learned new games so they could play together, who made sure she always had the things she wanted.

She was pretty sure she would worship the dirty, filthy Dom who would make her every kinky fantasy come true.

She turned and noticed this was a thoughtfully made table. It came complete with handles halfway down so the sub who rested against it would have their ass in the air and ready for plugging. It also allowed her to let her cheek sit against the padded table. She was grateful to have something to hold on to when she felt him move in, heard the sound of the lube squirting.

"Does that cool off your pretty backside?"

He was a sadist. "Yes, Sir."

At least it wasn't ginger. She would definitely prefer chill to cool.

"Can you relax for me? If you're good, I promise you a treat."

She knew exactly what that treat would be. Along with the plug she'd seen a vibrator. She knew she wouldn't get his cock. Not yet. He wanted to make this last, but he could give her the orgasm she craved. Besides, she had other things she wanted to do with that man's cock. She'd never gotten it in her mouth, and that was a shame. He'd been especially generous with the oral. It was time to pay her guy back.

Naturally she would have to keep the plug in, but she'd never backed down from a challenge.

She stayed still as she felt Kyle press the lubed plug against her. Another drop of the lube and it was sliding against that intimate place, making her bite her lip in anticipation of that moment when he would breach her and fuck that tiny hole with the plug. She whimpered at the pressure.

Kyle put a hand on her lower back, holding her down.

Something about that flat did it for her. She knew she could stop him at any moment, but there was something about him dominating her that made her whole body sink into a submissive state. It had been fun to play before, but this was truly intimate because of the emotion that flowed between them.

As easily as the lube. She bit back a smile at the thought. Such an old MaeBe thought to have, and it felt good to be able to view the world through those weirdly colored glasses again. The world had been colorless without him, black and white. Or perhaps it had been her trauma that stole her humor, but it was coming back, and she wasn't going to let it go again.

He circled her hole with the tip of the plug, gaining ground with each turn. She felt her whole body tighten as he came closer and closer to sliding that sucker home.

She groaned as he gently fucked her with the plug. It felt so big, so fucking hard.

The plug slid in and filled her, stretching her and making her so aware of her body. He seated the plug deep inside and attached the straps that would help hold the plug in. She liked the feel of those, too. They were soft and hugged between her thighs, snaking up to her waist and holding her tight. She twisted her hips, but the plug held tight.

Kyle gripped the vibrator. He placed it over her clitoris and the low hum started, sending waves of sensation through her body. He was gentle at first, letting the head of the vibe get wet with her own arousal.

His big body was behind her, arms encircling her as he rubbed that vibrator right where she needed it.

MaeBe forgot about everything but the magnificent pleasure that broke over her. She rubbed against that vibration, feeling it in her pussy and reverberating into her whole body.

She sighed and let her body relax.

Kyle moved behind her, giving her space so she could carefully turn. She looked up at him.

"Please, Sir. Please let me thank you for the discipline." She gave him her widest eyes and ran her tongue over her bottom lip.

"Such a brat." He stepped back and nodded.

MaeBe prepared to serve her Dom.

* * * *

She was going to kill him. She was so fucking gorgeous. Her skin was flush with the orgasm he'd given her. She'd shuddered and rubbed her clit against that vibrator, and his dick had responded by getting so hard it hurt.

He might find some relief in the next couple of minutes because his sub had that glint in her eyes that he'd come to realize meant she was serious about something. And this time that something was sucking his cock.

He'd never felt her mouth on him before. He'd always been too eager to please her or get inside her. He'd spread her legs wide and licked and sucked her but never felt that in return, and here she was offering him everything she had.

Everything except her heart, but that would come. He suddenly knew it. They would be okay, he and MaeBe. It was his choice. He'd been the problem all along. If he was the man she needed him to be, this would all work out. If he was brave, if he loved her enough to trust her, he could get everything he wanted. And everything he wanted was a life with her, a future with her. Come what may.

He helped her gently drop to her knees, amused at the way she grumbled about the plug. She'd taken it beautifully, and watching her tiny hole open for him had damn near made him come then and there.

It wasn't much easier watching her reach up and untie his leathers, pressing the sides away and revealing his cock. It was upright and weeping with arousal. She swept her thumb over the head and then sucked it into her mouth, her eyes closing as she tasted him.

She was the sexiest woman in the world.

He reached down and gripped the back of her head, sinking his fingers in. "I know why you did it, but I hope you color your hair anything you want soon. You are beautiful with any color, but I love the light in your eyes when you love your hair."

For a moment her eyes shimmered. "I don't know what they did to you in Wyoming, but you figured out what to say to me."

She leaned forward and took his cock in hand, stroking him up and down.

Fuck that felt good. He watched as she used that small hand of hers on his cock. She moved from base to bulb, her palm tight around him. After a moment, she leaned forward and swiped her tongue across his cockhead.

He groaned and tightened that hand in her hair.

She loved the bite of pain. It was there in the way her eyes went soft when he pulled, how she gasped and her breasts bounced, nipples tightening to hard pink points he intended to suck and nip on later this evening. The gold rings that pierced them gleamed in the low light of the dungeon. He loved the way she squirmed when he twisted and played with them. Their needs dovetailed so perfectly.

She was perfect.

He held still as she sucked his cockhead behind her lips, lightly scraping him with her teeth. The sensation threatened to send him over the edge, but he wasn't ready for that yet.

She hummed around his dick, and he forced himself to breathe.

She took him deep and then released him, pressing little kisses along his dick, making him crazy with all the different sensations. "So what shall we do for the next couple of days? We'll be stuck here in Sanctum at night, and you promised never to play here."

That was good. He'd had the briefest image of that time he'd walked in on his mom and Sean, and he suddenly wasn't so close to the edge. That was helpful. "You know the reason I don't play here, and they're in New York and will be through next week. You can safely assume you're going to be on display Saturday. We'll avoid my uncle as much as possible. And when we get to DC, we'll be staying at Drake's club."

The Court was as secure as Sanctum and had more than once acted as a safe house for kinky operatives.

She licked a long path down his cock. "So I should pack my fet wear?"

She didn't need it. She could stay naked all the time as far as he cared.

Her eyes narrowed. "I'm not staying naked all the time."

She knew him well. He couldn't stop the smirk that hit his face. "Hush, sub. We'll work it all out."

MaeBe growled as she sucked him deep again, and all thought beyond how her mouth felt fled. It would be okay. They would work this out because they were meant to be together. He was the dumbass who'd screwed it up, and she was the one who opened her heart again. All he had to do was stay close, be good enough for her. He wanted to spend the rest of his days making life easier for her, being her true partner in all things.

He tightened his hands on her hair, wanting to control her movement. He wasn't going to come down her throat. He wanted to get inside her pussy, to fill her with his cock and feel that plug against him, wanted her to feel him everywhere.

One more long pass of her tongue and he tugged gently on her hair. "Come up here, baby."

She rose, only wincing the tiniest bit. He leaned over and kissed her, tasting his own arousal on her tongue. He kissed her over and over, his hard cock rubbing against the soft skin of her belly. He wrapped himself around her, loving her scent and taste and the feel of her in his arms.

He was never letting this woman go. If she couldn't forgive him, he would stay close and be her friend. He would honor her boundaries, but if she ever needed him, he would be there.

Her nipple rings rubbed against him as she moaned.

It wasn't going to go that way. He could win her back with sex and trust. His uncle had been right. He couldn't let fear rule him one second longer.

This—this magnificent feeling of belonging—should be the only thing that led him through life.

He moved her back, getting her to the massage table he'd been sure would be perfect for what he intended. "Turn around."

She whimpered but turned.

He pulled on the straps, able to fuck her with the plug without touching it. He could tug on the straps and make her squirm. "Tell me how it feels."

"Like I have a cock in my ass, Kyle," she replied with a bratty tartness.

That earned her a slap to her pretty ass. It was already pink. "I can turn this red if you'd like."

"Maybe later, babe." Her head was turned, the sweetest smile on those lips. "How about you give me something else now? Like your real cock. I can pretend you're a sexy beast with two cocks and I'm the pretty princess you caught in a trap."

The books that woman read... "I'm your beast. Only yours. Spread your legs."

She moved her legs apart and tilted her ass up, offering him everything he needed. He shoved his leathers down and grabbed the condom he'd prepped. He managed to drag it on his dick and then he moved into place. He let his eyes roam across her back, fingers tracing her spine. He leaned down and set his lips on the back of her neck, kissing her gently before he gave her a nip.

Her gasp and low moan let him know how much she liked it. She gripped the sides of the table as he let his hands roam down to her breasts and those nipple rings he adored. He tugged on them as he rubbed his cock against her pussy.

"You're killing me, babe."

He loved it when she called him babe, loved being hers. He was safe with her, and he wasn't going to feel less like a man because he thought that way. He was going to revel in it, live the rest of life in this magnificent place where he loved MaeBe Vaughn. "Never. But I will tease the hell out of you. We've still got a couple of days here, and then we'll be at The Court. You should understand I intend to take advantage of the fact that we'll be living in clubs for a while. I'll do nasty things to you every single night, and you have to obey me when we're playing in a club. Hell, when we get back, Julian Lodge has some apartments over his club. We could live there."

"We are not living at The Club. We are finding a nice starter house with a game room and a big backyard so we can entertain."

The words came out fast enough that he knew she meant them, had thought about them. "I mean if we stay together."

The Kyle of three days ago would have backed off. He would have taken his hurt heart and walked away. Instead, he was going to respect her process and be involved in it. He toyed with her nipple rings, making her go up on her toes and probably shifting that plug at the same time. "If we stay together, we'll find a starter house with a beautiful game room. Now stop thinking about anything but this."

He brought his hands back down and held her hips as he started to fill her pussy.

His eyes nearly rolled to the back of his head as he started to thrust into that tight wet pussy. So fucking tight because he could feel the plug drag against his dick.

MaeBe squirmed, obviously trying to accommodate him.

"You okay, baby?" He could make himself stop if she didn't like the sensation. They could start over. It would kill him, but he was never going to take pleasure when she didn't feel it, too.

"Don't you dare stop." She could barely get the words out. They were breathy and sexy and made his dick swell even further. "It feels perfect."

That was all he needed. He thrust up and seated his cock deep, holding her hips. She would be able to feel him everywhere. "You're the one who feels perfect. MaeBe, I know we're playing and I'm supposed to give you space and time, but even though I don't say it, I still feel it."

"Say it, Kyle. No matter what happens between us, this part was true. This part was always true."

"I love you. I love you so fucking much. You're the best part of me." The words felt right.

She growled, and for a second he thought she was going to tell him to stop. "I love you, too. Now stop being the sensitive guy and fuck me, Sir."

Oh, his uncle was such a bad influence. He slapped her ass and then gave her exactly what she wanted. He dragged his cock out and then thrust back in hard. He let one hand wind around her waist and down to her clitoris. He rubbed her there, finding a rhythm that had her moaning and pressing against him. Backward, forward, any way she went he would be there. That had been his plan, but he was caught in it now, too. He loved surrounding her, making sure she received pleasure from everywhere.

It didn't take long before she shuddered and cried out, her body clamping down around him.

Kyle let himself off the leash and pounded inside her, giving her everything he had and letting the orgasm briefly become his whole world. It was safe and warm and beyond all expectations. This was sex and something so much more, something he'd never had with any woman but this one.

As he came down from the wild pleasure, a peace filled him.

He would do whatever it took to keep her.

Whatever it took.

Chapter Seventeen

By Saturday night Kyle was almost certain everything was in place. This was going to work. He glanced up at the clock. It was almost ten, when Sanctum would get going, and he was excited to get to tonight's play. It might be the last time they played here. He was serious about never seeing his mother in fet wear again.

It was okay. They could play at The Club.

Although MaeBe loved it here. He might have to negotiate with his stepdad. That was weird. Negotiating with one's stepfather as to who got to go to the sex club on which night was weird.

He was going with it. He was going with all of it because this was his family, and he was happy here.

Where they played didn't matter as long as MaeBe was content. They could play for the rest of their lives wherever she wanted.

"You look entirely pleased with yourself." Drake leaned against the locker door.

"What's not to be pleased about?" He stopped. He'd been in a happy cocoon for days. He couldn't forget there was danger out there and they were about to fly right into it. "Sorry. Julia. I'm not pleased about her. But the rest of it, I'm pretty okay with."

Drake's lips kicked up. "Good. It took way less time this go around. I was worried about you."

"What do you mean?"

"I mean Julia kicked the shit out of you. The first time around it took over a year for you to start being Kyle again. This time it was mere weeks, and it's not because you're smarter than you were before."

Now he understood and he agreed. "It's because of Mae. And when you think about it the fact that I managed to get that woman means I am smarter than I was before." He sobered a bit because while he'd been betrayed by Julia, Drake had spent his whole life with her. She was his sister. "Are you okay with what's going to happen?"

"You mean am I okay with my sister being assassinated by the group we're about to take down?" Drake sighed. "I have to be. It's what's going to happen. I could try to catch her and put her in jail, but you know what they'll do to anyone who could testify against them."

Julia would die in that cell or she would die in some random place—wherever The Consortium caught up with her. "You've thought about trying to bring her in?"

"Taylor and I have gone through pretty much all of the possible scenarios, but they all lead to one thing. Our mother's status could potentially protect her if I could trust her to testify," Drake admitted. "But I don't. She would use whatever time we gave her to manipulate her way into a position where she could do more damage. I know who she is now. I just also remember who she seemed to be. That's the problem. But don't think I'm not fully invested in this op."

"You better be because she'll try to use that relationship against you," a familiar voice said.

Damn it. They needed to be better spies. He realized Joseph was walking up behind Drake. He was dressed in the khakis and polo shirt he'd bought when he'd finally realized he was stuck here. Not stuck, exactly. They'd gotten comfortable enough with the Canadian that they'd offered to let him go home. He could take himself back to the great north, but he'd decided to stick it out.

"She can't. There's no relationship left. She was willing to kill our mother." Drake's eyes had gone grim. "I watched her. She was going to use her murder to test a new recruit. Our mother, who never stopped hoping she was alive and could come home. No. She can't use a familial relationship with me because we no longer have one. I miss the child I thought she was, though now I look back and see how selfish she could be. I think my father took those impulses of hers and turned them to his advantage."

He forgave himself for not hearing the guy walk up since at that precise moment a shout went out. Someone had scored or not scored or a bad call had been made and every man in the Man Cave was having their say about it. Sportsball. That was what MaeBe called all of it because she did not care. Baseball. Football. Basketball. It was all sportsball to her.

And yet yesterday when he'd sat in his uncle's office and caught the last half of the Mavericks game, she'd joined him. They'd taken to staying late at the office before they carefully made their way to Sanctum, a couple of guards with them at all times. MaeBe—who did not do sportsball of any kind—had brought him a beer and laid down on the couch, her head resting on his lap as she'd read a book on her tablet. She hadn't watched the game, but she'd stayed there with him. She'd brought him peace and comfort, and it had been lovely.

"Julia had a complicated relationship with your father, from what I could tell," Joseph was saying. "She didn't talk a lot about her past, but she did tell me her father was the reason she got her position in the organization. I got the feeling it was something she and your father worked toward for a very long time."

"So the Canadians knew my father was a bad guy but they didn't tell us," Drake said, his bitterness plain. "I'm sure my mother would have liked to know before she ended up nearly dying in a London hotel room."

"He worked for the Agency." Joseph sat down on the bench, and if he felt the pressure of Drake's emotion, he didn't show it. "You work for the Agency. We've been over this. We're still assessing how deep the corruption goes."

"Does that mean you haven't cleared us?" Kyle wouldn't be surprised, but he also wasn't upset at the thought. It made him believe Joseph. He would have to be careful.

"Oh, I've cleared you," Joseph said. "You're too connected to your uncle. Ian Taggart has an impeccable reputation as an asshole who doesn't deal with organizations like this. Ever. The McKay-

Taggart team knocked the legs out of this group for over a decade. It's only been the last few years that they really managed to get back into power. I'm honestly not worried about you, Drake. Or your mother, but my colleagues need more convincing. Hence I'm here for a while. It would help if you didn't leave me behind when you go to DC tomorrow."

Kyle sighed and let his head fall forward.

"Well, Kyle, I am a spy. It's what I do, and before you worry I was eavesdropping or hacking into one of Hutch's brilliant systems, I wasn't," Joseph explained. "The company that services the private jet called in. They apparently are treating this like an everyday corporate event. Which is smart because that is a small world. There's a lot of talk that goes on in private aviation. By treating it like an everyday event, your uncle ensures there's no talk. However, it also means he has to allow the normal protocols to proceed. I was walking through the lobby this morning. Your receptionist was going over the luncheon menu. It's steak and potatoes. It sounds excellent. I wouldn't mind some of that. Don't blame her. She didn't understand I wasn't supposed to know. And honestly, I knew you would try to leave me behind. It's only the timing I figured out."

He was going to have to talk to his uncle. Although maybe not. The man was running a damn company, not an intelligence agency. "You know why we're not taking you."

"You still don't trust me." Joseph stood and sighed. "I suppose I can understand that, but I want you to think about what's at stake. It's more than your war with Julia. Lives are at stake. My people. Your people. The Consortium will always exist. The name will change. Collective, Illuminati, The Star Room. It's just a different name for the same point one percent who will do anything for corporate profits. We can only hold them down for so long, but in that time, we can make progress. That's all I ask. Think about how you use that information and who you share it with."

Sometimes it was hard to remember how much was at stake. It seemed like the problem with Julia was his whole world, but there was so much more. The kids would be going out in the world soon. His sister and brother. His cousins. A whole bunch of them would likely be going into the military, and groups like The Consortium would view them as cannon fodder. They manipulated wars and placed the youth on the firing lines so they could have access to more oil, more diamonds, more consumers.

"I will remember that there's more at stake." One day he and MaeBe might have kids, if she wanted them. He had to think about their world.

Joseph stood and straightened his shirt. "I'm staying down here until the night's festivities are over. Let me know if you need anything. While you're gone, I'll monitor the Julia situation. I don't like a few things I've seen in the last couple of days."

"How are you monitoring Julia?" Drake asked.

"The Dark Web," he replied. "I've been working with MaeBe. I showed her a couple of the accounts I've grown over the years. I started one of them when I was barely eighteen. That's the key. You can fake a lot of things, but time is not one of them. Back then I was working with local law enforcement to identify militia groups in the area. I've since moved that persona into black ops around the world. I try to keep an eye on any mercenaries Julia might hire. It's been handy because I want to know who I'm going to have to work with. I know Julia's habits. I believe she's moved. I think she's in DC, but I also believe she's working off The Consortium grid. About an hour ago I found out she's hired a group of mercenaries I 'work' with. They've been hired to kidnap a girl here in Dallas. I think they might try to take MaeBe again tonight."

"At Sanctum?" He knew he should be more upset, but he wasn't sure why Julia thought a group of mercenaries—even good ones—could get through Sanctum's security. There was a reason so many high-value targets had been safe here over the years. "Please tell me she's coming along."

If this could be over tonight, he would thank the universe. If they took out Julia, the mission to find Don Radcliffe's intel wouldn't feel so fraught with danger. They could take their time and do it right.

"I don't think so. Julia never risks herself if she doesn't have to." Joseph glanced around. "I don't think she understands what she's up against. She can be arrogant. It's a weakness you can use against her. But I also worry that Julia is at her most dangerous when she's desperate. I don't like to think about what she'll do to MaeBe. I've come to like her quite a bit. Julia won't play around with her this time. Or rather she will, but in the nastiest way. If she gets her hands on MaeBe, I don't think she'll come back whole. I wanted to make sure you know I think she'll be waiting for you in DC, and she wouldn't do that if she wasn't sure she'll have leverage."

"My mother is secure," Drake promised. "We've changed all her guards, and the new ones are Taggart approved. If Julia tries something here tonight, we might be able to keep one of the fuckers alive and figure out what she's planning."

Joseph's head shook. "They won't know. Half the time she didn't tell me what she was planning until we were almost ready to go. And I'm sorry to spring this on you now before your...play time. I only verified the intel right before I left the office. Do you want me to talk to Mr. Taggart or do you want to do it?"

"I'll handle it." Kyle nodded Joseph's way. "Thank you. And I promise I will keep you updated, and you will get the information you need."

"Consider yourself our ground crew," Drake added. "You'll stay in touch and monitor the Dark Web for any intelligence about Julia and what she's planning. In exchange, you can remotely monitor our missions. You can work with MaeBe as technical support."

"I appreciate that." Joseph gave them what seemed like a genuine smile. "I think I'll grab a beer and hang with the guys for a while. I like this group. They're fun to be around. It's been a long time since I had any fun at all. I like the way Taggart runs his teams."

"Please send him back here." His play tonight might have to wait. If Julia was coming for Mae again, it would be prudent to move her now. The security was excellent here, but nothing was foolproof. His uncle had already had to rebuild this place once because an enemy had blown it up.

Joseph nodded and walked out.

"Where do you want to go?" Drake asked. "We can let Ian fortify the hell out of this place, but I know you. You'll want to move her."

"I want to move all of us. We can go to Julian Lodge's building. It's closer to the private airfield anyway." They might need to get tricky about this. "We should change up our plans. I think heading to your dad's golf club in South Carolina might be a good idea."

Drake seemed to think about that for a moment. "Yeah. He still has a locker there. We're supposed to clean it out, but he'd paid for the year. It's a logical place to look. Or rather a good distraction. One she'll believe."

"Then we get in a car and drive to DC." He could go old school when he needed to. "It'll be a long day, but we can still meet your mom and get those keys."

"Okay." Drake closed his locker. "I'll go and let Taylor and MaeBe know what we're doing. Can you call Lodge? We'll need a secure vehicle, too."

He was used to handling logistics. "Yes. Tell our ladies we'll move out in an hour or two."

He wondered if he could get to The Club and still have time to tie up MaeBe and torture her for a couple of hours. Probably not. Drake walked away and Kyle's brain started working on how the evening needed to go.

"What's going on?" His uncle rounded the corner. "Tell me it's something I can punch because right now I'm losing a bet with Jake. The Longhorns need a new coach, damn it."

"Apparently Julia's going to move on MaeBe tonight."

"Here? At Sanctum?" his uncle asked.

Kyle nodded.

Ian threw his head back and laughed. "Oh, that's going to be fun. All right. Are we looking at hired mercenaries or a whole bunch of Johns? I love that they call all their male operatives Johns. Gives it a classy flavor."

Kyle was about to respond when Alex McKay showed up at the end of the row. It wasn't the appearance of Alex that threw him off. Alex played most Saturday nights. No. It was who was with him.

Cooper McKay was a gangly kid. At fifteen he was almost six foot two and seemed to be all arms and long legs. And worried eyes.

"Ian, we need to talk," Alex said with grim resolve. "Or rather my son needs to talk."

"How is Cooper here?" Ian frowned and glanced down at his watch. "It's late and he doesn't drive."

"Tash drove me. I know she's not supposed to leave the house, but we had to look for her," Cooper said, his young eyes filled with tears he seemed to be trying so hard not to shed.

Ian's whole body went stiff. "Where's Kala? What the hell was she doing outside the house? Damn it. She was going to your house, wasn't she?"

"Apparently she's been doing it almost every Saturday night for three months," Alex explained. "This one here figured out how to manipulate the security system so I couldn't tell he shut it off to let her in and out."

"Nope, that was Kala, too," Ian said with surety.

"She came over and then we had a fight because she can be so..." Cooper began and then seemed to think better of whatever he was about to say. "Anyway, she left but I called to make sure she was home and she didn't answer. So I called Tash and we were going to drive around and try to find her, but Tash got worried and came here. She didn't think you would have your cell phone on because of...because you're here."

He turned to Kyle. "I'm sorry. I have to deal with this. It's not the first time Kala's gotten angry and given her whole family a heart attack. We need to figure out where the closest late night boba tea place is. It's her version of a bar. Damn it. She's never getting a car of her own."

"I can help." He didn't want his little cousin running around Dallas at night. Kala tended to think she was far more indestructible than she was.

Ian's head shook. "No, you can't. You need to move MaeBe. I thought a fight would be fun tonight, but it'll have to wait. We're shutting down. Go talk to Wade. Tell him what's going on. We have protocols. I need to get dressed and tell my wife. You take a couple of guards with you and go to Lodge's. I'll text him and let him know you're coming. His place is smack in the middle of downtown. They won't be able to move freely down there. Text me when you're safely in for the night."

Kyle started for the door.

It looked like playtime was done.

* * * *

297

MaeBe put the finishing touches on her makeup and considered the fact that soon she might be able to color her hair again.

Blue. She hadn't been blue in a long time. Or maybe a vibrant Little Mermaid red.

Taylor sat down at the vanity next to her. The women's locker room at Sanctum was like a giant fabulous space dedicated to self-care. Even the showers were luxurious.

"I love this place." Taylor set her makeup bag on the table and adjusted the lights. "I know Drake loves The Court, but this place is nicer. I might have only been to a couple of clubs, but I can tell this one is special. Are you sure you want to leave it for the other one?"

They hadn't talked about it, but technically Kyle's membership was to The Club. Of course hers was here. "I don't know. I think we might do a best of both worlds kind of thing. Sean and Grace don't play here every single night it's open. They're usually here Thursdays."

Taylor's lips curled up. "So you admit you are thinking about what could happen down the road."

MaeBe sighed. She'd kept up the fiction that she was floating through life, living in the moment. Despite what had happened between them, she still worried he would find a way to ship her off to safety. Hopefully after they left for DC and she was still a full member of the team, she could trust that he was ready to change. "I'm practically planning a wedding, and I think that might be a problem."

"I don't. I'm happy for you. Kyle is...he's so much happier than he's been since I knew him. He's pretty much a different person. The Kyle I met was bitter and nervous all the time. He's calm and patient now. I like this Kyle."

She loved this Kyle. "He changed a lot over the time he was here. When he showed up, he was shut down. He was standoffish with most people."

"But not you."

"A little with me, but not the way he was with the others. Even his mom." She knew that because Grace had talked to her about it. It had been at the Christmas party at Top, and Grace had teared up when she'd thanked MaeBe for making Kyle so happy. She'd told Grace they were friends, but Grace hadn't believed her.

They'd never merely been friends, but friendship had certainly been a part of their relationship.

"He was still processing what happened to him. I should know. It took me a long time to come to terms with what happened to my dad. It still hits me from time to time but when it does, I go and sit with Drake and be with him. He can't do anything, but he can be there for me. I'll do the same for him. I worry about him. I don't know what's going to happen when he sees his sister again."

"Hopefully we'll find what we need and let the authorities take care of things." If they got the intel, they would forward it to anyone who would listen. Putting it out there was the safest thing to do, they'd decided. Of course only after they'd thoroughly vetted that sucker to make sure it wasn't something Radcliffe had made up.

"Hopefully." Taylor ran a brush through her hair. She wore a scarlet corset and a short skirt. Unlike MaeBe, she had on killer stilettos. "But if she shows up, you need to understand, I'm going to shoot first and not even care about the questions. If I have a shot, I'm going to take it."

"You know we could always have our own channel." A plan was working through her head. The truth of the matter was, she was worried about Kyle, too. He'd already killed Julia once, and it had wrecked him. Oh, she knew he would tell her it was all about the relationship itself and all the lies, but deep down she knew it had affected him deeply to turn a gun on a woman he'd thought he'd loved.

Had loved. It might have been a reckless, transitory emotion, but he'd cared about her. She'd given him something he'd needed in that moment, though what he'd needed was to be self-destructive.

She had to face the fact that Kyle Hawthorne might never get over the mistakes he'd made.

"What do you mean?" Taylor turned her way, and then the light seemed to dawn. "You mean a channel so we can talk without the guys listening in?"

"I'm not trying to cut them out, but you know they'll try to deal with the situation any way they can." MaeBe would be in the overwatch position, taking over all the cameras at the bank. She'd already mapped it out and could do it without a hitch. She would also have an eye on the security cameras and traffic cams within three blocks so if anyone tried to jump them at the bank, she would know. "If I see Julia and there's a way to get you into position, I'll do it."

"Then I don't have to argue with Drake." Taylor nodded. "Yes, I like this plan."

They weren't sneaking around, merely putting a fail-safe into place. Something played around in her head. She'd thought about something and the idea had sparked…another idea. What was it? It was right there but she couldn't quite put her finger on it.

"Hey, you two." Charlotte walked up to them looking stunning in her pure white short shorts and bra that was really more of a bikini top. "Drake is at the door. He says he needs to talk to both of you. Joseph found some intel that you need to hear."

"Thanks. We'll be right there." MaeBe winced as Charlotte walked away. She'd wondered what had been going on with Joseph. He'd stayed at the office when the rest of them had come down to the club. He'd told her he had a couple of things he wanted to wrap up, and there had been a bodyguard willing to hang with him.

"We spent most of the day trying to figure out where Julia is right now," she admitted. "He's got some great profiles on the Dark Web. The Canadians know how to build a presence, and some of them have been active for ten years."

Taylor stood, towering over MaeBe because Mae was a barefoot sub. "That's amazing. I'd like to take a look at those."

MaeBe grabbed her robe, slipping it on. "Do you think she's on her way to DC?"

"I think that's highly likely but not all that surprising." Taylor strode toward the door.

MaeBe waved at a couple of friends who'd just gotten in. She would miss Sanctum while she was gone, but she was eager to see The Court. Unlike Taylor, she'd only ever been to Sanctum. When they got back she hoped Kyle would take her to The Club.

That was wrong. There was no hope about it. He would. He was already talking about it and all the things they could do together over the holidays. He was acting like it was a foregone conclusion that they would be together in a couple of months and enjoying Thanksgiving at Top and the holiday weekend out at the lake house where the Taggart kids would run wild and the adults would drink and eat and watch over them. They would sit around the firepit and enjoy the cool weather. She would cuddle on Kyle's lap and stare up at the stars.

Yeah. She was fooling herself if she thought she wasn't right back in a relationship with Kyle.

And that was okay. It was okay that he'd made a massive mistake and might make it again. She understood why he'd done it. Time and distance from what had happened would help him enormously. Being apart would not.

She loved him. She was going to trust that would be enough, that they could be enough.

She followed Taylor out of the locker room. Drake stood in the hall, and he hadn't changed yet. He still wore the jeans and button-down he'd had on while they were working.

Her hopes of playing tonight were rapidly diminishing.

"Hey, what's going on?" Taylor moved in, brushing her lips against her boyfriend's.

Drake growled a little, his hand finding her waist. "Trouble, of course. But first, you are stunning and I can't let a second go by without telling you how gorgeous you are."

Taylor practically glowed. "You're not half bad yourself. Even out of leathers."

Drake's face fell. "Yeah, the leathers are going to have to wait. You two need to get back into street clothes. We've got to move."

"What did Joseph find out?" There was only one reason they would be moving.

"Julia's planning on making a move on you tonight." Drake's words confirmed her worst fear. She'd known Julia would try again. The only question had been when. "Joseph found out she hired a group of mercenaries to kidnap you tonight."

"She's moving on Sanctum?" That didn't make a lot of sense. Sanctum was practically a fortress, and since they'd started using it as a safe house, Big Tag had upped the security. After the fiasco with the parking garage, he wasn't using anyone who didn't directly work for McKay-Taggart, and she'd noticed he was only using guards who'd been around for years. "It would have made more sense to attempt to take me when we were moving from the office to here."

Taylor nodded. "Or she's somehow figured out we're flying out in the morning and she's going to try it then. We should have a big presence at the airport."

"I'll get on that," Drake promised. "But until then, Kyle and I have decided to move over to The Club for the rest of the night."

"I'll go and get dressed," MaeBe agreed. "And I'll take a quick look at the security cameras to make sure we don't have any unwanted guests too close to the building."

If they were moving in, she would be able to tell. She'd been trained to look for the clues, and they had security cameras that covered the areas they would need to review. Her recent training hadn't all been physical. Erin Taggart had spent a lot of time going over tactics and military theory, including urban warfare.

If she was going to make a hypothetical run at Sanctum, she would obviously wait until it was closed, and she would come in through the back gate where they had a small basketball court. It was the easiest point of ingress, though it was still secured.

"Joseph also thinks Julia is in DC and will be waiting for us when we get there. It's likely she planned to kidnap MaeBe, so we hand over the intel in exchange," Drake explained and immediately pointed a finger her way. "And do not suggest we let this happen so you can be on the inside. The only thing you would be on the inside of is a cell and a whole bunch of torture."

Did he think she was ridiculous? "I was only willing to do that when I had a friend on the inside. I certainly don't intend to let Julia break my bones again to prove a point. Although I might be able to take her if she didn't have a gun."

She was pretty confident when it came to close unarmed combat. And if she had a good line of sight, she could totally shoot that woman. But she wasn't going to put herself in a terrible position for no reason at all.

"I need you to understand that Kyle would lay down and die if anything happened to you." Drake had gone gravely serious. "It's not that he doesn't trust you."

Drake seemed to have missed all the changing and growing and learning things that had happened over the past couple of days. "He doesn't trust the world, and more than that, he doesn't trust himself. We're working on it. I am fully ready for him to freak out at some point and lock me in a closet somewhere so I can't get hurt. You should understand that my response is going to be to break out of that closet and still watch his back."

"I'm going to help her," Taylor said with a grin. "I've been practicing my lock-picking skills. Also, we're pretty sure we understand enough physics to bust through a door Kool-Aid man style."

Drake sighed. "I'm just going to ask you to be careful and remember the men in this op are going to constantly be on edge until it's over."

Which was a good reason to let her and Taylor take over the majority of it. If she had her way, she would leave the dudes behind and take Erin and Charlotte Taggart and Tessa Hawthorne with her. All girls. No drama. Well, except over who got to kill Julia. They might argue over that, but otherwise, it would be smooth sailing and Julia wouldn't stand a chance because not one of those women would listen to her bullshit. She wouldn't be allowed to monologue or cause a scene. Straight bullet through the brainpan at the first opportunity. It was the only way to go.

But she wasn't going to tell Drake that. Or Kyle. Men were sensitive.

"Well, hopefully we get it right the first time and this can be over." She was ready to get on with her life, with the life she could have with Kyle.

All they needed was the data.

There it was again. There was something about the data. A route that they hadn't considered.

"I hate to tell you to go get dressed when you are so beautiful, but…" Drake began.

Taylor kissed him and turned. "But it's time to go back to work. You should understand that we're going on vacation after this is over. Somewhere tropical, and I'm going to sit on a beach and drink fruity cocktails and think about absolutely nothing."

MaeBe nodded Drake's way and followed, her brain trying to work through the problem. "You can have the beach. I'm going to Disney World. Kyle was supposed to take me to Disneyland, but I think we're going full on World, and I'm going to make him take me to all four parks."

303

Taylor looked deeply amused as she held the locker room door open. "I would not have taken you for a theme park girl."

"I am a complex and interesting woman." Julia didn't seem so complex. She seemed focused on one thing and one thing only—getting Kyle back. Well, and keeping her position. MaeBe followed her back. "You've seen Julia in action. Does this sound like a plan she would make? Storming Sanctum?"

Taylor's heels clicked along the floor as they made their way back to the lockers, passing the women who were getting ready for a fun evening. "Are you asking if I've worked up something like a profile on her?"

"That would be handy. Kyle's been talking to Eve about Julia. She used to profile for the FBI." She'd had to convince Kyle they needed to know more about Julia. Eve McKay could give them valuable insight into what Julia might or might not be capable of.

"Yes, Drake talked to her today as well. He's going to talk to his mom about letting Eve interview her." Taylor stopped at the locker she'd been assigned. "It's going to be hard, but he thinks it might be cathartic for her. He thinks Eve might help his mom understand she didn't do anything wrong. Sometimes the people we love do terrible things, and we can't stop them."

"And sometimes terrible things happen to us and we did nothing to deserve it. That's what I'm trying to get Kyle to understand." He was starting to get the message. The very fact that he was here and he was trying meant he was getting better. MaeBe moved three lockers down, to the one she'd used since her training days. "I can't help but wonder what Julia could be thinking."

"Well, she tried it before."

But that had been different. "She thought I would be alone with West. West, as I'm sure she knows, is fairly new at the bodyguard business. She intended to kill him and take me into custody. She'd planned it out. She took her time with it. Think about it."

"Well, we know she rented the space in the building across from yours the month before," Taylor mused. "She had to have someone waiting there every day to see if you returned. According to Joseph, she'd been planning it for a while, though he was left out until the very end."

She rather thought Joseph had tried to be the voice of reason, and Julia wasn't having it. "She also had the parking garage security guard in her back pocket for months before. She had several options to use, but Joseph didn't think Sanctum was one of them."

"But you pointed out Joseph was often left out of her plans when it came to Kyle."

She was right. "It still feels slapped together for Julia. I've watched her work and while I know she can be unhinged, this plan has little chance of actually going right. There are so many ex-soldiers in this building."

"I would suspect she intends to move on the club after hours." Taylor expertly undid the laces of her corset. "They'll sneak us over to The Club, and then I would bet Taggart is going to try to trap the mercenaries and see what he can get out of them."

Something still didn't sit right.

"Charlie? Baby, I need you to come here."

MaeBe glanced back and the door to the locker room was open. Big Tag had pulled a T-shirt over his chest, but his legs were still covered by his leathers.

"Do you think Ian would shut down the club for the night?" Taylor asked. "I worry if he does, she'll know we're on to her."

"I don't care." MaeBe went to her locker and pulled out her laptop. She could throw her clothes on over her fet wear if they needed to hurry. She wanted to take a look at the security cameras. She sat down on the bench and quickly had them pulled up. "I'd rather have everyone safe. If Ian's closing us down, I trust his instincts."

"Do you see anything that worries you?" Taylor had slipped a sweatshirt over her head that matched her leggings. "Didn't you do a deep dive into all the real estate around here?"

"It was all fine." After what had happened at her apartment, she'd wanted to make sure no one had recently taken up residence in one of the buildings around Sanctum. "No one's rented any space in the three buildings that could potentially be used as sniper nests. And anyone coming from those buildings can be seen by our security cameras, so it wouldn't be smart to launch an op from there. The only thing they could do is drive right up and start fighting. That's why it doesn't make sense. No sane person attacks this building. She doesn't want attention. Not from the authorities, and a firefight is the only way to get into this building."

Taylor took a long breath as she stared down at the computer. "Then we should consider alternatives. This could be her way of getting us out of the building, and she'll attack the car on the way to the new location. Though it would be far easier to do that coming from the office."

"Or she's planning something else, and this is a complete distraction."

Taylor sat down beside her. "All we can do is check everything fifteen times. Do you think we should cancel tomorrow's flight?"

She wasn't sure Kyle would allow that to happen. "I think we should talk about it. I've had this plan playing around in my head since I sat down with Joseph. Julia wants the intel. We don't have the intel. She's never seen the intel."

She was going to continue but Charlotte chose that moment to walk by, Serena Dean-Miles following close.

"I'm going to kill that child," Charlotte said, her face flushed. "She was grounded."

MaeBe stood. "What's going on? Is everyone okay?"

Charlotte stopped, and that was one mad momma. "My daughter is what's going on. Kala, of course. Apparently she's been sneaking out of the house to meet Cooper every Saturday when we're here at Sanctum. She's not allowed to leave the house, much less without one of us knowing where she's going. And now she's mad at Cooper, and she's disappeared on him. They had a fight, and she didn't go home. I swear that child is going to kill me."

"You know how she feels about Cooper," Serena said.

"I know that she's gone too far this time." Charlotte started to walk back to her locker. "And I'm the dumbest mom in the world because it's been going on for months and I didn't even see it. When I find her, I'm going to lock her up. She won't see the light of day until she's eighteen."

MaeBe stood there, her feet planted and body unmoving as her mind made nasty connections.

Julia had been monitoring Kyle's family for at least a year. She'd had people watching them, learning their habits and weaknesses, and she'd used them.

Julia needed someone to make Kyle come to her. Oh, she could pretty it all up by saying she wanted the intel, but what she truly wanted was Kyle.

Julia couldn't get to Carys or Lucas or David. They were too well protected. She would never get close to Kyle's mom. Now she couldn't get close to MaeBe.

But Kala had been sneaking out, making herself vulnerable because that child didn't understand the meaning of the word or how fragile she could be.

Tears sparked, and fear blazed through her.

Julia hadn't been coming for her. No one would storm the doors of Sanctum tonight because Julia already had her prize.

"What's wrong?" Taylor asked. "You went so pale."

"It's Kala. She wasn't here for me this time."

It was Taylor's turn to pale. "You don't think she would…"

Oh, but MaeBe did. She rushed to get to the next row of lockers where Serena was helping Charlotte out of her corset. "Charlotte, Julia Ennis hired mercenaries to come to Dallas tonight. We thought they were coming to Sanctum."

Charlotte laughed at that. "That's ridicu…" Charlotte put a hand to her heart. "Oh, god. She's been watching us all. She knew what Kala was doing, knew she would be vulnerable tonight. I have to tell Ian. We have to call the police."

Yes, there would be no keeping the authorities out.

She had to find Kyle. MaeBe took off, praying they could find Kala in time.

Chapter Eighteen

Kyle thought about going down to the women's locker room. He could grab MaeBe and not let her leave his side until…well, until Julia was dead and they were safe. He could keep his eyes on her so nothing could possibly happen and she couldn't get away from him the way Kala had gotten out of her very secure house and caused a shit ton of trouble.

Except MaeBe was a grown, competent, thoughtful woman who knew how to take care of herself and wouldn't put her team in danger but would explain to him the meaning of the words *infantilize* and *marginalize*.

So he turned the opposite way as he left the men's locker room and started toward the security office like he'd promised his uncle he would.

Behind him he could hear his uncle talking on his cell phone. "I'm sorry. I know you're busy but I need you on this, Chelsea. I need all the cameras between my house and Alex's pulled up, and we need to go through them for the last four hours. Yes, I've already sent someone to where her phone signal is. It looks like she's at a park, but I want to cover all our bases."

It was going to be a rough night in the Taggart house.

He turned into the lobby, and there was one of the people who was having a rough night. Tasha Taggart stood in the lobby dressed in leggings and a big T-shirt with some K-pop band on the front of it. She had a jacket on, her hair up in a messy ponytail.

"You okay?"

She looked up, worry plain in her eyes. "I don't know. Did I do the right thing? It's not even eleven. She could be home by now. I might have panicked."

He understood her predicament, though he'd never had to cover for his brother. His brother had been practically perfect. The worst David had done was stay up past bedtime to practice his moves for chess club. His brother had been such a dweeb, and he was going to hug the hell out of him because now he realized how hard having a rebel sibling could be. "You did the right thing, Tash."

"I always do the right thing. It doesn't make me popular. Kenzie's angry with me. She thinks Coop and I are being overly dramatic, and Kala will sneak back in when she's ready," Tash explained. "But something feels off. She texted me back and it was weird."

"Weird how?"

"Kala tends to text in emojis and GIFs. This time she used like whole sentences. It was weird. Kenz thinks it's because she's so mad at Cooper. I tried getting her to text again but I got nothing. That's why I came here." Tash wiped a tear from her eye. "I think something's really wrong. What if she's not planning on coming back?"

"She's not running away." For all Kala's flaws, she wouldn't run. He hoped. "You need to tell your dad when he comes out." He put a hand on Tash's shoulder. "And you need to follow your instincts, Tash. Your sisters will get over it. It's a bad time for Kala to be sneaking out. Your parents have enough to worry about. Do not leave this lobby without your dad. Do you understand me?"

"I'm not going to do anything foolish," she said with a sad sigh. "I never do. I'm every parent's dream child, haven't you heard?"

"There's nothing wrong with following the rules." He couldn't stand how helpless she looked. "You're not trying to get your sister in trouble. You're worried about her. That makes you a good sister. Not a bad one."

"Tell it to Kenz." She sat down on the bench near the window, her keys in hand. "And Kala. She's awfully good at revenge. After what my parents are going to do to her, she'll likely have a lot of time to plan it out."

He wasn't sure what to say to that since he was aware Kala could plot. She could be ruthless and thoughtful in her plans. But she was a teenaged girl, and she could also be reckless, as this evening's adventure proved. "Keep your head up, Tash."

She gave him a watery smile that dissolved as Cooper McKay appeared and settled in next to her.

"Remember what I said about staying inside." He moved to the hallway that led to the security office. The music that floated down from the second floor completely disappeared as the doors closed behind him.

The security office was small, but from here the guards could easily get to any part of the club, including the third floor. He glanced down the hallway to ensure the red light over the back door was still on.

He opened the door to the security office and found West Rycroft sitting at one of the two desks. His brother's office was behind him, the door closed and the lights off.

"Hey, I was just about to come and look for you," West said.

So he'd already been informed. "We need to figure out the best way to get MaeBe out of here without picking up a possible tail."

West's brows rose. "You're moving tonight?"

Or he hadn't been. "We have reason to believe Julia's going to try to take MaeBe tonight."

West huffed. "That woman is not one to give up."

"No. She's not. She's obsessed, and she'll keep going until she gets what she wants or dies."

"And what she wants is you. Are you sure she's not moving on you? Why take MaeBe when she can take what she actually wants?"

"She might want to get me under her thumb, but I assure you she wants the intel her father left behind more," he explained. "From what I've learned, her bosses are not happy with her. She wants to use that intel to secure her place with the group."

"How would that secure her place? Wouldn't that be bad for her?" West asked. "Or am I misunderstanding what this intel is? I thought this was information on the people who run The Consortium. Wouldn't they be suspicious of anyone who had that?"

"By turning it in, she proves how loyal she is." Although there were other reasons she could want the intel. "She could also want it so she can blackmail important people. It's a perfectly acceptable way to move up in The Consortium. You can't go by normal reason in that world. It's different."

"So she can prove she's loyal?"

"I know that they would have been angry that her father died. He gave them access to parts of Washington they'll be lucky to get close to again. He had direct access to a couple of presidents over the years. An everyday CIA agent might be useful to them, but Radcliffe was invaluable. I'm sure they'd intended to place Julia in that position someday, or maybe they thought they could eventually get to Drake, but what happened between Julia and I screwed that plan up. The way I see it, she's got two choices. She could deliver that intel and prove her loyalty. Or she could use it to try to protect herself. That's the scenario I worry about. If that's what she's planning, then she'll have no one to oversee what she does. She'll also be desperate, and when she gets desperate, she gets reckless."

It was something they should all remember. A cornered Julia could be deadly.

"I'm glad I'm just a bodyguard, man. I hate all the spy crap. I still wonder why she thinks you would be better at finding the intel though."

"I think she's counting on Drake finding it. And you know I did work in intelligence for years. I wasn't terrible at it." Though he'd mostly been muscle. He was good in a fight, excellent from long range. He could use a computer, but not the way MaeBe or Taylor could.

"Do you think she'll use MaeBe to find the data?" West asked, proving he could find the right questions when he wanted to. "I would assume at some point you'll have to figure out passwords or codes, and that's exactly what MaeBe does. She specializes in being able to hack almost anything."

Because that was an excellent question. Did Julia want MaeBe for more than mere torture? Why would Julia expect that he would be better at finding the data than Mae? This would be a tech heavy op, and Mae was far better with tech than he was.

It would probably be more sensible to kidnap him and make

MaeBe find the data. Of course, kidnapping him would be more difficult.

"She might," he conceded. "It's all the more reason to keep MaeBe safe, and I didn't need another reason. We're going to need a secure way out. We're going to Lodge's building. I've already got the go-ahead, and he's got a secure underground garage so they can't be sure who gets out of the car. We need to make sure they don't know who gets into the car on this end."

"All right." West picked up his cell phone.

The door opened and West's brother Wade strode in. "Hey, we're closing down the club for the night. Big Tag's orders." Wade Rycroft looked over at Kyle. "I'm working on transportation. But first I need to make sure no one is about to storm the club. I wasn't around for the first time this place blew up. I do not want to oversee building this place a third time. West, pull up all the traffic cams around here. Give me a four-block radius."

West nodded and started to move over to a laptop. "Sure thing. And Kyle, some courier showed up with that package for you about an hour ago. I signed for it. Not sure why you had it sent here."

He hadn't. He hadn't had anything sent here.

"Don't you fucking open that." Wade gestured for him to move back and then glared his brother's way. "What the hell are you doing accepting packages? We don't get supplies on Saturday night."

"What was I supposed to do? I recognized the courier. It's the same one the lawyers use when they need to send us stuff at the office." The package West had pointed out was more like a folder. It was slender, the envelope mostly flat, but with a slight bump toward the end.

"It's not a bomb." Kyle's gut twisted. He knew what that was. "It's a phone. Has it rung yet?"

Why would Julia send him a phone? That wasn't the right question. He knew why, but the timing was off. He would think it would come when she was sure she had MaeBe.

It didn't make sense to send it beforehand. It would tip him off that something bad was about to happen.

He needed to go find MaeBe.

"No. It hasn't done anything. Why would it ring?" West asked. "I didn't open it. The courier said it was for you. I was about to come and find you. I don't think it's a bomb. I know what a bomb looks like."

"No, you fucking don't," his brother shot back. "Though it is small for a bomb. You think it's a phone? You think Julia's trying to call you? I would assume she doesn't have your cell number."

He didn't have a proper cell anymore. He had an endless set of burners he ran through like water. That was why she'd had to call into the office before. But if she knew he was at the office, wouldn't she figure out he was spending his nights at Sanctum? Why would she let him know she knew where he was?

Unless she thought she had a way to make him do what she wanted him to do. "Is MaeBe still in the building?"

"We've got the alarms on. No one's come in or out since Alex met Cooper and Tasha in the parking lot. Tasha's car is the last one to come in," West said. "Alex walked out and you can see him pacing, and then Tasha and Cooper show up about two minutes later. Alex's rage pretty much shook the cameras. I'm shocked the kids stopped. At their age, I would have rolled right on by and lived my life out elsewhere."

What the hell was happening? Nothing made sense. He pulled out his burner to call his mom and make sure everyone was accounted for up in New York. "Hey, West, can you call my brother and tell him to be careful tonight. Better yet, call Tessa and let her know what's going on."

West nodded and pulled his cell phone, disappearing into the hall. Kyle needed to make sure everyone was safe and where they needed to be.

But someone wasn't.

A cold chill went up his spine.

"Wade, go and find Big Tag. Right fucking now. This is so much worse than Kala walking off on her own."

The big Dom went still and then breathed out a long sigh. "Fuck."

Wade jogged out toward the locker room.

That was the moment the package began to vibrate.

Kyle had been wrong. Julia's timing was utterly perfect.

This plot hadn't been about stealing MaeBe. It had been all about him. It had always been about him.

He glanced over at the security cameras and noticed a black SUV had stopped in front of the parking lot, pausing on the street.

It was here for him.

He had mere seconds to do what he needed to do, but the truth was he didn't need more. A weird peace settled over him. This was it. This was what he'd waited for since that moment when he'd realized how brutally he'd underestimated Julia Ennis. From the second he'd realized she was alive, he'd been waiting for the moment he took her out again, waiting to pay the price for his mistake. That price—he'd always thought—was his joy, his future, his life. He'd known he would face her alone.

But he wouldn't. Not even close. That had been arrogance on his part, the masculine belief that he would stand alone against the face of evil.

MaeBe would laugh at him if she knew that thought had gone through his head.

He opened the package after writing a brief note on the notepad in front of him. He pulled the cell phone out and started for the door. "Hello, Julia. Is Kala alive?"

He wasn't sure what he would do if she said no. He would never be able to look his uncle in the face again. He walked out the door and into the hallway.

"Of course she is. She wouldn't be much use to me dead." Julia's words came over the line with what sounded to Kyle like a slight hiss. Like a snake who knew she had her dinner in view and she was waiting to swallow it whole. "Now let me tell you how this is going to go. You have less than a minute…"

"Proof of life." He moved to the lobby where Tasha and Cooper still sat waiting parental judgment. They looked up but he moved past them, walking out the door.

A sigh came over the line. "Well, I don't have her here with me. She's knocked out but she's alive. If you want to keep her that way, you'll walk outside and get into the car I sent for you. If you don't, I'll be forced to decide that this was all a huge mistake and I'll clean up my mistakes. I'll have them kill her and go underground and you won't ever feel safe again. You'll never see me coming."

"I'm on my way." He believed her. He would give them no excuse to kill Kala. She would be there to keep him in line, and he would be used to make MaeBe do whatever she could to find the intel and turn it over to Julia. A big man stepped out of the SUV, his face covered in a balaclava. He held the door open for Kyle. "She's just a kid."

"Just a kid?" Julia chuckled over the line. "She gave five trained mercenaries hell. They had to put her out. Don't worry. One of them is a medic. I've been assured she's fine. And don't bother trying to use her dad's name to freak them out. They know. They don't care. If you're a good boy, you'll be allowed to stay awake and watch over her on the flight. I don't know that I trust them to not...well, she's a pretty girl. I've given instructions, but you know how mercenaries can be."

He hadn't even thought about that. Fuck. He couldn't fight. If he had a clear chance to get them both to safety, he would, but he had to prioritize Kala's safety above everything else. And he was going to play this smart. She had a delusion. He could feed into that. Carefully. "I won't cause trouble. Thank you for that, Julia."

"Well, I'm not a monster. I don't want some kid to get abused."

He could argue she'd already done that by kidnapping her, but if she needed praise for not allowing a kid to get molested by her own hired soldiers, he would give it to her. "I appreciate it. I'm getting in the car now. I'll see you in a couple of hours."

"Kyle, you sound almost okay with that." Her voice had turned wistful.

She needed so much help. Perhaps at some point in time that help could have come in the form of therapy. Now that help would be a bullet. "Well, I think it's time." He settled into the backseat. If Kala was in this car, he would try to delay. Big Tag could work miracles, and he would know something was wrong. He glanced around. "She's not here, Julia."

"She's at a private airfield. I assure you I have eyes on her," she promised. "I'm not joking, Kyle. I would kill her, but I wouldn't torture a kid that way. I wouldn't torture any woman that way. Not ever. You'll be allowed to watch over her."

So he would have to go. "All right. I hope you're telling me the truth."

"I won't ever lie to you again, my love. I'll see you soon."

The line dropped and the car door closed and the car took off.

Kyle felt cold metal click around one wrist and simply offered up the other. It went against his every instinct. He wanted to fight, wanted to get out of this car and burn the world around him.

But too many he loved could get caught in those flames.

There are some games that reward aggression. They can be fun. We like to call them fuck-your-buddy games. But my favorites are cooperative games. I like playing something where the whole team has to rely on each other. You have to trust that the people on your team have your back. Isn't that kind of what makes life worthwhile?

MaeBe had said those words that first night when they'd sat in his uncle's office drinking his secret Scotch. He hadn't understood the appeal of board games, but then he'd pretty much been thinking Monopoly. She'd explained it to him in a way he'd understood, a way that had made him want to see the world through her eyes.

"You seem pretty comfortable for a kidnapping victim," the man driving the car said. "I guess the crazy bitch was right. She said you were actually her fiancé and you had cold feet."

The man sped down the road.

"Not at all." He sat back. Patience would win this game. Sometimes the hardest thing to do was wait for your turn. "She's absolutely kidnapping me and using my fifteen-year-old cousin to keep me compliant. It's okay. My girlfriend is going to kill her."

And his uncle and aunt would take care of the rest of them.

Kyle sat back and waited, perfectly secure that MaeBe would come for him.

* * * *

"Where the hell did Kyle go?" Ian was stalking down the hall when MaeBe walked out of the women's locker room. He had a whole group behind him, including Alex McKay.

"He's in the security office." Wade Rycroft walked beside Ian.

"Julia has Kala." She'd thrown a T-shirt over her corset and pulled on the pajama pants she'd intended to change into at the end of the night before she and Kyle walked upstairs to go to bed.

"So I've been told." Ian stopped and looked back at the locker room door. "Does my wife know? Never mind. She knows."

The door had slammed open, and Charlotte Taggart strode out.

She'd changed. She wore black pants and a black pullover sweater. She'd gone with flats instead of her normal heels and her strawberry blonde hair was in a bun on her head. She walked out, checking her semiautomatic.

"Is Chelsea on this? She needs to check all the security cameras between our house and Alex and Eve's." Charlotte's voice was tight, her face expressionless. "And we need to figure out how they're planning to get her out of the state. We need to figure out where she is right now."

She had to be terrified, but it was obvious Charlotte was going to hold it together. They all had to hold it together.

"According to all our intel, Julia was in London. Now we think she's heading to DC," MaeBe explained. "DC is the best bet for where they'll take her. From everything I know about Julia, she'll be hands on when it comes to her plans. Joseph was right about the fact that Julia was coming for someone. We made the mistake of thinking it would be me or Kyle. We've known for a while she was watching Kyle's siblings. We didn't realize she was watching the rest of the family, too."

"Well, she wouldn't have learned much about the rest of my kids," Charlotte replied in a monotone. "Clearly Kala had some secrets she was keeping."

"She was being a teenaged girl," Tag argued under his breath. "She didn't think she was going to get kidnapped."

"Well, then we raised her wrong," Charlotte shot back.

"She's going to want either Kyle or me. I have to suspect she's going to use Kala to get one of us to come in willingly." MaeBe walked with them toward the lobby. "I promise I will get her out. I'll do whatever it takes. If I can negotiate a trade, I will."

"It's not going to come to that because I'm going to find Julia Ennis and take her head and put it over my fireplace," Charlotte said with a nasty twist of her lips.

"She's been wanting to redecorate." Ian had moved close, putting a hand on his wife's waist and leaning over to whisper to her.

Whatever he said had Charlotte nodding and seeming to relax slightly.

MaeBe moved into the lobby, her heart pounding in her chest.

She wouldn't be able to breathe until she saw him, knew he was okay. Not that any of them were okay.

Tasha stood by the door, her eyes wide. "He left. He went out the door and got in a car. I don't think he knew them."

MaeBe felt her heart threaten to stop. "Who?"

"Kyle." Tasha looked so lost. "He didn't even say good-bye. He was talking to someone on his phone and he left. Why would he leave when Kala's missing?"

He wouldn't. "I need you to tell me everything that happened."

Tasha nodded. "He told me to stay inside, but he walked out. There was a big guy with something over his face, and I think he had a gun."

Fuck. Fuck. Fuck. Julia already had him. She'd found the perfect way to make him walk willingly into her trap.

Cooper looked so young. So damn vulnerable. "It's something to do with Kala. She's in real trouble. She's not sitting in a ramen place waiting for me to show up, is she?"

Alex stepped in close to his son. "It's nothing for you to worry about. I'm going to have your mom take you home. She's changing right now."

Cooper's hands fisted at his sides. "Don't. Don't you tell me I shouldn't worry. I'm old enough to make the decision to completely ignore all of your rules. I'm old enough to worry that doing that cost my...cost Kala. She could be dead. She could be... I don't want to think about all the things she could be. I know you think I'm a kid, but don't tell me not to worry."

"You are a kid and you did something reckless and you will have to face the consequences. I know you're scared, but do not give me more to worry about. You have to trust that Kala's father and I know how to deal with this. You will go with your mother and you will do everything she asks you to because you don't want to be the reason someone has to take even a second away from trying to find Kala," Alex said.

Kyle had left her again. She understood why he'd done it, but he'd left and he hadn't even sent her a text or told one of the kids to say good-bye for him. Julia had called and he'd gone.

Because he had to save Kala. He did exactly what you would have done.

"Was she in that car?" Charlotte asked. "I'm getting in mine and following. Tell Chelsea to call me with updates."

Ian's jaw tightened. "Baby, I know you need to do something, but if you chase them, they will do what they have to. You risk getting into a wreck or a shootout."

"You can't expect me to sit here," Charlotte argued.

Ian simply moved close to her and wrapped his arms around his wife, holding her tight. Charlotte was still for a moment and then her arms went around him, and a shudder went through her. They held each other, giving each other strength.

"I'm going to the security office." She didn't have anyone to hold her because Kyle had walked away once again.

It wasn't fair. In her head a calmer voice kept telling her to slow down, but the part of her that still ached from her father's abandonment was louder.

She needed to get to work. She would pull up the security cameras, see if they could get a plate off the car. She needed to check all the private airfields between here and…Oklahoma City? All the way down to Austin? Or should she check to San Antonio?

She found herself walking down the hall as Ian was issuing orders. He said something about finding Joseph and making sure he hadn't left the building. She heard Adam talking and Charlotte on the phone.

She kept walking until she made it into the security office.

West stood there behind one of the two desks the guards used, the landline in his hand. He held the receiver up to his ear. "I don't know if that's a good idea."

Oh, she knew who that was. Julia had already had her talk with Kyle, so she would know exactly where to find MaeBe. She would call into the security office because on a play night, it was the only place where a phone would be monitored.

"Does she want to talk to me?" It was a stupid question. She knew the answer, and it shouldn't have been a question at all. That was old MaeBe talking. "Give me the phone, West."

"I should go get Kyle," West hedged. "I'm not sure where he went."

"She's already got Kyle." MaeBe held out a hand. "Julia kidnapped Kala and then Kyle. Give me the phone, West."

319

West handed her the receiver and stepped back.

"I didn't have to kidnap Kyle," Julia purred over the line. "He walked right out of that prison you had him in. He's on his way to me right now."

She was crazy and that didn't matter. "What do you want, Julia?"

"Don't want to play, then?"

She wasn't playing with Julia at all. She was right back in the same position she'd been in. Kyle took everything on himself and left her behind. He would always do this. She had to get him back, but how could she trust him when every single time something went wrong, he left her? "I don't have the intel yet and you took part of my team, so it's going to take longer."

"Oh, we both know Kyle was never going to find my father's files. My boy is gorgeous and knows how to treat a lady, but smarts were never his strong point," Julia said with a laugh. Like they were girlfriends discussing the guys they dated. Not like one of them was a criminal who kidnapped people. "It was always going to be you or my brother, and I don't know if I can trust my brother. If he thinks that intel can help our mother, he might not trade it to me. He also might decide I'm not as strong as I really am. It can be hard for him to accept that I do what I need to do."

"I think your brother perfectly understands how far you'll go. He knows exactly who you are."

"You'll forgive me if I trust my own instincts when it comes to my family. You don't have one of those, do you?" Julia seemed intent on taunting her. "I can see where it would be hard for you to understand the bond between siblings. You're alone in the world. You can cling to the Taggarts all you like, but you won't ever be one of them."

She wouldn't be a Hawthorne, either. She took a deep breath and paced. "I'm asking for terms, Julia. You have Kyle. Let Kala go. You don't need her anymore. And you don't need the scrutiny that comes with a nationwide manhunt. We won't call the police over Kyle. We will over Kala."

"I wouldn't if I were you," Julia replied. "If I get a hint of police involvement, she'll be too hot to handle, and I need her to chill out very quickly. You know the minute they find a body, they'll stop looking for me."

MaeBe grabbed a pen and then reached for the closest notepad. Someone had already written on it.

Save us, MaeBe. You're our only hope. Love you.

Tears blurred her vision for a moment.

There was a scenario her trauma-addled brain hadn't considered. A scenario where Kyle had walked away because he trusted her to save him. To save them both. A scenario where Kyle left it all in her hands because he believed in her. Loved her. Trusted her more than anyone on earth.

She sniffled and covered the receiver, glancing back at West. "Go and tell Ian not to call the cops yet. Tell him I'm on the line with her."

A hopeful confidence coursed through MaeBe's whole being. Kyle had walked out without saying a word because he'd left her the message she'd needed. This was her op now. He would handle things from his end. He would deal with Julia and protect Kala. He'd walked back into his own personal hell because he knew she would get him out.

"All right. No cops. I'm going to need proof of life, and I'm going to need it soon."

"You're in no position to negotiate," Julia countered.

"I have two freaked out parents with more firepower than you can imagine and ties to most of the intelligence agencies around the world and at least one Russian syndicate. If you give me proof of life, I might be able to calm them down and convince them I can handle this situation for them. If you do not, they won't care what happens to anyone but their daughter."

A low growl came over the line. "Fine. I suppose I can understand that, but I'm serious about them coming after me. If I get a hint of the authorities getting involved or the Taggarts sending assassins my way, I'll make sure the kid goes down with me. She's out right now. I had to drug her, but the medic assures me she's fine. What the hell did they do to that kid? She almost took out two grown men. Luckily I sent five."

Good for Kala.

She glanced up, and Ian and Charlotte stood in the doorway. They held hands as though they needed to touch in order to get through this.

"Can I talk to Kyle then? Is he with her?"

"You would love that, wouldn't you? You would love to talk to Kyle and play out all your sad-girl fantasies."

"I would love to talk to Kyle so I can prove to my boss that his daughter is still breathing. You're the one bringing emotion into this, and I thought better of you. I rather thought you could be a professional for five minutes, but if you prefer to taunt me, I can turn this whole thing over to Ian."

A huff came over the line. "Fine. I'll have my men send proof of life. You get a picture tonight. Tomorrow I'll let the girl talk to her parents over a secure line. You will not be talking to Kyle ever again. Do I make myself plain? You'll get the girl back if you do what I ask, but Kyle is mine."

She had to play this properly. Julia had to believe she'd won a victory. "Well, given how quickly he walked away again, I suspect that's true. I'm sick of competing with you. You were right. He hasn't gotten over you and I'm tired of being your stand-in. I want Kala back. I'm doing this for her."

Julia was quiet for a moment. "That was easy."

"He pretended to be dead. I tried but I can't forgive him for that. And he walked right out those doors the minute you told him to." Now that she was saying the words out loud, she understood how ridiculous they were. Kyle had done what he had to do, and she would never question that truth again. She would get her man back and move forward in life with a clean slate. The mistakes he'd made were wiped clean by that silly *Star Wars* referenced note.

"Remember that. Stick to nerds. They're easier to control," Julia advised. "You should leave men like Kyle to women like me. You'll have your proof in an hour. Tell the Taggarts to stand by. And MaeBe, this is in your hands now. She lives or dies based on how fast you can get me what I need."

The line went dead.

"MaeBe, you have to know that Kyle…" Ian began.

MaeBe held up a hand. "I know what Julia needs to hear. Everything I said was for her benefit. I'm going to get my man back. I'm glad he went because I do not want Kala to be alone. Did you already contact the police?"

"Derek Brighton knows, but he's going to keep the investigation private for now," Ian replied. "I've put in calls to a couple of others who might be able to help us. Hutch and Chelsea are already working on traffic cameras and the private airfields."

"And I've got a message in to my cousin. He's going to find the mercenaries who took her and make them pay," Charlotte added.

She needed to make herself plain to these people she thought of as family. Julia had tried to get a dig in. She'd tried to make her feel like she wasn't worthy because her father hadn't loved her enough.

But what she'd come to realize was that was his problem. Not hers. She'd done what she could and then she'd moved on and found another family. She'd found good people to surround herself with. People she could fight beside, could live this life with.

In the end she knew the loss of her father would always make her ache, but she could be more than content with the family she'd found. She could be joyous.

"I need you to understand that we will get Kala back. Kyle will protect her, and I will find the intel we need." She glanced toward the door and Taylor and Drake stood there.

Her team. She would work with everyone, but Taylor and Drake were the Team Kyle had left for her. Drake had so much knowledge when it came to intelligence and his father. Taylor was brilliant when it came to constructing an identity. Not that they would need that.

MaeBe stopped because that thing that had eluded her all day, that itch she'd been unable to scratch, was suddenly so clear to her.

She knew exactly how to get Kala back quickly.

And when Kala was safe and with her parents, MaeBe would end this, and her first gift to the man she loved would be his stalker's heart on a silver platter.

Chapter Nineteen

Kyle came awake to the jarring bang of the small plane hitting the landing strip. At least he hoped that was what they were hitting. After the night he'd had, he wouldn't be surprised if they were crashing. He tried to stretch but was reminded that his hands were in cuffs.

Actually, if they crashed, he might have a shot at getting himself and Kala out of here.

Kala. He had to think of Kala and how scared she was going to be. Whatever those fuckers had given her had kept her out the whole night. He'd been the one to carry her onto the plane, praying to anyone who would listen that she was okay. For all her ferocity, she looked exactly like what she was when she was sleeping—a fragile young woman.

He had to reassure her he was going to protect her.

"I blame you."

He turned slightly and blue eyes stared back at him. Kala was a little worse for the wear this morning. Her hair was a mess, and the mascara she'd worn formed circles around her eyes.

She did not look terrified. She looked pissed and a whole lot of that was directed at him.

"Me?" It was odd how easily he slipped into the aggrieved sibling role. He and Kala had zero blood or DNA between them, but he'd been around when she was a baby. He'd gone on family vacations where he'd amused the kiddos. He felt like her sibling. "I'm not the one who snuck out of my perfectly safe house to visit my boyfriend."

"He's not my..." Kala sat back as the plane started to taxi toward whatever airport terminal they were heading to. "Well, not anymore because he's an asshole like all men. But this is about you, isn't it? At first I thought it was someone who was pissed at my dad, but then I woke up and you were here. Unless you've turned super villain. Have you, Kyle?"

"No."

"Then that psycho ex of yours couldn't get to Carys or Lucas or David, so she kidnapped me," Kala deduced. "And you're the dummy who fell for it."

"Yes. I'm the dummy who decided to save your ass."

"You can't save my ass if you're beside me in prison." Kala glanced around the small jet, and her voice went low. "There are only five of them. I think we can take them."

She was going to give him a heart attack. "No. We're not going to *take* them. We're going to sit on our asses and wait for MaeBe to come up with a brilliant plan to save us."

"Or my parents to blow up enough shit that this person of yours shoves me back out in the world and asks them to go away." For the first time, Kala looked like she understood this was serious. "They're going to be so pissed at me. It might be better to die."

"Don't say that. Don't joke right now." He needed to get ready because he was about to have to deal with Julia, and that would take every bit of focus he had.

"I'm not necessarily joking. Dad I can probably handle. He'll try to inject me with some sort of tracker, but he'll chill after a while. My mom will never forget. Never. She's the one who saved me from the tracker the first time around. There was a lot of talk about bodily autonomy, but she will let that go now. She'll hold my ass down and put the collar around my neck. Or they'll lock me in my room. Forever. I guess they know I ditched all their GPS devices. Like I couldn't find that in my shoe. I know all their tricks. They're going to kill me."

They came to a stop and one of the massive, muscled

mercenaries stood and walked toward the front of the plane.

"Hope your wife's got insurance on you because my mom is going to kill you," Kala said, raising her voice.

The man turned, his dark eyes on Kala. "Keep talking. I would love an excuse to spend some time with you."

Kyle stood. "You'll go through me first."

"I don't think that's going to be much of a problem." A nasty smile hit the man's face.

"Do you know who the little bitch is?" A dark voice rumbled from the back of the plane, a deep Russian accent flowing with menace.

The obviously American asshole shrugged. "Don't really care."

"She's a Denisovitch bitch. It took me a while to connect the two, but she's the second cousin of the head of the syndicate. Whatever this woman is paying us, do you understand what the other syndicates would do to get hold of her? We could make millions selling her," the Russian said.

The American raised his pistol, and Kyle shifted to try to get his body over Kala's as the American shot the Russian, the sound an explosion in the small space.

Kala started to shake, but she didn't scream. She simply went still behind Kyle.

"And now I have to share less money, so in a way he was right." The American stared at the body for a moment before turning his gaze Kyle's way. "Do you want to say anything? I'm going to warn you, I'm not afraid of her father or whoever the hell her cousin is. I'm auditioning for a job, and I'm going to do it right."

"Should I call you John?" Kyle kept his cool even though he wanted to fight. He knew exactly what job the man was auditioning for, but he should be very afraid of Kala's parents.

"There's only four of them now," Kala whispered.

If he kept her alive it would be a miracle.

There was loud banging as the door came open and the stairs were pulled down. A man he hadn't seen before strode inside. So she had more mercenaries here.

"What the hell happened?" This mercenary was tall and wiry, with a thin mustache over his gaunt lips. "Why did you kill the Russian?"

One of the mercenaries had also been the pilot of the plane. They'd driven long into the night to get to the small airfield in Northern Louisiana, right across the Texas state line. It was likely just far enough that MaeBe wouldn't be able to find them in time. She would have been forced to search every small airfield, and this one hadn't looked like they cared about keeping proper books.

"The Russian wanted to take the little girl and sell her to one of the Russian syndicates." The new John kept his pistol at his side and his eyes on Kyle.

"I'm not a little girl," Kala said, but under her breath.

"You need to be a girl who keeps quiet," Kyle whispered back. "Your bravado is going to get both of us killed. Stay behind me. We're not going to let them separate us."

Then the wicked witch of the world floated in on those ridiculous heels she preferred to wear when she was sure she wouldn't have to run. Julia strode onto the private plane with her recently purchased face and her bought-long-before evil soul. She wore a designer suit and that necklace he'd bought her. Or rather a copy she'd forced another man to replace for her since she'd lost the one he'd given her.

Julia looked over at the dead Russian, a brow rising over her cold eyes.

New John shrugged. "He wasn't getting with the plan. I thought I'd save you the trouble and fire him. You told me to watch out for the kid. I didn't like the way he looked at her."

"And now you have one less person to share the pay with," Julia said with an approving nod. "Well, he's yours to clean up. After. For now I want you to take the young Miss Taggart to the limo. Don't take your eyes off her. She's smarter than she looks."

"I'm not letting you take her. You promised me I could stay with her." Kyle faced off with the woman who'd pretty much dragged him into hell.

"Well, she's not getting far, and John seems to know how to handle anyone who doesn't understand how I want my underaged prisoners treated." She frowned and sighed, a frustrated sound. "She's going to go sit in the limo so we can talk. I'm not going to send her off somewhere. I have a room ready for you at my house, and I will allow you to share it with her. Maybe you can keep her under control. I have no idea what the Taggarts have been teaching their kids, but that one is practically feral."

"You should remember that." Kala spit some bile Julia's way.

Julia's lips curled up. "She reminds me of me at her age. Except I was better with manners. Her father should beat her more."

"Hey," Kyle began.

Julia held up a hand. "I thanked him later. It prepared me for torture, which as you know in our line of work is an everyday kind of thing. Now, Glen, if that's your name since I don't care to know it…"

"Glen works," the slender mercenary said.

"Excellent. Why don't you and John take Miss Taggart out to the limo while I talk to my fiancé."

Kala's eyes rolled. "Oh, my god, lady. You are delusional. He's not your fiancé. He's practically married to MaeBe."

"No, I'm not. Mae's never going to forgive me for leaving her. We don't have a relationship anymore." He had to keep that falsehood going.

"Well, if that's true, you screwed that up. MaeBe is awesome. Kyle kind of sucks. He makes everyone in the family go to his lame funeral and he didn't even respect us enough to actually be dead," Kala complained.

He didn't like to think about the fact that his mom and stepdad had let his uncle have a whole, awful funeral, and there was a coffin somewhere with a blow-up doll in his place. And his Xbox. Yeah. That pretty much sucked.

"At least I got an Xbox out of it," Kala continued.

Hah. He knew his mom wouldn't have thrown out an expensive piece of technology, but she would hand it over to someone else.

"It was inevitable that any relationship Kyle tried would fail," Julia said with a prim set to her mouth. "He was already in the most important relationship of his life."

"Yes, with his Xbox. He loved that thing, and now it's mine." Kala couldn't seem to help the sarcasm.

Julia's eyes narrowed.

The woman could be incredibly cruel when she wanted to be. He needed to keep Kala as far from her as he could, and that meant trusting her the slightest bit. "I need you to promise me she won't be hurt and you won't separate us for more than a few minutes."

She stepped closer, her hand coming to his chest, and he had to fight the nausea that rolled through him. "I think you want me to get her back to her parents at the first opportunity. But yes to everything you asked. She will come to no harm unless new John here doesn't want his job."

"I don't want to hurt a kid." John stepped around Julia. "Come on, kid. Try to remember I'm the one who took you down."

"Only because you had backup." Kala's head came up, eyes going steely. She looked so much like her mother, but that stubborn set of her jaw was pure Ian.

"I still have backup." John gestured for her to go first. "If we get back soon, I can make us pancakes."

"Like I would eat poison pancakes," Kala snorted.

"They're not poison." John followed after her, the gaunt guard trailing them and leaving only the pilot behind.

He could take Julia down. He could get the gun she carried and kill the pilot, too, but he didn't have Kala. If Julia wasn't alive to pay them, it wasn't like the mercenaries would throw up their hands and walk away. No. They would try to cover up the crime by killing them both and burying the bodies, and he would never do that to his aunt and uncle. Or his mom and dad.

Where had his death wish gone? For so very long all he'd wanted was to push the world to its limits and go over that edge so he could find the peace he craved.

The peace he craved wasn't in the afterworld. It was right here. And that peace wasn't some thing or place. That peace had a name. Mae Beatrice Vaughn.

"You didn't fight me," Julia said quietly, studying him with solemn eyes.

"You knew how to get me to move. You don't need Kala." He took a step closer to her, staring down. "I'm angry with you, but I think you might be right. I haven't enjoyed my life lately."

"You looked like you were."

"Do you honestly think I could be happy forever with board game nights and hanging out watching *Star Wars* with a bunch of geeks?" He was a geek. It didn't matter that he had great abs. He could now have an hours' long discussion about how Marvel could properly align the X-Men universe with the current MCU. He had achieved geek status. He loved sitting around a board game table trying to figure out how to block Hutch or Deke from getting the points they needed to win.

But Julia would never understand what it meant to have a group of people who loved her, who took care of each other. All she'd ever had was a well-meaning but absent mother and a stepfather who was a fucking monster from what he could tell.

Julia's lips curled up and she stepped in, coming close and tilting her head up as though waiting for a kiss. "No. I never thought you could be happy in that world. You weren't meant for it, my love. You were meant for mine. Have you thought about how we could rule The Consortium?"

Yep. There was the bile in the back of his throat. He hated the fact that this had worked on him once. He'd thought she was gorgeous and sexy, and he'd been attracted to her darkness. Now that was all he could see. "I don't know that I want to rule The Consortium. I don't know what I want at all except I don't want my uncle to come in here and kill us. He'll do it. I assure you he's out there plotting your painful death right now."

Julia pouted like a child who'd been called out for some minor bad behavior. "That seems rude of him. Up until now all I've done is give the girl an adventure. It's not like she's some cry baby. Trust me. She'll be fine, and when I'm done, Taggart won't be able to touch me. Now stop talking about the girl who is not your family. You don't share an ounce of blood with her."

"You didn't share an ounce of blood with Don Radcliffe, either."

He knew he'd made a mistake when she stepped back, her eyes going cold again. "He raised me. He loved me. You were an adult when you met Sean Taggart. It's not the same thing at all, and I killed him to save you. He was the only person who ever knew who I truly was, the only one who wanted me to be as great as I could be. I destroyed him because I love you. You need to think about that. Don't try to get me to let go of the girl again. I'm not stupid, Kyle. I know what you're doing, but what you don't get is that I will win you back. I'll peel back all those happy, normal layers you've taken to hiding under and I'll find the man I fell in love with again."

"And if that man is gone? If I'm exactly who I say I am and he was always the mask?" That Kyle had masked his pain, his fear. Now that he'd faced both, he didn't need a mask at all.

"You better hope he's in there somewhere," she said, venom in her tone. "For you. For that kid you're trying so hard to protect."

She turned and walked out of the plane.

"Come on. It's time to go." The pilot pointed a gun his way.

He prayed MaeBe would work quickly. He was afraid their time was running out.

* * * *

"Let me see if I understand what you're saying." Ian Taggart looked older this morning. It was clear the man hadn't slept at all the night before. He'd barely been home long enough to shower and talk to the kids and make sure they moved over to Alex and Eve's for the time being.

MaeBe sat at the other end of the big conference table, her heart aching for this entire family she'd come to love so much.

After Julia's call, they'd all come back to the office where it would be easier to gather the intelligence they needed. Derek Brighton had shown up along with a friend of his from Dallas's FBI office. They'd gone downstairs to the Miles-Dean, Weston, and Murdoch offices once Adam had assembled his team.

While Ian had talked to Adam's team, she'd huddled in with hers. Drake and Taylor and Hutch. Noelle had shown up with Deke and Maddie, bringing them all much needed coffee and snacks. She'd forced herself to eat the sandwich her friends had brought her despite the fact that her stomach was in knots.

By morning, she'd known her plan could work. But she had to make Ian and Charlotte and the rest of the crew comfortable with what she was proposing.

"She's asking the right questions and coming to proper conclusions. If we wait until we actually find the data, it could be weeks. I can't let that happen." Charlotte couldn't seem to sit still. She paced the length of the conference room in her bare feet, a coffee mug in one hand. "Does Julia know what's in her father's files?"

"I would bet my life that she doesn't," Drake replied. "If she did, she would have used the information. My father was a deeply selfish man. If this intel exists—and I believe it does—he didn't share it with anyone. It would have been far too dangerous. That intel my father gathered on The Consortium was only to be used if he needed a safety net. Consider it mutually assured destruction. If The Consortium ever decided to terminate him, he would use it as a shield. He wouldn't have shared that with my sister because he knew damn well she would use it in a different way. For all that he trained her, I don't believe he truly trusted her."

"She'll want to take power," Taylor continued. "Has everyone read the profile I gathered on her? It's a compilation of Agency information on her over the years and Eve McKay's updated profile."

Ian tapped the folder in front of him. "Yes, I've gone over it again. It's pretty much my personal nightmare. I'm going to be honest, she's not who I would have selected had I been given a choice in which criminal kidnapped my daughter."

"I'll be honest, it gave me some hope." Charlotte set her mug down. "She's ruthless but she's got some hard lines she hasn't crossed yet. She could have killed MaeBe. She didn't."

"I don't think she kills for pleasure. She's angry with me, but she views most people as sad sheep who need her leadership," MaeBe replied. "Some of her advice to me was actually helpful. I'm not saying she's not a monster. She is. But I don't think she'll torture Kala. I think she'll happily trade her back for the intel and keep her real prize. Her greatest flaw is she thinks she's way smarter than she really is. She believes if she hands over Kala unharmed, you'll be so happy to have your daughter back, you won't come after her."

"In my sister's mind, there's no reason for you to come after her. She will view this as a transaction," Drake stated. "We have something she wants. She has something you want. Once the deal is done, she won't understand why you would be angry."

"I'll explain it to her in thorough detail," Charlotte promised.

She couldn't imagine how hard these hours had been on Charlotte. It was one of the reasons she'd come up with her plan. "Julia believes she's the smartest person in every room. She's a true malignant narcissist, and we can use that arrogance against her. If Julia has never seen the intel in her father's files, why shouldn't we make it all up?"

That was the plan that had come to her. They thought they knew where the data was, but until they got into the bank, there was no way to be sure. They could be running across the US and parts of Europe chasing after this intel, and she wasn't willing to leave Kala or Kyle in Julia's tender care for any longer than necessary.

Adam chuckled, though it wasn't an amused sound. "You think her ego will be satisfied with getting her way, and she won't question the data."

"I think I know how my father worked," Drake corrected. "And Taylor knows how to fake data so no one will even question it. MaeBe and Hutch are damn fine at it, too. So is our guest, who is being helpful, but he's not happy about his confinement."

Ian had immediately put Joseph under twenty-four-hour guard despite the fact that he'd been right that Julia was going to attack. He'd simply been wrong about the target, but Ian couldn't risk Joseph roaming free. "I've talked to the Canadian. He can leave once I have my daughter back. We can't be sure he's not a double. I don't care what the Canadian authorities tell me. The Agency would have said the same thing about Julia Ennis a few years ago."

Joseph had been calm about the guard. He'd offered his services and his opinion on whether or not they could fool Julia. He thought they could, but he was also under the assumption that Julia would trade Kala but not Kyle.

However, if Kala was out of the equation, Kyle would be free to do whatever he needed to do.

Once Kala was safe, MaeBe would be able to move in and then the real game could begin.

"Explain this process to me." Charlotte finally sat down beside her husband.

"We're going to take everything we currently know about The Consortium and a whole bunch of things we think we know and put them into a group of reports and faked surveillance footage that will look like a burn file," MaeBe explained.

"I know how my father organized the one he had on his Agency enemies," Drake admitted. "He kept detailed blackmail-like material on many rivals at the Agency and in politics. My mother would call it opposition research, but my father used it for something different. So I know how it should look. We simply have to properly organize it and make the data in the reports as airtight as possible. We've already begun. Normally we would take weeks, but we've got several talented people working on it. Chelsea alone has faked enough documents to make a go of this, and MaeBe is shockingly good with the deep fake."

"Hutch is, too." They'd spent the night faking video evidence of a couple of known Consortium CEOs committing acts of sexual deviance that would likely get them ousted. Not that she thought there was anything wrong with a dude who liked it rough and with a surprising amount of bodily fluids, but the world had not caught up on the live-and-let-love-kinkily philosophy. "We're matching up times and places so everything looks good. It should take her far more than a casual perusal to figure out it's fake. She'll have to dig deep to catch any flaws."

"We think it should take her days to go through what we're going to give her," Taylor explained. "It's not reasonable for her to verify the data before she releases Kala. We think she'll trust Drake enough to be willing to exchange Kala for what we give her. She'll still have Kyle after all."

"My sister doesn't think I'm ruthless. She underestimates a lot of people, but you should understand that she will be well organized at this point," Drake said. "I know you're well versed at military operations, but she'll be prepared for that. I'm not saying you can't take her…"

"But until we have Kala out of the line of fire, anything can happen," Charlotte said, seeming to take control of her emotions. Ian reached out and took her hand in his. "When we have Kala, there won't be anything to stop us from taking care of the situation." Her eyes came up. "I'm sorry, MaeBe. That call should be yours."

"Kyle will be waiting for us to storm in. He'll be ready, and he wouldn't want to stay with her any longer than he has to in order to protect Kala," MaeBe replied. "He told me what he wanted me to do. We move as soon as we can, and we finish this."

"I've talked to our law enforcement contacts, and they've agreed to allow us to handle this as we see fit. They're putting their careers on the line for me because this is not protocol," Ian said, his voice grave. "So we need to keep this entire operation as quiet as possible."

"No one's going to talk," Adam promised. "I've already wiped any security cam footage of Derek and the others coming into the building, and Chelsea will make sure there's nothing to be found on our end. She also thinks she's figured out where they flew out of. She believes they drove to a small airfield west of Shreveport, Louisiana. According to the records she's managed to recover, the plane was a private jet registered to a company with known Consortium ties."

"Where did it go?" Ian asked evenly.

"According to the records it flew to Upstate New York. Chelsea didn't believe the official record," Adam explained. "They had to have filed one or they wouldn't have been allowed to land, but they can go back in and hack records. Chelsea believes the plane landed at Winchester Regional Airport in Northern Virginia."

"One of the places Joseph told us to look was in Winchester," MaeBe pointed out. "It's an hour and a half out of DC."

"My father's family had a house out there. He sold it after his mom died. I'll get you the address," Drake replied. "I wouldn't be surprised if my father found a way to fake the sale and use it as a safe house. If he put it under an alias, it would be hard to track who actually owns the place, and my mother wouldn't have asked questions. It had some interesting architectural features that no one talked about."

"Why?" Charlotte asked.

"Because they're historical and could potentially caused the whole estate to have been declared a historical landmark and then it would be worth less money because it would be so much harder to redevelop it," Drake replied. "No one wants to live in a house they can't renovate without going through a historical society. If I remember we made a couple million off it, but my father apparently kept large sums of cash hidden. This could have been his way to ensure he had a completely hidden safe house. She wouldn't have cared about anything but the cash. She was in a tight race at the time. I argued that I wanted the place, but I was fourteen and she wouldn't listen to me."

"What made it historical?" Ian asked.

"Tunnels." Drake sat back. "Several well-kept tunnels that moved in and out of the property. The estate was a stop on the Underground Railroad, and later my relatives used it to move booze during Prohibition."

"And you know these tunnels well?" MaeBe could already see the wheels turning in her bosses' heads.

"There's no formal map of the tunnels, but I remember them," Drake replied. "I can get us in and out. Once Kala's safe, we can attack her from there. But we need to do some recon. It's been years. There's likely some security. I know my father wouldn't have closed the tunnels. He would have wanted a way in and out. If this is where she is."

"It's far too much of a coincidence." Ian reached for his cell. "She's gone to someplace familiar, someplace where she feels like she's in control. The fact that she likely doesn't know Drake has any idea his father had control of it would make her even more likely. She would enjoy putting one over on her brother and mother. Adam, start checking records to see if we can verify who owns the house. I've got someone who can do some recon on the place."

"He'll have to be careful," Drake said. "My father was a tricky man."

"Yes, Ten is aware of how dangerous your father could be. He worked for the man for years," Ian explained. "Not directly under him, but he and Ten's foster dad were not on the best of terms. He knew to watch out for Radcliffe. And despite me calling the man soft, he hasn't lost a beat. He's already on his way to DC. I called him last night, and he's working on getting back to the States. His first flight was this morning. He should be on the ground in DC sometime tomorrow."

Tennessee Smith was a legend at the Agency. He'd left many years before to work with McKay-Taggart around the world. Ten often got the roughest of assignments, and he never failed. He split his time between Dallas and his wife's clinic in Sierra Leone. If anyone could get in and out of those tunnels without tripping Julia's security, it was Ten. He would get them everything they needed to move in when they could.

"We leave tonight. I've got the plane ready. I need you to do everything you have to do in order to make this look good," Ian continued. "I've got to think she's going to have eyes on us. It won't be a surprise Charlotte and I go with Mae, Drake, and Taylor, but we have to keep this team tight."

"I think we should send a second team to New York and have them drive to Virginia," Charlotte added. "Sean's getting a car. Theo and Erin are meeting them there tomorrow morning. It's a six-hour drive, but we think it's the best way to avoid anyone who's watching. We want all eyes on this team. Not on Ian's brothers or Ten."

"I can give her a good show," Drake promised. "I'll call my mother. We can meet in public, and then there's zero reason for us to go to that bank quietly. We can march right in. I can assure you if Taylor and I meet my mother at her country club, Julia will know everything we say."

"All of her attention will be focused there," Charlotte mused. "I like that idea. If we can get good intel from Ten, we might be able to get Kala out early. But we need proof she's in that house."

"We'll do whatever it takes," Ian promised.

And she would do whatever it took to get her man back.

Chapter Twenty

Julia felt comfortable in Virginia. It was oddly peaceful here, though she had some terrible memories. This was where her father had brought her to train. His methods had been brutal to say the least, but effective. Still, she also had good memories. She and Drake would play here for hours, exploring the tunnels when they could. Her mom used to be happy when they would visit. It was the only time she slowed down enough to remember she had children.

If she had her way, she would live in this house most of the time. Not every day, of course. She had to travel far too often for work.

But in her mind she saw a different world—the one she should have had. A world where she and Kyle lived in this house and they were happy. They took a train into DC, and she oversaw operatives at the Agency and helped her father with his work. Kyle understood why it was important to make as much money as they could and accrue all the power they were able to. He supported her career and never talked to his family because she was all he needed.

She didn't have to have nine guards to ensure he didn't misbehave.

Was she doing the wrong thing? Had her father been right and Kyle would never love her the way she deserved to be loved? Not that he'd put it like that. He'd said something more along the lines of *stop thinking with your pussy*, but her mind changed the words to something softer, more fitting.

"Ma'am?"

She turned away from the big bay windows that showed the vibrant green of the well-kept backyard that led to the woods not a hundred feet from the house. New John was here, and he was like all the other Johns. Helpful. Seemingly subordinate. The slightest bit untrustworthy, but that kept her on her toes. She missed old John, but it was better that he was gone because Kyle didn't need to know that their relationship had included an intimate level. She wouldn't ever touch new John. Theirs would be a completely professional relationship. The higher she went in the organization, the better his placement would be as well.

"Yes? Is the meeting taking place this afternoon?" It had been two days since she'd gotten Kyle back, and it looked like there was finally some movement from the Taggarts.

"Your mother left her house about thirty minutes ago, and we tracked her to her club," John explained. "We've got good surveillance there. Your brother and Taylor Cline just arrived. If things go the way we think they will, your mother will turn over the key to the safety deposit box to him."

Drake had sent her his thoughts on where the intel would be in exchange for letting the Taggarts have a thirty-second video conference with their daughter. It was the only time she'd seen the girl cry. Such an interesting girl. It would be almost cruel to send her back. There was greatness in Kala Taggart, but it would be quashed by her parents' bourgeoisie values.

"Good. If they can record the meeting, I would appreciate it." They had several operatives at that club since it was frequented by DC's wealthy and powerful. It would be easy to use some of the tech The Consortium kept for its own personal use to surveil the meeting. "Do we know where MaeBe Vaughn is? She'll be somewhere close, listening in. She'll be working the meeting from the tech end."

She wouldn't hate killing MaeBe. Especially if she could do it quietly and have some cover for the crime. DC could be a dangerous place. She wasn't sure she bought Kyle's story. It would be better if he had nothing to go back to.

"I didn't have the manpower to look for her. We had to stick with your brother," John replied. "I could call in and get some more help in the field."

And then The Consortium would know what was going on. Or at least they would know something was going on. It was precisely why she'd been using mercenaries. She had her father's hidden funds to help her out, but they wouldn't last forever. She needed to get back in The Consortium's good graces and soon.

Although she did have access to a cool million. A million she'd earned. She'd thought she would need it as leverage to keep Kyle close, but having him access the funds himself would do nothing but strengthen her case against him.

"You don't think you can do the job with the men you have?" She put a chill in her tone.

This John was taller than the last one, a bit more intimidating physically, but he'd been trained the same way. If he was upset she challenged him, he didn't show it. "I'm stretched thin. I need you to prioritize what you want, ma'am. Do you want me to look for Vaughn? I can pull a couple of guards off the perimeter."

No one knew where she was. The only people who knew this compound was still in her possession were dead. Without her father or the old John, no one would even consider this place as a possibility. Kyle and the kid had no idea there were tunnels, and they had plenty of security cameras. "I want five guards on the house. You can take the rest. No one's coming in those tunnels."

Her father had made sure those tunnels had been forgotten. His family had kept things quiet over the years and not given into the need to aggrandize themselves for their parts—both good and bad—in American history.

"I agree," John said with a nod. "I can monitor the security cameras. Mostly it's deer and the occasional hiker, but no one has found the entrance to the tunnels. I have ensured that the way is clear and the lights are functional. I did that myself since we're working with mercenaries. They don't need to know the secrets of this house. They could talk later."

"Oh, I thought we would kill them when we're done," she said with a wave of her hand. "They charge too much anyway. Now where is my fiancé?"

John shrugged off his future murder assignment like a pro. "He's taking a shower, but the kid said she was hungry so one of the guards took her into the kitchen."

Julia frowned. "She's alone with a guard?"

"I thought we were supposed to feed her. It's okay. I left a guard on Hawthorne's room, too."

Kyle would lose his shit if he found out his precious, not quite a cousin had been left alone with a guard even if it had been the girl's idea and not hers. She would be blamed. She hurried out of the office. "You should have asked me. I made a deal with Kyle that she wouldn't be without him. Also, I think you might be underestimating her. She's likely planning to murder the guard since there's only one of him now."

"I know she pulled some crap back in Dallas but that was because the guards weren't ready for her. Now they all know she's got some skill. I think they can take her. She weighs a hundred pounds soaking wet," John argued.

"Yes, because small equals harmless." She moved into the kitchen, pressing through the old-fashioned double doors. There was no open floor plan in this house. The people who cooked would be kept far from the rooms used for entertaining. The guard was staring at his freaking cell phone, and Kala had her head in the refrigerator.

Julia let out a long sigh. Good help was so hard to find.

The guard stood up straighter the minute he realized she was standing there. He was young. Younger than she would normally use, but beggars couldn't be choosers. He had to be in his twenties, and from what she'd overheard, he'd been kicked out of the Army for drug use. Again. Beggars. Choosers. "Ma'am. The girl said she was hungry."

Kala slowly closed the refrigerator door. It was the way she'd went still that made Julia suspicious. Kala wore the clothes she'd had on days ago despite the fact Julia had offered her clean ones. Stubborn thing. "Not that you have anything to eat. Can we get some pizza or something?"

Sure, she'd come in looking for food. Julia glanced toward the knife block. Perhaps she should step out and see if the girl could actually take this guy. He pretty much deserved it, and he would be dead by this time next week anyway. "Where are the knives, Kala?"

"I don't know. Where are the knives, Julia? Why would I have knives?" The girl was good. Her expression didn't change, and despite the pale shade of her skin not a flush went through her.

"Do I have to have one of these guys manhandle you? I would rather not. I've been in that position, and it feels like shit. I'm trying to ensure you get out of this experience with as little future dysfunction as possible," Julia said. "But we can do it your way. I've found kids sometimes need some trauma. John?"

Kala's hands came up. "It's in the fridge behind the almond milk. I don't have a place to hide it. Next time I'll wear cargo pants when I get kidnapped."

That information tracked since there was only one knife missing from the block and there were no other knives that would be deadly in the kitchen. She nodded to John, who moved to the fridge and pulled out the big butcher knife.

"All right, I'm going to help you out, child." Julia was feeling magnanimous. She gripped the big knife and Kala took a step back, her combat boots squeaking on the floor. It was good to know she had a sense of self-preservation. "This is too big for you to wield. You should have taken one of the steak knives. They're easier to conceal, but they're sharp enough to do some damage if you know what you're doing. If you had come at me with a knife that big…well, I would take it from you and run you through with it."

Kala frowned. She was developing an excellent resting bitch face. "Not if I stabbed you first."

Julia held up her left hand, showing off the wicked scar there. "A man in Hong Kong tried to stab me with a knife about that size. I took it in my nondominant hand and managed to wrestle it away from him. Then I had his knife and I killed him. Should I show you how?"

"Uhm, boss," John began.

Julia sighed. "I wasn't going to use her. I was going to use the idiot who was about to either get murdered by a teenager or kill her himself."

"Sorry. She reminds me of my sister." The mercenary didn't have the same control as Kala. He flushed quite easily, and his eyes narrowed. "I didn't know the kid was so violent. It wouldn't have worked. I would have taken her down. You think about that the next time you try something stupid."

She might kill this one herself. "Yes, because it's stupid to try to get away from the people who kidnap you. So foolish of her. Don't fuck up again or I'll let her try. And don't call her a bitch."

"Thanks," Kala said. "I don't like it when people call me that."

"You haven't earned the title yet, honey. But you will." She looked back at John. "Give us a bit of space. And let me know when the meeting is done."

He leaned in. "Do you want us to steal the key?"

She shook her head. "No. My brother will have much better luck getting into the bank. I can't. I'm dead. Even if I wasn't, I don't have the same face anymore. But watch them. Find out where they go, and scout a good place to meet with the Taggarts. If they find the intel, I want it in my hands this evening. And call in for pizza. I'm hungry, too."

"No sauce." Kala's expression softened slightly. "It upsets my stomach. And I know it's weird, but I like anchovies."

"You heard the girl. And Kyle will want something with a lot of meat." She would share with him like they used to. Many a night they'd sat up late and eaten pizza in bed. Usually after an op. They would throw down and then get hungry because they burned a lot of calories.

If Kala was back with her parents tonight, would Kyle be happy with her? Could she remind him of how good it could be between the two of them?

"Did you really do that thing with your hand?"

Ah, so Miss Taggart was curious. She had to admit it. She did like the girl. It wasn't often she found a young woman who wasn't a complete braying sheep. She would bet the kid's other siblings were and she was considered the troublesome one. "I did. It hurt like hell, but what are you going to do?"

"I wouldn't know what to do," Kala admitted. "My dad won't train me. He sent me to karate but the dude teaching the class was an asshole, so I left."

"You should find a woman to teach you." Julia opened the fridge and grabbed two bottles of water, handing one to Kala. "At least the basics. When you get comfortable, you'll need to spar with men. Don't let them hold back on you. Take the pain. Take the losses. The pain and loss will teach you more than beating the shit out of a hundred well-matched opponents. Figure out how to take on the ones you shouldn't be able to. Why won't your dad teach you? From what I understand he's trained everyone else."

"Pretty much. I thought he might let me sit in on some of..." Kala moved back to the table and sat down. "Well, I thought he would let me sit in on some recent training sessions."

"You mean you thought while he was training MaeBe Vaughn he might care enough to train you, too?"

"Something like that. My dad cares. He cares too much."

"Does he?" It wouldn't hurt to challenge the girl's thinking. "Mine trained me. He wanted me to be like him. I think yours wants something different for you. Isn't it funny, though? In both instances neither man cared what we wanted."

Kala leaned in. "I don't know about that. I think he and my mom had it hard, and they don't want the same life for me."

"I'm sure they don't, but it's your life. Shouldn't you have a say in it? Why should your father spend all his time training a new generation when he neglects the one in front of him, his own child? I bet it would be different if you were a son."

Kala chuckled, but there was no amusement behind it. "Hah, my brothers aren't ever going to work intelligence. They have zero interest in what's happening in the world beyond their video games."

"Yet I bet your dad would teach them if they asked him to. You are a smart girl, Kala Taggart. You could be someone great. You can be one of the real people of this world."

"Real people?"

"The ones who aren't asleep. Most of the people in this world look away from what's real. They don't understand the truths of humanity. They don't really live. You don't have to be one of them. You can see the world as it is." It occurred to her that Kala Taggart might be important someday. It wouldn't be terrible to make a connection. It was obvious Kala struggled to fit into her parents' suburban paradise. "I was a lot like you as a kid."

"I doubt it."

"No, I was. Tell me if I'm wrong. Your sisters are far more popular than you are. Your mother's always worried. At least she calls it worry, but it feels more like she's embarrassed. They have much easier relationships with the others. Sometimes you wish you didn't exist at all. It would be easier on everyone else if you didn't."

Kala looked away.

Julia softened her tone. "I understand you because I was you. And I'm here to tell you screw making things easier on people. Other people don't matter. For all it's worth, they don't truly exist except to serve your needs. You can be a god in this world. All it takes is belief. You are smarter than they are so they don't count."

Kala's eyes found hers. "I am not like you."

But she could see she'd hit a nerve. A live nerve that flinched when brushed against. Yes, there was a spark inside Kala that could grow if she let it. She'd had the thought that she was superior. "Like I said before, you haven't earned any titles yet. And if you don't want to be like me, why bother going into intelligence work? So you can be like Daddy?"

Kala's jaw went tight. "My father is a hero."

"Some would say. It's all about point of view, isn't it? That's what I'm trying to tell you. When reality is flexible, we can all be heroes. We can all get what we need." She didn't see why this was so hard. "When you no longer care what other people think, you're free. When other people don't matter at all, you're completely free to remake the world the way you want it. Some people would call that evil, but evil is a word used by the weak. You and I don't have to use that word. All that matters in the world we make is that we get what we want. Think about it, kid. Once you let yourself be who you were born to be, you won't sit around and worry why you're not like your sister."

Ah, there was the second set of tears. Yes. She could break this girl's sad ties to a senseless morality the world tried to force on her. It was the gift her father had given her.

"Kala?" Kyle raced into the room, nothing but a towel wrapped around his lean hips.

That was such a glorious man. She deserved him.

Kala's face screwed up in an expression of utter horror. "Eww. Where are your clothes? Eww. Maybe I don't need pizza. Eww."

She stalked out, and thankfully Julia caught sight of John striding after her. Kyle's guard moved in, watching him with expressionless eyes.

Kyle turned on her. "I thought she wasn't going to be left alone with the guards."

"I was with her almost the whole time." She wanted to reach for him, to put hands on him. "She convinced her guard to let her come to the kitchen and then she stole the butcher knife. Don't worry. I got here before she hurt herself. Now I've had John order her pizza. Honestly, she'll remember this whole thing as a fun party because she hasn't been hurt. She could use a shower though."

Kyle started to go around her.

"Kyle, seriously, I'm not going to hurt the girl. Shouldn't I get some credit for that? I'm trying."

His brows rose. "Are you fucking kidding me? You want credit for not beating the shit out of a teenaged girl? That's a pretty low bar, Julia."

Anger rose. She'd been practically perfect to this man. "Watch how you talk to me. You have to know that even if you somehow manage to get away, I'm done playing. You'll honor your promises to me, or I'll send all the information I have on your crimes to anyone who'll listen. How will your precious parents feel when you're outed as a double agent? I can have you brought up on treason charges. How will your heroic stepfather feel about you tarnishing the Taggart name?"

He shut down. "I'm going to check on Kala."

"You won't have her around much longer. Once I verify the data, I'll let her go and you're going to have to deal with me. Drake is going to the bank today. Think about that," she warned.

Kyle stopped at the door, but he didn't turn around. "I doubt I'll think about anything else."

He moved on, and she was left alone.

Maybe she was keeping the wrong one. Maybe Kala would be a more charming companion.

She took a deep breath and banished the thought. Once this was over, Kyle would come around. He had to.

And maybe she would keep Kala, too. It would be fun to have a little one to mentor. It would be smarter to kill the Taggarts. Despite what she'd said to Kyle, she didn't truly think they would leave him here with her.

She groaned at the thought. There were a lot of Taggarts. But then, it could be a fun game.

Kyle seemed to like games now. He would find out just how ruthless she could play.

* * * *

Kyle walked back into the small prison where Kala sat on one of the two cots inside.

"Thank god, you're dressed. Were you trying to blind me?"

As jail companions went, he could do far better than Kala. It was like being locked in a small box with his uncle, but she didn't have her father's discipline. "Well, you nearly gave me a heart attack. Don't do that again. I don't want you alone with any of these people."

She seemed even moodier than usual, staring at him with her arms crossed over her chest and a deep frown on her face. "You're the one who had to make yourself all pretty for your girlfriend."

He glanced over at the guard and decided to not have that discussion with her. Julia was already suspicious. He didn't need for her to decide he wasn't worth the trouble before he even had a chance to get out of here. MaeBe would come, and he didn't want her to find his corpse.

"Sorry," Kala said under her breath.

He sighed as the guard closed the door, locking them in.

Only Julia would have a prison cell in her vacay house. He'd hoped he would have many opportunities to escape once they got to Julia's hideaway, but this place was pretty much impossible without help. They were in the basement, and the door down was well hidden. She'd flicked a light switch in a particular way to get the panel to slide open and reveal the steep steps that led down to this detention center. He'd wondered how many people had been visitors over the years. It was well equipped with a small bathroom and shower that could easily be monitored with one guard, but Julia had two on them at all times.

He'd made the mistake of thinking he could take a quick shower and everything would be okay. He'd nearly lost his shit when he'd walked out and the cell door had been open with no Kala inside.

"I was hungry," she said.

"Why didn't the guard bring you something?"

"He said he wasn't my mom and if I wanted food I should cook it myself," she replied. "I think he's lazy. Or he doesn't like being stuck down here anymore than I do. I won't do it again. I think they're going to order some pizza. What did you ever see in her?"

The guard who was monitoring the security system looked half asleep. He was relying far too much on technology. He thought he could relax because there was no way they could escape from the high-tech cell, and for now he was right. All of that would change if MaeBe could sneak onto the system. His hacker could handle anything. "I was in a dark place. She was exciting at the time. Bad choices were made."

"So she's evil, right? Like there's nothing good about her?"

He wasn't sure why she was suddenly interested in his past relationship with Julia. She'd been mostly quiet, only speaking to ensure him this was all his fault and that her life was pretty much over because her parents would punish her forever. "Well, I guess some people would say she's good at her job."

He'd hoped to make her laugh, but the words seemed to send her deeper into herself.

"Hey, what's going on?" He sat across from her, keeping his voice low. "Did she say something to you?"

"She was actually pretty cool," Kala replied. "I mean in a really evil way, but she didn't say anything that wasn't true."

"Yeah, that is something she's good at. She's excellent at manipulation." This was another reason he hadn't wanted Kala to be alone with her. "She points out things that seem to make sense, but she's warping the truth. She twists or turns it so it serves her purposes."

"Doesn't everyone do that? I know my parents do."

"Not everything is manipulation. That's what I had to learn. Your parents love you. They want the best for you. I don't think your dad tries to manipulate you in any way. He's very blunt about what he expects from you. That's pretty much the opposite."

That earned him an amused snort. "Truth." She sighed and sat up, leaning toward him. "She said I reminded her of her at my age."

So that was her game. "That is bullshit, and you know it. Kala, do not let her get in your head. It's a game to her, and everyone else is a player to move around. She doesn't love anyone. She's not capable of it, and I know damn well you are."

"Am I? I can't seem to do the things the people I love want. What if I can love, but I'm not lovable? What if that's what happened to her, and I'm going to end up in the same place?"

He hated the fact that Julia had even an inch of space in Kala's head. "That won't happen. Can you honestly see yourself working for a group that actively harms the world for profit?"

"There are days when I could. There are times when the whole planet could explode for all I care. Usually after I get dress coded at school or some idiot cheerleader says something nasty and I get suspended for punching her. School is turning me evil. I should quit."

"I'm serious, Kala."

She sighed, a weary sound for someone so young. "No. I don't want to work for some evil group. But did she when she was my age?"

"I'm sure she wouldn't have put it that way, but yes. She wanted to be as powerful as she could be, and she didn't care how she got there. I don't know if she was born that way or if her stepfather stoked that part of herself until any real conscience she had was gone."

A huff came from his cousin. "Tash says I don't have a conscience."

"I'm sure she said that because she was irritated with you. You do have a conscience. You do care about people. You are not Julia. She's killed many, many times, and for profit. Not to protect people. She was a double agent."

"I wouldn't do that," Kala said, her tone firming. "My parents think it's a bad idea for me to go into intelligence work. Do you think it's because they worry I would do something like that? Do they think I would betray my country?"

He wanted to strangle Julia even more than usual. "No. I think they worry you could get killed. They do not think you have the capacity to do the kinds of things Julia's done. They're trying to protect you, but they don't understand there are some things no one can protect you from. You're going to have to make those decisions for yourself, and like me you're going to have to live with the consequences. What I've found is it's so much easier when you talk about the mistakes you make with people who love you. You can share the burden that way."

She sniffled, the first sign of her emotional state. "Yeah, well, now I can compare notes with Tash on how shitty it is to get knocked out with ketamine. I didn't think that would be something we bonded over."

Tasha had once been used by a man who could have taught Julia a few things about manipulation. The fact that this had happened twice to his cousins made his heart hurt for his uncle and aunt.

The door above buzzed and then opened, and he watched as Julia descended the stairs.

"I wanted to let you know that it looks like Drake's going to come through," Julia announced. "My guys are going into DC to meet him tonight and get the data."

That didn't seem right. "Are you taking Kala with you? Are you delivering her to Drake? I want to be in that car, Julia."

"I'm sure you do, and that's precisely why I'm not going at all." Julia ran her fingers over the bars separating them. "I'm staying right here, and so is Kala."

"That was not the deal we made."

"I'm not negating the deal, merely changing it a bit," Julia admitted. "I want to see what Drake finds. I can't do that in some parking garage where Taggart will probably be lurking or setting me up to get sniped. I'm not that foolish. I've tangled with his guys before, and he tends to win. I'm going to make sure I have what I need and then I'll release the child into the wild. I'm sure she'll figure out how to contact her dad."

"Sure thing. Just give me my cell phone and I'll be out of here," Kala replied.

"Honey, I had them throw out your cell a long time ago." Julia shrugged. "You'll have to beg to use someone else's. I know that's hard, but I believe in you. Unless you want to hang out here."

"She does not." He wasn't going to give that idea a chance.

"The kid wants to be a spy. Her dad won't train her. I could."

"She is not staying here, and it's insane of you to even suggest it. Her father will find you," Kyle warned.

"I think I should probably finish high school first," Kala said quietly.

"Your loss." Julia sighed as she looked Kyle over. "Be ready to move. We're going to leave the country for a while, you and I. After we get the intel we need and ditch the kid, I think we'll go somewhere nice and tropical. It can be the honeymoon we never had, or I can kill you there. It's up to you. Be ready."

She turned and walked away.

"You used to have terrible taste in women," Kala said with a shake of her head.

He had absolutely no answer for that.

* * * *

"I have her. I can verify that Kala is in Winchester." MaeBe smiled for the first time in days. "Tell Ten he's got the go-ahead. She's there."

Charlotte stood, her eyes hopeful. "How can you be sure? Were you able to trace yesterday's video call?"

She'd had no luck with that. "No. I told you I didn't have time. This is going to sound weird, and I hope you can believe me, but I've been monitoring pizza places around the town."

Now she had Ian's attention. He'd been staring at the computer screen where he'd been monitoring Taylor and Drake at the bank. It was all performative. They already had the information they were going to give to Julia, but they'd decided if they showed up without all the bells and whistles, Julia would get suspicious. "Pizza? Are you hungry?"

They were ensconced in the top floor of a posh DC hotel. They'd turned the series of suites into a mobile base camp. Big Tag and Charlotte were monitoring Drake and Taylor as they moved into the bank, though it was Hutch who was in Drake's ear.

That was because MaeBe thought she was onto something that would allow the Taggarts to move earlier than they'd hoped. Julia had proven troublesome. She was demanding that they turn over the data and then she would verify the intel and give them instructions on where they could pick up their daughter.

Charlotte seemed almost certain if they passed over the fake intel, they would be picking up a corpse. Of course, she was fairly certain it didn't matter if they turned over all the real intel in the world. Julia couldn't be trusted.

So she'd come up with a better plan, one that involved finding proof that Kala was exactly where they thought she was. "Pizza is the easiest way to feed a big group of people. It's cheap and fast, and you can eat it hot or cold. No one questions a big pizza order, and you can have very little contact with anyone."

"All right, I can agree with that," Ian said slowly, as though trying to work his mind around the problem. "But how does pizza fit into this? This is the DC area. There have to be hundreds of places to order from."

"But not in Winchester. There are three, and only one of them recently delivered a pizza without sauce, double anchovies."

Ian stood up so fast she thought he might turn the desk over. "That's Kala."

Charlotte wrapped her arms around her husband. "She's still alive. MaeBe, that is brilliant."

"It was delivered to the same house?" Ian asked.

MaeBe nodded. "Yes. Around an hour ago, and then I took control of the traffic cam that's pointed at the road that leads to DC. The pics are grainy, but I think Adam might be able to tell us who's in that car. I think she's on the way here to get the intel. She obviously knows Drake and Taylor met with the senator earlier today."

Ian kissed the top of his wife's head. "Okay. If we're sure, then Ten's ready to go into those tunnels. We can be in Winchester in thirty minutes. The helicopter is standing by. Ten made that happen, too. My brothers and Erin are waiting for a go."

"What if she's not in that car?" Charlotte asked.

"Baby, if you want to wait, then we wait, but my gut is telling me the longer we leave her there, the worse it's going to be. That woman isn't stable. If she thinks for a second she can get something out of killing Kala, she'll do it."

They'd been agonizing over this for days now. When did they move? Did they wait until they got Kala out? Until the exchange was made?

How long would this vetting process of Julia's take?

Charlotte nodded and stepped back, wiping her eyes. "If we can separate her from even a couple of her guards, we'll have a better shot at it. Joseph thinks she might try to kill us, too. I know Drake thinks he knows his sister, but we have to weigh that against her obsession with Kyle. There has to be a reasonable part of her that knows we'll never leave him with her."

Adam strode in from one of the other rooms. "Hey, I talked to Drake. He's been given a meet spot to turn over the intel. I don't think Julia is planning on being there, and that means neither will Kala. She's not in this car, but I identified the driver. He's a known mercenary. I think these are our guys."

"She split her troops. Worst plan. Never split your troops unless you have to," Ian advised. "Do we know how many she sent to DC to pick up the intel?"

Tennessee had been watching the house, but up until now, they hadn't been sure it was Julia. They'd only identified three men who could be mercenaries. There were probably more. He hadn't physically gone into the tunnels yet because of the security. They would get one shot at those tunnels. They needed it to be the right shot.

"According to what Joseph found out on the Dark Web, he thinks she hired at least seven to ten, and she's probably already got a new Consortium assistant," MaeBe explained. "He's the one we have to be careful of because the rest might lay down arms when they realize they've been caught, but he won't."

"I don't intend to leave any of them standing," Ian vowed. "All right. When is Drake meeting with her men?"

"Seven," Adam replied.

"Good. It'll be dark then." Ian picked up his cell. "I'm going to tell the others to be ready. I'm sending Ten in. We need to know where they're holding Kala and Kyle and how hard it's going to be to get them out. We have to hope Julia is distracted by the handoff."

A terrible plan hit MaeBe. Terrible, but also likely excellent. What was one distraction when they could have two? "I can give her a distraction. I assure you, you'll be able to walk Kala right out. You can come in from the tunnels, and she won't be bothered with the security cams."

"MaeBe," Charlotte began.

She shook her head. "I get to make this choice. It's mine and I'll do it not for you but for Kala and Kyle. And I'll do it for me. I need to face her."

"We will move as quickly as we can," Ian promised. "I won't leave you with her for long. If you get a shot to kill her, take it. Do not monologue. Do not play with your prey."

"I'll handle it," she promised. "And she won't ever see me coming."

MaeBe walked into the other room to get ready.

It was time to end this.

Chapter Twenty-One

The light from the streets had long since faded but the moon above was full, and MaeBe knew that meant there would be plenty of opportunities for the security cameras to pick up on the fact that a team of Taggarts was about to move through the tunnels. Earlier in the day, Tennessee had carefully sent a small drone through. It was disguised as a mouse, though anyone who paid real attention would have been able to see the way the thing moved was different than any natural creature. Still, it had done its job, and Ten had been able to map the tunnels. They now knew they could get into the house, but they had to get through the security system inside.

"Hey, you know you don't have to do this." Hutch's voice came from over the small device in her ear that she would ditch before she actually started the op.

She kept her voice low. The house was still a hundred yards or so away, but she wasn't taking any chances. "You know I do."

"I can cause some chaos," Hutch promised.

They'd been over this a million times since she'd come up with this plan. Hutch had gone over all the ways they could distract Julia so they could extract Kala. Ian and Charlotte had understood the situation. When she'd gone over it with Drake, he'd agreed this was the way to go. Hutch had fought her.

"Chaos alone won't distract the whole group," she explained for the hundredth time. Her patience didn't wane because she understood how hard it was to be at the other end of the connection. It was worse because she was about to dump that connection, and Hutch would be left helpless to do anything but the job. "Julia's not dumb. She's a good tactician. If we don't overwhelm her on an emotional level, she'll make the right calls, and then we're all in trouble. I'm the only one who can push her that far."

"You can push her to kill you."

"She's a predator who likes to play with her food," MaeBe replied, watching the yard around her. So far she hadn't seen any evidence that there were actual humans patrolling. Julia was relying on tech.

That was a mistake.

MaeBe had written the protocols that would break the code on the door that led from the tunnels to the basement. It wasn't biometric. The tech on the door was surprisingly dated. Likely because if they switched it out, they had to bring in people and questions could be asked. From what Joseph had told him, Julia and her father had always been paranoid about keeping their safehouse as private as possible. The Consortium board didn't know it existed, hence they had outdated security on the tunnels. Ian had recognized the system. It was one he'd put in a thousand times before, one he trained all his employees on, so they knew all the backdoors. Still, it could take a while to break the code, and she was going to have to buy them that time.

Likely with pain and blood.

"I don't like the idea of her playing with you," Hutch said over the line. "She's going to hurt you, Mae."

Nothing would hurt worse than not getting Kyle back. Than knowing she hadn't done everything she could for Kala. "I can handle it. She's done it before. I survived. I know how to keep her angry, but not so angry she kills me. And once they get Kala, they'll come for me."

Ian would never ask her to take a minute's more pain than she had to endure. She'd found a family that would never leave her behind.

It was enough.

And then she and Kyle would cuddle up, and someone would

take care of them while they healed from whatever that woman was about to do. She would likely find herself right back in Grace's pool house, curled around Kyle and taking a whole lot of pain killers.

It wasn't such a bad place to be because this was only time, and it would be finite. The pain would pass. Her love would not.

"We'll all come for you," Hutch promised. "Now if we're going to do this, it's time. The mercenaries she sent to meet with Drake and Taylor can't get back for at least another hour."

Adam had identified four men in the SUV. Why Julia had sent what might be half the men on her team had been debated over, but she accepted Drake's explanation. Julia feared Taylor. Julia had tangled with Taylor and didn't want to come out on the wrong end of that fight again. Taylor had pricked Julia's pride, and she wouldn't underestimate her.

She would not feel the same way about MaeBe. It was exactly what she was counting on. "I'm going silent. Let Ian know he has a go."

She took a deep breath and pulled the device out of her ear. Hutch would let Ian know she was going in, and he could start the countdown.

MaeBe stood just outside the security cameras on the big lawn that ran down from the highway to the house. The place was thick with trees, and anyone driving by wouldn't know there was a house here at all, much less the estate that had been in the Radcliffe family for well over a century.

Kyle was somewhere in that rambling mansion, and so was Kala.

She had to hope this house wasn't about to be her tomb.

The phone in her hand buzzed, letting her know the message had been received and she had a go.

MaeBe let the cell phone drop and then eased around the big tree. She had to make it look good, like she was trying to stay off the security cameras, trying to sneak up to the main house.

She had several guns on her, but she didn't expect to make it far with them.

She moved to the side of the house, inching around the cameras so it would catch a glimpse of her.

That was when she set off the perimeter lights. They came on, flooding what was previously dark with harsh white.

She dove for the side of the house, out of the cone the light created. She wished she didn't have to be so dramatic, but she was selling a scene. Julia wouldn't believe her if she simply walked up to the door.

She had to make this look good and hope the men Julia had left behind were paying any kind of attention.

Ian and the team needed every single eye away from the security cameras when they started in. Hutch was going to cut their Wi-Fi and switch the feeds to a loop they'd made and then Ian could move in freely.

But those eyes needed to be on her for the ten to twenty minutes it would take for them to get into the house or they could get cut off coming around a corner, and she wasn't willing to risk a firefight in the narrow tunnels. They would be caught, and if someone came up from behind…

She wasn't going to think about that. It was time to put away worst-case scenarios and only deal with what was real and happening in front of her.

A door opened above her, and she realized someone was paying attention.

Joseph had told them Julia preferred to work with small, well-trained teams. Sometimes because she killed them rather than paying their wages. He thought there would be no more than ten men on the team, and four of them were heading to DC.

Six men, give or take a few, and Julia.

"What the hell?" The guard was a big man, and he looked more like he was ready to work out than get into a shootout. He lifted his Glock, holding it in a way that let her know he was good with it.

She let hers drop to the ground.

Hopefully she would be showing off the skills Ian and Erin had taught her, but she wouldn't be doing it right now.

Right now she would pray this guy didn't simply blow her away.

She held her hands up. "I'm in the wrong place."

"You are definitely in the wrong place," another voice said. A man who was slightly smaller than the first stepped out. He had dark hair and was dressed in tactical pants and a T-shirt. He looked her over, assessing every inch of her for threat, and then sighed, a tired sound. "Who are you and what are you doing here? This is private property."

The first guy kept his eyes on her. "Hey, she's got a gun. A couple, actually. You think she's a fed?"

This was the part she had to do well. "I'm not law enforcement. Julia's really here? They didn't believe him. They didn't want to risk anything…"

"Him?" The second man stepped off the big wraparound porch. "Who is *him*? I was told no one knows about this place."

The first guy kept his gun up. It was obvious he wasn't falling into the trap that she was small and no threat. "I knew it was a bad idea to send John and the others off. She should have made the meet spot closer. They're too far away. Slowly take that gun out of your shoulder holster and kick it my way."

The second guy looked back. "You honestly think we can't handle her? She's maybe one twenty, and I will be shocked if she knows how to use the guns."

"Hey, I meant what I said," the first guy reiterated in a hard voice. "The gun, now." He turned back to his coworker. "Don't underestimate her. We should call the boss."

"Or we could have some fun with her." Second guy seemed bored and ready to do something about it.

She was far more worried about the first one. She might have to show her hand.

Well, she'd come to make some chaos. If they were chasing her, they weren't paying attention to the group.

When the man put a hand on her, his lips curling up, she knew exactly what to do.

She quickly brought her hand up and in a moment had the guard's gun in one hand, his wrist in the other. She twisted him exactly the way Erin had taught, making his big body her shield. His body jolted as the other guard reacted far too soon. He'd seen her moving and thought he could take her out. Instead, she'd gotten his friend in front of her in time to take the bullet that would have been a head shot for her.

It lodged deep in his chest. She fired under his arm and took out the big guard's left lung. One more shot and he wasn't breathing anymore, shuddering as he hit his knees and then the hard wood of the porch.

It wasn't how she'd thought it would go, but she had been taught to be flexible.

She let her shield drop. The guy was way too heavy.

That was the moment when she realized there was a red dot hovering over her heart. She glanced up, and Julia was on the balcony overhead.

"Don't you fucking move."

MaeBe forced herself to go still.

Another man showed up on the porch, his eyes looking at the two guards she'd taken out. His weapon came up, and MaeBe realized she could die. This could be it.

"Don't you pull that trigger." Julia held herself steady.

"She killed Hank and Bill," the guard said, his eyes flashing hatred.

"And I'll kill you if you don't obey orders," Julia replied. "This is Mae Beatrice Vaughn. I would like to know how she found me and who else is out there in the woods."

Mae shook her head, her hands in the air now. "No one. I came by myself."

"Sure you did. I want an explanation of how you found us, and I want it now. How did my brother know I still own this house? Our father did an excellent job of hiding this place."

This was where she had to make some choices.

"Drake didn't know. He didn't believe it when we were told we should look here. Neither did my boss, but I had to check." Her heart beat against her chest so hard she was almost certain she could hear it. "Drake didn't know you still had this place, but John did. Does."

"What?" Julia stood, the rifle coming down as she stared at Mae.

If Julia hadn't had the high ground, Mae thought she could have taken the new guard. He was distracted by the bodies and getting too close. She could see the move play out in her head. Kick up and catch his balls. Then when he bent over, she would bring the flat of her hand up to crush his nose and send the cartilage up into his brain.

Instead, she stayed where she was, holding her hands up to show she was no real threat. "The man you called John is alive, and he told me where to find this place. Like I said, no one wanted to listen, but I had to come see for myself. I had to find Kyle. No one cares about Kyle, so it has to be me."

"John died," Julia stated, no emotion to her tone.

MaeBe shook her head. "He didn't, and he had a lot to say. Take me to Kyle and then I'll tell you what he said and who he really was."

This was what she was counting on. Julia stood there for a moment, staring down at her. Mae knew what she was doing. She was calculating whether or not she could believe Mae, deciding if she even had a choice.

"Bring her inside. Restrain her first, and check her for any weapons," Julia said with a frown.

He gripped her arms, placing zip ties around her wrists that he tightened far more than he should. They bit into her, and she would lose feeling if they were left on for too long. "You have made a big mistake coming here."

The lights flickered off and then on, and she knew Hutch had cut into the power and the Internet. The power was already back but the Internet wouldn't be, and they would all blame the brief power outage. By the time they'd reengaged the security system, Hutch and Adam would be inside, changing the code and feeding the monitors with the hour of footage Ten had taken by carefully placing his own cameras near the ones that protected the tunnels.

She was right where she needed to be.

Julia had briefly looked back as the power flickered. "Perhaps we should…"

She couldn't allow the woman to send someone to check on security.

"John saved me from being taken in by your first team," MaeBe announced. "In fact, he was the one who took them all down. I'll tell you why if you let me see Kyle."

"I thought John was the guy in charge after you," the guard said, his hand curling around her arm and squeezing her tight. "If he's talking about the group you work for, we have a much bigger problem than the girl and your boyfriend."

"He's dead. He would have come back to me if he hadn't died," Julia replied, but it was easy to see she'd been shaken by that news.

Yes, she'd known this would be the way to buy the time she needed. Julia had to be hyper focused. The need to recheck her security was gone in the face of a situation that was much more horrifying. And immediate.

"How do you think I found this place? Your former assistant told me about it. Drake said it wasn't true, and Ian believed him. They don't want to trust Joseph, but I did," she stated, letting her chin come up and showing her stubborn will. "And I'll tell you all about him if you let Kyle go."

Julia's eyes narrowed. "You'll tell me everything, and I'll enjoy getting the information out of you. Bring her inside. I want her in the guest room. She'll tell us everything we need to know. And if anyone else shows up, shoot them on sight. And check her for a tracker. If you find it, cut it out of her and flush it down the toilet. I need to know if someone else is coming. I'm going to call John."

Pain screamed through MaeBe's shoulder as the guard wrenched her along. It was a close thing to stay on her feet.

She prayed Ian worked fast.

* * * *

Julia couldn't believe that bitch had walked right up to her safehouse. It was a bold move for such a sniveling little girl. And a liar.

John couldn't be alive. John wouldn't have betrayed her like that. Never. John had been with her for a long time. He'd been an excellent assistant, always doing what she needed. He'd been a halfway decent lover. He wasn't Kyle, of course, but he'd gotten the job done.

Had he betrayed her because he was jealous of Kyle?

She stalked through the familiar halls, her mind whirling as her cell rang.

It was the new John. She stared down at the phone. Could she trust him? Could she trust anyone at all? She slid her finger across the screen to accept the call even as she made it to the landing where she could watch the big guard she thought was named Ken drag

MaeBe in. Usually she didn't believe in letting men hurt women unless it was absolutely necessary, but she would allow this one. This act of anger and misogyny would let MaeBe know what was going to happen when a real expert had her.

"Did you get it?" There was only one thing that mattered more than whatever knowledge MaeBe had.

"I have it, and I've already looked through some of it," John said over the line. "I can verify a couple of the items in this report. Some it's going to take time. However, if this is true, your father had a lot of material on the board. What the hell was he planning on using this for?"

She didn't have time to explain things to him. The truth was, she might have to deal with him sooner rather than later. It might be time to work on her own.

John couldn't be alive. MaeBe was lying, and she intended to find out why.

"Get back here and fast. I need you to deal with the Taggarts," she said as she took the stairs quickly. The guest room was code for torture chamber. It was really an interrogation room, but her father had taught her that interrogations went so much faster when there was torture involved. "They won't wait long."

"We need to talk about this," John insisted. "This is dangerous information. If The Consortium ever…"

She cut him off, anger rising. "We'll talk when you get the job done. Get back here and contact the Taggarts. Give them some bullshit about picking up the kid in thirty minutes somewhere in DC."

"Well, I don't have the kid," John pointed out.

He wasn't as smart as she'd hoped. "I didn't intend for that to be the actual pickup spot. I'm not an idiot. If we give Taggart a real time and a real place, he'll have a whole team waiting for us. But I need him to think this is happening now. Then we'll leave the kid somewhere in the woods. I'm sure she can find her way out. It'll keep her parents occupied while we move Kyle to the island. Get everything ready. We'll leave as soon as we dump the kid."

She was no longer considering keeping the kid around. Up until a few moments before it had been an actual thought in her head. She could use something like family, and the girl would be an excellent way to keep Kyle in line until she could get through to him. She could teach the girl as her father had taught her. It could be fun.

But the thought that John wasn't who he was supposed to be had unsettled her.

Luckily she'd caught another little fish who might do well. The question was how many others had she brought with her?

Though it would be like a man to not listen to a woman. She could see Taggart ignoring poor MaeBe's warnings. It wasn't like she herself hadn't dealt with men who didn't listen to logic. Drake would have told her to follow whatever plan he'd come up with. Another man who thought he knew everything.

"You're probably correct about Taggart," John was saying. "But we're going to have to talk about what's on this drive. I'll make the call now and set the meeting at the Lincoln Memorial. It'll still be packed at this time of day."

It would be chaotic, and that was exactly what she needed. "Good. I'll talk to you when you get back."

She hung up. She was going to have to figure out how to deal with the new John. The old John would never have questioned her. He would have verified the data and passed it over to her.

Had that perfect obedience hidden his real agenda?

"Ma'am, the power is back on, and I rebooted the security system." There was a guard waiting at the end of the stairs. "It's working now. I think there was a glitch in the system, but not long enough to go to the generator. Do you want me to go and do a perimeter check?"

Something wasn't right. It pricked along her spine, that feeling that something was about to happen and she wasn't ready for it. She should lock everything down.

And then the guard dragged MaeBe in, and all she could feel was rage.

MaeBe's head came up. "Just let me see Kyle. I'll tell you what you want if you let me see Kyle."

It had all been a lie. MaeBe had told her she couldn't forgive Kyle, but here she was, a pathetic creature begging for love from a man who shouldn't be bothered to look at her. She wasn't beautiful or exciting or even intelligent. She was nothing compared to Julia.

Was this what Kyle wanted? This mewling idiot?

The instinct that she was in trouble dimmed in face of the real threat. Nothing was more important than Kyle and proving to him once and for all who was the right woman for him.

"Take her inside."

Julia wanted to be alone with her adversary.

Only one of them would walk out of that room.

Chapter Twenty-Two

The minute the lights blinked on and off, Kyle knew the game had changed and he had to be ready.

He looked over to where Kala had been lying on her back, seeming to nap, but now she shifted, turning to her side, and easing up to sitting.

He would give it to his cousin. She was a cool customer. She glanced over and the guard was yawning. He might not have even noticed.

How many guards were in the house right now? He'd counted a solid eight, but had overheard two talking about who would be going to DC to take the drop-off.

When he'd heard the word *drop-off*, he'd known they were moving into the most dangerous time he and Kala would face, and it had happened far faster than he'd thought it would. He'd expected at least another couple of days.

Unless they'd found the intel exactly where they'd thought they would.

Or…unless MaeBe had found a way around it all. Giving Julia the intel was dangerous to the world. Keeping it would be dangerous to him and Kala.

So the only way MaeBe could meet both needs would be to fake it all.

His adrenaline started pumping as the door above came open.

"Hey, everything okay down there?" a deep voice asked.

At least two. Two guards close to them. There would be more, but she would have sent several to protect that all-valuable data. Julia was paranoid and almost certain there were other Consortium operatives watching her. If they'd started with nine, they would definitely be down to at least six. Maybe less.

The guard sat up straight and tried to cover a yawn. "It's fine. What's going on?"

"You didn't see the lights flicker?" the mercenary asked. "Are you fucking sleeping again? I warned you about that. Check the security cameras."

"Fuck. It looks like the Internet is out. I've got to reset it." The guard moved over to the bank of tech equipment.

"I have to go to the bathroom." Kala stood up and moved to the bars.

"In a minute, kid." The guard sighed as he looked over the many high-tech blinking boxes with their lights and multitudinous switches.

"Is it back up? You know she's going to freak out if some power surge knocks out her cameras," the guard above said. "I don't want to deal with her. John's not here, and she's a mean bitch when he's not around."

So she'd sent John.

Kala's hands held on to the bars as she looked out. "I really have to go."

Something was about to happen. He knew it. That power surge wasn't a coincidence.

"We've had three surges since we got here. It's an old house," the guard argued as he flipped a switch and then waited.

Or it could be coincidence.

Either way, he needed to be ready.

Could they have figured out where Julia would take them? Yes. Absolutely. MaeBe could find him. If anyone could, it was her, and if she could, his uncle and aunt would come up with a plan. If they had any doubt at all that Julia might not honor the deal, they would do what they had to. For some people that would mean bringing in the authorities. For his family it meant taking matters into their own well-armed hands.

Which meant this all would go down very quickly.

"Dude, I'm going to pee myself if you don't let me out of here," Kala insisted.

The guard growled and went back to look at the monitors. "She should have put a fucking bucket in there." He glanced at the security cameras which appeared to have come back online. *Appeared* being the operative word.

How would they come in?

"The cameras are fine," the guard said.

"We have a situation up here," the man on the stairs announced. "Check the locks and get your ass up here. Someone's on the grounds."

They must be down to a small team if they were leaving he and Kala alone.

"What do I do about the kid? I don't think we have anymore clothes, and I don't want to sit in a car with her if she's covered in pee."

"She can wait." Kyle didn't want to get separated at this point.

"No, I can't." Kala managed to squeeze out a tear and look an awful lot like her sister. Despite the fact that they were twins, it was always easy to tell the difference between them. Kala was hard where Kenzie was soft. Some of that vulnerability her twin never hid was coming out right now, and he could see it was working on the guard.

"Hurry," the upstairs guy said. "Something's happening. If this goes south…" He left that dangling.

"Kala, I don't think you should leave right now."

She frowned but kept her eyes on the door in front of her. "The bathroom is right there. Do you want to humiliate me?"

The guard quickly put in the code, his gun up. "Hurry. You've got two minutes."

Kala was back to her bratty self. "Awesome."

She disappeared into the small bathroom. It was a tight fit, with no mirror and only the toilet, sink, and rudimentary shower that did not have a drop of hot water attached to it.

What was she doing?

And then he realized what she was doing when he heard a

gentle snick coming from his left.

He groaned, trying to cover the noise. He wasn't sure how or why, but there was something happening along the wall opposite of him. Maybe they were coming in through the vents, but he had to make sure the guard didn't check. Kala had done her part. She'd realized her parents were coming and she'd hidden so they didn't have to worry about her.

The rest was up to him.

"Hey, how the fuck long are you planning on keeping me down here?" He got loud. It might throw the guy off since he'd been a model prisoner up until now. He hadn't tried a damn thing, and he was pretty sure the guy thought he was as much of a threat as Kala.

He wasn't as hyper, likely-helped-out-by-steroids muscled as this guy, but he could handle him.

"Keep your voice down, asshole."

He could hear something shuffling. Was someone moving inside the walls? "Why? What are you going to do?"

The guard stopped as though he could tell something was happening.

"I asked a question, you piece of shit."

That got the guard's attention. His nostrils flared like an angry bull, and he turned away from where the sound was coming from, giving Kyle his full attention. "You want to play, asshole?"

That's what he needed. He needed this dude wholly focused on him. Perhaps then he wouldn't notice that Kala wasn't coming out of that bathroom and someone was moving around behind that wall, looking for a door that might be there.

Had MaeBe discovered that, too? Had she found this place and learned there was a secret way in?

Julia had always told him she wouldn't live anywhere she didn't have a way out of. She said her father had taught her that.

"I don't think you can play at all," Kyle taunted. "I think the lady upstairs has your balls in a vise, and you can't do anything about it. She tells you what to do, and you do it like the lapdog you are."

The guard's shoulders straightened, and he probably had the instinct to beat his chest or something. "Fuck you. I do what I want. I don't let any bitch tell me what to do."

That was the moment the door opened and Charlotte Taggart moved in, her body encased in all black and a gun with a suppressor in her hand.

"Die." She pulled the trigger and the guard went down quickly. Charlotte stared down at him. "This bitch seems to have been able to tell him what to do. Kyle, where's my daughter?"

Ian had moved in behind her, his brothers and sister-in-law flanking out from the small door that had been revealed.

The bathroom door opened. "Mom!"

Kala ran out, hurling herself into her mother's arms.

Theo and Erin carefully moved around them, covering the stairs. Ian joined his wife and daughter, wrapping his big arms around them.

"I knew it was you," Kala said, her head resting on her mom's shoulder. The tears had come now, and she looked more like the kid she was. "I knew when the lights went out that you were coming to get me, and I knew I should hide so you could do what you needed to do, but I couldn't get Kyle out and I thought he would be smart enough to take cover, but I don't think he did. I don't think he knew."

"I knew." He'd been a damn CIA operative. "I absolutely knew."

His stepdad moved in front of him. Sean looked so different, like this was a side of him he'd never seen before. He was in all black and looked exactly like the badass Green Beret he'd once been. But his eyes softened, and he was Sean again. "Hey, son. You okay?"

How much had his mom and stepdad been through the last few days? Emotion threatened to choke him. Why had he ever considered leaving this family for a freaking second? He nodded, reaching a hand between the bars. "Yes, Pops. I'm good. I kept watch over her. Uncle Ian, I take back everything I've ever said about you. You are a saint of a man."

He wasn't going to call him Sean again. He couldn't call him Dad. That place was forever enshrined to the man who'd raised him as a child. But Sean had taught him so much about how to be a man. Pops would do.

Sean took his hand, pulling him against the bars into as much of a hug as he could while Ian kissed the top of his daughter's head and then frowned, sniffing the air and finding out his daughter hadn't bathed in days. At least he'd taken a shower.

Sean sighed as though something had settled inside him. "Okay. We're going to get MaeBe and get you out of here. We brought along some C-4. Ten is going to take Charlotte and Kala back out."

That was when he noticed the lanky man in the back. Tennessee Smith. He'd met the man before, but he looked different today. He looked leaner and harder than the man who smiled and told jokes at family get-togethers. This was the Ten Smith who'd existed before he'd met his wife and had a bunch of kids.

"She only left one guard here?" Ten frowned as he looked down. "That wasn't smart."

"MaeBe was right. She isn't thinking straight," Charlotte said, taking a deep breath and stepping back to look at her daughter. "Come on, baby. We're going back through the tunnels with Ten. We'll wait for your dad and everyone else out at the cars."

"Where's Mae?" Was she holed up in a van monitoring the situation? He wanted her far away from here, but he wasn't going to tell her to run. Not this time. He was going to trust her.

He was kind of surprised she hadn't left Hutch to do the overwatch work.

Kala turned to her dad. She stood up a bit straighter, as though trying to be professional. "I'm pretty sure you're dealing with less than five tangoes, and they're all mercenaries. Two of them are former Marines. I think the rest are ex-Army. This is a job to them. We think Julia sent the dangerous ones to the meet site. Well, I do. I don't know that Kyle thinks a lot."

She was the worst. "Go. Get her out of here so you can find a way through the security code on this sucker. Can I talk to Mae? Do you have her on the radio?"

Charlotte took her daughter's hand. "I'll leave that explanation to the rest of the group. Ten, we're ready. Theo, you can start working on the code to the door."

Theo Taggart had a familiar device in his hand. It was a modified tablet that Hutch and MaeBe used to bust codes on security systems. It could sometimes take hours.

He could be here for hours. The thought should freak him out.

He should be chomping at the bit to get out of here so he could face Julia and finally end this madness. He couldn't let his uncle do this for him.

Except he really could. He didn't care who killed Julia as long as she was out of his life and he could be with Mae. It didn't matter who brought Julia the justice she deserved. All that mattered was he got to start his life with Mae.

"Mom, please. Like I didn't watch." Kala stepped up to the keypad of the lock. She closed her eyes as though trying to remember exactly what she had seen.

Another reason she'd asked to go to the bathroom. In the chaos of the power flickering and whatever was happening upstairs, the guard hadn't covered the keypad.

Kala had watched his fingers move.

Oh, if she got this open, he was never going to live it down. He hadn't even thought to watch the guard.

Maybe it was time to accept that he wasn't the superspy he thought he'd been. He'd been a soldier, and that was okay. Now he just wanted to be a husband and—if they decided together—a father.

He prayed his child was easier than Kala Taggart.

The lock clicked and the door opened.

But there was no question that one day Kala Taggart was going to be magnificent.

"Hey, kid." His uncle put his hands on Kala's shoulders. "I love you. We're going to sit down and have a long talk when this is through."

"Yeah, and I'll be grounded for life," Kala replied with a sigh.

"Oh, you'll be grounded, but we're going to talk about more than that." Ian leaned over and kissed his daughter's forehead. "You want training? I think it's time. You might not like it, but I know when fate is probably punching me in the face. Go with your mom. You two be safe."

Kala's head tilted up. "I love you, Dad. Kick her ass. She won't stop coming after Kyle. Not ever. You have to kill her. If she's alive, she'll find a way to hurt Kyle and MaeBe. We can't let that happen."

So like her father. A hard outside, with real love and caring behind it.

"We won't let that happen," his uncle promised.

Kala started to walk toward the secret door, Ten Smith holding it open for her and her mom. Charlotte went first, placing Kala between her and the ex-operative.

"Faith and I will be waiting for the all clear," Ten promised. "You give it and I'll get her in as fast as I can."

Faith Smith was with them? It was good that they were so prepared they'd brought along their own doctor.

Ian nodded and the door closed behind them.

His Pops handed him a Glock. "I don't suppose I can get you to go with them?"

He wasn't leaving his family to handle this alone. He might not care who killed her, but he was going to back them up. "Nope. But I do want a comm. I want to hear MaeBe's voice."

Ian and Sean seemed to try to communicate through a series of grunts and the narrowing of their eyes.

Theo sighed. "Guys, come on."

"Dude, how do you think we managed to get in without a firefight? MaeBe is distracting her, and if we stay down here protecting Kyle's tender feelings, she's going to need more than Faith." Erin never spared a dude's feelings.

Kyle felt bile threaten as Erin's words sank in.

"She's here. She's with Julia." He had to say it out loud to understand that this was not a drill. This wasn't some nightmare he would wake up from. "She's the reason Julia didn't notice the lights going off and on, the reason she didn't protect her perimeter the way she should have. She's not defending the house because she's too busy torturing Mae."

"It's been roughly five minutes," his stepdad said in what was probably supposed to be a soothing tone.

There was no soothing this. It was five minutes too long.

"Erin, you have a go. Theo, take her six. Proceed with all caution, and try to make as little noise as possible." His uncle, like the others, wore a vest over his big chest. "You put that on before you run through the house like a maniac. She did this to make sure you and Kala came out of this alive. Do not make her sacrifice be in vain."

His stepdad had opened the big bag they'd brought along and handed him a vest.

He had to stay calm. MaeBe needed that dark, ruthless side he'd been trying to quell.

But the dark, ruthless side loved her, too. Perhaps the only part of himself he needed to quash was the self-absorbed kid who was still so afraid he would make a mistake and lose everything he loved, the one who tried to control everything because he didn't believe the world could be trusted.

The side of him that was flat wrong. He'd been given a wonderful family, and MaeBe was a freaking gift from the universe. All he had to do was put his trust in her, let her be his partner in all things.

"Tell Hutch to release the security cameras." He had to be cool and smart. "We can do our recon through them. I don't expect the rest of the group back for another hour or so. We need to take out her guards and then we go for her."

His uncle touched his earpiece and relayed the instructions to Hutch.

Kyle took a deep breath as the cameras came back online and all his nightmares were made real.

* * * *

MaeBe hissed as she hit the floor in what looked like an interrogation room. The floors were sealed concrete—the better to easily mop up blood—and there was a chair complete with restraints for her arms and legs.

She needed to avoid that chair.

Her knees had flared with pain when the asshole guard had shoved her inside.

She welcomed the tears that came with that pain because she needed to appease Julia's sadistic side. The more she cried, the less she would look like a threat.

It was easier now. Her emotions could flow, and she could tap into them.

Her emotions—love and joy and worry and even fear—they were a gift. They were tools for her to use in any way she needed. Being able to cry, to feel something beyond that awful numbness she'd felt for months and months, was a relief.

Although she got the feeling she was going to wish she was physically numb in a couple of minutes.

"What do you want me to do, boss?" The guard who'd shoved her around stood in the doorway as Julia made her way to the small closet. "I'd love to help you break her. I can't believe she managed to kill Hank and Bill."

"They were obviously morons. I'm going to assume you're not." Julia's tone could have been made of ice. "The good news is you'll get to split their pay. And I don't need help breaking her. It's going to be the fun part of my day. What I need you to do is go and ensure we don't get extra company. I don't know how much I believe a word she's saying."

"You think someone's on the way?"

Mae knew better than to protest. This was the fine edge she was walking. "Yes, they are. Ian Taggart should be here any minute. He won't leave me here."

Julia turned, her eyes rolling. "Well, which is it? Does he believe you or not?"

She forced herself to stand, her hands in front of her. They were turning faintly blue. "Whichever one means you go and deal with the problem instead of using whatever the hell that is on me."

She knew exactly what it was. Julia was holding a cattle prod in her hand. But anything to keep her talking.

Ian and Erin had taught her how to take a punch, but neither one of them had ever sparred with her while holding a cattle prod. Also, they tended to not bind her hands so tight she couldn't feel them.

They had taught her how to break those bindings, but then the fight would really start, and she needed to buy time.

"I think you were telling me the truth the first time." Julia flicked the prod on, the sound charging the air around them. "I don't think you know how to lie."

Julia had never seen her play *Sheriff of Nottingham*. MaeBe had lied her way to a win more than once.

She held her hands in front of her—another mistake that guard had made. "My boss will be here soon."

"I don't think he will. I don't think he would risk his baby girl for your instinct. And it was instinct because John died. John was loyal to me. John has been with me for years."

It was time to throw her off. MaeBe braced for some pain, but it would be worth it. "The way Kyle was loyal to you?"

Julia's eyes flared. "Don't talk about him unless you want me to use this on you."

She really didn't, but she didn't think Julia was going to call for tea while they had this discussion.

"What do you think you're going to do with him? Are you going to keep him in a cage? That's your version of love?"

"You have no concept of what happened between me and Kyle. You can't understand us. You're so far below us, it's impossible for you to know what love means between two soul mates. He's killed for me." Her lips curled up, eyes going soft as though the memory brought her great pleasure, or perhaps this was Julia's version of comfort. "You have no idea the amount of blood on his hands, and he did it for me. Not you."

"I would never ask him to get blood on his hands." She suddenly felt a pulse of sympathy for this woman. How hard must it be to go through life and not be able to understand what it meant to be in a genuinely loving relationship? It didn't matter if Julia had been born without some essential part of her soul or if she'd been robbed of it by an uncaring monster of a father figure. It was still sad that they were here, that Julia was about to die and she would have never felt real love. There was no marriage and kids and game nights and family holidays at the end of this for Julia Ennis. There would be no Taggart army rushing in to save her. There was no one for her except mercenaries she had to pay and people she had to keep in cages to amuse her.

"Then you don't know him at all because he loves it," Julia insisted. "He loves this work. He'll come around."

"No, he won't. That's another one of your delusions," MaeBe replied, and she didn't mean it unkindly. Behind Julia, the guard hadn't quite completely closed the door. She watched as a familiar figure moved across her line of sight. The woman moved quickly and didn't make a sound. She was there for a moment and then gone, only the hint of curly red hair poking from under her black cap. Erin.

Her team was here, and all she had to do was give them the few seconds they would need to secure the outer area and they would be here for her. She would be shocked if the guards weren't all either dead or incapacitated.

She was minutes away from rescue.

"I'm not the one living with delusions." Julia edged around the table, that lightning stick in her hand.

MaeBe backed up. She didn't want to yell out because she didn't know where the team was or what level of secrecy they were still working at. Erin would have noted that door. She wouldn't have moved past it if she hadn't needed to. They were making sure Julia was the only one left, and then they would deal with her.

Julia's face seemed locked in a frown. She picked up the small radio left on the table and pressed the side. "Ken, I'm going to need you to come back in here and secure our prisoner."

That wasn't going to happen, but MaeBe's heart rate picked up because this was about to get real. Julia had lost the rifle, but she still had a semiautomatic in a holster on her hip.

She put the radio down and focused on MaeBe. "He'll be here in a moment, and you're going to take your place on that chair. I haven't decided if I'm going to kill you or break you and let Kyle see what he tried to replace me with."

MaeBe got ready to move. Any minute now. Any minute. But she was going to take these last few seconds to impart a simple truth to the woman who'd once given her advice while she tortured her. "He doesn't love you. He never loved you. You talk about him picking me because he couldn't handle losing you, but it was honestly the other way around. I was never the placeholder. I'm the woman Kyle Hawthorne was born to love, but he lost his way. He couldn't handle losing his friend. He got stuck, and for a while you distracted him from that pain, but he was always going to find me. You were nothing but a bump in the road on his way to me."

"I'm going to take you apart," Julia snarled, not noticing the door behind her opening and the object of her affection beginning to come through.

Kyle was there, a Glock in his hand.

It was time.

MaeBe raised her hands above her head and brought them down as hard as she could, using the strength she'd gained from the long hours of training with Ian. The zip ties cracked, and her hands were free if still numb. She wasn't sure she could properly punch, but she could kick out.

Which she did, knocking that cattle prod away as Julia started to reach for the gun at her side.

"Don't do it," Kyle warned.

She stopped cold, her head swiveling and eyes widening. "Kyle?"

He stared at Julia, not taking his eyes off her for a second. "You have her, Uncle?"

That was when she realized the Taggarts were in the house. Ian moved in behind Kyle, with Erin and Sean flanking him. Charlotte had likely gone to protect Kala, and it looked like Ten Smith had their backs.

She teared up because this was her family. Hers.

Julia was still, her eyes on Kyle, and MaeBe wondered if there was some music swelling in her head because somewhere in that brain of hers this was what love looked like. Somehow she'd decided this was her epic love story.

Kyle relaxed, bringing his gun down and walking right by Julia on his way to MaeBe. He wrapped her up in his arms, and wasn't that the cruelest thing of all for Julia?

In the end, she didn't matter.

Kyle wrapped his arms around her, focusing all of his attention on her. He looked down where the ties had bitten into her wrists. "Baby, are you okay? I was so fucking scared. Who did this?"

"It doesn't matter," Erin pointed out. "We killed them all. Hope there's a freezer around here somewhere."

"Kyle, this is about us. Don't you pretend to ignore me," Julia warned. "This is our fight."

"Julia, he's not fighting with you anymore." It was odd how sad she felt for the woman. "There's no more fight. From here there's peace and life, and he's not ever again giving you a second of his time. You don't get mine either."

Julia's face had gone a florid red, and she drew the hand with the gun up. "If I can't..."

Four shots went through her body.

"She can have a minute of my time," Sean Taggart said, his tone deep and dark.

Ian frowned even as Julia's body hit the ground. He pointed. "What the hell was that? That was not a kill shot, Sean. Even Theo had a kill shot."

The Taggart brothers started arguing about who had the best shot, but Kyle was picking her up and hauling her close to him.

"I want to leave this place," he said. "Will you go with me?"

She loved this man so much. He'd proven once and for all, he loved her. He hadn't needed revenge on the woman who'd torn his life apart. He'd only needed to ensure the safety of the woman he loved.

"Theo, I think that cattle prod is on. Don't touch it," Erin was saying.

And she loved this family of theirs. "I'll go anywhere with you."

He walked them out of the room and never once looked back.

* * * *

Three days later MaeBe sat beside Kyle in the conference room at Sanctum as Drake went over the data they'd found at his father's country club locker in South Carolina.

She'd been pretty spot on when it came to some of it.

And then some of it was a complete revelation. "I never knew how ruthless the organic produce business could be."

Big Tag sat back. "Yeah, I think all business is war when you're in The Consortium." He'd come in for this meeting with Drake and Taylor, but he was staying home with his family for the next couple of weeks. The Taggarts were going through some things, but they would get through it the way they always did—together. "Have you identified the double agents?"

Drake nodded, his expression grim, but the fact that Taylor was at his side gave MaeBe hope that he would get through this, too. He'd had to bury his sister, and while she'd been a terrible person, he'd still shared a childhood with her. "I've got positive IDs on fifteen agents across five different intelligence agencies. Taylor and I have already been in touch with some people in government who are going to help us clean house, so to speak. Now the question is what do we do with the rest of the intel?"

"Work with our allies to take down as many of the fuckers as we can." Ian closed the folder in front of him. "I'll send this down to Adam's team. They might have some suggestions on how to use the information. We'll likely funnel it to the proper authorities and The Consortium will go underground. For a while."

They were never gone forever. Another group would inevitably fill the power vacuum, and someone would have to take them down again.

She was pretty sure Tag worried it would be his kids who would someday tangle with the next version of the group.

But that was another problem for another day. "Is Kala doing okay?"

A ghost of a smile played on Ian's lips. "She's using the whole thing as a way to get me to train her properly, and damn, but it's working. I have to hope this is a phase she'll get over. I want my kids to go to college and have easier lives, but I've been told they get to choose for themselves. That should come on the packaging. There should be a warning."

She was pretty sure there had been plenty of warnings about the dangers of having kids, but she was glad Big Tag had ignored them all. Those kids would save the world one day.

"Has anyone seen or heard from our mysterious friend?" Kyle asked.

When they'd gotten back to Dallas, Joseph Caulder had managed to slip away from Sanctum and his guards. He'd proven he was every bit the spy he'd claimed to be.

"Oh, we have, and the Canadians are not so happy with us," Drake replied. "Taylor and I are flying to Toronto next week to meet with his bosses and share some of this intel with them. Hopefully we can repair that relationship. He wasn't happy to be left behind. I might have trouble with him in the future."

"Luckily, I'm out of the game." Big Tag pushed back his chair and stood up. "At least for now." He pointed a finger Kyle's way. "Nephew, are you sure you want to do this?"

Kyle's hand found hers, threading their fingers together. "Yes. I've never been more sure of anything in my life."

They'd spent the last few days in bed together, barely coming out of the apartment to do more than gather food and go right back to being alone together again. It had been marvelous to have everything out in the open. No more secrets. No lies. Only love between them. And plans. They had lots of plans. "I think he's teasing you about where we're going."

Kyle got the goofiest grin on his face. Since the pressure had been taken off of him, she was starting to see news sides of the man she loved. He could be goofy and fun and so tender it made her heart ache. He'd relaxed in the last few days, much of his guilt and anxiety sliding off him like a coat that no longer fit.

"I did not take you for a big Disney fan," Ian said with a shake of his head. "Are you two eloping?"

She was sure that was exactly what they wanted to do. "I might try to convince him to make a quick stop in Vegas on our way there."

"Already have the tickets," Kyle said. "I do not intend to let her get away from me this time."

She gasped. "Me?"

Kyle laughed and tugged her hand until she was sitting on his lap. "Definitely you. I've learned from my uncle that revising history can be the best way to go."

"Then my work here is done," Ian announced. "You two enjoy the next couple of weeks. Kyle's moving up to investigations when he comes back, and I'll expect some work out of the two of you. I want to keep track of what happens with The Consortium fallout."

The boss left to go back to his family.

And she was with hers. She wrinkled her nose his way. "I was not the problem."

"Not how I remember it. And who will believe you?" Kyle asked. "Who will believe that a dude like me would ever run from such a gorgeous woman? Also, I love your hair, baby. It's beautiful on you."

She'd gone full on purple, and it felt great. She wanted to look like herself for her wedding pictures.

"It is gorgeous," Taylor agreed. "I'm thinking of some fun hair for myself. So, we were wondering if you two needed some witnesses? I would say let's all get married, but I think Drake's mom needs a distraction, and a big society wedding for her son will do the trick."

Drake brought her hand to his lips. "And I appreciate that." He glanced over at Kyle. "The least we can do is take you two out to dinner after the ceremony. After all, it's not like you have a ton of cash."

They'd had the cash, but the first decision they'd made as a formal couple had been to give away the million Julia had stashed in his account. He'd located the family of the man he'd killed on Julia's orders and ensured they would not need to sell another piece of land again.

It was the start of his healing, and now he was out of the business. The world needed spies, but he'd done his time, and now he would find some peace. She intended to make sure of it.

"I will take you up on that offer, my friend." Kyle winked at her. "Pick someplace expensive, baby. It's on moneybags."

"Yes, enjoy it because you'll be eating corndogs the rest of your honeymoon," Drake teased.

That didn't sound so bad to MaeBe.

Epilogue

Dallas, TX
Ten years later

Kyle Hawthorne was known as the happy guy around the office. He was the dude who would always help out—even if he sounded way too much like his uncle most of the time—the guy who gave sound advice.

But he could be ruthless at the gaming table.

He looked at the *Ticket to Ride* board, watching carefully as each of his opponents claimed their spaces.

"How is the new girl working out?" Michael Malone was gobbling up the train routes in the west. His wife, Vanessa, seemed to be interested in the routes further north. "Isn't she related to you?"

He'd asked the question of MaeBe, who was definitely trying to connect New York to New Orleans. "She's my stepsister." MaeBe grinned, an expression that still made his heart pound. She tucked a strand of her electric blue hair behind one ear. "It makes my stepmom insane, but once my stepsisters got out in the world, they pretty much came straight for me. They said they'd always been curious about me, and we turned out to be pretty good friends. Audrey has always been fascinated with computers but her mom wouldn't let her study them so I helped her out. She changed her major and worked her way through college. So now I have a brand-new help desk manager who wants to learn more."

And she had two young women who looked at her like she was the sun in the sky. Her stepsisters had gotten close to MaeBe. It was a little ironic since their mom had cut them all off. Now that their mom was pretty much out of their lives, MaeBe's stepsisters brought way less drama than his own siblings and cousins.

One day he would figure out what had gone wrong between his sister, Carys, and Tristan Dean-Miles. There was big drama as they approached her wedding to Aidan O'Donnell. He'd always expected Tristan would be there, too.

Hutch took a green and a red card. "I think the more interesting thing happening at the office is how the twins disappear all the time." Hutch looked over at Kyle. "I'm surprised Big Tag didn't kill Drake for that."

"For what?" Kyle asked, hoping he sounded truly innocent since what Kenzie and Kala were doing was super classified. Though he'd been happy when his uncle hadn't killed Drake, too. He'd been worried when the twins went to Drake with the proposal to form their own CIA team that Drake would end up stuffed in his uncle's mythical freezer. Instead, Drake had explained that while he would be the twins' liaison with the higher-ups at the Agency, their dad would be handling them on a daily basis.

He kind of wished he'd been in that meeting.

Drake and Taylor would be getting the tight team they'd dreamed of, and Kyle trusted those two to treat the new recruits right.

"We all know why Kenz and Kala disappear," Hutch said with a shrug. "Lou and Tasha, too."

Boomer leaned in. "My daughter does not work for the CIA."

His wife hid a grin. "Nope. Definitely not."

Their daughter, Louisa, was totally on that team. As far as he could tell it was Tasha, the twins, Louisa, Tristan, and Alex and Eve's oldest, Cooper.

And there it was. Yes. They were closing in on the end of the game, and he was behind in points. He wasn't sure he could make up the points in routes, but he could cost the leader some points. He claimed his spaces.

His wife's gorgeous eyes narrowed. "You knew I needed that route."

He had. After many years of marriage, he knew his wife's tells. He also thought she was sexy when she was irritated with him, but then he pretty much thought she was always sexy. He gave her his most innocent look. "I thought I was cutting off Hutch, baby. Not you."

Hutch snorted. "Sure. She's going to buy that one. Hey, Armie, that is a bookshelf. Not Mount Everest." Hutch scrambled out of his chair to save his son from himself. "I swear that kid got his smarts from me."

"I'm not even sure he's mine," Noelle said with a grin. "I think Hutch cheated with the mailman."

"Well, our boys are right in there helping him, I'm sure." Maddie Murphy sighed. "It's too quiet in there. Something's happening."

Deke grinned and pushed back his chair. "I'll go check."

Maddie blew her husband a kiss. "Stop by the kitchen and bring me one of those cupcakes of Daphne's."

Boomer's wife had brought along a big box of new cupcake flavors from her bakery, Daphne's Delights. They sat at the second table in the big game room Kyle had spent years perfecting for his gamer wife. It was large enough for two big gaming tables and shelving space for her overflowing selection and all her bobbleheads. He was pretty sure they were the only family in the neighborhood with a giant red dragon head hanging proudly on the wall alongside the light sabers they'd made on their honeymoon. He'd never expected to live in geek world, but he loved it.

"You know I can't complete my routes now," MaeBe complained.

This was his every Thursday night. Game night at their place. Everyone brought the kiddos, and they had pizza or tacos or whatever they could scrounge up and played games. Friday night was their date night, and they usually ended up at Sanctum or The Club—depending on who was playing where that night—but he loved game night, too. He loved being surrounded by his friends and their families, loved the fact that his own kids had this group to run with. "I think you can still find a way to win."

"You can do it, Mama." Their youngest was already in her PJs, and she climbed onto her mama's lap, snuggling close.

MaeBe's expression softened as she looked down at Diana Hawthorne. She was four and two thirds, as she put it, and the most adorable kid he'd ever seen. She was going to be so much trouble one day, and he couldn't wait. Their son, Rand, would be in the other room with the "wild boys" as he called the group of friends.

MaeBe kissed their daughter's head and seemed to breathe her in. Their eyes locked, and for a moment they were in complete harmony. There were times when she looked at him and he knew exactly what she was thinking. She was grateful for the life they'd built together, for the time they had, for all the love around them.

For their son and daughter. For their friends and family, and for all the adventures to come.

MaeBe broke the moment as she hugged their baby girl. "You know what? I think I can still win. Let's play."

She drew a card and Kyle sat back. It was her move, and he would be ready for anything.

* * * *

Meanwhile in Toronto

Ben Parker was eager to get to work.

He stared out over the Toronto night, the lights all around him, but he preferred the shadows. It was odd to think that once he'd planned on playing professional baseball. Everyone wanted him to play hockey until he'd proven how well he could pitch. He'd planned on spending all of his time in the sunshine when he inevitably moved to the States for his pro career.

Not so much. Now he had a different goal.

"Ben? You can come in now," a familiar voice said.

Joseph Caulder was his brand spanking new boss. He'd been the one to recruit Ben out of the Army and into his newly formed intelligence agency.

The world was getting more dangerous, and Canada needed protection. Ben was ready to start.

"I'm very pleased with your efforts in Tokyo last week." Joseph wore a three-piece suit and looked like he was auditioning for the head of MI6 in a James Bond film. Ben pegged his boss's age in the mid-thirties, only a few years older than he was, but then Joseph had been in the business from a young age. "You brought us excellent information."

"Thank you, sir." He'd been tracking a couple that had been identified as having ties with an anarchist group that had been staging deadly "protests" across the globe. He'd gotten the proof that they were meeting with certain media professionals who didn't seem to care that the group they worked with had caused at least fifteen deaths. "Are they in custody?"

"Yes, I talked with my contact at PSIA, and they've moved on your intel," Joseph explained, sitting down and offering him a chair across from him. His big desk was in between them. "It looks like they were planning a major event in Tokyo to coincide with the Ueno Cherry Blossom Festival. They've sent their thanks as well."

"Excellent." He was happy he'd been able to help avoid more chaos, but this wasn't where he wanted to be. He had much bigger fish to catch. A particular fish who wanted to set the world on fire and play in the ashes.

Joseph stared at him for a moment as though assessing him. "What would you say if I sent you to Australia?"

He felt his gut tighten. "I would ask you to let me talk to you about Emmanuel Huisman."

Manny. His childhood best friend. Dr. Huisman, the most dangerous man on the planet.

"I've read the files," Joseph said not unkindly. "I agree the doctor should be monitored. I've got some eyes on the whole Huisman Foundation. I don't think we're at a point where I would send you in. Unless you believe you can use your former relationship with the doctor to get on the inside, so to speak."

"I think he would rather shoot me on sight at this point." His one-time best friend wouldn't allow him to get close. Not ever again. No one ever said Manny didn't have excellent survival instincts.

"Then let me gather some intel on him. Right now, I don't think there's enough to take to the chief. I promise I will keep you up to date, but I need you in the field. We're working with the Americans on this one, and I don't know the operative they're sending," Joseph explained. "She's new, and the reports I'm hearing about her are intriguing, to say the least."

"You want me to assess what kind of an agent she'll be?" He had to be patient. He couldn't go after Manny on his own. He needed the full force of his agency behind him.

Joseph handed him a folder. "I want you to get to know her. Let me know if she's an ally or a roadblock. The word around is that she'll be sweet as pie one minute and the next she's walking out without sharing the intel she promised. I think she might be dangerous. There are groups on the rise, and they'll have doubles in every agency. It's a simple job. I just want your thoughts."

He opened the folder and stopped because there was a picture of the single most gorgeous woman he'd ever seen. She had bright pink hair and wore a dress that clung to her every curve. That woman was made to drive a man insane, to make him forget his every responsibility. "Tell me they call her Miss Pink."

Unlike the CIA, Canadian Intelligence didn't use the color system.

"I believe she goes by Ms. Magenta when she's working with military or foreign assets." Joseph sat back, a brow arching. "Do you think you can handle her?"

Oh, he would love to handle her, but he wouldn't. She would be strictly hands off. "I can take care of the situation, sir."

"Excellent. Then let's go over the op," Joseph said.

Ben sat back and shoved aside his immediate attraction to a woman he didn't know. He would be professional and decide whether or not Ms. Magenta was a threat.

If she was, then he would take her out.

* * * *

All the Masters and Mercenaries will return in Masters and Mercenaries: New Recruits: *Love the Way You Spy*, coming September 19, 2023.

Love the Way You Spy
By Lexi Blake
Masters and Mercenaries: New Recruits
Coming September 19, 2023

Tasha Taggart isn't a spy. That's her sisters' job. Tasha's support role is all about keeping them alive, playing referee when they fight amongst themselves, and soothing the toughest boss in the world. Working for the CIA isn't as glamorous as she imagined, and she's more than a little lonely. So when she meets a charming man in a bar the night before they start their latest op, she decides to give in to temptation. The night was perfect until she discovers she's just slept with the target of their new investigation. Her sisters will never let her hear the end of this. Even worse, she has to explain the situation to her overprotective father, who also happens to be their boss.

Dare Nash knew exactly how his week in Sydney was going to go—attending boring conferences to represent his family's business interests and eating hotel food alone. Until he falls under the spell of a stunning and mysterious American woman. Something in Tasha's eyes raises his body temperature every time she looks at him. She's captivating, and he's committed to spending every minute he can with her on this trip, even if her two friends seem awfully intense. His father will be arriving in town soon, and he's excited to introduce him to a woman he could imagine spending the rest of his life with.

When Dare discovers Tash isn't who she seems, the dream turns into a nightmare. She isn't the only one who deceived him, and now he's in the crosshairs of adversaries way out of his league. He can't trust her, but it might take Tasha and her family to save his life and uncover the truth.

Author's Note

I'm often asked by generous readers how they can help get the word out about a book they enjoyed. There are so many ways to help an author you like. Leave a review. If your e-reader allows you to lend a book to a friend, please share it. Go to Goodreads and connect with others. Recommend the books you love because stories are meant to be shared. Thank you so much for reading this book and for supporting all the authors you love!

About Lexi Blake

New York Times bestselling author Lexi Blake lives in North Texas with her husband and three kids. Since starting her publishing journey in 2010, she's sold over three million copies of her books. She began writing at a young age, concentrating on plays and journalism. It wasn't until she started writing romance that she found success. She likes to find humor in the strangest places and believes in happy endings.

Connect with Lexi online:

Facebook: Lexi Blake
Twitter: authorlexiblake
Website: www.LexiBlake.net
Instagram: authorlexiblake

Sign up for Lexi's newsletter at www.lexiblake.net/newsletter

Made in the USA
Middletown, DE
05 October 2023

40321337R00231